BLOOD BROTHERS

The Unveiling (Book 1)

Ethan E Westwood

Copyright © 2022 Ethan E Weswood

All rights reserved

The characters and events portrayed in this book are fictitious. Any similarity to real persons, living or dead, is coincidental and not intended by the author.

No part of this book may be reproduced, or stored in a retrieval system, or transmitted in any form or by any means, electronic, mechanical, photocopying, recording, or otherwise, without express written permission of the publisher.

Cover design by: Solid Earth Art

PREFACE

The story that I am about to share with you is my own account of the memories that I have shared with my blood brothers, and others. Memories shared through blood exchange. Most especially the memories of James Kalin, who is the oldest of us. My memories may not be completely true to other peoples' recollection, but I have recorded them as I understood them.

James Kalin is mostly referred to as Kalin by those who know him. His origins are in the beautiful land that is now known as Croatia, the cradle of ancient civilization. He believes he is of Illyrian descent, and his age is remarkable with his memories gaining clarity around 1200BC.

Croatia stretches from the slopes of the Alps deep into the Pannonian valley, and from the banks of the Danube River to the Drava River. Though there is very little mention of ancient Croatia at first, it eventually becomes our place of refuge. Throughout, I have used the modern names of places for ease of reference.

There are seven of us as I start this tale. The twins, Romando, and Benedikt are originally of Roman descent and were resident in Croatia during the Roman occupation. They hail from Dalmatia on the Adriatic Sea coast. Nadan used to run with Kalin some 3,000 years ago and lived on the island Hvar, which was at that time occupied by his family. He was lost to the brothers in recent times and is rarely mentioned. Caeron comes next and is of Irish descent. David follows Caeron – he is of Celtic origin. Hadrian is a more recent brother, but not as recent as I am. I am the seventh to join the brotherhood. Later in this tale, we will become eight in number.

I have changed the names of most of the people written about, especially where there is a need to protect the person mentioned. The brothers have permitted the use of their real names as they have now gone underground for reasons you will discover.

This is my own bloody account, told from my own perspective as well as that of others involved. I have endeavoured to share with you our unspoken and sometimes horrific lives that we lead in parallel to humankind. Bear with me as my story unfolds ...

PROLOGUE

From Kalin's memories

In an early epoch, when the ages were still dark ...

Kalin ran panting, his lungs rasping in exhaustion and pain. He briefly paused to look back over his shoulder. His pursuers were closer, as he could now make them out in the distance, the mist still cloaking their ever-increasing numbers. They saw him pause and began baying out their excitement, urging their mounts to greater speed. Again, he loped on. They had been following him now for a full day, mercilessly whipping the horses that they rode. Never before had he had to call upon such hidden reserves of stamina - stamina that was rapidly dissipating in his need to rest and feed.

At this time of the season, just out of the winter months, the Lazac meadow offered little cover. The grasses were short cropped by the grazing animals that had sought out the new shoots after the winter famine. Only the perunika had managed to break through the frozen soil but were not yet in flower. The meadow was dotted with isolated trees that had ventured out of the forest: lone sycamore, maple, elm, and ash. The days were still short and, even though they were warmer, the night air drove away any remembrance of the daytime comfort, bringing forth the icy, biting winds from the mountain. Pockets of snow still covered the valley in cold patches.

In the distance loomed the Risjnak Mountains: the refuge that he sought, where horses could not easily follow. He loped on howling to himself as his burning muscles threatened to refuse his demands. In vain he commanded his tired brain to reach out for his kin, to wing his thoughts to them wherever they were. As he continued running towards the foothills, he left behind him the bloody marks of passage that told the story of his suffering.

A sink hole appeared before him. The icy water fed by a mountain spring. He had smelled it before he saw it. The spring gurgled into the hole teasing his thirst unbearably. Without hesitating, he threw himself into the deep dark water, and gulped thirstily before he sank below into the hidden depths. The galloping footfalls of the pursuing horses could be felt, even in the water. They drummed out a relentless beat and the ground shuddered with their coming. Their hounds, noses to ground, followed the bloody prints of the C'raether, as the brothers were then called.

Kalin found a place in the water where submerged rocks formed a subterranean resting place. Slowly he sank to the rocky ledge, legs drawn up to his chin. Even though his heart beat wildly in his chest he began the meditation - the slowing of his body's rhythms, the taming of his pounding pulse. It was a discipline well learnt. His eyes remained open but sheathed themselves in a membrane of protection. In this state of suspended animation he remained, heedless of the inquisitive aqua species that pecked at him in curiosity and of the chilling eddies of the water that twisted his hair about his face. So he stayed within the suspension of his physical needs, his senses ever keen.

The hooves of the horses crushed the meadow gravel in their haste. Loud masculine voices called to one another in anger and astonishment. One horse pawed his eagerness, and the dull thud of its hoof permeated the water. The hounds yapped in excitement as they milled about the icy cold and uninviting water-filled sink hole. Soon the water was filled with the sounds of their close passage.

After a while all became still as Kalin's

pursuers continued their hunt. He remained at rest, his lips turning blue not only from the cold, but from the lack of oxygen. All that moved were the masked eyes that fluttered weakly in the dark murk.

CHAPTER 1

Present day

Kalin looked at the five brothers seated about him. "My friends," he said, "I have finally made contact!"

"Ah, we have waited long Kalin. The time is right," Romando sighed.

Kalin's eyes shifted to each of the brothers. "You will find him well worth the wait. He is perfect and has remained intact, as we trusted he would. The first seed is planted. He acknowledges without knowing why, but the acknowledgement is encouraging. Hadrian, I am tired and would trust you to take up further vigil, but I fear that your power might be too much for him at this time. You have yet to learn to harness your gift, my friend – being still so young yourself.

"Instead, I ask for the invitation to take succour from you all as it is the seventh day. I am sure you will have hunted and my need is such that I ache. I have been about our business in a most discreet manner and have been out of touch with you all. Accept my apologies brothers."

"Kalin," Romando replied, "You need not ask, even though I know you must. Please, we are yours today as we will always be. Our flesh, like our blood, which was once theirs, is yours. The soul that has chosen its freedom with us is new and its memories fresh. Take, and with taking, ecstasy will be ours." All nodded their agreement.

Kalin approached, and Romando held out his arms to him. The room fell still to the primeval rush the sharing brought. The rest moved towards the pair. It was the seventh day - the day of blood sharing. Aural emanations filled the room with the power that had them in its thrall. As one, they howled their rapture.

Benedikt turned, his hunger now sated, feline eyes brimming with ecstasy. With clenched fists he left the room, beckoning for Romando, his brother of blood and conception. Hadrian followed the twins, bliss on his face. Caeron and David smiled their happiness and expectation as they reached out to simultaneously touch the forehead of the other.

Kalin watched his adherents with a love that could get no deeper, except perhaps for one of the C'raether of the true blood – his own blood. "Ah, Ethan, my lamb, our time is near. I have waited too long!"

†

Ethan

As I lie here in bed, still too weak to get on with my life, my hand buried in the thick fur of Thalem's neck, I try to piece together what happened. I decide that it had all started on that day ...

†

It had been a sun-drenched summer day of red wine, music, and good company. I could feel a warm glow emanating from my face, in harmony with the last rays of the setting sun that seemed to caress the summit of the buildings in the street, forming in a way 'buildings with blooded linings'.

I lived with my girlfriend, Megan, in a flat on the west side of London. Our building was older and trendy, and the small garden at the entrance always seemed neat and clean. I never knew who kept it that way. A red rose climbed a trellis just next to the blue front door. I noticed that Megs was out because her ancient Mini wasn't parked in its usual place in the street. With a quick glance in the mailbox in the lobby and a nod to a neighbour who was laboriously negotiating the stairs with a prammed baby and toddler in hand, I made my way up the stairs, two at a time, much abused guitar case in hand, to the third floor where we live.

Once inside, I leaned my guitar against the wall, took off my jacket, and grabbed the hi-fi's remote control. The flat was always filled with music. The first compact disc came on, and soon Nick Cave asked mournfully, "Do you love me?" I danced over to the fridge, peered in for a tomato juice, and poured myself a glass that I gulped down in one breath. I then went over to fetch my guitar case. I flipped the catch and, as always, felt the pleasure of taking out my beautiful semi-acoustic Gibson. I'd strum along while I waited for Meg.

The day had filled me with feelings of remoteness and well-being, which was a welcome relief from the confused emotions that I usually experienced. This was the way I had always been, with extreme emotions: highs compensating for lows, and vice versa.

Time seemed to slip unobtrusively away, and Nick Cave crooned that the plain gold ring had a story to tell. This brought my thoughts back to Meg, who should be arriving home soon in her usual flourish of shopping bags and smiles.

Let me tell you about Meg. She is a confident person, with a fun but sensitive character. She gives before she takes, and today is my only remaining and devoted follower. I met her, personally, in a hospital waiting room, but recognised her as having been in the audience several times when I'd played gigs a couple of years earlier. She was then part of my 'built-in support battalion' - one of the necessary accoutrements to my limited fame. In fact, Megan was one of the very people that, in their devotion to my music, had made my acknowledgement possible.

It'd been about two years since I'd been involved in the music scene on a professional, or should I say full-time, basis - thanks to my regrettable drug problem. A problem that I finally believed I had under control - let's call it the nightmare of my white mare.

Back to the hospital waiting room ... Meg came into my life at a time when I was at my lowest and loneliest. Right place and time I guess. Anyhow, she was exactly what I needed - generous with herself, sympathetic, caring, and above all, she loved me. I must have needed that! I was so busy coping with my emotional and drug problems that I can't say I had much energy left to reciprocate her love with anything as near, or as intense, as hers for me.

Meg is special; I know that! She is soft-natured - yet she's an eccentric dresser, which certainly makes her stand out in a crowd. I often wondered how she could express herself to such an unconventional degree and yet remain so devoted and loyal to me. If I think about it, it must have been hard for her as her interest in me was so much more than friendship - and she made it obvious. But friendship and companionship were all I could handle at that time. Maybe it was the mundane I needed, y'no, the permanence - something to lock on to without giving the essence of myself.

Well, Megan had invested in me, and within a few weeks of knowing her she had tentatively invited me to move in with her. I was okay with that, so I packed the few belongings I had and took her up on her offer. It's not like I had anything else to do. At that time our relationship remained, as I chose, platonic; although I knew she would have liked to develop it into one with all the trimmings and commitments that go along with that sort of thing. There were times when I was tempted to buckle in and just go with the flow. It would have been easier, but something always held me back. And by this I don't mean that I didn't find Megan desirable, or couldn't see myself committing to her, but something else - possibly the fear of a physical relationship or maybe the time just wasn't right or conducive to a deep emotional attachment on my part.

With these thoughts, I heard her arrive at the door in the expected rustle of packages. I jumped up to open the door. She glanced up in surprise when the door opened, and she saw me - her hand still searched for the key in her bag. An immediate smile creased her face.

"Ethan! You bugger, you startled me."

"Hi," I smiled and leant forward to give her a light kiss on the cheek. "Here, let me get those for you!" I bent to pick up the grocery packages that were on the floor by the door, first transferring my cigarette to my mouth, where it dangled precariously.

"Hey, watch it; you're burning your hair on your cig." She reached out to tuck the tendril of hair behind my ear.

I grunted, and without much success tried to roll the fag to the other side of my mouth. Then I shuffled through to the kitchen with the packages.

Megan was left to do what it is women do best in kitchens and expect men to be able to do without feeling domestically uncomfortable. She soon appeared with a tray with two plates, placed them on the centre table, and returned to the kitchen for two glasses of ruby wine. I'd already had enough 'red' for the day but didn't say so.

"How did your audition go this morning luv?" She sat down on the floor next to me and began poking a fork in her food.

"Not too bad," I replied. "I'll be playing on trial with the chaps, starting tonight. They want to see how I handle it. You know, if I like what they're doing and all that. I've been out of it for a while, Megs - don't know if I can cut it. Sorta worries me; just dunno what they're expecting."

"Of course you can do it!" She assured me with a mouthful. "You're good and the music is still there inside you - didn't just go away." She swallowed and waved her fork about at me. "You'll find that after a couple of nights it'll be the same as it was before. You were really good Ethe, and still are." She popped another forkful of food into her mouth. I smiled my thanks.

Silently, we both ate our food and drank our wine, glancing at each other over our wine glasses.

"Carry on; what were you saying?" she asked.

"I said I'm only going in as rhythm, until I get to know their numbers better. Hope it'll be okay, and I don't lose it. We spent today going over a few things and worked well together. Are you going to come through tonight, as a sort of pre-converted appreciator?"

I hadn't meant to ask her to come as I would be under pressure and didn't need the extra burden of having to be attentive to anyone.

"Of course I'm coming, what a question." With a smile she bent forward to plant a kiss on my cheek. "Yours forever, remember. But I'll see you quite a bit later 'cos Andrea and I are going to a 'hen party' at the local tonight - do you remember me telling you?"

A bit of the pressure left me. It would be better if she came later when I was well into the feel of the venue and people. It was with a small amount of relief that I answered her. "Nah, but that's alright."

As she stood up, I reached forward to make a playful grab at her, but she side-stepped and walked towards the bedroom, glass in hand and singing to herself in an off-key voice. Her voice was one of the things I liked about her - it made her real.

"Luv, what time do you start playing tonight?" she called from the bedroom. I could hear the taps running in the bathroom. She continued, "I'll probably be there round eleven.

Do you think they'll let you do any of your own stuff?"

"Maybe - see how it goes!" I called back, my breath destroying the smoke ring I was creating. I was getting good at these rings and could blow one through another and then another through those. It'd taken me years to master this.

Her voice had faded as she moved into the bathroom. "If you do, save Massacre Molly for me, okay?"

"Yeah, sure!" I called back. "If the band is interested in doing it. You still like it?"

"Always will." Her voice was clearer. "Great stuff - it's what made me like you in the first place!"

Nick Cave droned on, "Tap, tap tapping with his cane ..."

Megan called again from the bedroom "Come here for a sec will you!"

I took my time, lit another cigarette, and went through to the bedroom. I had been smoking far too much since I'd given up the dope.

She was half in the cupboard, obviously looking for the right layer of clothing for the evening. Her voice came muffled from somewhere amongst the clothes. "Grab my bath luv, if you will, before we end up with a flood. Want to bath with me?" She was obviously warming to the wine.

I killed the cigarette and walked through to the bathroom to turn off the tap. From where I stood, steam billowed out the door framing her in a wreath of mist. The moment seemed unreal as I watched. Very desirable! I had to turn my back on her to control it. Still don't know why I always made such a concerted effort to control my natural urges.

I was still a virgin at twenty-six and had absolutely no intention of relenting after all the years of private suffering to keep it that way. Why? Fuck only knows! I just somehow knew it should be like that. The more I did it, the more of a challenge it became, until it was almost obsessive. I would have thought less of myself had I succumbed. Don't think that I didn't feel the urge, I did - I was a man, there was no doubt about it. Something just held me back.

I turned again to look at the way she arched her slim neck as she considered the array of clothes. The wardrobe was just outside the bathroom. Self-consciously I wiped the hair back from my forehead. She was now tapping at her mouth with a long finger; then leant forward to dig out some shoes at the bottom of the cupboard. With the wine dulling my inhibitions, it was all becoming too much for me. So with a shrug to pull myself together, I returned to the lounge.

Another truth that I was loathe to admit, was that I couldn't quite put a finger on my lust - it was tinged with desires that I felt might be abnormal and I was just a bit afraid of giving in to them.

I was pulled out of my reverie by the hurt in her voice. "Ethan, come back, what's wrong?"

"Nothing," I croaked in a voice I barely recognised as my own. "Nothing." To myself I said, "If I can't understand it, you never will."

CHAPTER 2

The clown

The doors opened at nine, and we were scheduled to start playing at ten. We arrived a couple of minutes before ten, parked right outside the door and began hauling in equipment that we had taken away with us that afternoon after practice.

Young people loitered around on the pavement against backdrop walls painted in psychedelic shapes and colours. Girls in chattering crowds glanced over at the boys and giggled. The boys pretended they didn't see the girls but made as much effort as possible to sit and smoke and lounge in just the sort of manner they thought cool and impressive. The whole thing was to look as "super-cool" as possible.

Cars hooted as the odd person ran over the road to greet friends. A couple of them slouched over to the van to greet us and see if they could help.

The heavy equipment had been taken along that afternoon when we had set up the venue, and so it was just the lighter stuff, like the guitars, that still had to be taken in.

We elbowed through the crowd and got the occasional pat on the back as we passed - they were obviously relieved that we had shown up at all. Although I was new with The Sock, they were notorious for not keeping to schedule. Their usual excuse was that they had forgotten about the gig. I could see how that could happen as they spent most of their time inebriated by one chosen poison or another. I was obviously well-suited to them.

People had already started arriving in droves, and drinks in hand, were expectantly crowding around the small stage.

We tuned and ran through a few scales to warm up. The crowd was the usual for this type of venue: young; looking for noise and action; printed T-shirts on which none of us were yet lucky enough to appear; and come-ons being body-languaged back and forth across the room. Mediocre and non-appreciative! I needed the job.

The band, with whom I hopefully had a short-term career, played most of their own numbers and opened with one I knew well. It was one to which, for showmanship, I was even able to add the odd flourish here and there without my efforts affecting the performance or popularity of any other member of the band. I had been out of it for a while and still needed to do a lot of work to bring myself up to scratch, and the rest of the chaps, well hey, they were good.

We played the usual alternative music that was much in demand by the crowd that frequented Exodus, interspersed with metal for the head-bangers. It went down well, the kids enjoyed it, and as the evening matured I felt better about being there.

As it got later and I became less inspired by my surroundings, I felt the start of a mood-swing. This wasn't what I wanted, as I had to get through this evening in one piece and keep my music on a sane note. The band broke for a drink, and I slipped out to the van to roll myself a quick joint. I felt it would help to mellow me for the rest of the evening. I vaguely remember seeing a man standing in the shadows of a building. He seemed to be watching me. It made me feel uneasy, but I reminded myself that I often experienced a persecution complex when I smoked weed. When I looked again he was gone.

Afterwards, I went back inside feeling more at grips, and then less at grips with myself, but smiling more than was usual for me. I greeted a few people I knew, refused a couple of offers of drinks, and jumped back up onto the stage. Two girls, most-surely under-age, sat ogling and admiring my grandeur - I say tongue in cheek. So, to keep myself amused, I decided to go on a mission to impress them. I ran through a complex blues number, and they seemed suitably in awe. Then I lost interest as my mind took an expansive leap elsewhere ... As I sat there, with what could only have been a foolish grin on my face, I couldn't help feeling like a white-faced, bulby-nosed clown, in full colour, waiting for the other clowns to arrive. I felt a blend of mirth, sadness and stupidity written all over my painted face and saw my hair as two tufts at the side of my head. The thought made me feel to see if my hair was still where it should be, and how it should be - not stuck to my head in tufted sponges of bright orange as I'd witnessed it in my mind's eye.

I remembered the two girls and glanced down with an embarrassed smile. They still looked on, the same awe written on their faces, probably waiting for me to do something spectacular. Seems that no time had passed since I had become the clown! I wondered what they expected, then forgot them again.

By this time I was convinced I looked like a clown and with that, lifted my clown face up, eyes painted in weeping tear drop lines, and looked across the room: expectantly, sardonically, somewhat sadly, mouth turned down at the corners (I could feel the pull at the edges of my mouth). Perhaps if I blinked my eyes would sparkle.

I wondered what they would think, down there - should I join the circus as the clown I was, or perhaps as the lion tamer, or whatever they called him. Perhaps the ringmaster was for me. But then again to quote - "See the clown playing fiddle to the boy, sad because he can't appreciate his toy, blah, blah and so on!"

Normality returned for a moment and my glance fell on a person, half-hidden in shadows at the back of the room, who watched my every expression. I felt rather foolish, wondering if I had been noticed for the clown I really was.

Where was the band? I cast a panic-stricken look around for them - needed some meagre support. Had I lost them? Ah, there they were, attempting to extricate themselves from friends at the bar and it seemed a friendly argument was also in progress.

My pathetic plea went unnoticed, so my eyes were again drawn to the man at the back of the room, different, and not part of the young audience. He still stood there watching, holding my eyes now with a fixed gaze. Then he became my obsession, my compulsion. As the superficial clown I was, I stared back in challenge, chin up, barely able to mask the chill that crept up my spine. A coldness of spirit that was accompanied at the same time by an inexplicable joy of recognition washed over me - I stood there emotionally naked and spiritually exposed.

"Come, my angelic friend. If it's a challenge you want, then it's a duel you will have," I mind-mouthed across the din. Hell, why did I say that? Our gazes locked and he smiled in acknowledgement. From whence this angel came I knew not - I sniggered at my cool language.

Raising his hand in salute, he bombarded my mind with his thought forms. I say bombarded because the attack came suddenly and unexpectedly. His entry felt like an icicle piercing and then melting its way through my aching head. My body became the ice of his invasion and my chilled hands dropped from the guitar.

My imaginary clown suit blew away in the confusion, taking with it the smile that had been painted on my pretender's face. It was at this point that my life changed. He spoke to me with those eyes, raped my soul with those eyes, and made promises that could sanely never be met, all in a matter of seconds. It seemed like hours. He left me barren, empty, a husk tossing wildly in a storm. I began to cry. When I blinked the tears from my eyes to find him, he was gone, and I felt my legs buckle.

As I fell to the stage, a grey and muted ethereality surrounded me. All that remained of my senses was the faint sound of the people whispering as they gathered about the fallen clown - me!

Everything to that point had been blurry, but what happened afterwards is vague. Faintly and with little clarity I heard the accusatory comments and the pre-suppositions but had no inclination or ability whatsoever to argue the point or protect my honour. I heard the words, and with the words came blackness.

That is what I remember of the day my soul was raped.

Megan

As I rushed towards Ethan, I saw Bryan and Blue shove their way through the crowd towards the stage. Andrea tagged along behind me. Ethan lay in a puddle of his own saliva, eyes wide and staring. I clambered up and took his head onto my lap, assuming he had overdosed. After all, what was new.

"For Chrissakes somebody, call an

ambulance!" I shouted hysterically, as I frantically rubbed his hand, and then wiped the silky hair from his wet face. All he'd ever given me was the ability to weep endless tears in his honour. I don't think anyone ever did call the ambulance.

†

Ethan is my life. He is everything and I feel that I've lost him even though I'm sure I never had him. He has always been elusive, rather mysterious, and incredibly beautiful. He is so involved in his psychological battle with who knows what, he never notices the heads turn when he walks by. The fact is Ethan is a wonder to behold.

At this point, Ethan is slipping further and further into a grey place. I don't believe he now feels any emotion at all. His presence has crystallised into something ethereal and has reached a point of causing discomfort to the beholder. And, when I say discomfort, I mean a physical pain jolts through the body of those of who gaze upon him, almost causing a loss of breath.

A couple of years back now, I heard the nurses at the hospital saying very much the same thing. People are confused by this physical manifestation and cannot ascertain whether it's a form of primeval and consuming lust, or pain at the perfection of his beauty.

They say that such uncommon magnificence rarely exists without repercussion. They also say that it is in the eye of the beholder. Yes I'm sure it probably is, but there's no doubt about Ethan's shine. To me there's an aura about Ethan that encompasses ages past, ages to come, the old and young alike, naïveté and wisdom. It isn't a cold thing, but warm and incredibly inviting.

Ethan impresses himself upon one but allows no impression on himself. It's almost as if his barriers have been erected, never to be glimpsed over. I often wonder what really lurks behind them but am afraid for too much ever being revealed.

Ethan can be warm and amusing. In fact, whether he chooses to do so or not, he has the ability to draw people like moths are drawn to a storm lamp. He then switches it off without excuse or provocation, leaving them once more floundering blindly in the dark, as if the light had never been there but had merely been a figment of their imagination all along. Then the lamp might give forth a glimmer of its former light, and as one reaches out to turn up the wick, it is quickly and secretly extinguished once again, leaving an indelible impression in the dark of the light that had once been - an impression that can never be forgotten.

Ethan accepts his strangeness without question. Well, I suppose it can be said that he has never known any different so probably doesn't see himself as strange. It is almost as if Ethan has been moulded for some divine purpose yet to be revealed.

Ethan was twenty-one when I first saw him, charming his small audiences with his looks, voice, and musical ability. He wrote strange music and had few permanent fans. Those he did have, and who genuinely appreciated his music, were mostly intellectual freaks and dropouts, obviously as strange as Ethan himself. They were his cult followers. Wherever shall Ethan go, so shall we! And so did I. Otherwise, of course, he had both male and female admirers slobbering over his beauty, wherever or with whomever he played.

But they all left Ethan at about the time I was just getting to know him. He had spent too much time away from his music and out of the spotlight, determined to conquer his addiction to heroin. It's not that they left him; it was he that left them, his flock. Not that the flock visibly seemed to care when the shepherd fell.

I was one of them, following him from venue to tiny venue, hoping and dying for a glance, a word, or a hint of having been noticed - waiting for those striking blue eyes to look my way, adoring, worshipping, and mourning. Never had I loved so much, been so smitten or suffered such heartache, as when I followed Ethan. I was the ultimate groupie.

The first time I touched him, he had knelt on the stage and stretched his hand out over a sprouting of hands that greedily grabbed for acknowledgement. Being right at the front as I always was, his hair had covered my face and I had drowned in the powerful ambience of smells and vibration that he exuded. He had smiled an apology and continued his performance without another glance in my direction. I was in love.

He told me afterwards that this was the first time he'd noticed me. Nevertheless, it was to be a full two years before Ethan and I spoke to one another again.

I had given up following him around and was sinking my energies into my chosen career of interior design. It was part of growing up, and I had soon realised that nothing was going to make my God notice me. Also, I wasn't feeling particularly successful creeping in and out of night-clubs to drool over a stranger who barely acknowledged me, except for that one smile.

Strange how things work out. I ended up

meeting Ethan in hospital, where I was visiting my brother who had been admitted for an emergency appendix operation. Smoking was not allowed in the hospital, and I had gone to have a cigarette outside. I was sitting, puffing away as quickly as I could, ingesting as much nicotine in as short a space of time as possible, when two hands clasped me from behind and closed my eyes. I thought it was one of my brother, Rory's, friends.

"Hey!" I yelled and let fly with a sharp elbow to the ribs, silently applauding myself for my quick reaction.

I heard a sharp intake of breath and turned my head to enjoy the pain I had caused to one of the many young men that frequent my mother's house.

Imagine my shock when I found myself looking straight into those blue eyes. My mouth dried up completely and my tongue felt stuck to my teeth; felt stuck to my lips. In fact, I became an immediate catatonic.

"You alright, luv. You okay? Can I get you something?" he asked, comic concern playing about his mouth. That mouth really did something for me. I found myself staring.

"Oh, hello!" I finally managed to blurt out, smoke billowing from my mouth. Foolishly, I repeated myself, "Hi."

"Don't I know you from somewhere?" he asked, moving around to face me.

"It's Ethan isn't it? Um, sorry about that smack with the elbow, thought you were one of my brother's friends. Yes, I've seen you play before - a while ago. Tell me, do you always grab strangers from behind and scare the wits out of them?"

"I'm sorry." He wiped the hair back from his forehead. "Don't know what got into me." I could see he didn't mean it. "Must be this place - been cooped up here for a couple of weeks. But I do know you - I've seen you around. Hey, I've got to say this, but you've got the most gorgeous blush I've ever seen. Now you've got to forgive me!"

I couldn't believe he knew me or that he meant a single word of what he said. What had I done to deserve this? He waited for an answer, a silly grin on that beloved face.

"Oh! I mean, yes of course ... forgiven!" Really at loss for words, I gulped, felt the blush heating my cheeks once again and then began to laugh wildly, as I always do when I'm nervous. Finally I managed enough self-control to continue, "I'm Megan by the way." I extended a belated hand, "Pleased to finally meet you." My eyes carried on laughing, betraying my pleasurable delirium.

The whole incident must have suddenly struck him as funny because he joined me, and we laughed hysterically - only stopping to suck in air and point at one another's' faces in uncontrollable mirth.

For both of us, I think, it was merely a means to relieve our own private tensions.

For the next week we saw each other every day, until my brother was discharged. Ethan had been admitted for a drug overdose and was being kept under psychiatric observation for a while. He said that the only reason he hadn't discharged himself was because he was enjoying seeing and talking to me. He admitted having noticed me those two years previously and said that if it weren't for the fact that one of his policies is not to get involved with the women in the audience, he would most definitely have tried to get to know me. He was glad for the opportunity the hospital had presented. Naturally, I soaked up every word of it.

Anyway, we spent long periods of time together and I became a worm at his feet, running to do his bidding and agreeing to everything he said. Fact of the matter is, I thought him wonderful, as you've probably realised by now. Most of the people with whom he associated seemed to hold him in the same awe, so for Ethan life must have held few true friends, as everyone just felt obliged to fall over themselves agreeing with him. He must have been very lonely now that I think about it.

†

What happened to Ethan at Exodus left me really worried. The chaps in the band said that they had seen him slip out to the van, and that he had been stoned when he returned. I wondered if he was back to 'riding the horse' (as I've heard them call it) again, so as he lay there, I had quickly pushed up a sleeve to check for the marks. No tell-tale punctures displayed themselves, only some older scars. I couldn't be sure, but bile rose in my throat, and pain twisted my heart. What had triggered this collapse? Had he spiked somewhere else to hide the needle marks? I wouldn't be able to examine his whole body.

He regained some semblance of consciousness, enough to ask me to take him home. My friend Andrea drove. I sat on the back seat of the car cradling Ethan's head on my lap and gently stroking his face. Spit drooled from his mouth and pooled on my lap. He was in a state of shock and seemed pretty unaware of my attention. From time to time he'd mumble something about a man but would then lapse back into a coma-like trance, sweat beading his white face.

By the time we arrived home he was sufficiently aware for me to ask whether he thought he needed to go to hospital.

"I'm okay. I'll be okay. Okay ..." He was obviously confused. Then quite coherently, "Really don't know what went wrong, Megs. That man, that ... I'll see how I am tomorrow, okay, and then perhaps go and see the doctor. Stay with me, Megs, please. Don't leave me alone, okay." His grip on my hand tightened.

Blinded by tears, I nodded. He seemed satisfied that I'd be there and drifted back into his silent world. His indication that he needed me was all the encouragement I needed to get rid of Andrea and spend the remaining hours before sunrise lying next to him, aware of his every breath, and loving him more as each stab of pain knifed its way across my heart. What was it with me? With his head on my shoulder, he slept through the rest of the night.

CHAPTER 3

The forgotten son

Two weeks passed without Ethan leaving the confines of the flat.

He woke every morning bathed in sweat, hair wrapped around his neck and across his face like writhing serpents attempting to strangle him as he slept. He dreamt dreams like he had never had before - dreams of beginnings, and dreams of endings.

Wiping his hair back off his forehead, he glinted through swollen eyes at the early morning sun. He patted the table next to his bed for his cigarettes and, whilst puffing, reached for his jacket, and dug into the inside pocket for his kit. 'No!' he argued with himself over and over, 'you're *not* going to do this. You're not going to get into this again!'

His head ached, and he reached for a pillow to smother the daylight. He itched all over and scratched his hands constantly. The dream of the night remained with him, attempting to invade the reality of the waking day.

†

Ethan had been himself, as much as he could be in such a dream, strolling through a forest of ancient and imposing trees. Sun dappled the path along which he walked, and the juice of the red pomegranate he clasped in his hand dripped from his chin. He could taste the bitter-sweet fruit and longed for more.

A tree seemed to reach out for him, as if this is what trees did. The tree teased with its branches, clasping, releasing, and stroking, as it slowly entwined itself about him. Then, with its arms of gnarled wisdom, it drew him in towards its throbbing core.

As it squeezed, Ethan felt himself diffuse into the broken trunk - become the trunk. He reached up with his arms into the tree's branches - and became the tree! Ancient wisdom took seed in his brain, and he was able to see all around him - the trees for what they were, and the forest in all its majestic glory.

Raging storms flashed their primitive strength through the heavens. Uprooted father-trees lay on their backs, aged roots openly displayed to the tumultuous sky. A dark foreboding brook cackled through the rocks. Lightning turned the forest into charcoal etchings. Be-knighted horses galloped under and through threatening boughs, flaring their blood red nostrils in defiance. Knights with the cross of the crusade!

Ethan, as the tree, witnessed this from the topmost leaf of his twisting and swaying branches. A leaf broke off that bough, and he was the leaf. He started his descent to the murky, damp forest floor.

†

Ethan threw the sweated pillow from his face, lifted himself onto an elbow, and with shaking hands reached for his cigarettes. His entire body ached, his stomach cramped, and he was beaded with what he thought was the sweat of addiction. He felt drained, as if not a drop of moisture remained. With parched lips and eyes crusted as if with the murk from the forest floor, he took a couple of deep draws from his cigarette and swung his legs over the side of the bed. He was still wearing the same crumpled clothes that he had worn the previous evening.

Like a sleepwalker and on unsteady legs, he made his way to the bathroom, splashed water on his face, wiped his hair back and brushed his teeth. As the water passed over his lips it made him shudder.

With the more tempting thought of a glass of red wine, he made his way to the kitchen and poured. The wine washed comfortingly down his parched throat like blood through a famished vein, bringing back memories of the fruit in the dream.

Between sips, he cast his eyes over the early morning city. The cars hooting in the streets below caused shards of pain in his head. All this intertwined with thoughts of blood and night-creatures that called from the memory boughs of his mind.

†

Megan must have already left for work without disturbing him. The flat was lifeless without her.

The morning passed, as had those of the past two weeks, with Ethan intermittently staring out of the window, smoking cigarette after cigarette, and throwing himself down on the floor to listen to music and to try to figure out what was happening in his life. Over and over again, the first line of a song he had written came to mind: *'The forgotten son sat in the corner, no beam to penetrate his futile fate.'* If only he could figure it out. It was as if a message was trying to get through, from where though, from whom? Just his daft mind, he supposed.

There were no answers, and he began to grow weary of looking for them. His head ached in its usual manner and his blood screamed out its torturous need.

With a final scratch in his hair, he walked over to answer the insistent knock on the door. He wasn't sure if it was a knock, or if it was the throb of pain that he could feel pounding his temples. With cigarette in hand, Ethan opened the door to find Blue grinning and bobbing as he usually did.

"Hey man," greeted Blue, then in the same breath, "where've you been at? You look like shit! I s'pose you know the guys found someone else to take your place. He's okay but lacks the feel for the beat that you have." He bobbed from foot to foot, waiting for an invitation to come in.

Ethan felt distant and unconcerned, wishing Blue would miraculously disappear. "Come on in Blue - not that it's really necessary, 'cos I'm sure you've told me everything you came here to tell. Sorry man, sorry - really, come in. I've been a bit out of it last couple of weeks. Excuse the mess."

Ethan turned and Blue followed him in, tapping agitatedly on the side of his leg to some imagined song. Ethan eased himself onto the floor and slowly and laboriously, battling to formulate each word, said, "Don't think the band's for me. Y'no, gotta do my own thing. Like something to drink?"

Blue had thrown himself down opposite

Ethan, cross-legged in front of the CD rack, and started sorting through Ethan's collection. "Wow, you've got some unreal music here man!" Then he answered belatedly, "Yeah, love something to drink."

"Red wine? Tomato juice?" asked Ethan, then ran his tongue around the inside of his mouth to dislodge the cotton wool that he was sure was clinging to it.

"Wine? Tomato juice!! Ah, come on, Ethe. Got a beer, at least?"

Ethan disappeared into the kitchen to search the refrigerator. There were a couple of beers at the back as far as he could remember. After rummaging around, he found them, took one out, popped the cap, and took the bottle back to Blue. He brought a tomato juice in the can for himself, with a topped-up glass of wine, and put both on the centre table and slumped back onto the floor and crossed his legs, both drinks within easy reach. He fumbled in the full ashtray for a cigarette stub and lit it.

"Hey Blue, where'd you get your name?" he asked, feeling his speech centre getting back on track and trying to be more sociable than he felt. He blew two smoke rings, one after the other, and gazed at Blue through the smoke. He looked down at his cig, it was down to the filter; he stubbed it out.

"Questions, questions. Dunno really, has sorta been stuck with me since school, ya know. Ethan, honestly you look like shit man. You know what you need don't you? You know I can help you out man?"

Ethan lifted his brows and nodded. "Yeah, I know exactly what I need; I need to shoot my fucking brains out!" He smiled weakly and added, "But right now I need another cigarette – I've run out. You got one for me?"

"Like I told you, I've got everything you need." Blue dug in his pocket for his cigarettes and shook one out.

Ethan wasn't sure he really liked Blue. Blue was just one of those people who chose to be too familiar and usually got away with it, leaving one wanting to object but not really knowing what the objection was. He watched as Blue got up and disappeared in the direction of the bathroom, taking longer than he should have.

Blue returned with a self-satisfied smirk on his face. He danced his way over to Ethan. "Got sump'thin here that you need, sump'thin that'll make you feel a whole lot better my man - got sump'thin here that'll make you feel excellent, but you're going to owe me. Just remember, this one's on the house, okay?"

"Jeez Blue, you know I've given up on that stuff, man. It's been quite a while now."

"Ah, crap, man! I don't believe you! Anyway, you can think or say anything you freakin' like. Once an addict, my friend, then always! Just think of it as a once-off - if you must - a favour from an old buddy. You can go back to pretending that you're the ultimate martyr afterwards. So, waddya say?"

He held out his offering to Ethan. Ethan felt his heart skip a beat at the sight of the already loaded syringe. He felt sweat prickle his top lip in a heated rush. Blue held it out to him with a knowing grin. "Now without further ado about nothing, relent fair knight and proffer your arm. Man, I can't waste this stuff - it's too good. Freakin' best there is. I tell you no lies."

Ethan had reached a point where he really didn't give a flying fuck anymore. In fact, his decision to hold out his hand for the syringe was prompted more by that of a masochistic urge than need. He needed the reality and pain of his former - and now seemingly to be newly resumed - addiction, to bring him back down to earth. Anything was better than the void he had been experiencing just lately – the confusion; the not knowing who he was.

With a sigh of resignation, Ethan killed the cig

then slipped the belt from his waist and wrapped it around his upper arm. As it tightened and his veins squeezed their way to the surface, he held out his hand for the syringe. This was something he always did for himself. His look was one of resignation. "I hope this is good stuff Blue. I really shouldn't be doing this! What about you, dude?"

"Plenty where this came from, you first" sang Blue, handing him the syringe. He had visions of making a lot of money out of Ethan again, as he had in the past. In fact he relished the return of Ethan's addiction, as Ethan was just too beautiful for Blue's personal comfort. He watched as Ethan slowly inserted the needle, and gloated in self-satisfaction.

The drama that then unfolded was just too much for Blue's fragile ego. As Ethan plunged the syringe, his body relaxed and within moments he had fallen backwards to the floor. He gasped a few times, and then started to turn deathly grey.

Blue panicked, and whispered hysterically, "Oh, for fuck sake, I've killed him. I'd better get outta here man. Oh fuck. Oh fuck me!" He fumbled in his pocket for the Naloxone he always carried, just in case. He jabbed the needle right through Ethan's clothes into his thigh, then scrambled up, sending a pile of CD's flying; slipped, struck his head on the table and finally, in a crawl, reached the front door. He looked back at Ethan. He thought he could see his chest start to rise and fall so he must be breathing. He wasn't going to stick around any longer to see if Ethan was okay. Being the kind of person he was, he decided to just get out and clawed himself upright against the wall, threw open the front door and skidded down the staircase as if Lucifer himself chased him.

†

When Ethan had lost consciousness, all was black for him.

†

Kalin, in his vigil, lived through the blackout and Ethan's slowed breathing. As the breathing ceased and the body lapsed into unconsciousness, Kalin entered and healed before the Naloxone had time to take effect. He absorbed all the impurities from Ethan's body and cast them out to join the ethers of the universe. He used the opportunity to plant a second seed in the brain of his prodigal son.

With love, he left and returned to familiar surroundings, his own body. He had entered without invitation, but under the circumstances no laws had been broken. All would be well, and Ethan was nearly his, was nearly theirs - and they were nearly Ethan's. They would all be one, as they should be. Their blood would flow together as it had in the beginning and as it would until the end. They had waited long enough - he, Kalin, had waited long enough. "Ah my son," he murmured as he returned to his body, "brother of ours."

†

Megan arrived home to find Ethan semi-conscious on the floor. His bruised eyelids were fluttering. "Ethan? My God, not again! Ethan please speak to me," she pleaded. She shook him hysterically. "Ethan wake up, for God's sake!"

He muttered, and she felt a wash of relief. Kneeling beside him, she cradled and crooned as she had done that night on the stage. His head rested on her lap, hair warmly covering her bare knees.

Megan looked around, and immediately noted the over-turned coffee table, the CDs all over the floor, an unfinished beer, full glass of wine, a can of tomato juice, and the puddle of saliva on the carpet. She didn't want to know what he'd been up to. He had been strange and sick just recently though, she reasoned with herself, and he was probably sicker than she had thought. Over the past couple of months she had had to make constant excuses for him.

Then she saw the syringe lying on the floor

where it had fallen, and another still sticking out through his clothes against his thigh. "Oh my God! Oh, forgive me Lord for using your name so often. Christ Ethan. Ethan!" She shook the silent form again, moved his head from her lap and stood up. She babbled to herself. "Don't tell me!"

Her heart sank. Ethan was her perfect God - she couldn't believe the stark reality that confronted her. She took an arm, now neatly folded on his chest, and lifting it, found the lightly bruised vein and tell-tale puncture mark. Her heart fell and a tear slipped down her cheek.

"Oh, Ethe, why? Why did you do this? What's making you so darn unhappy? Hasn't my love been enough? What do you want?" She shook his arm hysterically and shouted, "What is it that you want? Tell me!" She ended with a whisper, and trailed her fingers across his face, gently wiping the tendrils of hair from his cheek.

Ethan stirred. "Megan?" he squinted through half closed eyes, bewildered to find her bending over him.

"Ethan are you okay? Dear Lord, thank you for answering my prayers. Ethan?"

"I think I'm okay, Megan." He sat up, and shakily wiped his hair back. "Actually I feel fine, Megs. What's wrong? What am I doing on the floor? Shit, where's Blue?"

"Ethan, I've been sitting here with you, beside myself with worry. Is there something I should be doing to help you? How do you feel? Must I take you through to the hospital?" The tremor in her voice expressed the panic she had been feeling. Tears burst from her eyes, and she wrapped her arms about him.

"I'm fine, really I am!" He abruptly removed her arms from about his neck. "Really I am, Megs. Shh, stop it. What're you carrying on about?"

In fact Ethan felt extremely well, and happier than he had in a long time. This was not a drug-induced happiness, he knew the feel of that - this was different. Vitality coursed through his veins, and he never gave a further thought to the drug he had so recently injected into his arm. He knew then that he was changing, and it felt good.

Discreetly, Megan picked up the syringes and wrapped them in old newspaper. "I'll make us some tea" she excused. She walked through to the kitchen and tucked the newspaper bundle in at the bottom of the bin, then switched on the kettle. She was nauseous with disappointment and hurt at the thought of Ethan back on drugs after so long? Sick at the fear of losing him! Fear of the devastation she had seen etched on his face over the past couple of weeks, and today, wonder at the face no longer filled with lines of worry but smooth and clear like that of a child.

Radiant in the peace of the moment!

For the first time in two weeks Megan could hear Ethan singing at the top of his voice in the shower like he used to. It sounded good to hear him happier, so she pushed the past couple of weeks from her mind and concentrated on the meal she had decided to prepare.

By the time Ethan had finished in the shower and had towel dried and fingered out his hair, Megan had the food ready, and more importantly the wine. She had opened a bottle of Boschendal, one of their favourites. She turned around with Ethan's glass in hand and found him framed in the doorway. He had a towel wrapped about his slim waist, and a drape of long black wet hair rested on his shoulder. A wolf tattoo raged on his bicep. He looked relaxed and healthy; quite fantastic really. The improvement in him baffled her.

He smiled contentedly as he picked up the wine bottle from the centre table to examine it and made a point of sniffing the air. "Ah, our favourite wine - cool! Food smells great too, Megs."

Grabbing her free hand, he gently eased her to the floor. "Come, talk to me. Let's chill for a while and catch up?" She crumpled down on the floor next to him acutely aware of his knee touching hers.

His face became serious, "I'm really sorry about my behaviour and mess-ups. Jeez, I can't seem to get anything right, but I promise things will get better. It'll be okay, luv. Anyway, you wouldn't have wanted to speak to me the way I've been feeling – I reckon you wouldn't have liked what you heard."

Somehow she couldn't find anything to say. What could she say?

"Megan, you still cross?" He pleaded, "Speak to me." He reached out and took her hand. Still silent she clasped his hand tightly, never wanting to let go.

So for the first part of the evening they sat together by candlelight, now empty dinner plates piled on the centre table and good wine in their glasses. They surreptitiously touched, sipped wine, and listened to music. Such a good normal evening! So right. So wrong.

As Ethan allowed Megan into his space and drank more of the wine, he could feel warmth diffuse through his body and, unexpectedly, the beginnings of a strange desire. Suddenly fascinated, he watched the smile that always played about her mouth; the dimple that seemed especially attractive on this occasion, and the soft flush on her cheeks. He watched the artery in her throat pulsing with each heartbeat, and he thought of blood. Something foreign was building up inside him. He didn't recognise it.

"What's been happening?" she finally found the courage to whisper. Her smile vanished and a small frown creased her brow. "I've been feeling so left out, Ethan. I can't help feeling that I'm losing you, and just don't know what to do about it. Help me – tell me Ethe!" she implored. "Are we still happening, or ... well where is this going?" As she waited for an answer, she watched as he swirled the wine round and round in his glass, now seemingly mesmerised by the whirlpool effect. Had he heard her? She took a small sip of her wine.

A fleeting breeze caused the candle to dance out a hypnotic rhythm of swaying shadows on the wall.

She reached out and wiped a stray lock of hair from his face. "Am I losing you Ethan?"

Without blinking he looked up. Even in the low light she could see his deep blue eyes and long dark lashes. He was so beautiful. He stared at her intently. "Truly Megan, I don't know. It's ever since the night I played at Exodus. Something happened, something I can't even explain to myself – a mind-fuck I don't understand, so don't know how to explain."

He broke his gaze, wiped his hair back from his brow and swallowed. He took her hand and squeezed it. Her stomach fluttered.

Slowly he leant forward, eyes fixed on her mouth, and touched his lips to hers - softly at first with small sensual pecks, and then, as his passion rose he began biting softly at her lips, and finally eased into a passionate full mouth kiss. The intensity of the kiss increased until Megan felt like her last breath was being sucked out of her body. She returned the kiss as best she could, but he was leaving her behind, consumed as he was by passion – the kiss becoming so much more than a kiss that it hurt.

A brief whimper of fright escaped from her mouth and, with eyes full of tears and the taste of blood in her mouth, she panted, "Ethan, don't, please, not like this, you're hurting me. I don't understand. This isn't right - you're not doing this right."

The ripe pomegranate passion on his cheeks enhanced the cold, now steel blue of his eyes. His grip on her arm was unnecessarily harsh. "Come!" he said, his voice cold but urgent. He rose effortlessly, pulling her up at the same time, but keeping a firm grip on her arm. He force walked her to the bedroom.

When she protested in alarm, he bent his head

and whispered against her cheek. "Sorry Megs, it's okay. I'll try to do this better? Let me!"

Although her legs were shaking, and her stomach was clenching in response to his lovemaking - if it could be called that - without knowing why, she was afraid. As he lowered her to the bed, her eyes widened with both passion and fear. Still he did not blink. Megan couldn't help feeling that her Ethan had abandoned her to be ravaged by this other Ethan that had taken over his body. She'd so wanted this, but somehow the scenario had played out differently in her mind.

He buried his face in her hair, slowly nudging it from her neck, and moved downward, licking and caressing; over her breasts, barely lingering; back up to her neck, biting softly, softly, pinching her skin between his teeth. She murmured in response. Again he worked his way down past her breasts to her abdomen, then to her side where he started sucking. Megan's groan of arousal soon turned to panic as he sucked, and sucked, until pain stabbed through her abdomen.

The pain awakened her from the almost hypnotic state he'd caused, and in a panic she tried to push him away. He eased upward and held her wrists above her head. "Ethan! No! Please stop". With a start, he surfaced from his euphoria and let go of her wrists, his eyes seemingly returning to a warm normal. She struggled out from under him and staggered away from the bed. Before he could pull her back, she stumbled through to the bathroom and locked the door behind her. Heaving sobs convulsed her body. This was the first time Ethan had attempted to make love to her, and she had felt no love in him, but something dark. A trickle of blood ran from her side where he had sucked, and another from the corner of her mouth. She reached up to touch her lips, gingerly feeling around the splits that had been opened. Her hand came away bloodied.

Megan expected Ethan to come knocking at the door with an apology, or even perhaps in anger. He never came and she heard nothing from the bedroom. An hour passed and still she waited sitting on the closed toilet seat. Then she started regretting her retreat and felt awful for having probably over-reacted. She should have led him more and showed him what pleased her, but she hadn't. He was still her God, and she didn't want to lose him. Fear, and the memory of just how unfeeling Ethan had seemed, were beginning to fade from her memory. So, feeling really foolish, she pulled a little face at herself in the mirror, opened the bathroom door and peeped out to see if Ethan was sleeping. The bedroom was empty. He had slipped out whilst she had been comforting herself in the bathroom.

†

As Megan pushed him away and ran to the bathroom, Ethan woke from his possessed state. Confused and disgusted both by his behaviour and by the intensity of the consuming passion that still coursed through his veins, he walked over to the bathroom door and stood listening to her sobs.

Revolted, but at the same time ecstatic, he pulled himself away and went over to the side table where his cigarettes lay. His consuming lust left him. He wiped the back of his hand over his swollen mouth, tasting her blood. He lit the cigarette, grabbed at the just opened bottle of red, and blindly walked out of the flat, fearful of seeing Megan's face and afraid of what he was becoming. He was confused by his own out of character behaviour!

The memory of those sobs remained with him the rest of the evening as he walked the streets. Feelings of guilt and lust exploded in bursts in his mind. He walked aimlessly, without getting tired. Thoughts of suicide slipped their tentacles, here and there, between the wedges of guilt and passion.

Snippets of his life re-played themselves over and over in his mind, memories of his family.

His father long dead, probably killed by the vast quantities of alcohol he consumed and the stress of keeping up with a business growing too quickly. His younger brother, Andrew, was now in Paris lecturing in art. It had been a long time since he had seen either his brother or his mother, as he had kept away since the time when he thought that his dependence on drugs must have become an embarrassment to the family. He no longer felt he could relate to them, or they to him for that matter.

He wondered if his mother, Anne, had managed to keep the business going after the death of his father. He supposed she must have because he still received a couple of thousand pounds every month, part of the trust and his small portion of the profits of the business. He felt feelings of guilt at having abandoned her.

Ethan examined himself in minuscule detail, something he had avoided for years. He had been living day by day and moment by moment. What he saw didn't appeal to him much. He saw a life devoid of true friends and empty of any close relationships. He felt like an abandoned raft tossing in the storm-waves of an uncaring sea of life. He wondered if he had brought this loneliness on himself, and wished he knew of a way to reach out and get closer to the people in his life. Something always seemed to hold him back. Perhaps the fear of getting hurt, or more realistically he just didn't care enough about any of them to really want to go to any great lengths to nurture friendships. Yet he craved a close relationship where he could feel as one with someone. But he always fucked it up.

As he walked, dawn saw the city start whispering its secrets to passers-by. The smell of eggs, bacon and toast wafted from an open window. A man in a heavy jacket and watering can poured warm water over the frost on his car window. People started oozing into the streets to start their day. A tabby cat darted across the road. A normal day was just starting. Ethan made his way home, devoid of passionate thought, singing to himself drunkenly and grinning in self-satisfaction. He flung the now empty wine bottle into someone's overgrown front garden, to join the other accumulated junk.

The flat was empty, and although Ethan half expected it, he was still shaken to find the note from her.

"Ethe, I think we need to think things over," he read. "I know you're going through some kind of a tough time right now and I don't know how to help. I don't know what you want, or if I play any part in what you want. Well, you know what I mean. I love you Ethan, what more can I say? I can't plead for your love or your sanity; it's really your choice. Think about me, about us. We'll talk again soon.

Yours, you know. Meg".

A drunken tear sprang to his eye. He was already lonely without her. But he wondered at his feelings. Surely if one loves, one doesn't have to ask if one loves, one knows, so they say. Or do they? "Do I love her?" he asked loudly of the old poster of Tom Waits on the wall. No answer. "Well, if you don't know, then who the fuck knows!" he shouted, pleased with his observation and the finality written on Tom's face. Ethan fell dispirited onto the bed.

†

... Ethan, as a fragile leaf, lay on the mouldering forest floor; afraid of the era it could see drawing to a close. It had lived a rich, full life. Is this how it would end, in decay and oblivion? It looked up at the leaves remaining on the tree, blowing in the wind of impermanence, and seeing what it had already seen. The time was now theirs to absorb life's energies.

Cold and damp seeped slowly into the veins of the leaf. Death's angel rampaged through the forest, nonchalantly crushing all underfoot.

A faint roar invaded the forest, and grew louder, and louder, until the roar became all. Gigantic waves of water rolled through and over the forest floor, sweeping up everything in their path. The waves' watery fingers pried and felt and searched.

The leaf was swept up into the wet plexus of debris, and sent tumbling and rolling, soon to be discharged into the great seething cauldron of a river. It rose to the top and floated for a while amongst the flotsam of the river. Eventually, the leaf began to absorb water and became heavier, slowly swirling, sinking - sodden. The leaf became the river and spread its veins into the eddies and streams. It caressed the riverbed and swiftly negotiated the sharp bends, to finally become tranquil and softly flow into the sea. The river became the sea. Ethan became the sea.

The tranquil sea had slumbered for millennia, an empty brine-womb. Now the creatures of its creation seethed and teemed within its bosom. Ethan moved through these waters of creation in quick bursts of energy. In time he could see a myriad of medusa around him, all pulsing in the ethers of life and moving towards the dawn of all that was to come.

He felt himself washed upon a beach and crawled on all fours in the thick, muddy sand to be enveloped by the sulphuric virgin air, only to be washed back with the tide and to remain, waiting for the next time. He crawled up again and, with an explosion of pain, took gasps of air into his lungs - the pain of the awakening. He sunk his claws into the soil to pull himself forward ...

CHAPTER 4

Kalin's kiss

Ethan awoke much as he had the day before. He rose, lit a cigarette, poured a glass of red, and walked to the window to look out at the river. This time there was no Megan, just the quiet flat. No sound except for a drip of water from somewhere, which splashed out a small regular beat; faint talking from an adjoining flat down the passage. He had a shower, got dressed and downed the last of his glass of wine. He left the flat, and the drip, and without over-thinking made his way to the pub, where he somehow knew he should be. With a small snort of self-amused laughter under his breath, he convinced himself that he was allowing fate to take its course. And of course, that is precisely what it was doing. Kalin followed, without permitting Ethan knowledge of his presence.

Ethan entered 'Ain't Nothing But the Blues Bar'. Two chaps sitting at the bar had watched him walk in and greeted him. He acknowledged them with a raise of his hand and a smile. Fellow musicians. So much for anonymity! He stood a little away from them and ordered a bottle of red. Conversation was the last thing he wanted. He leaned against the bar and sipped his wine. By staring intently at a wet ring on the counter before him, he was able to avoid prying eyes or conversation. There was a scrape of a barstool next to him, but he ignored that too, hoping the person would not try to engage him. Kalin sat down close to him, leant forward on an elbow, and looked at him intently with a small smile. Ethan felt uncomfortable, as he could sense he was being stared at. His space was also being blatantly invaded. Fury started bubbling up inside him, surprising and unsought. After a while of ignoring the unwelcome intrusion, he looked up, ready to glare and move somewhere else. He recognised the benevolently smiling man sitting opposite him. But from where? The memory was fuzzy. He began to feel the fresh invasion of his psyche, as the peculiarly familiar eyes burnt into his soul - the rush of the awakening! His heart leapt in his chest as he locked eyes with Kalin - as he remembered.

"You found me!" he whispered excitedly, eyes darting over Kalin's face, eye to mouth and back again. "Strange thing is, I knew you would, even though I don't know who you are. Yet I know you as I know myself. I've waited! Honestly, I've waited, not even knowing what I was waiting for. What is it you want of me? Who are you?" His voice broke with his rising passion - the passion of the moment - the warmth of *his* nearness.

"Ah, Ethan, my brother; my son. Do not fear. All will be explained in time." The voice was syrupy. "Now, we must leave, come!" He took Ethan's hand in his and started to rise. Ethan offered no resistance but rose willingly. He drew strength from Kalin's hand. He felt strangely at peace and was content to follow.

They left the dimness of the pub, and under the streetlights Ethan was able to see Kalin properly for the first time. As before, Kalin was expensively dressed in a black suit with a loose white shirt open at his throat. At first glance he looked as young as Ethan but was obviously much older.

To Ethan, Kalin was as perfect as any human being could be. He had a fine bone structure, striking hazel eyes, and rich black hair not unlike Ethan's. The face displayed a combination of everything: wisdom, innocence, peace, love, and a something that couldn't be described as good yet could never be thought of as evil.

Although Kalin lacked Ethan's ethereal qualities, he was striking. People stared in open wonder as the two of them walked by; but they were unaware of the attention riveted on them. Both walked with a smile, soaking in the presence of one another.

They stopped at the door of Megan's flat. Ethan entered and looked back with raised eyebrows and enquiring eyes at Kalin, who waited expectantly on the threshold. "Please, come in. We need to talk" Ethan said.

"Thank you, yes we do need to talk!" Kalin replied. He followed Ethan, barely glancing at his surroundings, attention riveted intensely on his prodigy.

Kalin opened his arms and beckoned as Ethan turned. Without stopping to consider the strangeness of his actions, Ethan walked into Kalin's embrace, sobbing on his shoulder all of his life-tragedy and relief. Kalin pulled him close and lay his chin upon Ethan's bent head. He projected empathy, harmony, and his love.

The heaving sobs stopped after a time, and Ethan pulled away. "I'm sorry," he whispered, "I'm so very sorry. I hope you will forgive me." A wash of tears coursed down his flushed cheeks.

"Ah Ethan, there is no need for an apology, and there is nothing to forgive. I have come for you, my lamb. I am here for you as I always was, and as I always will be!"

In wonder, Ethan realised that they had been speaking without words. "You know my name? How? I would like to know yours!" he mind-voiced in return, surprising himself at his new-found ability.

"I am Kalin! You will know me well in time to come, as I know you."

"How did you do it, Kalin? How did you enter my mind? It was you, that night at Exodus, wasn't it?"

"Yes, it was me. It was time. It could be no other way, as you are mine. I could never have entered without your invitation - without knowing you invited. I have waited long!" Whispering against Ethan's cheek, he stressed, "We have waited long - too long!"

"My invitation? You're talking in riddles, and I don't understand."

Ethan could feel the first webs of anger. He wanted answers; needed answers. Invited? He didn't believe that the rape of his soul had been by invitation. Is a soul raped so willingly? It was the seduction of his soul - it had been Kalin's need, not his.

He pulled from Kalin's embrace. "How can you call it an invitation when it was more like an invasion? Why? You left me empty and devastated. You left when I needed to understand, so I substituted. You've made me hurt Megan in my ignorance!" Ethan released the anger of his twenty-six years. "How? Tell me who the fuck you are! Some kind of weird stalker? Maybe you should just get the fuck out of here, because this is fucking with my mind!"

Kalin waited for the anguish to vent itself; then consoled, "Shh. Ethan, my lamb, come here! Come close and I'll show you. Trust me - we're on the same side you and me. I love you Ethan, like no other. *Come!*" He invited with an outstretched hand.

Ethan moved slowly towards him, entranced by the invitation of the open arms. He knew himself to be the sacrificial lamb of his own desires.

As Kalin took his hand, the last vestiges of Ethan's anger drained away. He was filled with rapture as Kalin lifted his compliant fingers to his lips. Kalin gently and lovingly kissed the slim hand he held in his - Ethan's hand, the hand of purity and love. He kissed his wrist, down his arm, and stopped at the needle mark.

"This would have killed you, my precious lamb, had I not saved you. Your friend was too late with his antidote. You were already leaving this life. If your life was in my hands then, do you think I would hurt you now? You should choose your friends more wisely."

Ethan had nothing to answer as the pleasure of the kisses enfolded him. The pleasure of Kalin enveloped him. As Kalin kissed his arm, he felt those same primeval urges that he had felt with Megan on the previous evening. He whimpered in pleasure, eyes closed in the perfection of the moment.

Kalin kissed over the puncture mark, and bit slowly into Ethan's arm until blood seeped into his mouth. He then turned his head and bit into his own wrist. With shaking limbs, he pressed his own wound against Ethan's gush.

As their blood rushed together, Ethan's rapture exploded warmly through his entire body. How could this be better than a heroin rush? But astoundingly, it was!

Kalin pulled Ethan closer, and whispered, "We are nearly one, and I shiver with excitement as I look forward to the finalisation of our union. As much as I'd like to stay, I must go now before my lust gets the better of me. Rest in peace my beautiful one; we will soon be together. Just not right now!"

Regretfully, he pulled away from Ethan. He reached into his pocket for a white handkerchief, which he wrapped about his wrist. With a final smile of farewell, and a slight finger touch to Ethan's forehead, he turned abruptly and walked out of the front door.

Ethan was left in a euphoric stupor. Blindly, he stared at the ceiling with his fists clenched and veins that stood out in knots on his arms and hands. His teeth ground against one another as he worked the passion from his being. When the pink fusion cleared from his eyes, he searched for Kalin's presence and found he was gone. Ethan wasn't even sure if he had been real, or if he had been imagined. He also knew that nothing would ever be the same again!

CHAPTER 5

Metamorphosis

Megan had hurriedly thrown the few things she would need for the weekend into an overnight bag and scribbled a hasty note to Ethan. She thought it best that she leave him to sort things out for himself for a couple of days. The note couldn't begin to explain how she felt, and so she left it mostly unsaid. He must know, after all, mustn't he?

Sometimes she felt as if she was fighting for something so elusive that she was making a fool of herself. She wished that the consuming love she felt for Ethan would miraculously disappear, and that instead she would fall in love with an ordinary nine-to-fiver whose greatest ambition was to become the ultimate yuppie and whose purpose in life was his mobile phone, his car, and the gym. But that did sound a bit boring. No, she decided, she enjoyed a challenge - but Ethan?

Her 1960's red mini was parked outside, as

always, on the pavement. She put her small suitcase onto the backseat, started up the car, and sat for a while whilst it warmed up. It was an old car and needed to be treated a bit kindly to function properly. Once the car was idling a bit smoother, she drove carefully off the side of the pavement and into the road. She was on her way and feeling happy to be doing so.

Megan hadn't seen her parents for a while and imagined their surprise when she arrived. The reason she hadn't seen them, of course, was Ethan. She had been too intent on not letting him out of her sight. Besides, she had been incredibly busy at work with a number of decorating assignments flowing into the weekends - measuring curtains, choosing wallpaper and all the small irritating chores that were sometimes best left for the weekends.

Megan soon left the city behind and turned up the volume of the car stereo system. She started humming to the compact disc that was playing. Sisters of Mercy sang, 'I don't exist if you don't see me, I don't exist when you're not there'. It brought tears to her eyes. Angrily, she brushed it away and with a dramatic sigh, ejected the compact disc to look for something a bit more cheerful, then after considering her options, decided against listening to anything. She wasn't in the right frame of mind and could cry at anything!

A hill loomed in the distance, sharply etching the small village that lay at the foot of the slope.

"Home," she sighed, pressing down harder on the accelerator. She just wanted to get home to where she always belonged, the place where she was truly loved. She so desperately needed some love.

She decided she'd better call Mom and Dad to let them know she was coming and was nearly there. She slipped her mobile phone open. They would be surprised.

She carried on with her ruminations. What would there be if there was no hope, she thought. Hope keeps us going - keeps us reaching out for the things logic says we can't have. Logic, on the other hand, smacks hands and says no - says you can't do it, says you can't have it. Yes, hope was the heart, and the heart is love, so they must be one. She grasped frantically for answers within her own heart.

A signpost announced the town. She took the turning and drove up a gravel road, almost to the very foot of McCreedies Hill, before it turned and veered back down, running straight into the small town.

Her parents' home was one of only a few of the heritage cottages in the area. Gnarled oak trees surrounded the property, lending partial shade in summer to the paddocks. Autumn bulbs were pushing their way through the already cold ground all along the paddock fence. Brown and golden leaves lay in thick blankets under the oaks. It was all so peaceful and normal.

She drove slowly past the paddock and called through the car's window to the horse that grazed within. "Misty, hey boy." He raised his head and nickered in recognition. He trotted up to the whitewashed fence, followed closely by Bray, his donkey companion. It had been too long! The peace of the scene and the welcome from the horse warmed her icy heart. She smiled, her dimple coming to life for the first time in a couple of days.

The sun had begun to dip behind the hillock, casting both brilliant late afternoon rays and sombre dusk shadows. The air was chilling in preparation for the evening. She saw Jim, the farmhand, entering the north side of the paddock, lead rein in hand, to bring Misty in for the night. Bray would follow. She waved at him, and he waved back. It was so good to be home.

Her mother and father watched her approach, spectacles lifted to foreheads and eager hands waving all the time as she drove down the slope. An aproned Marge and braced Paul came amenably down the front steps to greet Megan and help with what small luggage she had.

"What a lovely surprise, don't you think, Dad?" Marge said as she kissed Megan on the cheek and gave her a hug.

"Lovely dear, just lovely." He gave Megan an embarrassed hug and took the bag out of her hand.

Marge hooked Megan's free arm in hers. "So nice to see you my luv. Come inside. I have more than enough dinner for the three of us, and dear you won't believe, it must have been premonition, but I baked your favourite today, a rhubarb crumble – even before you called. Dad has been saying for a while now that he just feels like one, and there you have it. Isn't that so, Dad?" She marched Megan into the house, leaving Dad to follow behind.

Homecoming was always like this, as if she'd never been away. Megan felt the weight of the past year lift from her shoulders and happily entered her childhood home. Familiar smells accosted her nose, and she delighted in everything being just as it always had.

The familiarity of it all and the comfortable feeling of being surrounded by love and acceptance assailed her.

With the smells of the stables wafting on the breeze through the window, and the rhubarb crumble just out of the oven; the constant dialogue between Mum and Dad; the sun pouring the last of its life over the hill; the oaks whispering secrets, and the bickering of the flock of birds that had come to roost in the eaves of the barn, Megan found herself smiling with pleasure and relaxed for the first time in weeks. She pushed thoughts of Ethan away. She'd allow them to re-awaken later, but not now. Not right now!

That evening under the care of her doting parents, Megan allowed herself to unwind - to become the child. After a wonderful and companionable dinner, Megan joined Paul in the lounge where he was pouring his usual glass of evening port. Marge would accept no help in the kitchen.

"Drink for you, my dear?" asked Paul, "Or perhaps some of your mother's After Dinner Mints instead?" She chose the chocolates and took great pleasure in nibbling them slowly while Paul rambled on about the farm.

Marge finished in the kitchen and joined them with tea for Megan and herself. She sat primly and sipped, while Paul spoke. But Paul was accustomed to early nights and soon, after swigging down the last of his port, excused himself to make his way upstairs to bed. He also knew the girls needed to do some catching up – girl chat!

Megan cuddled up on the old couch, in her special blanket that they always kept folded-up neatly on the side table for her and smiled at the gossip Marge shared. She tried not to let thoughts of Ethan spoil the evening, but every so often his face would spring to mind, or she would hear his voice where there was none. More than once she found herself tempted to call him to see if he was okay, or perhaps just to hear him speak.

Marge soon realised that Megan had stopped listening. "Well, lovey, what is it? I can see that something's wrong. You're not yourself. You're pale, you've lost weight, and you're all sad and miserable. That's why you're here, isn't it?"

"Yes Mum, you know me so well. I don't know if I can speak about this without starting to cry. It's just …" She swallowed to stop the tears that were brought on by Marge's sympathy.

"It's Ethan, lovey, isn't it?" Marge took her hand.

"Yup, couldn't be anything else, could it? Ethan!" The sound of his name meant everything to her.

Marge knew about Ethan but had only met him briefly when she and Paul had popped in after a completed shopping spree. They generally followed a policy of not interfering with their two children's private lives. Marge wasn't prepared to judge Ethan, as she felt she didn't know him well enough. In fact, Marge usually refrained from judging anybody until she knew them better. All the same, Megan was her daughter, and, in her very private opinion, she feared that Ethan would do Megan no good. Although she had always felt secretly wary of Ethan, she didn't know much about his background and felt that she couldn't assume that, as he was a non-earning long-haired musician, he was probably irresponsible and unfaithful. That wouldn't be fair. But he was not the person she had imagined her daughter ending up with. She wouldn't have said so, but she was just a little disappointed with her Meg's choice.

Well, it seemed from what Megan was telling her, that her daughter might not end up with him after all. Nevertheless, she respected the feelings Megan had for him, and reasoned that he must be of some worth if she could find so much to love, so she listened sympathetically whilst Megan poured out her problems.

Megan told Marge everything, from her viewpoint, and then how she imagined it would look from Ethan's side. Finally she stopped, and with a sigh, asked, "Well what do you think, Mum?"

Marge got up without a word and disappeared into the kitchen. Tea was always part of the solution. Megan waited patiently. It was one of the things she respected about her mother, she always thought things through before she opined.

Marge came back with the tray, set it down on a table, poured them each a cup and then looked up at her daughter. "Meg, this man has been living with you for nine months and has only made this one aborted attempt to make love to you. Don't you find it a bit strange? Are you sure he's not using you, or perhaps he prefers men?"

"Mum, Ethan is far from homosexual, believe me. I just don't know about the rest - I'm not sure if I see things realistically anymore. He seems to remain faithful to me, in his own way. He has very few friends, and no lovers that I know of. If he does have spare time in the evening he inevitably spends it with me - that is, if he's not playing somewhere. Well right now he's not playing at all, as the band that he started playing with again has found someone else, after the episode at Exodus that I told you about." She droned on ...." I just don't know, he sits at home doing nothing, hardly eats, and gets thinner and more withdrawn. It's as if he no longer finds reason to exist. I haven't spoken to him since the other night's love-making, or supposed love-making - whatever one would call it - and I don't even know what he's thinking about right now, or any time for that matter. Maybe I should phone? What do you think?"

"Meg, leave it as it is for now. Why don't you give him a couple of days to be without you? You'll probably find that everything is fine when you get home and that when he found you missing, he realised how much he feels for you after all. If nothing has changed when you get back, then I think you should re-think your relationship with him.

"You see, dearie, from what you tell me, it all seems very one-sided, and I don't want to see your heart broken any more than it already is. If things work out a bit better, why don't you bring him out here to spend a couple of days with us? Maybe the fresh air and some fussing will do him the world of good. After all, if you love him we'll make every effort to do the same, naturally.

"In fact, dear, stay here for a couple of days and then phone him with an invite to join us. You say he isn't working now." Marge was making every effort to both comfort Megan and suggest answers.

Megan could always rely on her mother to come up with something. Already she was feeling better and thought that she was probably over-reacting to the whole thing.

"That's a great idea, Mum. In fact, that's exactly what I'll do then, if you don't mind - give it a couple of days and then call. It's probably what we need, the two of us, Ethan, and me. I haven't had a break for ages. I wonder if he'll come. How would he get here anyway, he never uses a car?"

Marge smiled at her eagerness. "Well, Jim is going through to the city to buy spares for the tractor next week. Perhaps he could pick Ethan up?" She turned her head towards the window, "Listen to that, the cocks are already starting with their early morning din. I think it's time for us to go to bed luv."

Megan was surprised to realize it was so late. "Mum?"

"Yes, lovey?"

"Thanks. Love you lots. I feel a bit better now. Sorry to burden you like this. I'm sure it's all boring."

"Not at all," smiled Marge, "as long as you're happy and this all sorts itself out."

They took the cups to the kitchen and made their way up the staircase.

After soaking in the bath for a while with lots of bubble bath - Mum always had a bottle of bubble bath on the side of the bath - she brushed her teeth, put on her warm flannel pyjamas, and climbed into bed. She snuggled up under the covers of her old bed, the one they had bought for her when she was about fourteen years old, and again went over everything in her mind. It took a while for her to fall asleep as she couldn't keep from rehearsing what she would say to Ethan on the phone, and then imagining all his possible answers or excuses. It was already becoming light outside when she drifted off.

†

Ethan had awoken from his apoplexy with only a faint memory of what had happened. The events of the past two weeks were vague, and he had to grasp at the illusive memories, trying to piece together who he was, what he was and where he was. He had only a faint recollection of Kalin, and an even fainter one of Megan and the state of their relationship. He knew he lived with someone as he could see her things in the flat but couldn't bring a face to mind.

He was afraid to leave the flat, as he couldn't remember where he should be going or who he knew. Nobody visited him and his mobile phone never rang. He barely ate, but slept and stared out of the window, waiting for a more substantial memory, not knowing if this was the sum total of his life.

On Tuesday morning his phone finally rang. He answered hesitantly as he didn't recognize the name or number that appeared on the screen, afraid of whom it might be and what they would ask.

"Hello" he said carefully.

"Hey Ethan, it's me!" There was a moment of silence and Megan was afraid that he would hang up on her.

"Hi!" he finally said, relieved to find he remembered that his name was Ethan.

She was encouraged because he didn't seem at all annoyed with her. "You sound funny, is everything okay?"

"Yes, everything's fine." He waited, not knowing how to continue or who she was.

"You sure, Ethe? Just sound a bit strange. Look I'm sorry I just walked out like that, but I feel better now, and Mum has asked if you would like to come down to the cottage for a couple of days. She thinks it might do us both the world of good. I think so too. What do you say? Don't you think it's a great idea?"

"Okay. Yeah, okay! Great idea!" He was confused, not knowing where the cottage was and racking his brain to remember. This was obviously the person who lived with him. She seemed to know him well.

"Great!" Megan almost shouted her relief. "Mum says Jim, he's the chap who helps them with the farm, is going to the city tomorrow to buy some spare part or other for the tractor. She says you could ride back with him. Is that okay?" Megan was afraid that he would refuse - afraid of what it would do to her already racing heart if he did.

"Yeah sure, okay. Did you say tomorrow?" Ethan played along until his memory cleared.

"Yes. Tomorrow at about midday, as it'll take a good deal of the morning for him to drive through. Then, of course, he has to buy that part. Hey, Ethe ...?"

"Yeah?"

"Love you! Listen, I'd better put the phone down before I start bawling."

The phone went dead. Like a five-year-old, Ethan went to see what there was in the cupboards that he could pack for his holiday.

"She sounds nice." He mumbled to himself as he eagerly crumpled some clothes, which looked like his, into a plastic supermarket bag. And so he sat waiting, even though the man Jim was only coming the following day. After all, he had nothing else to do. With hands clasped between his knees, he waited, eyes filled with anticipation. He fidgeted, stood up, took a woollen cap from the hat stand, pulled it over his ears and tucked his hair up inside. A tuft of hair poked out the side of the cap behind one ear. He looked like a derelict homeless waif. He waited.

†

After she ended the call, Megan stood staring at her phone. Tears of relief poured down her face - he was coming! He still wanted to be with her!

Marge made her way through to the hall where Megan was standing propped against a wall, still staring at her phone. Marge noticed the tears and the shaking hands. Clucking her concern, she went up and put her arms around her daughter. "And now what, lovey? Doesn't he want to come?"

Megan smiled. "No Mum, he is coming. I'm just so happy!"

They stood weaving together, the daughter sobbing and laughing, the mother clucking and patting. "Come, let's go and have a nice hot cup of tea and some biscuits. Wouldn't that be nice?" Marge offered.

†

Jim was a plump, sombre man - not one for

words. He knocked at the door, squinting down his superfluous red nose at the piece of paper he held in his hand. Whilst he waited for a reply, he took his handkerchief out of his pocket to wipe the sweat from his brow, and then for good measure, blew his nose with a loud honk. He wiped back and forth over his hairy nostrils, pocketed the handkerchief, and knocked again, muttering under his breath.

Slow footsteps approached on the other side of the door, and then someone fiddled with the latch. The door opened.

Ethan looked out expectantly, bag in hand and cap pulled right down onto his eyebrows. "Hello," he beamed, "are you Jim? I'm Ethan!"

"Yeah! That's me. Ready to go I see." Jim looked Ethan up and down, barely able to hide his disgust.

Ethan was dressed in a pair of well-faded blue denim jeans with a rip on the knee. A large baggy tee shirt, that sported the face of an obscure rock star, hung from his bony shoulders. Grubby black hair hung from a laddered woollen cap, and a plastic shopping bag was clutched in his hand. Even though an angelic face with thickly fringed blue eyes peered out from under the cap, he made a sorry picture.

"I'm ready, let's go," said Ethan

enthusiastically. He pulled the door closed and began to walk down the stairs, glancing back at Jim in a friendly way just to make sure he followed.

For Jim the drive to the farm was something out of his worst nightmare. The imbecile asked him questions from the minute they got into the truck until the time they pulled up at the front door. Jim wondered what on God's fair earth this idiot boy was doing with a girl as lovely as Megan.

Ethan on the other hand was pleased to be able to use the time to ask as many questions as possible, to find out where he was going and who he was going to see at the other end. He asked with enthusiasm and paid keen attention to the short answers supplied by Jim. He knew Jim thought he was either mad or stupid but couldn't help beaming his excitement.

The van pulled up in front of the cottage and Jim hooted twice, impatiently. He couldn't wait to get rid of Ethan. Megan appeared at the front door and walked slowly towards them, her heart beating so frantically that she was sure Ethan might hear it. Her legs felt weak. Marge and Paul followed and then stood on the porch, not wishing to interfere with their greeting.

Ethan sat as still as a statue, wide-eyed,

staring out at the people that he presumed must know him. The younger girl was walking towards the van. She had nice legs and really pretty hair and, well the rest of her body was also nice. His eyes opened wider as she approached the side of the van and peered in through the window.

"Hey, just going to sit there?" she spoke softly and nervously through the open window, wondering if she should lean through to kiss him. Memories of the way he had savagely attempted to suck out her insides stopped her, more out of embarrassment than anything else. As his eyes rested on her face, a grin playing about his mouth, a sharp pain of response twisted her gut. She forgave everything in that instant, yanked the door open and nervously grabbed his hand in hers, pulling him from the van.

"Hello," he answered softly.

"Come," she said, "Mum and Dad are waiting. We can talk later."

He walked with her towards the house, glancing furtively at her body and face and trying to remember. His senses reeled with her smell. Never before had he smelt anything so sharply or so wonderfully, and he would have liked to bury his face in her neck to absorb more.

Yes, she was certainly worth knowing.

Marge and Paul greeted Ethan with an enthusiasm they didn't feel.

Marge approached, wiping her hands on her apron. "Hello, Ethan. I'm so glad you could make it, dear. Come in. Megan, show Ethan to the spare bedroom so he can put his belongings down and freshen up before lunch. You can show him around after we've eaten."

Paul extended his hand to shake Ethan's. Marge had made him promise to be kind if nothing else. Make the boy feel at home for Megan's sake Paul, she had said. Ethan shook his hand, and Paul noticed the bruises on his arm; the vestiges of Kalin's bite. He shivered in revulsion and pulled his hand away. It was as if Ethan had a contagious disease that would leap across as soon as they touched.

Ethan also saw the bruises for the first time since his memory loss and wondered at them. A slight light-headedness washed over him at a snippet of memory that crossed his mind - of Kalin.

Megan pretended she hadn't seen her father's rejection and found herself chatting away falsely to Ethan as she led him upstairs. Marge had put Ethan into the bedroom next to Megan's. Ethan followed amiably behind Megan, looking at the way her bottom moved in the jeans she wore. She walked with him into his bedroom and softly closed the door. He stood looking at her, wondering what she was going to do next and trying to remember. He stared intently at her face and lips, never blinking.

"What?" she asked, feeling herself blush.

"What do you mean?" Ethan asked, lifting his eyebrows.

"Here, sit next to me." She patted the bed. "Ethan, I wanted you here so we could sort things out. If anyone loves you, I do! So speak to me, Ethan, I'm confused - everything's muddled. What's happening? Are you doing drugs again, is that it?" Once said, Megan regretted her words, sorry she'd started on him almost as soon as he'd arrived. She should have waited for him to settle down and unwind a bit. He had a lot to cope with, and she caught herself making excuses for him again.

His look was clearly puzzled. "Drugs?" he enquired softly, looking down at the wounds on his arm. And then he thought he understood. "So that must be it", he said, "I'm a junkie?" He looked back up at her, surprised at this revelation. "Okay, let's talk. You start ..."

He hadn't known what else to say and was still trying to absorb what it seemed he was. The thought just didn't feel right, and he wondered if she had him mixed up with someone else. He could vaguely remember being bitten by something. "It was a dog", he said with a confused expression.

"What?! That's a lame one – you're joking, aren't you?"

"Huh?"

"You're stoned again, aren't you?" she asked, tight-lipped.

"No, I'm not stoned," he spat out angrily, instinctively defensive. It was not like he even knew himself, or fully understood the reason behind her accusations, or how either of them should feel about anything. For a second, the old Ethan emerged, and he whispered under his breath, "What the fuck!" Just loud enough for her to hear, as he intended her to. He was still there inside himself, somewhere.

Megan was about to voice her frustration when Marge called that lunch was ready. Ethan followed Megan downstairs not knowing if he was still welcome, or if she still loved him like she had professed earlier. He couldn't remember just what the nature of their relationship had been before this day. He felt the anger dissipate, replaced with insecurity and confusion.

Ethan and Megan ate in silence, eyes averted from one another. Marge chattered on about the farm and the goings on of the past week, trying to keep the atmosphere from freezing over completely. Paul also ate in silence, eyeing first Megan and then Ethan, and then Marge. Ethan unashamedly examined them all intently, each in turn, making them feel palpably self-conscious. Megan looked up at Ethan's face and didn't know him anymore, this beautiful young man sitting next to her in her parents' kitchen.

†

Ethan's whole being had begun crystallising into something fragile. A faint glow issued from his pale skin, almost as if a light was reflecting from the purity of it.

Marge found herself uncannily attracted to him, something she had just discovered, and now she blushed every time he looked her way. Paul found him ghoulishly appealing but would never have said. He was also frightened of Ethan, as he sensed something strange emanating from him that was not of this world, perhaps an enticing evil. Paul would never have admitted the lust Ethan inspired or the invitation he stirred. Both Marge and Paul thought him quite strange as he eyed them one by one, smiling, going about his food, examining, and smiling again. He was a strange one, they acknowledged to one another as their eyes met across the table, but yes, they could see why Megan worshipped at his shrine. And they fell in love with Ethan without wanting to, and never knowing how the attraction had arisen.

†

Megan decided to leave well alone and spent the rest of the week showing Ethan around the farm, and actually enjoying the attention he lavished on her. She still thought he was acting strangely, but left him to explore and poke around, ask questions and do little chores for Marge. Ethan fell over himself being helpful. This wasn't the Ethan she knew, but she liked it.

In the evenings, Ethan avoided direct conversation with her. After his habitual shower, he would collapse into bed. No dreams came to haunt his sleep, and every night she sat in his room and watched him, curled up on his side, knees almost touching his forehead, sleeping dreamlessly and quietly. He would wake up in the morning bright and happy, ready again to explore.

This was Ethan's incubation period; a period of suspended awareness; a chrysalis time in preparation for his metamorphosis; a time to recover and grow.

Within the week, the needle and bite injuries

to Ethan's arm had mostly disappeared. His skin had taken on a rosier glow, and he had put on a bit of weight. Marge thought it was her cooking, while Paul thought it was the work he had been assigning Ethan outside in the fresh air. Megan thought he was finally unwinding. She watched him carefully for any sign of drug use and was satisfied with what she found. Without wanting to admit it, she had to acknowledge that this wasn't the composed and 'cool' Ethan she knew, but someone quite pleasant that she was enjoying getting to know. He was like a child as he went through each day, discovering things she'd only noticed when she was much younger. Perhaps she was being given a second chance with him, she considered, and wished these days could go on forever.

All this time, Ethan never made any physical advances towards Megan. As much as she dreaded his physical attention, given what had happened the last and only time that he had been interested in her in this way, she so longed for his touch that on the last night they were to spend there she crept from her bedroom into his and slipped in beside him.

He mumbled in his sleep, turned over to hold her, nuzzled his face into her neck, and she slept in his arms for the rest of the night. He awoke in the morning surprised to find her there, smiled, but never asked why or how she had got there.

Megan was elated to have been with him the entire night, but bitterly disappointed at his lack of interest in her as a woman.

They were to leave that day, and still hadn't spoken of everything that had happened prior to their little getaway.

They said their goodbyes, and Marge and Paul waved them all the way up the road. Mist shrouded the surrounding area, and dew dripped from the foliage. Crows, in a cacophony of cawing, welcomed the day.

Even though the world was a bright and beautiful place, they drove back to London in silence, with Megan starting to feel uncomfortable and troubled again. She both looked forward to and dreaded the time when they would arrive home. Things would then get back to normal, and they'd have to sort out their feelings and relationship.

Ethan, on the other hand, revelled in the beauty of the world about him, the blindness of the years before wiped from his face like long-forgotten spider webs. He looked at Megan and wondered at the aura surrounding her body. He wondered, enthralled.

CHAPTER 6

Genesis

Kalin vaguely remembered the beginning - the dawning of man. In the passed down memories, he had experienced, as had they all, the genesis of his kind. Over the centuries they had remained few, as there was no need for procreation. They preferred it this way, given the very essence of their nature. Their development had paralleled that of man, very much the same, and also very different. Predation was part of their nature, taking where they could of the bountiful souls provided, and as they took they grew in wisdom and guile.

As time passed and they evolved, nature had focused upon them the creation of perfection by developing both their physical beauty and the heightened sensory perception that was imperative to their survival.

The blood of his last victim coursed through his veins. The psychic energy of the robbed soul pulsed through his being and, in so doing, ingrained its memories upon his mind. The last seven hours of this soul's life flashed before Kalin's eyes as he sat cross-legged on the floor of his chamber. He prepared himself, as he had so many times before, to filter those memories that he would take upon himself, and those he would permit the departing soul to take to its heaven.

Kalin was the oldest of the 'brothers' and though they shared in all, he had taken it upon himself to initiate Ethan - his lamb – his son.

They had been seven for as long as he could remember, their immortality ensuring their survival. Nadan, the seventh, was no longer with them. His loss had saddened and devastated them, as would the loss of any of the brothers. Each loss was catastrophic to their immediate harmony. He believed that they needed to be seven. It was their number.

They had claimed Ethan upon his human birth, and had watched and waited, ensuring the perfection of their kind be reflected upon him. Kalin was well pleased with their prodigy, a seeding they had only had to make once before in this century when Hadrian had birthed. He trusted that they would endure as they now were, Ethan in their midst. Much energy went into the seeding of a new brother but was made easier if the brother was of C'raether ancestry, as was Ethan.

In Ethan, the seed had been planted. The seed of Kalin's soul had been sown in Ethan's, and in sowing, Kalin had taken from him much of his essence, replacing with that of his own, although it still slumbered. Now they waited for the butterfly to emerge in its splendour, for the final blood sowing when Ethan would be admitted in turn by all six brothers, again to make seven.

Kalin rose from where he sat, and with outstretched arms gathered together the thought projections from the others. They needed to join in preparation for the final seeding.

In response to his summons, they came together noiselessly in the room.

"Kalin, what news?" asked David.

"As expected, he has been away and in so doing has had time to recover from that part of him that is human – from his human essence and error. His soul has been cleansed of impurity. We cannot leave it any longer and need to initiate him before his psyche is clouded again by the feculence of human nature. Come my friends, let us take hands; let us share of our souls, together today in a somewhat small celebration for what must come soon. I need to take sustenance from each of you for the time ahead. I thank you for your invitation."

They linked together, Kalin, Romando, Benedikt, David, Hadrian and Caeron, permitting the ebb and flow of life's forces to course through their joined hands. One into the other and spiralling through them all as they shared blood. They became one and re-established their kindred spirit. With closed eyes and clenched jaws, they raptured as the passion of the coupling energised the ethers about them.

†

The sun was setting by the time Megan and Ethan arrived back. Megan felt uncomfortable with Ethan. At the farm it had been easier to accept his strangeness. In their home environment she waited expectantly for the other Ethan to surface.

Ethan looked around, lit a cigarette that he couldn't smoke and wondered why he had lit it. Feeling obvious, he stubbed it out and looked at Megan as she walked from the lounge into the bedroom.

"Something has happened," he wondered softly as if to himself. "I don't know where to start. I'm not sure who you are, or who I am. There is a lot I do know, but don't know how to put it together into a whole, if you know what I mean? I feel wrong being here. Do I belong here, is this where I stay?" He wiped back the hair from his forehead in a familiar gesture and sat himself down on the edge of the settee.

The shock of what Ethan was saying had her momentarily dumbfounded. "I beg your pardon?" she asked as she walked back into the lounge, "I'm sure I didn't hear that correctly?"

"I asked, *Who am I? Who are you?*" he responded, louder this time, a frown creasing his brow.

"Ethan, what are you saying?" Her voice shook with disappointment. Dare she entertain the idea that he could be schizophrenic? This just hadn't occurred to her before, but it made sense. She decided to play along and see where this went. She just wasn't sure what would be the right thing to say. He did look like he was being honest and appeared to be as confused as she was.

"Did something happen to you last week?" She asked. "Are you telling me you don't remember anything? Are you having me on? You're not kidding around with me are you, Ethe?"

He fiddled with a guitar pick from the table, then raised his eyes to hers uncomfortably. His look convinced her that he was being serious. She sat down next to him on the couch and pried his one hand away from the other. She held it tightly and squeezed reassuringly. "You're telling the truth, aren't you, luv?"

"Yes, I am". He searched her eyes. "Your eyes are beautiful, you know!" he said in wonder. "They have little amber flecks in them".

"That's the first time you've ever noticed my eyes, you know."

"Well, then I'm sorry, but it's the truth - your eyes; my not knowing. Any other truth, I don't know right now."

"Ethan, listen to me. There's something not right. You need a doctor. You need help. Stay here, I'm going to call Andrea for her doctor's number. He's a therapist of some kind, from what she says. Perhaps we can get an appointment tonight or early tomorrow – at least see what someone else has to say about this. I don't know what's going on!" She started taking her phone from her bag, hands shaking.

"I'm okay," he said, eyes on her hands and bag, but wasn't sure he believed that he was okay. He felt okay, even though he didn't know who he was.

She turned her head, and consoled him, "It's all going to be fine; I promise. Everything will be sorted out. Just sit there, take it easy and let me get hold of the doctor for you."

Megan walked through to the kitchen whilst dialling. As she left him, panic poured bile into her throat. He could hear her from the lounge.

"Andrea, hi. It's me. I need your doctor's number. Who? No, the shrink guy. No, I'm okay! I said okay! Alright then, I'm not okay. It's Ethan. Yes I know it's always Ethan. This is different. Well he's okay but ... I know, I know, but we can't get into this now." She started writing on an unopened envelope in the kitchen. "Thanks. Okay. Chat later. Yup, you too. What?"

A knock sounded on the door. Ethan got up to answer, not catching the rest of Megan's conversation. Kalin stood at the door, and Ethan smiled in acknowledgement.

"Come, my lamb, come!" Kalin extended his hand. Ethan took it, and they walked out of the flat. He was going home at last, and all would be revealed.

When Megan returned, Ethan was gone.

CHAPTER 7

The Brothers

Ethan

I walked out with Kalin, knowing him by name. As he took my hand, relief flooded my being and all confusion left. Instantly my memory returned, and I cast off all that had been, knowing I no longer had need of those memories. They seemed like a chapter of an incomplete and discarded book. I took nothing with me, and I gladly followed him out into the evening of my awakening.

Thoughts of recognition passed between us, and we had no need for words or questions. A grey limousine awaited us in the road, blending with the city lights as they reflected off the paintwork. The door opened, and I crouched as I climbed into the rear of the car after Kalin.

We settled down, and the driver pulled smoothly into the traffic. I sank down into a body-moulding leather seat. My one hand rested against the smooth aromatic leather.

Kalin and I smiled at one another and said nothing. I waited in anticipation and trust, using the opportunity to observe him and to re-establish my memory links about our previous contact. I remembered it fully and in detail as if it had just happened. Still I did not question his intent but instead marvelled at the perfection of his aural glow, phenomena in people I had only recently discovered. He looked ahead, aware of my examination, but allowing me the privilege.

After a time we left the city behind us, driving into the suburbs of a cleaner and more upmarket area of large houses. The streets were lined with large old trees, high walls, and wrought iron gateways, behind which long driveways could be seen winding their way up to houses set in forested gardens.

The limousine pulled up to one of these houses, and the gates swung open to admit us. The driveway meandered through a garden; its perfection barely lost in the dim light of the evening. We alighted from the car, and the intense and heady smell of jasmine enveloped us. The driver pulled away and we were left standing alone before the house. A beautiful house, I acknowledged. Mostly dark but with the patio lights on, as well as a soft yellow glow from a downstairs room.

With his hand on my back, Kalin steered me onto the lawn. "Before we go in, let us sit a while in the garden," he said. "This is the time of evening most suited to my nature and provides a peace of mind that many people seek elsewhere."

I gave a short nod, wiped the hair from my forehead, and walked beside him to take a seat on an iron and cement garden bench set in an alcove of vine. We sat for a while enjoying the silence of the night, which was only broken by a dog howling in the distance. He turned towards me. "Ethan, there are things you do not yet know that I would like to discuss with you before we enter tonight. You have only yet had experience of me, but I am more than one, as are you. We are seven now with you – seven again." I nodded as if I knew exactly what he meant.

"Also be warned," he continued in his low voice, "there is no turning back once you cross the threshold. You must make the choice to sacrifice your individual soul as it is now, to be with us and become one with us - our group soul - our collective spirit. It is then that I will invite you to join us and complete what you know has already started. What you were born for." I blinked, swallowed self-consciously, and gave a small nod. Born for?

"I have passed to you the memory of our beginnings and, before the evening is through, you will receive all our memories as each brother in turn allows you access to his essence. With this sacrifice by each of us to you, you will be expected to obey our unspoken laws with undivided loyalty and without question. It is the least that can be asked of one who will be carrying, as do each of us, a portion of the soul of the other.

"Once you have been allowed admission, and once you have admitted each of us in turn, you will become part of us, and us of you. You would only be betraying yourself should thoughts of leaving or betraying us ever enter your mind.

"Ah, but I procrastinate as you do not yet understand the urgency and love with which we await you. Come, will you take these steps with us?"

My mind started clearing, as if his voice alone had cast the mist aside, as if the past years of my life were but a preparation for what lay ahead. My future lay before my eyes in all its glory. My search for kindred spirit, my confusion, my inability to form deep and lasting relationships with the people I had known, all this merely the foundation for the truth of discovery. Yes, I knew all too well what the sacrifice would be, it would be the sacrifice of my loneliness for that of belonging. It seemed a good trade to me.

"I will come happily and accept what you are offering. I understand." I agreed and stood up to show my eagerness to follow him.

Satisfied, Kalin touched his finger briefly to my forehead in approval then led me up the stairs to the door of the house.

I had expected something out of the ordinary as I entered but found it to be a very everyday house with a mix of traditional and modern finishes. Kalin hung his coat on a hook in the hall, then turned in a formal way to beckon for me to follow.

We entered a room. Books in mahogany cases lined the walls, and a highly polished table, in the same dark wood, stood in the middle. A small pottery lamp cast a comforting glow from one corner. As we entered, a door opened on the far side and five men entered, one by one, and they seemed soundless in their grace and beauty. It felt as if the stage had been set, and I was the principal player.

Five pairs of eyes stared intently at me, as had those of Kalin during the short space of time I had had contact with him. Not one resembled the other except for two of them, who could have been the same person, yet all were Kalin incarnate and in an uncanny way, all were me.

Each of 'The Brothers', as I would come to know us, came forward in turn to introduce himself. The order seemed random, with no apparent hierarchy amongst them. One by one they came, placing a finger upon my forehead and projecting their acceptance and love. I was consumed by a feeling of serenity and belonging. As each touched my forehead, he whispered his welcome and name in his own fashion.

"Good evening, and welcome brother. I am Romando."

"Hi, and it's about time. I'm David."

And then a complete replica of Romando stepped forward, "Welcome to our fold, ecstasy will be yours." He smiled and added his name, "Benedikt."

Another - "Ah, well chosen!" as he looked over at Kalin, "I am Hadrian, and will be your companion for a while. I look forward to running with you."

Finally in a soft Irish voice, "G'd evening. You are as lovely to behold as I expected. I am Caeron."

I grinned my happiness around the room and wondered if this was it.

Kalin spoke, "Ethan you have now met us all, and again made our number seven. Introduce yourself, invite us in, and we can begin. This night will be long, and I trust you have heart for it!"

I felt rather foolish now, and nervously pushed my hair back from my forehead, wishing for a cigarette to keep my hands busy. Ah yes, I remembered cigarettes.

"Well, I'm pleased to have met you all!" I felt ridiculous – it was such a foolish thing to say, and my grin slipped. I continued honestly, "I don't know what to expect, but would choose nothing else. I'm overwhelmed at the cool way you've, um, made me welcome. I don't know what to say. I am yours." Now didn't this sound even cornier?

But all the same, I couldn't stop the tears that I had kept in check all my life - tears of loneliness, rejection, and tears of failure slipped out of my eyes and down my cheeks. I lifted a hand and wiped across my face. But somehow I knew that this display was acceptable. I could see it in their faces. I had come home. I mattered.

They came closer, and in turn embraced me, allowing me to sob out all the grief and hurt that I had built up over the years. They cried too.

Kalin came last, and as he placed his hand upon my forehead, I felt the tears dissipate. He drew me towards him, and I could feel him tremble in anticipation. With his free hand he started pulling the other Brothers closer. Wide-eyed we closed up together, each showing his eagerness in a different way.

Hadrian stepped forward first, licked his lips in what appeared to be a nervous manner, grabbed a chunk of my hair in his impatience, and pulled me towards him. "My blood brother," he whispered hoarsely, "let us share first, as I will be running with you."

Instinctively, I put out my hand to fend him off, and instead found myself grabbing for his wrist to pull him closer. I could feel his sweet breath on my cheek.

"Not too hasty my friend," admonished Kalin, "you will startle Ethan and be rejected."

Hadrian stepped back, and I unwillingly released his wrist from the death grip in which I held it. The first trickle of fear twisted my insides. But I chided myself, as I knew I had no need of fear. We were one, and it would have only been the fear of myself.

I turned, and Kalin took me to himself. As before he kissed me on the shoulder in a tender fashion, moving down my arm to where he had bitten before. I waited with a mixture of trepidation and fear for the pain.

Even though I saw him rip through the skin

and flesh, the pain never came. Instead, I felt the beginnings of the ecstasy that I had previously experienced with him. Eagerly, I grabbed his wrist and bit into it. As the blood began to flow, I pulled the wrist towards my ruptured arm and pressed it, with Kalin's help, against the ebb.

Our blood flowed together, and the rapture began. I was blind to those about me as my body convulsed in passion but was aware through a sea of blood that each in turn bit at his wrist and held it to my arm. As one pulled away and another took his place, my rapture increased, until I thought I might go mad with passion and euphoric delight.

I knew each in turn - knew them as I know myself. As our blood mingled, so I relived each of their lives with them, and they lived mine. As we wallowed in the spilt blood on the floor, the dream continued.

I crawled from the sea of tranquillity on all fours, gasping for air and pulling myself forward with claws not yet adapted to earth. Pain exploded in my lungs as I took in the world's virgin air. I blinked my eyes to clear the water from them, simultaneously averting them from the sun to which they were not accustomed.

Intermittently I returned to the water and then back to the land to grub, until such time that the attractions of the land outweighed those of the water; and then I stayed.

As I gained strength, time passed in flashes before my eyes. I now trotted strongly and steadily on all fours, scouring the undergrowth with eyes well accustomed to the light, senses so honed that I could smell and hear my prey from far distances.

As the prey grew more cunning over the centuries, I began running with a pack of my own kind. In a group, we could achieve our predatory ends far quicker and more efficiently. The bond between us grew and we became inter-dependent, one upon the other.

The moon hung low in the crimson sky whilst volcanic eruptions lit the horizon, bathing the scene in a blood red glow. Sulphuric smells intermingled with that of the prey.

We loped silently through the primeval forest, communicating without sound. I glanced sideways at my companion. Foam flecked his lips in his effort to keep the pace.

We could see the prey up ahead, running on two legs. Habitually, when there was no urgency, we did the same, but come the hunt, we dropped to four to increase our speed and stamina.

The prey was disadvantaged by his stance and was fast tiring. His intelligence could not match ours as he peered out from under his small protruding forehead. We were drawing closer, and I could smell his fear and feel my heart pounding wildly in excitement. He dropped to his knees, emitting noises of panic and terror as we closed in.

Our intellect was such that his end came quickly. We gorged on his flesh and blood, taking unto ourselves portions of his spirit that could hasten the evolutionary growth of our kind. Sated, we again stood upright, disappearing into the forest from whence we had come.

We were seen as the gods of that time by these inferior creatures, and they often sacrificed their own to us, leaving us with no need to hunt.

Our predatory nature remained a successful part of our evolution.

There had been no need for us to turn to vegetation as our prey reproduced at an alarming rate and kept us sated.

We were few and remained that way, as we had no need to procreate. Our development was such that in essence we became immortal, as our cells regenerated and took on the properties that we needed to remain youthful from the blood of our prey.'

Throughout the night the memories shared by the brothers cascaded through my mind. By the time morning arrived, I was exhausted and hungrier than I could ever remember being. As dawn broke and we shared a last touch, each left to sleep away his exhaustion and depletion. Hadrian remained.

"We are now truly brothers, Ethan. Come, I have prepared a chamber for you to rest. Later I will show you the hunt so that our hunger may be assuaged. This night has been a wonderful time and it is with relief that we welcome you to our fold. We have been without the seventh for many years now and have waited patiently for your arrival."

Even though many questions had been answered, I longed for more. "Hadrian, I understand through the dreams, but where do I fit into this, and why me? Am I going to be staying here? What is the purpose to this?" My mind was too exhausted to put together, into a whole, the experiences of the past night.

He opened the door to the room that was to be mine. "Ethan, you have an eternal future for discovery and an infinite past to remember, so take this time to rest, as later we hunt. I will be back for you at sunset." He left me in the room, closing the door quietly behind him.

The room was decorated in a way that made me feel immediately at home and comfortable. A large bed rested in one corner, lit by a beam of sunlight that came through the main window. In another corner, a writing desk and chair stood to one side of a small porthole-type stained glass window, and a comfortable-looking leather easy chair next to the fireplace paid further compliment to the sparse furniture. There was a wooden wardrobe set into one wall. I got the immediate impression of warmth, possibly brought about by the amount of rosy wood that was apparent in the furnishings, as well as the stunning autumn-coloured rug that lay casually sprawled across the floor.

On the desk, I noticed a sealed envelope, addressed to me with a mere *Ethan* in Gothic scrawl across the front. No texting here ... besides, I had left my mobile phone behind. It was a short note of welcome, with a further message for me to cover my tracks and let friends or family know that I was fine and needed time alone. It was signed by Kalin. As I ran a finger over the writing, a queer feeling of the wonder of Kalin washed over me. In fact I was totally in awe of everything.

A sweat-beaded pitcher of milk stood to one side on a round table near the door. I drank thirstily, gulping until streams of the cool liquid ran down the side of my mouth and the sharp edge of my hunger dissipated. With feet that I could hardly lift from weariness, I shuffled over to the bed and collapsed into its enfolding warmth.

I woke in the late afternoon to a cooling sun and made my way down the passage to find Hadrian. I found him in his room, thumbing through a book. I rapped lightly on the door to draw his attention.

He looked up. "Ah, I see you've woken ... did you sleep well?" he enquired.

"Yeah, it was great; I was dead to the world!" I wiped the hair back from my forehead.

"Good." He smiled. "Until later when we go out together, please feel free to come and go as you please. The car and driver are available to you as none of us have need of them this afternoon. I am sure there are personal items you would like to collect. You are staying, aren't you?" He stated more than asked this, with a warm smile, knowing without asking that I would stay, without a doubt.

I smiled back, enjoying his humour. "You're right, there are a few things I must sort out that can't be left longer than today, so I'll take you up on the offer of the car. Thank you." Hadrian smiled and looked back down at his book. I was temporarily dismissed. "See you later then," I said, "unless of course you'd like to come with me?"

He stood up and came towards me, laid a hand on my shoulder, and looked me deep in the eyes. "The things of your past life are for you to terminate on your own. I had no part in that life and do not belong there."

I felt his love flow over me. My hand lifted of its own accord and touched his forehead in farewell - our ties were re-established.

With a feeling of satisfaction, I left to find the driver. I still had to accustom myself to the close bond that existed between the brothers.

†

We pulled up in the limo outside Megan's flat. She had obviously not gone to work, as the windows were open, and her car was parked in the street below. At that moment I felt no bond with her whatsoever, nor any feelings of betrayal or regret. I got out of the car, pushed my hair back and climbed the stairs two by two, not stopping to think how I must look to the outside world. I was in such a euphoric state.

As I was about to knock, the door opened. She stood looking at me, tear-streaked white face, and trembling bottom lip. "Thank God!" she said in a broken voice and, like a sleepwalker, turned slowly back into the flat. I followed.

"I'm not even going to ask," she said woefully.

"I've called everywhere, Ethan. Hospitals, police stations, you name it. Where the hell have you been? By the look of you you've had a pretty good night of it. You're a mess! You've begun to scare me." Her voice took on a harsher tone.

All this time she was looking down at the floor as if it held some fascinating answers, now she glanced up red-eyed. Tears once again filtered down her swollen cheeks. She waved her hand in the air, from my head to my toes, indicating my seemingly awful mess.

I shrugged my shoulders and turned away - made no attempt to talk to her, but kept my eyes averted as I walked through to the bedroom to throw some clothes into my backpack.

The full-length mirror in the cupboard told the story of the disappointment I had seen on her face. The lacerations, although already healing, started on my neck, disappeared under my shirt collar, and ended on my wrists. I was as surprised as she was when I lifted my shirt and found the bite and rip marks all over my torso. Blood caked the shirt. I took it off and threw it into the bottom of the cupboard.

Megan, now at the doorway, held her hand to her mouth in horror. Suddenly the situation struck me as insanely funny, and I couldn't help bursting into hysterical laughter. If only she knew the pleasure these wounds had caused in their making! The more horror I saw reflected on her face, the funnier it seemed. I laughed so much I could hardly breathe, and pains stabbed my sides.

I lifted my eyebrows at her and said, "Bad news, hey?" Again, I pealed into laughter. "I'm leaving, so you won't ever have to worry about me again." I sat down on the floor, gasping in manic mirth for air. "I'll take my bloody body - get it, 'bloody body' - away from here, never to be seen again. Gone for good." I laughed harshly. The other, kinder, Ethan was gone for now.

She turned and ran out of the flat. It would be many months before I saw her again!

CHAPTER 8

Elation

That evening Hadrian and I left the house with a sense of expectation and hunger. He chose a busy area, and together we retrogressed until we were the primordial creatures from my dreams. We stalked, she complied, and Hadrian killed and took upon himself the soul of our victim. Together we devoured her flesh, having given little heed to her terror and cries once she realised what it meant to offer herself so willingly.

We were the predators that nature had intended us to be. There was little to learn. It came naturally as if I had been born to it. Well, I had been born to it.

We returned home filthied by the murder and revelling in our elation. The high I experienced had no rival. The details of the 'kill' are not worth mentioning, as there were more exciting ones to come. This one merely appeased the hunger.

Over the weeks that I ran with Hadrian, he showed himself to be a spontaneous hunter, choosing his victims at random and caring very little how they succumbed. Hadrian was as ruthless as I was uncertain.

He had devised a number of ways to kill quickly and efficiently but seemed to prefer to strangle his victims. They would still be in awe of his very presence when he would reach out, pulling them close, and as their elation grew he would effortlessly enclose their necks with his strong hands. He never took much from them except for the few bites and blood from the belly - or solar plexus area - that we need to prolong our immortality and provide us with the rush.

I, on the other hand, felt ravaged by hunger, and greedily helped myself to the flesh and blood from any part of the body that provided the quickest satisfaction. In time, this insatiable hunger would appease, and I would become more discerning. It was the novelty of feeling free to succumb to my darker desires.

In retrospect, it became an addiction worse than that of the Heroin from my previous life, more consuming and more destroying if not available - destroying because it was one of the essential elements that kept the brotherhood together and kept them sharing so willingly. Of course, there was the advantage that it came for nothing and provided an inexplicable high. It can only be described as the ultimate rapture - the infinite trip - of which I have since had many.

Although I loved Hadrian as much as I loved all the brothers, and even though in the first couple of weeks of my stay with them I spent most of my time in his company, he was definitely the least refined of the brothers. In saying this, I realise that this is probably the reason why he was assigned as my companion. We were very much alike, having come from the same era and having experienced human life in a similar manner. I was as bestial as he was, I suppose.

So, even though we viewed the hunt differently, we both revelled in the goriness, and would inevitably arrive home bloodied and sated like war-painted cannibals. We would barge into my room laughing like maniacs at any small twist of conversation, put on loud metal music, and gyrate the next few hours away throwing our heads about until we gasped for breath.

At these times, energy flowed through our bodies from the stolen essence of the victim coursing in our veins, and we never stopped to relish the memories the soul offered us. At some point after each kill, we would always share with the others, as is our nature.

A month passed, and during this month I spent most of my time with Hadrian, adding to the memories I had of him, the reality of his everyday being. Little of our time was spent in killing, but more in discussion and play. By the end of the month, Hadrian started going his own way. We gradually began relating more with the kindred spirit of the brothers in their entirety, and less on a personal level.

Every seventh day, the brothers would come together, much in the same fashion as we had come together on my initiation, and share of themselves, to re-establish the ties and our bonds of devotion. Ours was a bloody but natural existence, devoid of guilt and emotional involvement with any but us.

I soon discovered that even though Hadrian and I had been permitted to run rampant whilst I learnt, such was not the law of the brotherhood. Discretion was important, and the ultimate sin was to over-indulge. It had been long agreed that only one kill every seventh day was necessary for our well-being.

As there were seven of us, in the future I would get to kill every seventh week but would return home to share the essences of that kill - its blood, flesh and spirit - with the others. And the next week, one of the others would kill and I would get to share and in sharing, our bond would always be renewed.

And so the weeks passed. I think I should add here that during this time I never personally killed but shared willingly with my brothers.

Although we had no favourites amongst us, as we were one, Kalin always provoked in me extreme mental lust by a mere glance in my direction. His power and wisdom far surpassed that of the rest, and it followed that he was the natural leader.

He always provided us with excellent council and maintained equilibrium that - given the animals we were, and the power with which we were endowed - must have taken extreme self-control to master. No more needed to be said. He was acknowledged, and none thought himself fit to take his place, nor wished to do so.

Because of the awe in which I held Kalin, he was the most difficult to be around. I was afraid of myself with him and needed to protect the slim feelings of pride I still had left. I suppose I was still harbouring old feelings of the fear of rejection, even though I knew that if rejection ever came, it wouldn't be from him.

†

Caeron was by far the softest, and therefore the hardest to keep in check. His emotions ran rampant, and he confused the primitive hunger that we shared with the parallel, if infantile, emotions expressed by the uninitiated.

He could often be found sitting at sidewalk cafés in the company of an array of different people, charming them with his soft Irish voice, golden halo of hair, and his brilliant aura of innocence and youth.

Although Caeron was one of the oldest, there was no doubt that he looked the youngest. His eyes, even though they perpetually twinkled with the good humour of youth, told the true story of his age to those that knew him.

Caeron was the true angel amongst us! Never let it be thought that he didn't kill with as much pleasure as we did, though. He is an old and accomplished hunter, absorbing more from his prey than we were able, and on his return, provided us with a rush better than any other. I always looked forward to taking from and sharing with him.

Caeron and I would walk together down crowded market streets, stop for a chat with his many friends, play chess over a cup of neglected coffee and discuss everything and anything that came to mind. It was on one of these evenings that I first accompanied Caeron on a hunt.

†

We sat at a sidewalk café, eyeing the people meandering by, and beyond them on the street, the rush of cars on their way home from work. It was the time just before sunset - the eve of the day - that I always enjoyed the most. It was a time when my blood began its own pulsing gush through my body.

I could feel the fever of excitement heat my brow as I watched the detached way Caeron's seraphic face contemplated the crowd. By his excited demeanour, I could tell that his hunting instincts had suddenly been triggered.

Even though it was his seventh day, I had expected him to hunt alone later that night. He had taken me by surprise with his invitation for me to join him, and I found myself extremely agitated and eager.

"Ethan, my lad. Come, let us go over to the bar for a drink. A real Irish whiskey is what we need to whet our appetite. I think a Tullamore Dew is the order of the day. What say you?" Caeron stopped talking for a moment, as his attention was drawn to some people a short way from us. I noticed his eyes narrow in concentration.

"Ethan, beautiful one, see over there. Quite a crowd has gathered, and I see amongst them a wallflower that will leave earlier than the rest. His aura shows his dissatisfaction, can you see?

Can you read his unhappiness with his situation? To be sure." His voice had turned to a whisper. An angelic smile spread across his face, and his hands agitated themselves with the buttons of his shirt.

Following Caeron's gaze, I looked over at the throng at the bar. They were laughing and cheering, downing drink after drink and being particularly noisy. There seemed to be a celebration of sorts in progress that had, from the look of things, been going for quite a while.

The men in the crowd were still dressed in their work attire - designer shirts, ties pulled loose, collars opened up and jackets slung over bar stools. A couple of them leaned against the bar in a competition to see who could down their beer the fastest. Three, belonging to the same party, sat at a table cheering and singing *For he's a jolly good fellow.*

The women in the group sat at the next table, often leaning forward to whisper to one another. Every so often, and with the ease of experience, they would touch up their lipstick in between joining in with the cheering.

They were all well on their inebriated way, and I could see their aural colours emanating hues of blush amongst others - the blush always indicative of the lessening of resistance and the rise of passion. Drink seemed to do this to people - always very willing to invite. It would now be much easier for the men to achieve their ends with these ladies, than it would have been earlier in the day. I looked for the person that Caeron had mentioned.

"Where, I don't see anyone that I think will leave before the others?"

"Come, when we get closer you will see. He sits alone and dejected just behind the ladies."

With a congenial expression, he made his way towards the party at the bar. I followed close behind but had time to smile at an extremely pretty girl. I bumped her chair, and she scowled at me with feigned anger. Her colours displayed her very obvious sexual attraction to me, and I felt a similar stirring in my loins. Not thinking twice about the strangeness of my physical manifestation, I pushed my way through the crowd, tailing Caeron. He elbowed his way to stand next to the targeted group.

"Whiskey, Guv!" He shouted above the din to the barman. "Two Tullamore Dew. Splash it over ice, and no water. I need to cool down my friend here."

He turned to me with a smile and made a space alongside the bar. I realised he had noticed my sexual attraction to the girl. He could read me like a book - I was that new and transparent to the brothers. I looked back to see her still looking at me.

"Ethan, you amaze me that you have the time or energy to flirt. We're here for a different reason. It's the first time I have seen such response from you prior to a hunt. Are you lapsing my lad?" He said this with apparent good humour, but I could see the black emanations of suppressed anger radiate in darts from his being.

A stab of panic pricked my brow and erased all sexual stirrings that I'd had. He handed me the drink and gestured with his eyes to the lone wallflower. It seemed that all had been forgiven. It would take time before I would fully understand my new companions.

The man sat alone just behind the girls, nodding in agreement when they happened to look his way. I could see that he was edgy and nervous. The evening was hot, and he wiped his forehead repeatedly with his handkerchief. In between wipes, he self-consciously sipped his beer.

He was different to the other men in his group and seemed to find it difficult to relate to them on this social level. One of the women turned to him saying something unintelligible from where we stood. Even with our superior hearing, the din in the bar drowned out the finer nuances of human speech. All the women laughed at her comment to him. His embarrassment was obvious, but he tried to laugh along.

She then called over to the men leaning on the bar. They responded with spiteful sniggers aimed at the plump, sweating man. He got up, excused himself, and jostled through the crowd to the gents.

"Caeron, is that the one? The fat embarrassed dude?"

"Yes. He's plump, only plump" Caeron answered, with pretended empathy. "The one they're making fun of, the bitches! Ethan my lad, my plans have changed. The chubby one doesn't deserve death - maybe another time, the poor bastard! Let's take that bitch instead - the one that's got too much to say!"

I realised that Caeron's anger had a lot to do with my earlier sexual revelation, and I wondered if he felt jealous, or if perhaps it had been infectious. Was it his way of hiding his own arousal?

Still, he waited for my reply. "Sure, why not," I replied, "I'm game!"

I knew that women found me physically attractive and decided to use this edge to atone for my earlier indiscretion. "Let me do this, Caeron. I'll persuade her to leave with me. Just give me some time to play the game, okay?"

He laughed loudly. "I'm sure I could do it for myself. You sure it's not just an excuse to express your lust, my lad?"

"No, of course not! The truth is I'm bored and need the amusement the situation offers. Okay?"

His mirth was genuine, and I laughed with him, reaching up to touch my finger to his forehead in a playful shove. I had picked up the forehead thing.

"Okay then. Will there be scraps left over for me once you've ravaged yon maiden?" It had already become a game.

"Trust me sir, wiles I have a-many, but the finale will be yours," I added playfully.

We toasted as together we looked over at the bitch. Just two friends planning some fair wenching.

It didn't take long for me to catch her eye. She was an attractive woman in her early thirties with pretty auburn hair, and a well-lipsticked rose-petal mouth that constantly pouted. She caught me looking at her. I turned my head away in pretended disinterest - merely a game to arouse her curiosity.

Caeron and I continued with an amiable chat about nothing in particular. All the while our excitement rose to fever pitch. A cigarette would have been appropriate, but I couldn't abide smoke anymore, so instead I downed my whiskey and lifted my hand to attract the barman for another – not Irish this time.

The first girl that I'd bumped into, on the other side of the room, smiled an invitation and I left the bar, new drink in hand. This, of course, was all in an effort to sufficiently arouse our target's interest. Ensuring that I walked around rose-petal lips, I brushed her shoulder suggestively as I passed. Without looking down at her, I ambled over to the pretty girl, all sexual feelings gone in the excitement of the chase. I crouched down next to her. "Hi, you still mad at me? You were, weren't you?" A small glimmer of a smile appeared on her lips. Encouraged, I continued. "Do I need to give you a clever opening, or is it just okay to tell you you're lovely and I'd like to buy you a drink?"

Not wanting to be left out, her friend nudged her to answer me. The pretty girl gave me her friendliest smile and, with a gesture that included her friend, said, "We're together. Oh, I'm Rebecca and this is Annie. Okay if she comes?"

"Yeah sure, the invitation was for both of you.

My friend is over at the bar, and we have two spare bar stools feeling pretty lonely. Come on over - drinks on us. Oh, and an apology for nearly knocking you off your chair earlier." This made her happy, and they rose to follow.

We weaved our way back to where Caeron stood staring at his drink. A muscle twitched in his jaw. I could see the excitement displayed in his aura. I introduced the girls, and Annie started making eyes at Caeron. He played along, but I could see his heart wasn't in it as he kept looking at the targeted woman, tongue flicking over his lips in anticipation.

"Hi sweetie!" Annie gushed. "Thanks for asking us over. We were just about to leave for more responsive hunting grounds."

Caeron chortled at her choice of words. "If only she knew!" he mind-voiced in my direction. I returned his grin.

"You're welcome," Caeron said seductively, warming now to the many-faceted game. "And what will you be drinking then, my fair lass?"

She turned to her friend. "Rebecca, what would you like to drink? Another wine?"

Rebecca nodded.

"We'd like a glass each of white wine, house special, and sweet please!" Annie giggled.

Caeron called to the barman and ordered for them. I chucked the dregs of mine down my throat.

Rose-petal's interest had been piqued. No longer was she joining in with her jocular friends. I made a point of catching her eye and practised my ever-increasing art of entering and persuading - a skill I was still attempting to hone, in honour of Kalin, who had done it to me with no effort at all. My arm slipped around Rebecca as I caught rose-petal's eye in challenge. I wondered how this could be so easy.

Caeron's pleasure was reflected on his face. He licked his lips and looked from me to rose-petal, to Rebecca, and then back to me again. Truly I was amazed that they couldn't see the blatant predation. He was literally death staring them in the eye.

We looked at each other, and he telepathized, "That wasn't difficult, Ethan, I see she's noticed you. Rebecca was unnecessary, but I understand your need to present yourself with a dual opportunity. Do you think you can get that bitch to leave alone with you?"

"Caeron, I feel her response and interest. She'll come. Are you questioning my motives?" I asked, a little embarrassed by the truth of his remark.

"I question you only because this is the eve of

my kill, and the need is becoming agony to bear. Don't prolong this little game of popularity you play for longer than necessary, or else I'll tire of it and leave to hunt alone. I'm sorry, I have been doing this for much longer than you've existed and I'm beginning to find this charade boring."

"Caeron, for Chrissakes, lighten up and enjoy. In your old age you've forgotten that life is full of wonder and anticipation. The others will wait, as they always do, for your kill. Relax. If I don't succeed with rose-petal, then this Rebecca will be easy prey. See how she blossoms from our attention. She blatantly invites without knowing yet that she does so. She'll be second choice."

"Yes but continue to target the bitch. Do not forget, she deserves it. There'll be no need for invitation here, Ethan my lad. We will take as we did thousands of years ago - with malice and no pity. This would suit Hadrian better, don't you think?"

I lifted an eyebrow in agreement. I pushed the hair from my forehead, and in readiness started redoing my ponytail that had become loose. Rebecca had a handful of my hair herself and was twisting it in her fingers. I had to pull it away from her. She was becoming irritating, as she hung all over me like an enthusiastic puppy. My impatience started to match Caeron's, so I dislodged her with a nonchalant shove, avoiding her adoring eyes. "Excuse me. I've got some business to attend to." I stood up and left without a backward glance in her direction.

Rose-petal smiled as I approached. I stopped at her shoulder and looked down into painted violet eyes.

She stammered, "You really needn't have gone through all that effort, y'no. All you had to do was come over." The truth of her observation surprised me. All the same, she was interested, so what the fuck did it matter.

I crouched down and she touched her hand to the side of my neck, gently pulling me closer. Oh sweet Jesus, her invitation was so blatant. I could smell her rose-petal perfume, her hair, her beckoning body.

With flared nostrils, I permitted her to reel me in, until my lips touched her neck. I kissed softly, saliva pouring into my mouth in hungry preparation.

It took all my self-control to pull away. This was to be Caeron's seventh - not mine, yet - and I respected that. My tongue was thick with its own pulsing blood, and I spoke hoarsely, "Come on then, let's go for a walk outside. Grab some fresh air. What do you say?" I took her hand and attempted to pull her up.

"Why in such a hurry?" she asked, playing hard to get.

I smiled, "Come on, don't be boring. Promise, it'll be the walk of your life. Or does that sound corny?" I tried.

"Man of urgency, huh? So you reckon it'll be the walk of my life? Big words there, my friend. I doubt that, but as you've asked so nicely, or should I say, so enthusiastically, yes, okay. Besides, it's getting stuffy in here and I need a breath of fresh air, and you're cute, so that's a big plus."

I took her hand and pulled her to her feet. She reached under the chair for her handbag, and then sent a victorious look across to Rebecca.

Again, I avoided Rebecca's startled eyes and spoke silently to Caeron. "It was easy, she's coming. Leave in about five minutes. We'll walk west. The road becomes quiet and there's a small garden. You'll find us there. The spot is well hidden from the street."

He nodded his understanding, jaw clenched in need.

The crowd roared about us like the life's blood that gushed hysterically through my pounding heart. My lips were swollen, and I licked them with growing anticipation.

As we left the pub, she entwined her arm in mine and we walked slowly up the road. She started the conversation. "I suppose you've heard this before, but you're really cute and a lot quieter now that we've left. Where are all the pretty words now?" she teased, and before I could answer, "Oh, don't worry, I like silent men, one never knows what they're thinking and that makes them more alluring. Now I'm giving away some female trade secrets, aren't I?" she giggled coyly.

I liked that. Cute! I grinned to myself. "Well, thanks. Never thought of myself as cute. Silent because I'm so taken with you" I gushed in my 'sexy' voice. "You're something else and, to be honest," - oh yeah, I thought, so honest - "I'm a little stage-struck right now. A question though, do you always go out walking with strangers?"

"No, not really, but there's something about you that I know I can trust. It's in your eyes." She made a show of examining my eyes, face peering up impishly into mine. "Hmm, they're so innocent. If you don't mind me asking, just how old are you?"

"Twenty-six." There was no reason to lie. Perhaps in another twenty-six years I'd have to start lying, I wondered.

"Oh, okay. Where're we going? Just walking?"

"Where do you want to go?" I offered, not caring where she wanted to go and steering her just where I wished.

"Walking's fine for now." She squeezed tighter, put her arm under my jacket and around my waist, then jabbered on, "We were having a farewell party for Mike, the fella with the moustache. He's been transferred from our company and will be doing a stint in Madrid, Spain - lucky devil! The other little chap, you know, the fat one, is the new guy that will be taking his place. Hell, I hope I'm not boring you ..." And she carried on and on, jabbering away endlessly whilst I stared fascinated at the rose-petal mouth that opened and closed and formed words that I wasn't listening to.

I glanced over my shoulder to see if Caeron had left to follow us. He was just walking out of the crowded doorway, apprehended in the process by someone he obviously knew. I realised she had asked me a question.

"Pardon, I didn't get that?" My heart was now beating painfully against my ribs.

"I asked for your name?" She replied. "I've gone walking with a stranger whose name I don't even know, even though I know his age."

It didn't matter if she knew my name. "Ethan. My name is Ethan!" I gasped through the pool of saliva that threatened to gush from my obscenely masticating mouth.

"Oh, that's unusual" she said. 'No it's not,' I thought.

She continued, "You know your face is familiar, have we met before? I work for a software company; perhaps we've met at the computer fair?"

"I don't think so. I'm not much of a computer man." I swallowed in an effort to control myself.

"What do you do then, I mean, for a living?" she asked.

I tried to concentrate on what she was saying. "I'm a musician. Well, I used to be a musician. Now I hunt!" I just had to say it.

"Are you hunting for a job?" I wondered if she'd chosen to misinterpret my words. "You know I could ask at the place where I work. They always have something or other going if you're not too fussy. I know jobs are hard to come by these days."

To change the subject, I pulled away from her and leapt over the small wall of the garden that I had told Caeron about. I reached for her and lifted her over. Women liked this sort of thing. I noticed my strength had increased a hundredfold since being initiated. I liked it. Lots of pain, lots of gain.

Leafy shrubs spread their branches into the small garden, forming an envelope of privacy. I could monitor Caeron's progress from behind the foliage without being seen from the street. The place was ideal, provided she didn't scream. My attention was drawn back to her. She was still speaking.

"Well thank you, I'm getting to like you more each moment." Obviously she meant having been lifted over the wall. "Wouldn't have thought of you as the old-fashioned type," she continued. She must've been quite drunk because she hadn't even noticed how easily I'd picked her up, right over the wall. Women!

She sat down on the oval of grass, and I sat beside her. As her arm encircled my waist again and I felt her fingers stroke the side of my leg, I caught sight of Caeron. He had finally managed to dislodge himself from his overattentive acquaintances and had started up the street. Before I lost sight of him behind a pillar, I noticed that his walk was relaxed and easy, but I knew that his excitement and fever, like mine, must be bubbling over.

"And what's your name, my rose petal?" I asked huskily, giving her my attention again.

"Rose petal? I didn't mean you to be that old

fashioned. My mother gave me a ghastly name, so I prefer to be called by my nickname, Muff."

"What could be worse than Muff?" I asked a bit cruelly, my blood pounding its need painfully against the walls of my head.

She squeezed my leg forgivingly and, with closed eyes, turned her head upward to be kissed. I kissed her full on the mouth, leaving an uncontrollable trail of spittle running down onto her chin and chest. Ye God, I was slobbering. At the same time, I looked over the side of her head to watch Caeron. He was halfway up the street and had broken into an eager trot.

I continued kissing her to keep her busy, but when I tasted blood in her mouth I knew it was time to stop before I lost all self-control. I gently pushed her away.

"I want you so badly," she whispered, amorously stroking up my leg.

So I told the truth. "I want you too Muff, you just wouldn't know how much." I pulled away, "Look, here comes Caeron."

With a disappointed sigh, she said, "Oh no, why now? Does he have to come? Can't we go somewhere?" She wiped a hand over her wet mouth and began rubbing her breasts against my chest.

Caeron came directly to our spot. I called out to him, and he easily jumped over the wall, pushing aside the foliage we were behind. He stopped before us and licked his trembling lips. I stood up in acknowledgement, took hold of Muff's arm, and lifted her to her feet. Caeron reached out, grabbed her by the shoulder, and with an inescapable hold pulled her towards him. Her eyes widened in dismay, and she called for me in a small voice, not certain of her predicament and not wanting to over-react. "Ethan?" Then she saw my face.

Caeron maintained his grip on her shoulder, his knuckles whitening from the pressure. Although Caeron was, by nature, a soft and compassionate person, I saw no remorse or pity in his eyes, the pupils of which had turned to perpendicular yellow slashes.

Her face had whitened in panic, and the skin seemed to pull tightly across her skull. Her mouth worked wetly because of all the saliva I'd left behind, and her eyes darted from one of us to the other. She tried to push Caeron away with one hand, and with the other tugged at my hand that still held her arm.

I smiled at Caeron. "What took you so long? I can't stand it anymore!" I didn't care enough to telepathize my question.

Caeron also answered loudly for her benefit. "Well, I'm here now to keep your promise to this bitch. The promise of providing her with the walk of her life; the ultimate experience, the final trip, a walk through death's doors. Join us immortally. Is that what you would like, you bitch, to walk eternally within us?" He said all of this in his most uncaring harsh voice.

She shook her head and tried to walk backwards, feet slipping on the damp grass.

I had to hand it to Caeron; he was getting more ruthless by the moment. My grin widened at his words. "Were you not telling Ethan here, only a short while ago, how much you wanted him? Well now you can have him forever. How would that suit you?"

Wildly, she looked from one of us to the other, seeing no pity on either of our faces but only the horror of our cruel and stony visages that I could see reflected in her eyes. I shuddered for fear of myself. Hah!

Caeron was losing his playful temper and pulled her closer, reached for her neck and gently pressed the side of her throat with his thumb. She collapsed. Out like a stone, soon to be stone dead. It was that simple, as he was the master of her demise. I stared in wonder and appreciation for the art of it.

He knelt down beside her body, and then turned her head around so that her face was pressed into the lawn. Obviously he found the staring eyes disconcerting. With a gentleness that belied his former beastliness, he lifted her blouse collar and bit deeply into her throat, gnawing greedily like the C'raether he was. With eyes that had become milky with ecstasy, he turned his cherubic face in my direction. "Ethan, what are you waiting for?" He lifted a bloodied hand and beckoned.

I needed no enticement to fall onto my knees on the grass, to lap at the thick life fluid that oozed from the wound on her throat. The sweetness of her dripped from my lips like ambrosia.

Caeron, in an impeccable display of manners, had stepped back to allow me full choice of his demised victim. He now came forward and took my besmeared face between his red hands, turned it sideways, and unceremoniously planted a bloodied kiss on my cheek. He said contentedly, "Come my beautiful man, we cannot stay here much longer. Take, as a final token, from the abdomen of this cadaver and let's be gone. Tonight we will both be there to share this kill with our brothers." Yes, she was dead.

CHAPTER 9

Missing

The telephone rang urgently in Detective Inspector Mick Courtley's office at the local police station. He grabbed for it with a free hand, clutched it between his ear and shoulder and continued flicking through the files on his desk. "Courtley!" he barked into the mouthpiece.

"Mick, hey, it's Megan!"

"Hello, my love, haven't heard from you for a while. How're Marge and Paul? Rory?"

"They're okay Mick, saw them a couple of months ago and nothing much has changed. Mum's still spoiling, and Dad's still contemplating renovations on the barn. Rory has been in London for a while now. I hardly ever hear from him. Another new girlfriend I believe."

Mick's mouth was squashed against the phone, but he still managed to talk. "I really must get to see your folks soon, just so damn busy."

She could hear him thumbing through papers. He continued, "This city hasn't heard that crime doesn't pay. Back to you love, are you phoning for a reason other than to ask me to lunch?"

"Both. I know you're busy Mick, but I really need to speak to you and, amongst other things, a caring shoulder to cry on. Could you make it today? Any time is okay. And before you answer, let me beg again, please make it today, I just feel it can't wait until tomorrow."

"Listen love, I'm pretty tied up until about four. I'm working tonight, so no one will bitch too much if I slope off for a couple of hours. Would you like me to pick you up, or …?"

"Mick, I'm at such a loose end right now that I'll walk down there to kill some time. Is that okay?"

"That's fine love. Just come right in. Tell them you're here for me. They'll probably ring through from the front desk."

"Great. Oh, and Mick, thanks!"

"Okay," he said distracted, and once again started shuffling and paging. "See you later then!"

Megan and Mick had been friends for years. She had been the adoring little girl at his knees at a time when he was in high school, earning a little extra cash on Paul's farm during school holidays.

On leaving school he had wanted to study law but had found that his grades were too low to achieve a university entrance. Instead he had joined the police force. Since then, he had worked his way up to being an extremely respected detective.

Mick had always seen Megan as a little sister and had affectionately known about her crush on him when she was seven. That had been a long time ago, and over the years they had settled into a close and long-standing friendship that could be relied upon by both of them.

†

Megan fiddled with her hair, dabbed her lipstick, grabbed her handbag, and nervously locked the door as she left her flat.

She had done a lot of thinking and waiting. At first she had hated Ethan, and then forgave him, and then loathed him and then loved him. She had turned the situation inside out to decipher his motives, his reasons, his mind, and her own feelings. Her conclusion was muddled, but she had decided that if anyone cared about what happened to Ethan, she was probably the only one. In fact, she was more than likely the only one that realised that 'something' could possibly have happened to him.

By this time she had ruled out drugs. That was old news and a problem Ethan understood, in his own way. She thought that he might be mixed up in something shady, or perhaps with another woman. But how would that explain the state he was in when she last saw him. How would it explain the marks on his body and the blood on his shirt? How would it explain the personality change, the way he avoided her eyes and his disappearance?

It was the disappearance that concerned her most. One minute they had been talking and the next minute he was gone. If Ethan had been at home, she could have worked around sorting things out, but he was gone, had disappeared into thin air and had not been seen for months. It was like he had never existed.

She had visited his old haunts hoping for a glimpse, called anybody that knew him, including his agent and family. No one had seen or heard from him, nor seemed to care one way or another.

She decided that even if Ethan didn't want to be found, she was going to see if she could, at least, find out if he was safe. So she had called Mick, hoping that he would be able to help her.

Megan was nervous as she walked down to the

police station. Nervous of how she would begin, and of how she would put the story together without having Mick take an instant dislike to Ethan. She needed his concern and his shoulder. Every couple of minutes she checked her wristwatch, wishing the time would go quicker.

The police station loomed before her, greyly. People scurried in and out, some in uniform, some civilian, some tramps. Cars squealed to a halt, people were dragged in and out, and shouts could be heard from the building. It seemed much busier than usual.

She felt uneasy in this environment. Threading her way through the myriad of people on the steps, she entered the building and joined the queue of hopefuls waiting to present themselves for scrutiny to the dragon behind the desk.

The person behind her kept on invading her space with his dirty unkempt clothes and red-chequered carryall. He grumbled continuously through his filthy beard and attempted to engage her in conversation. She made a point of ignoring him but couldn't help feeling bad about her lack of empathy. She wasn't in the mood for empathising with anybody but herself. She smiled at the thought of how pathetic she was.

"This could be Ethan," Megan thought to

herself. "For all I know Ethan could have landed up like this. Well, actually, that would be the more acceptable thing to have happened. At least he would be alive. I don't even know if he is alive. Oh God, please help me I beg you, please help Ethan." And that was how she occupied herself until the policewoman behind the desk called.

"Next. Hurry up I haven't got all day!"

"Hello," offered Megan, "Um, I'm here to see Detective Mick Courtley. He's expecting me. I'm Megan Sands."

With her small piggy eyes, the woman scrutinised her, sweat beading her top lip. She oozed out of her uniform like dough rising out of its tin. "D'ya have an appointment? The detective is a very busy man!"

"Yes, as I said he's expecting me and said to tell you that you could phone through to his office for confirmation."

"Do you know where his office is, then?" Stupid question to ask, in Megan's opinion.

"Just down that corridor and to the left. I've been here before."

Miss Piggy shook her head and reached her podgy hand for the phone. "Mick, there's a lady down here to see you. She's waiting! You'd better come and fetch her. Sez she's been here before, but I'm not letting anyone go wandering off by themselves." She put the phone down and growled, "Next please!"

Megan stood to one side to wait for Mick. The policewoman was going out of her way to be unpleasant to the dirty man.

"Speak up!" she shouted, as if he was deaf. "Can't understand what the fuck you're on about. You must stop coming down here Arch, there's nothing, and I repeat, nothing we can do for you. Approach Prisons Department. Write them a letter. Do anything, but don't come in here again. Now get out of here!"

The man shuffled away, still mumbling under his breath.

"Next please! Just fill in the form."

†

Mick Courtley was a man of presence. As he came striding down the corridor, people greeted him and then shifted out of his way. The men called him "Sir" and the ladies made sheep eyes at him.

Unconcerned, he barged his way towards where Megan stood, with a grin creasing his open face. "Hullo love, sorry about the crush." He gave her a bear hug and she disappeared into his shoulder. "Dave!" he called out to a policeman walking by, "I'm going out for a while. See you in about an hour or two. Hold the fort, okay?"

He guffawed at the comic look that appeared on the young policeman's face. They obviously shared a private joke.

"Hello, Mick. Missed you." Megan stood on her toes to peck him on the cheek.

"Well, I hadn't realised it love, but I missed you too." He placed his arm protectively about her and ushered her out of the large doors.

Mick took up a good bit of the stool on which he sat, his well-muscled arms leaning on the counter of the coffee shop that they had chosen. He took a half-doughnut bite whilst he contemplated Megan's drawn face. With a mouthful he asked, "So what's up?" He gestured with his other hand, "Best bloody doughnuts in London huh?" He grinned, and then gulped the other half into his mouth and added a slurp of coffee.

"Jeez Mick, except for the fact that you've got bigger you haven't changed a bit. But I'm glad of it. It just seems so kind of ordinary to be sitting here with you. You know, like nothing terrible has ever happened."

"I'll always be the same, just waiting for you to change your mind and make me a happy man. So what's so terrible anyway?"

"It would spoil a wonderful friendship and you know it - you and I as a feature, Mick. Besides there's someone else, or maybe I should say there was someone else, and that's the reason I'm here."

"Yeah! I can see it coming, love problems. I suspect you need some advice from a 'well versed in the ways of love failure' person like myself. If its love you want to know about, I'm probably the wrong person to be on the receiving end of your woes. Anyways, I'm all ears love, so spit it out."

"It's not as easy as that," she said, "but I'll try if you have some time?" She absent-mindedly stirred her coffee.

Mouth full of icing, he said, "I told you, I'm here to listen, and never let it be said that 'Michael the mighty lover' wasn't the confidante he professed to be. So love, in all seriousness, what's the problem? You look pretty miserable. Lost some weight too, haven't you?"

"Yes, I couldn't get more pitiful if I tried. Anyway you hit the nail on the head - love problems. His name is Ethan. I don't know where to start telling you about him. He means almost everything to me. I love him, Mick.

She started, "He's a musician - not your type

of music. Alternative rock-metal type stuff. Had a drug problem a couple of years ago, which it seems he might have started again. He's walked out on me, Mick. Well, didn't actually walk out with a great farewell or anything, just disappeared right out from under my nose. One minute he was sitting there with me, and I went out to make a phone call. Next minute when I came back he was gone.

"A day or two later he comes around to my flat, well 'our' flat, smeared with blood and acting weird. He just packed a few clothes and went. Mick, he's a musician - he didn't even take his guitar.

"I haven't seen him for a couple of months, well about seven weeks, and just don't know what to think. This sounds rather corny, doesn't it? I'm worried sick though."

Mick broke his silence. "Stop, you've said it all. Dump him, Megan, if he hasn't already dumped you, and that's how it sounds. Enough has been said; I know the type. In and out of jail, never really off the dope, losers, lazy, and must I go on? Little bleeding heartbreakers - families in shreds. No, this already sounds like bad news for you." He stuffed the rest of the second doughnut into his mouth in finalisation of his statement and watched as her face dissolved into tears. He relented and eased closer to put his arm around her. She sobbed out the months of heartbreak in streaky moisture over his collar.

"Whoa baby, I'm sorry. It's as bad as that is it? Well c'mon then, let's hear the whole story. There's a good girl, stop crying." He asked the waitress for a wad of serviettes to swab Megan's face. "There, that's better. Better?"

"Oh Mick, I'm sorry" she sobbed, "I really hadn't wanted to do it this way, but it's just so wonderful being with you. Sort of makes me feel all sorry for myself, and just looking at you makes me want to cry." She gave a heave, dabbed at her pouring nose, and continued. "Believe me there's more to this or I wouldn't have asked you to come. I suppose I started all wrong. Just the thing I was afraid of doing."

"Well here I am, and I still love you even with that snotty nose and red eyes and the fact that you want to cry just by looking at me. So, out with it then." He also dabbed at her nose and wiped a stranded tear from the bottom of her chin.

So she told the story as she knew it, not leaving any details to imagination. Mick listened, with a grunt now and then to indicate he was following the tale of woe.

With a final sigh, Megan came to the end of her missive "... and that's the whole sorry story.

What do you think?"

"It's a tough one love, and I really don't know what to think. Honestly, I think this guy sounds like he's had one too many, but the blood on his shirt and his seeming disappearance interests the investigative side of me. Would you like me to look into this, discreetly? You never know what I could dig up. At least you'll have peace of mind when you find that it's nothing more than a kinky lover, or something else that he has got himself into. Do you have a photo of him? It would help." He grunted, more to himself, "There's so many of these good-for-nothings out there."

She chose to ignore his comment. "Yes I do. Hang on; it's here in my bag." She scratched about in her large sack of a bag for her wallet and extracted the photograph gently from one of the pockets. "Here, look. Pretty gorgeous, isn't he? He was a bit younger when this photo was taken but hasn't changed that much."

"Very pretty boy for sure, but not my type love."

"I should hope not! Mick, thanks. I appreciate this. So when do you think you'll be able to start looking or whatever?"

He slipped the photo into his shirt pocket. "I can't promise when, but I'll see who's in and not too busy tomorrow, and who can have a bit of a snoop around. Things are hectic down at the station, and there are a lot of pressing things keeping me sleepless at the moment. So I'll try for tomorrow but can't promise. I'll keep you in the loop though, okay?"

"That's fantastic, thank you so much". She reached out and squeezed his arm. "So I'll wait to hear from you. At least I've got more reason to wait now."

She paid the bill, and they walked out together, stopping on the sidewalk to say their goodbyes.

"You owe me one next time," she said, "A cuppa and a doughnut. Let's hope it will be a celebration."

"Sure, cheers love - and hey, give us a little smile." He reached out and lifted her chin affectionately.

She smiled up at him, and then gave him a quick kiss on the cheek. "Bye Mick - and thanks again. You're my hero for the day."

He watched as she walked forlornly up the windy road. A flying paper bag followed her closely, as lost as she was. Megan looked back briefly and gave a small wave, tendrils of her long hair blowing forwards to partly cover that sad face. He shook his head, put his hands in his coat pocket, and turned to walk in the opposite direction.

†

The next day Mick did as he promised. He thought that David would be the best man to do some snooping around – he could be so charming. Think of the devil, and he walked past Mick's office.

"Hey Dave, come in here a minute bud, got something to chat to you about." He held up the photograph of Ethan and waved it at the police officer.

David poked his head in the door, a pencil hanging from his mouth. "Wazzat?"

"Come in and sit for a sec." Mick pointed to the visitors' chair.

David came in, and with his usual casual grace pulled out the chair and made himself comfortable. He took the pencil out of his mouth and stuck it behind his ear.

Mick grinned at him. "So how's it going with the Harvey case? Anything happening there?"

"Looks good, Boss. Whole thing's coming together nicely, and that bastard of a witness has finally agreed to testify. It took some smooth talk though. We should be able to tie up the loose ends this week. Why?"

"Feel like doing a bit of poking around for me, strictly off the record and casual?

"Sure, got some time. Why off the record?"

"Family stuff" answered Mick. "I would've done it myself, but I'm up to my eyeballs. I'll just say you needed a few of days off after the hours you've put into the Harvey case. Okay with you? You can use my car to get around. You've been wanting to take her for a spin. Now's your chance. Just treat Sally nicely – like she belongs to Moses. Leave your squad car for me. I'll blue light it for a while."

"Sally?" David queried with feigned surprise.

"The car – I call her Sally".

"Sure Boss, sounds cosy. I'll look after 'Sally'. Let's have the case details, or not, as the case may be." He chortled at his play with words.

"I haven't got much. His name is Ethan Westwood - 26 years old. He went missing about seven weeks ago - last seen by his girlfriend, my very good friend Megan Sands, in her flat. He was covered in blood, seemingly from wounds to the upper torso, like dog bites. Then he took off without as much as a goodbye and I'll see you. No one has heard from him since, as far as Meg knows, and he hasn't hung out at his usual haunts. Ex-junkie rehabilitated about two years before his disappearance. Seemed he might have got back onto the stuff just prior to his disappearance, which makes me wonder if it could be a gang drug thing. Check that out. Check out his contacts, his friends, and the musos he played with. Check with his family. You know the usual stuff?!

"Also check him out on the network, maybe we've got something there. He could have left London for all we know. London is a huge city to easy to lose oneself in. Speak to people at the train station. Show them the photograph – they may remember him because of the pretty face. Check out the airport and flight details for the last seven weeks. Look hip and hang out at the night spots where this type of person would go. You know what I mean? It's a 'go out and enjoy yourself' type of job." He smiled conspiratorially.

"Yessir, Boss, but this'll all take more than a couple of days." David leaned back in his chair and examined the photograph. "It shouldn't be too difficult. With a face like this, he's bound to have been seen around. Pigs' teeth, who could miss him? Real pretty boy."

"Yeah, well, if you like the type. Anyway, get to it, Dave, and keep me posted. Take about two weeks if you have to. We'll sort it out afterwards.

I'd also prefer it if you keep away from the girlfriend, Megan. She's a close family friend. She's already upset, and I don't want to bother her until I've got something definite. I don't have a good feeling about this."

"Ah, I get it, okay, off the record. I'll keep away from her unless I clear with you first. Okay?" Without waiting for a reply he got up gracefully, pushed the chair in, and walked out whistling a little tune to himself.

Mick liked and trusted Dave. He was one of the dedicated few.

†

David tied up the few matters that needed his attention, and then put his feet up on his desk. He sunk back in his chair, and again examined the photograph of Ethan.

"So Ethan, my man, we must find you. Believe me, I need the break. Thanks, pal."

He whistled tunelessly to himself as he started going through the motions of looking for Ethan. He took a blank file out of his drawer and slipped the photograph into it, made a few phone calls to friends in the business and keyed in the necessary for computer enquiries. There was no information whatsoever on Ethan - no prior convictions, nothing.

David telephoned enquiries to see if he could track down Ethan's family. They confirmed a couple of families with the surname Westwood. He was particularly interested in a Mrs A Westwood living in a small town on the south coast. Mick had told him that the family was fairly affluent, and that Mr Westwood was deceased.

He called the 'A Westwood' number, and a female voice answered the telephone. "Hello. Westwood residence."

"Hello, this is David Jacobs. I am an old friend of Ethan Westwood. Is this the right number for the Westwoods related to Ethan?"

"Yes it is, but Master Ethan hasn't lived here for a long time, and the Madam hasn't heard from him. Heartbroken she's been, poor lady."

"Well, I haven't heard from him either and it seems he's gone missing."

"Hold on then, Mr Jacobs. She's outside in the garden. You're lucky to find her here today, what with her running the business n'all"

The phone went quiet, and David waited. He could hear the echo of footsteps in the background, and then faintly, voices. After the voices, a small silence; then he could hear someone walking towards the phone.

"Hello. This is Anne Westwood," a voice finally said.

"Mrs Westwood, thank you for taking my call. My name is David Jacobs, and I'm with the police department. My apologies for not being forthright with your employee, but I was afraid you wouldn't want to take my call." He waited for her reply.

A short silence while she seemed to be making up her mind how to respond. "Well, how can I help you Mr Jacobs?" she asked in a reserved aloof voice.

"It concerns your son Ethan, Mrs Westwood. His girlfriend has reported him missing. At this point in time we're not launching a major manhunt as we're not sure if he is missing or not, but there are people who are concerned. I would appreciate it if you could spare me some time for a chat. Possibly this afternoon? I could drive through soon."

"Mr Jacobs, you obviously don't know my son like I do, but yes, come if you must. I doubt, though, that I'll be of any help. We haven't heard from Ethan for close on three years now."

"Well, I'm so sorry to hear that Ma'am, but thank you. Would it be in okay for me to see you in about two hours?"

"That's fine, Mr Jacobs." The phone went dead without a goodbye.

He looked at it quizzically, and mimicked in a sarcastic feminine voice, "That's fine Mr Jacobs".

The drive through to the Westwoods' was a pleasant one, and David whistled to himself in his tuneless way, and in appreciation of the peaceful surroundings. The town was situated on the coast, and the sea air was clean and refreshing. He had needed an excuse to get out, as the oppression of the police station was weighing heavy on him just lately.

Although he excelled at his police work, it really wasn't what he planned to do for much longer than the next five years.

David was a nature lover, revelling in the wonders of life and the simplicity of the animals that inhabited the world with him. He related on a most personal level with the beasts, and they with him. David had no close ties and, in fact, he hated most people as much as he loved animals. So police work suited him just fine, and over the years he had become an excellent actor, playing out the scenarios that people expected. On the surface, David appeared more normal than most people did. This was part of his play.

†

She was reclining in a garden swing chair, large hat shading striking blue eyes. Eyes like Ethan's. Anne Westwood was definitely one of the most attractive women that David had ever seen. He whistled to himself under his breath.

"How do you do, Mrs Westwood?" He leant forward and offered his hand.

She smiled and took it. "That's me, and I presume you're the young policeman I spoke to earlier?"

"Yes, I'm David Jacobs. I expected someone older, so forgive me if I'm speechless for a while. You're as striking as your son, Mrs Westwood."

"Thank you. Yes, you're right; he is a lovely boy to look at - has been since tiny. Please call me Anne."

"Okay, Anne it is." He proffered his most charming smile.

Anne smiled back from under her superfluous hat, held out her hand, and he helped her to her feet. "We have some fresh tea inside. May I call you David?"

"Well, that's my name. The tea would be great."

As he followed her inside, David couldn't help but appreciate what he saw. She was a most arresting woman.

†

Anne's story was nothing out of the ordinary. "Ethan was adopted when he was a week old, as I thought I couldn't have children. As far as the family is concerned, Ethan is a Westwood. He even bears a striking resemblance to my mother's side of the family. Anyway, he grew up as most boys do; an ordinary teenager, if a bit spoilt and strange in that he kept very much to himself. Ethan's intelligence has always been above average, and he excelled at school, achieving exemplary grades for music. He's a very talented boy, Mr Jacobs - and I'm not just saying that as a proud mother.

"But to continue - he had only a few good friends, and they were gradually estranged from him after he left school. By the time he moved out of home, none of his old friends were around anymore. It was almost as if he'd purposely ensured that no one would miss him when he went. He was twenty years old then.

"Within two years, Ethan was entrenched in the local music world and was beginning to make a name for himself. Quite an achievement, if only local. I know this because the newspaper ran a short success story about him.

"By the age of twenty-four, he had reached

the height of his popularity and, tragically for him and devastating for us, we heard that he had become addicted to heroin." Anne stopped at this point in her narration to collect herself. She stared out of the window thoughtfully, and then continued, "You know, David, we never could help Ethan, though believe you me we tried. He has so many guilt feelings and seems to flit between being a caring and tender person, to another who just doesn't care. He can switch on and off at a whim. It seems he truly believes we'd reject him if he opened up to us. In fact, he believes emphatically that we have done just that, rejected him. This really isn't true. We love him very much, Andrew and me. He has a lot of issues that we don't understand, and quite a fragmented personality, which is one of the reasons we don't worry too much when we don't hear from him. Even for so long. Without him knowing though, we do keep an eye out for him."

"You mentioned Andrew? Your husband?" David enquired.

"No," she smiled proudly, "my other son. A year after we adopted Ethan, I fell pregnant. Something we never thought would happen. Needless to say we were thrilled, all of us, including Ethan. They have always been extremely close - that is Andrew and Ethan.

"Andrew is in Paris, lecturing in art. Ethan's

downhill plunge started at about the same time that Andrew went away I believe. The drug thing! We struggled to understand it. Before that, Ethan had always seemed to be in control of what he was." Her voice trailed away, and then she added, "He's always been my little angel. Just don't know why things went awry! Well, David, back to the point: what is it you want to know, exactly?"

"Anne, I'd like a list of people Ethan may have contacted, as well as their contact numbers if possible. Also where Ethan may have gone; a familiar or favourite place, perhaps. People often run away to favourite holiday places they went to as children. Compile a list of any family members with whom he was particularly close. Andrew's contact number would be helpful. Also, habits that he might have - excuse me, I don't mean to be rude - excluding the dope habit, we know about that. Oh, and also the name of the newspaper that ran his story. Maybe one of their reporters has kept track of his progress, or lack of it. In fact, Anne, anything you think might help at this point."

"David, you're serious, he really is missing?" Her hand daintily adjusted her hat. David noticed a slight tremor to both her hand and mouth.

"Well, as far as his girlfriend is concerned. She last saw him about seven weeks ago, and after that he just disappeared into thin air. Apparently she was the only one to whom he was even vaguely attached. Well, that's as far as she's concerned."

"Who is this girl you mention, David? We've been left out of my son's life, and I didn't even know he had a girlfriend."

"I only know that her name is Megan, and they shared a flat. I don't know the full details of their relationship, and Mick, my boss, really only gave me brief notes to work from. He isn't taking this too seriously yet. Seems to be doing it more as a favour to Megan. She's an old friend. On the other hand, it would be taken a lot more seriously if you filed a missing person report, Anne."

"Megan says he's been missing for seven weeks, David, but to me he's been missing for a couple of years. I haven't seen or heard from him for that long. I wonder if this girl knows him as well as she thinks she does. I think that perhaps Ethan has chosen to go missing for reasons only known to him. Probably on the binge again. If you must, then file the report.

"Oh, there is one way you can check up on him. There is trust money from his father's estate. Every month, his bank account is credited with a couple of thousand pounds. He also gets a small share of company profits. If he's still around, which I know he is, he will have to live, won't he? He'll need the money, especially if he's gone back to his drug habit. I suggest you check this out."

"Yes, thanks, that's really helpful. I most certainly will check it out. Can you let me have the account number and where he banks? It'll be a great help. You can text through the other details I asked for. I think, Mrs Westwood, you have probably solved this case for us, and I'm glad I came to see you. Well I've taken up enough of your time and thank you for your kind hospitality." He made to get up.

"Please stay for a moment. I will get the banking details for you before you go. They're filed away in the study, so I'll only be a few minutes. Please feel free to help yourself to another cup of tea while you wait." She disappeared for a few minutes and came back with the banking details on a sheet of paper that sported the Westwood crest. She gave it one fold and slipped it onto the table opposite him.

David stood up again and picked up the account details and put them in his pocket. He extended his hand. Her handshake was warm and business-like, unlike a woman's.

"Goodbye, David. Thank you for coming over. Let me know if you hear anything."

She walked him to the car and turned to walk away before he'd even started the engine.

✝

The sun was already setting as he drove back to the city. His excitement grew as he contemplated the hunt with Ethan that night.

CHAPTER 10

Inhumanity

Ethan sat alone in the garden, tortured thoughts plaguing his mind. Over the past couple of months there had been little room for introspection. All had been blocked by Kalin's presence; Kalin's seed planted deep within the recesses of his spirit. His mind's eye relayed, in flashes, his deeds - their deeds, during the time he'd spent with them. And he questioned if he was wholly and entirely Ethan.

Kalin found him seated so in agitated meditation, emitting a troubled and erratic aural glow. He read Ethan's condition; it was what he had been expecting. He sat down beside Ethan on the grass, smiled peacefully and took Ethan's fidgeting hands in his own.

Ethan gasped, "Why, Kalin? I have been happy, but now this blackness is overwhelming me, like it used to. I thought I had finally rid myself of this depression."

"The growing takes time, Ethan. The excitement and novelty of your situation are now dimming, as the reality of what we are permeates your being. You will come to accept and understand."

"But it begins to seem like I have embraced my own ultimate madness and desire - that we are all the victims of our own desires."

"Let me explain. You see, Ethan, my lamb, what is chaos to one is order to another, and so it is that what is order to one is chaos to another. The very planet we live on was created out of chaos that became order. So one might question which one is order and which one is chaos. Or is there such a thing as order, or is there such a thing as chaos.

"Similarly, what is good for one man is evil for another man and vice versa. Hate and love are similar emotions but then again, dissimilar in their enacting. They are akin to one another and can change from one to the other.

"One then contemplates the order of things, or in other words, is there a universal law that pertains to all living creatures? It is really a matter of perception at the level to which we have evolved.

"Humankind has evolved on a parallel with - and to - us, as you have discovered in the collective memories of the brothers. But in so saying, all creatures have evolved in the same way and are very much alike, and then again dissimilar in the ways that they physically and mentally express themselves. But they are one with us, and us with them. Our evolution is still in its infancy, though, and thus the need to act ritualistically amongst ourselves, the brothers, to re-establish kindred bond."

"Kalin, I still question our right to kill to maintain our own immortality," he offered, obviously confused at Kalin's missive.

"Have you not yet realised that all creatures are immortal. That in fact all we're doing is providing them with a medium to better understand their immortality. It's really just a transferral of energy. All creatures share a universal flow.

"You are only twenty-six years old, Ethan, and yet you have experienced, through us, the birth - the creation of all. So have all creatures. Their memory is yet untapped. That is why it is more important for us to take of their soul and their memories, than their blood and flesh. There are many times when some of the brothers allow the excitement of the kill to regress their souls. When the primeval ritual we enact - and the consequential rush - become to their minds the aim of the kill, when it is not the aim at all."

"So if there is no good or no evil, no order nor chaos, Kalin, what is there? And, from what you say, is the hunt necessary? Surely if the essence is the most important, it is the essence we must take. We have the power, as you have proved to me by your actions, that we may share another's essence without taking the mortal body."

"Ethan, my beautiful one, you are learning fast. That is the whole aim of the brotherhood. We have taken upon ourselves physical immortality. This is a vanity, our vanity, the fear of dying. But we realise now that there is no death for any one creature, only for the particular body they inhabit at any given time. So in saying this, is it evil to take from them? Is it not good to provide them with the opportunity of our immortality?

"We are ruled by our nature, do not forget. We were made so, and at this time must live by the rules according to which we were made. This is our survival.

"We are not the only creatures that consume the flesh of another creature. Humankind consumes the flesh of many of the creatures with which they have evolved. They breed them for that purpose, those creatures of kinder and gentler souls. Do they first ask? Do they wait for invitation as we do? No! So, then, if there is evil, as perceived by humankind, is this not evil?

"Why should we perceive ourselves, then, as eviller than others? This is a fallacy. We are not much different, but different inasmuch as we take the flesh and essence of the most intelligent, successful, and resourceful creatures with which we share and inhabit this Earth of ours - with their permission. And in their success, our survival has been their choice. Surely this is more intelligent? Do we not have more to gain from taking human life than killing the ignorant and dumb as humans do?

"Remember Ethan, every time we kill we share. We share the blood of our victim. This is physical. But more importantly we share his soul. He becomes us, and in so becoming, we allow him the opportunity of living immortally within us. A wonderful opportunity, wouldn't you say?

"But my lamb, I repeat myself in my endeavour to gain your understanding. What say you? We are not a human creature, and it follows we will not express ourselves as humankind do."

Ethan knew that Kalin had rambled on without answering his question why they had to kill. He chose to ignore it.

"Kalin, what about our sacrifice of love? I mean the love that two people share. You know, the bonding of man and woman?"

"There is nothing stopping any of us from bonding with a human. We are so like them that it is possible. Procreation is possible. After all, Ethan, you are part human. It has been a parallel evolution, one with the other and the bond is already forged. In any event, we have learnt that it is not necessary. We understand that the passion felt between two human beings, usually but not limited to a man and a woman is destructive by its very nature. The eternal bonding of two people, one to the other, is not a natural law.

"Between us, the brothers, we have a purer love, a love that has nothing to do with the sexual act, which is primitive in its very doing. We have perceived that it is not necessary for the establishment of soul mates. We are kindred spirit Ethan - we are one.

"We have no sickness nor the diseases that plague humankind, a symbol of their weakness brought about by their destructive thought patterns." Kalin smiled tranquilly, pleased with his explanation.

Ethan sat silently for a while considering what Kalin had said, or chose not to say. He felt he must agree. "What you say is true, as I have never felt more in harmony with myself or others, but I ask, surely the very destructiveness of humankind's bonding is an education in itself - their opportunity to expand and grow their souls? This is what I've been thinking. With every failure there is the urgency to succeed, and as they taste success, they strive for further success. Will they not overtake us in their spiritual evolution? Perhaps we stagnate in our nonchalance and euphoric stupor? Their very ageing process is a lesson within itself - an opportunity, perhaps, for the soul to feel all creation and the reverse thereof, in one lifetime; a lifetime that sees an end and might look forward to a new beginning. This we do not have."

Kalin grunted in disgust at what Ethan said. "Ah, but Ethan, that is the sacrifice we made for our immortality. There is always choice. Choice, when all is said and done, is what it's all about. We made the choice and have to live and learn within - and in harmony with - our one immortal life. We will not have the pleasure of dreading the end if there is one. It was our choice, and we were chosen for this path.

"Ethan, my lamb. I hear some notes of discord I feared to mention. This surprises me, even though I expected it. Your soul has never hummed with the same rhythm as ours, although I have seen it battle to achieve this end. Never have any of the brothers questioned the choice we made. It has been our ultimate reality. Think well before you further your path with us.

It is not too late, blood of mine. You have the 'choice', as I told you before you initiated with us. Think, brother, and we will talk again."

Kalin stood, making it obvious that the discussion was at an end. Ethan wondered if Kalin really knew all the answers but loved him no less. Simultaneously, he felt the trickle of guilt as a pain over his heart. He began to cry, deep inside, in a panic of loneliness and abandonment.

The alarm had barely materialised when Kalin, aware of Ethan's agony, turned and took him into his arms, emanating love and peace like Ethan had never felt before. All questions were gone, and they found solace in their love, individual being, and in being as one.

Ethan knew there was no choice, he was the chosen and conceded to his choosing. The last vestiges of Ethan left, as the seed of Kalin vanquished with its dark and soulless inhumanity.

CHAPTER 11

Galleria des Artistes

Benedikt wound his way through the gyrating throng of humanity, with Romando close on his heels. Heads turned in recognition, as the carbon copy of the one shadowed the other. They were well known at this club that they often frequented.

The two were of the brotherhood but were also brothers by conception. Identical in their looks and imitating in their ways, they charmed and threaded their way to the table at the far end of the room.

Both brothers emitted a morbid humour and the same dark good looks. Black eyebrows fanned equally dark eyes, which searched the throngs above well-defined cheekbones and aesthetically perfect noses. They smiled in unison, magnetically drawing the ladies with their striking appearance and the men in their envy.

Romando focused his gaze on the one remaining drunk at the table. The drunk scrambled up, grabbing at his drink as he did so. He afterwards thought that perhaps, in his drunkenness, he had imagined the yellow slit in that strange fellow's eye, or perhaps he had imagined the threat to his very life portrayed on that sumptuous cruel mouth. In any event, he hadn't stayed to find out; life was hard enough as it was. He had gulped down the remainder of his drink and staggered his way through the people, thinking that home had never before seemed such a safe and wonderful place to be.

The brothers chuckled and then seated themselves. They had perfected the art of getting rid of unwanteds. In fact they were both of good humour and not the evil caricatures envisioned by the drunk. They were congenial fellows, ruled, as were the others, by their nature. But pleasant and warm in their acceptance of what they were and with the wonderful bounty that life had to offer. Life was good, and they made the best of it.

At home they sat quietly, enrapturing to strains of medieval music. But here they permitted the beat and excitement of the modern club music to reverberate through their being, thrilling their primal need in preparation for the diffusion of energies that would take place. Their euphoria would have been obvious to any silent, committed observer, if there was one in this place of loud music and drug-crazed visitations.

"My hunger burns, brother," Benedikt chortled in high humour.

"Then drink up and let us dance," smiled Romando, "There are many doting ladies here tonight who would do us the honour. They are a wonder to behold, brother: all these bright butterflies awaiting our attention, begging for their wings to be clipped and mounted upon our wall of ecstasy. But look over there, a young man of equal attraction; the king of butterflies - and he looks our way."

The young man smiled his innocence and invitation across the room.

"Let me invite that young man to join us," said Romando. "Your company grows tedious, and the bambino emits his loneliness." He locked the eyes of the young man, enticing and magnetising even though he was already winding his way towards them.

The man approached their table with a timid flutter of hands about his head to tidy his hair. "I see you have a spare seat here; would you mind terribly if I join you?" He spoke with an Australian accent, obviously from out of town.

"Be our guest," said Benedikt. He stood, pulled

out a chair and extended his invitation with an outstretched hand. "Romando was just saying that my company grows boring."

The young man took the chair and offered a handshake across the table. "Hi, I'm Greg. You must be brothers?"

They nodded and turned to smile at one another.

"I am Benedikt, and this ugly person next to me is Romando."

Greg beamed and turned so as to obtain a better view of the dancers. "This is the first time I've been here." And again in embarrassment, "Yours were the only two friendly faces in the crowd. I'm afraid that I just homed in. Please say if I'm interrupting anything?" His eyes questioned each in turn.

Romando's smile had never left his lips, but it now increased its width and his eyes twinkled. "No, no, not at all. Please, you're more than welcome." His Mediterranean accent revealed itself in the emphatic "No, no."

"I hear you're not from around here either," remarked Greg in a relieved voice, pleased to have found something in common with his chosen comrades.

"Well, yes and no," offered Benedikt, "We're

not from here originally, but have been here for some time. You are obviously new to our city, and with permission, I observe that it seems that as yet have no friends?"

The young man blushed and stared into his drink as if the lump of floating ice held the answers of the galaxy. "You're embarrassingly direct," he stammered. "But yes, you're right. Friends are difficult to make, and it took a lot of courage to come here to you. Somehow I felt drawn here though, almost as if I had no choice."

"No, you had no choice. Your loneliness took your hand and led you over. But it is fine, and we are glad of your company. So, think no more on it and let us celebrate our newfound friendship. Salut!" Benedikt raised his glass, and the lights of the dance floor reflected in sparkling patterns of portent on the three faces.

✝

Their friendship with Greg came fast, and all three slipped into a relationship of easy-going and bantering camaraderie. There was no further thought of harming Greg. They never harmed their friends. They liked Greg. His loneliness matched theirs that they had kept hidden all these years.

At that time, the brothers did not know, as they took Greg's friendship, that it would contribute to their undoing. An undoing that had already sown its seed with the taking of Ethan to their fold; a destruction that had started its growth deep within the recesses of each of the brother's souls; a seed of discontent, so discreetly sown as to be invisible to their collective spirit. Kalin had made his first and final mistake. An error so grave, that they would never know how it had begun. Ethan was the harbinger of change to their kind, with Greg his Judas.

†

Greg

Greg decided he really liked the two brothers. Their humour, though a trifle dark and melancholic, was catching. As he followed them from the club on that particular night, he felt happier than he had in a long while.

This city had attracted him with its historic feel. A place so unlike his hometown, Sydney in Australia, that it left his senses reeling in the richness of its ambience.

He would be here until his canvases told the full story of this city and its cultural heritage: the people, the cathedrals and the churches, the palace; the winding streets, markets, and high-end shops; the pubs and, last but not least, the Thames. Already, he had completed two large paintings that captured the timeless city and its people in bright, bold colour. He had made statement upon statement with furious brush strokes.

People interested Greg, and the more his interest in them as individuals was piqued, the more he became intent on their discovery and finally their capture within a frame, to be forever defined by oil and turpentine.

Romando and Benedikt did not inspire the artistic side of Greg as they were too European. He had come for the local English culture that as yet had not found popularity in the galleries.

The warm friendship of the two brothers was welcome, and he needed the temporary escape from his studio - if one could call it that - whilst he searched for new subjects and subject matter.

Home was a small two-bedroomed flat above a pawnshop, with one room converted into a studio. It overlooked a market, and so provided Greg with an unending cacophony of chatter and noise just outside his window.

The building housed the usual elderly that had lived there since times when the area was up-market housing. Elderly people who tottered up and down derelict stairs to various strains of new music emanating from the nooks and crannies of the building they now shared with a new-age population. Peeling paint; cooking smells; and small scruffy Maltese poodles trotting and sniffing to the pervading wisps of incense and weed.

Greg was of the new age and enjoyed his surroundings. He was an animal of both empathy and compassion; well-read, and politically and culturally aware. Each day provided him with the wonderful opportunity of discovery as he savoured the experiences that presented themselves and that could only be enjoyed through the eyes of an artist.

†

Greg woke on the morning following his meeting with the brothers with a feeling of well-being. The sun was already streaming through his window, bright beams providing passage to heaven for the dust particles that traversed in slow but sometimes erratic movements, back and forth.

He checked his watch, and then there ensued a mad scramble of dressing and rushing. The two completed and now dry paintings stood against one wall, wrapped in thick brown paper, ready for their delivery to the gallery where they were to be exhibited the following week. Greg picked them up and regretted that he had not taken up the gallery's offer to have them collected. But they were his children, his pride and joy, and he was afraid that they might get damaged.

He struggled down the stairs with his bulky packages and burst out into the already busy street. Even though the gallery was just a couple of blocks away, his struggle with the two pictures took him close on fifteen minutes. He begged for some assistance from a passer-by when he got to the gallery door.

"Hello, Guido." he puffed to the gallery owner who had rushed forward to help when he saw the struggling artist. "These are the paintings you're waiting for. Hell, they're heavy with the frames on – I should have had them framed here."

Guido was a short squat man, balding with wispy hair that hugged his gold necklaced neck. Today, he wore an open-necked shirt with red tulips flowering their way across his breast.

"Gregory, you silly man, I told you we would collect," he said in his dainty voice, as he kissed Greg on the one cheek, then the next. He turned with a flourish and called back into the interior of the gallery, "Simon dear, can you help this darling man." He turned back to Greg, "Gregory, truly, I have so looked forward to having your work here. Do hurry. I wait with bated breath darling."

Simon appeared from the back of the gallery. He was a tall thin man with a thick crop of curly blonde hair. "Oh, hello, Greg. Good to see you again," he said shyly in a well-educated voice.

Greg grinned at the two of them. They were a well-matched couple, that had apparently been together now for many years. He had met them soon after his arrival in the city.

Guido had taken Greg under his wing, immediately impressed by the quality and originality of his work. Greg fully appreciated the luck that had thrown him in Guido's path.

"Thanks, Guido. You've done me a hell of a favour! How about you put the kettle on whilst I catch my breath? A cuppa would be great. I was in such a rush this morning I didn't have time to have a bite or anything. Got something to eat, or should I buy?"

"My dear man, of course I've got something for you to eat. Simon baked last night, and I've brought some of his delicious cake in today." He turned to Simon with a proud smile, "Much to your embarrassment, my poor darling. Simon dear, I'm going to let Gregory sample a slice of your culinary masterpiece as soon as these paintings are stowed safely away. Go now, help him, and I'll cut and pour."

By the time they returned from the back of the gallery, Guido had moved aside some of the clutter on his desk and a tray of tea and cake had been placed in the middle of it all.

"Gregory, now tell me, do I detect red eyes there, and just a hint of alcohol on your breath? Did you go out last night, and who did you meet?" His eyes twinkled with curiosity. "It's about time that you pulled yourself away from your paintings, darling."

"Well, actually yes, I did go out. You're a crafty old devil, Guido." Greg was just a bit embarrassed, and discreetly put his hand over his mouth to hide any remnant of alcohol breath.

"Don't say old, Gregory. I don't like it much, you know that. One is only as old as one feels, and I think you know how I feel - crafty perhaps, but old ...?" He turned this question to Simon whilst he poured. Then he took a cup over to Greg. They sat down, cross-legged on an Afghan rug. There were no chairs.

"Well, did you meet anybody?" Guido asked, bursting with curiosity.

"Yeah, I did." He slurped eagerly at his tea, keeping the couple in suspense. "You could never get old, you know, Guido." He peered over the rim of his cup at Guido's expectant expression. "Okay, I actually met two really nice guys. Don't get ideas now! No lady, though, and I know that's what you meant."

"Yes, but the two gentlemen sound exciting, darling. Tell me more." He put his cup down and leant further forward towards Greg.

"Oh, just two really great chaps. Brothers. I had a good time, Guido, and in fact I'm meeting them later on today for a drink."

"You're not!" exclaimed Guido in delight. "I want to hear all about it. He patted the space next to him.

"Simon, come here. Greg's got something to tell us."

Greg had to narrate the entire evening from start to finish. Once Guido and Simon were satisfied, had exclaimed, oohed and aahed, giggled and nudged Greg, it was back to business.

"Not that I want to change the subject darling, but the exhibition is on next weekend and will open at 9 am. I'd like you to be here, as we're expecting quite a few people throughout the day. Most by invitation, but you know how it is - word gets around; even some Frenchies coming. Oh, and dear, we'll be starting with a champagne breakfast. Isn't that so, Simon, darling? It's Simon's idea, of course." Simon nodded, and blushed. "Oh and Gregory, the more the merrier darling. Why don't you invite your two new friends, and more? Place for anyone who might buy. You know we'll have some spectacular works on display."

"Thanks, yes. Perhaps I'll ask them. Well, I'll see what they say later. Maybe they're not interested in this type of thing." His gaze fell on Simon, "Hey Simon, make sure Guido gives me prime display area, okay?!"

Simon flushed and tittered at being addressed directly. "Sure, Greg. Guido, did you hear that?"

"Yes, yes. You know you're one of my favourites Gregory. Keep your panties on darling," Guido chided.

Greg chuckled, "Very nice Guido, very nice!" He dabbed his finger in the last of the cake crumbs on his plate and popped them into his mouth. "This cake is fantastic, Simon." He meant it.

By 11am, they'd finished discussing the display position of the two paintings, and Greg made his apologies. "I have to get going, 'cos as I told you, I'm meeting Romando and Benedikt. They're closing their shop for lunch in about a half hour, and I said I'd be there before then." He stood up to emphasise his statement.

"Very well, darling. What romantic names!

Are they Italian, or something?" asked Guido, still very interested.

"I don't know, Guido. Will keep you posted, though!" He moved into the doorway, "Until later. Cheers, Simon. See you next week then. I'll be there at nine sharp. Prime display, remember!"

†

Greg left the gallery and decided to walk the few blocks to the brothers' shop. He arrived as Romando was winding up the outside awnings.

"Well, hello, Gregory. We were wondering if you would not regret your decision to come. Glad to see you. Give us a hand and grab that cord on the other side. Pull when I say."

"Hello. You mean this one?" Greg took the cord in his hand.

"Yes, okay. Pull!"

They pulled together, and the yellow awning slowly lifted to umbrella itself against the plaster of the building.

"Come inside. Benedikt is finishing up," beckoned Romando.

They walked into the shop. Designer shoes lined the tastefully decorated shelves. The backdrop of the shelves was lit by low, hidden lighting. Large loose mirrors were hung on the walls. The reflections in the amber glass were those of the beautifully crafted Italian shoes and the plush red carpet that covered the floor. Low ball and claw stools were arrayed here and there for fitting. Greg was suitably impressed.

"Wow, this isn't what I expected! This is great!"

Benedikt looked up from the desk where he sat, gold fountain pen in hand. "Ah Greg, hello! Thank you. Have a look around, maybe you will find a pair of shoes for a lady friend. I must warn you that they're pricey. Romando and I fly to the shows every season to choose these shoes, so I say with some pride that they're the best this country has to offer."

Whilst Greg looked around at the exquisite merchandise, Romando and Benedikt finished off whatever it was they were busy with.

"Let's go," said Benedikt, "all is done, and a cup of espresso is just what I need."

As the trio ambled their way down the street, with the two brothers heatedly discussing the business of the morning, Greg found himself examining them and wondering how old they were. They certainly seemed a lot older than they looked. He kept his thoughts to himself. They were good company, and he looked forward to his lunch with them

The pavement café offered excellent espresso, open sandwiches, and a birds-eye view of the passing populace. Greg noticed the interest the brothers caused, as their fellow patrons gawked at their similarity and foreign dark good looks. They seemed unaware of the scrutiny and continued to chat and jeer at one another in their easy-going manner.

"So Greg, where did your morning take you?" asked Romando, turning to look directly into Greg's eyes.

Greg was momentarily taken by surprise. The black eyes seemed to look into the very depths of his being, and suddenly he felt a small tendril of panic creep up his back. The panic was interlaced with a primordial lust. Unhesitatingly, he found himself reaching forward to pull Romando closer. He withdrew his hand and shook his head to clear his over-indulgent imagination.

"Greg, I asked you what you did this morning. You've hardly said a word."

"Uh, oh sorry Romando, or is it Benedikt?"

"You're right, I am Romando. Remember that Benedikt is the ugly one." He laughed warmly and looked over at Benedikt.

"Ah, you want to play a game with me

brother?" Benedikt quipped, an affectionate smile on his face.

Greg grinned his enjoyment from one to the other and wondered how he could have felt, for that one moment, so uneasy - so aroused. "Sorry, I've been deep in thought. It's become a habit just lately. Not used to company."

"And why is that?" asked Romando with interest, and a knowing glance in Benedikt's direction.

"Well, I've been busy with some paintings that I needed to finish for an exhibition next week. That's where I was this morning - taking them over to the gallery. Galerie des Artistes, just a couple of blocks up the road from your shop."

"Ah, I know of it. Well, we have passed it from time to time, but have never gone in. So you are an artiste?" Romando asked playfully, a lift to his eyebrows.

"Well, yes. A struggling one though, but hopefully something good will come out of the exhibition. I would like it very much if you'd both come along, you know, some moral support and all. That's if you have the time? It's on Sunday morning, and Guido is starting the day with a champagne breakfast. They're expecting quite a few people, you know, the artists themselves and the buyers. Maybe you could meet some potential 'shoe shoppers'? Just joking."

"Ah, but Greg, you are right." Romando turned to Benedikt. "What do you think brother, should we go along to give our friend the support he requests?"

"But of course we will come, and perhaps we will buy. Do you not think we need a 'piece de resistance' for the shop, or even for at home. The others can come along too. They enjoy meeting new people, don't they brother?"

"They most certainly do," answered Romando.

Greg noticed that once again the brothers were caught up with each other, almost as if they spoke without speaking, of things that he would never hear or know. He couldn't figure it out, and their strangeness seemed more noticeable than ever.

Greg shuddered and reprimanded himself. "The others? Do you have more brothers, or do you mean your families; friends?"

Benedikt answered seriously "Yes, we have several other brothers - not of conception, but of blood. We are all of the same blood."

Greg didn't understand what Benedikt meant, and felt he was treading on holy ground here. He said no more on the matter, but his curiosity was extremely piqued.

The rest of the afternoon was spent in light-hearted banter and Greg was glad of the mood.

†

That night, Romando and Benedikt hunted. They quenched the desire that had been burning deep within them for the past two days; a desire born of the age-old longing; a longing that was part of their everyday life. The flesh and blood they needed to quench the rising tide within them, to return to them the acceptance of the brotherhood and the sharing of spirit.

They returned home, and all met. Once again, the seven took hands and permitted the flow of the universal spirit, the ethers of one to the other.

Ethan bit into Romando's arm, and the ecstasy of their sevenfold union coursed through his veins as he put his own ravaged arm against that of the brother next to him. All thoughts left his mind as it soared once again like an eagle. He sobbed out his happiness to all, and they to him.

CHAPTER 12

Fatal attraction

Ethan

On the morning that we were invited to attend Greg's exhibition, I was in unusually high spirits. The previous day had been the seventh time that we had killed since my arrival. It was July, and a warm but wet summer's day. Having just hunted, it was a time of elation for the brothers.

Kalin and I were the heroes of the day. Me, only because I had accompanied him on the hunt. By this time, I had already hunted with each of the brothers, but not with Kalin.

The time with Kalin was the best I had yet experienced. It was so special that words could never describe the skill and creativity with which Kalin killed. Even though I would have liked to believe that I had no favourites, it would be an omission of conscience not to acknowledge that Kalin was the master - the gourmet chef.

†

The limousine picked us up about mid-morning.

Since I had taken up my new way of life, we had never all been out together, as the singular that we were. We were all happy, sated from the sharing of the previous evening - compliments of Kalin and me. The mood of celebration reflected in each of our eyes as we fought to control the feline pupils with which we were endowed. Needless to say, my fight was the hardest, and I became the joke of the morning, with Romando and Benedikt constantly teasing me and my disobedient eyes into submission.

Kalin sat scrutinising us with paternal pride and love, as if each of us were more like his child than his brother. I wondered at this.

Hadrian was, as usual, planning his next kill, and enthusing over a potential victim. David was involved with the ways and means of us going unsuspected for our murderous deeds - not that we had ever fallen under suspicion before. Caeron, with his seraphic face, was quoting the odd line of poetry that seemed to fit in with each comment and the occasion.

Then of course there was me. Well, I am just

Ethan, and happy for once in my life. Happy in my acceptance and the camaraderie; happy to have finally found what it seems I had always been searching for; and happy to have a family of my own. Once Andrew, my familial brother, had gone to France, I never believed there was place for me among the Westwoods.

I really missed Andrew and intended contacting him no matter what decision I had taken with this life of mine.

As I wondered if it would be acceptable to the brothers for me to see Andrew, Kalin spoke to me without words, as is his habit. "Ethan, you are still of this time, and naturally you have ties that have not yet been broken. As long as the sanctity of the brotherhood is respected, you are free to contact whomever you wish.

"You would, however, do well to remember what I have told you: with human love comes human sadness. Beware! We do not want the melancholy of humankind invading our equilibrium - as you feel and as you experience, so will we."

"It is a difficult choice Kalin, but he is my brother as I am yours. Of my own free will, nothing will change the way I feel about the brothers and especially you. I will always be yours. I think you know that."

"I am confident, Ethan, and trust that you will make the right decision. I will always be here for you by a mere extension of your thoughts in my direction, as will we all." He turned to look out the window and said out loud, "I see we have arrived."

Kalin's thoughts had ceased their rapport with mine as the limousine pulled up and parked in the road opposite the gallery.

†

Even though the brothers were attracted to one another, the nature of the seduction was that of 'like attracts like' or 'like a moth to the flame.' Each of us was a moth and each of us was a flame, and that was the attraction we had for one another. I'm sure Caeron, with his poetry, could more aptly describe it.

I have never been attracted to another man - er, human man - but must confess that when Greg walked out to welcome us to the gallery, I felt a chemical attraction to him. I suppose an attraction of fate. Or maybe I should say, "A fatal attraction". It may have been his aural glow. It reflected peace of mind and happiness, not to mention the purity that was not revealed by any of the brothers' auras. That confused me, as were we not pure in our very making?

I glanced sideways at Kalin, always reading

my thoughts. He had a frown on his face. I questioned whether he could read the emission of Greg's aura. He only shook his head in acknowledgement but refrained from answering my silent question. I could read that he wished his thoughts on the matter to remain his own at this time. There were tears in his eyes.

Romando and Benedikt cheerily greeted Greg with a genuine display of friendship, and briefly introduced the rest of us as we each climbed out of the limousine. As we followed the twins into the gallery, I noticed that their aural glow reflected more humanity than I had ever seen before, when they communed with Greg. The brothers were old souls. This was well reflected in emanations that usually emitted little of the light of humankind.

The change was startling, and I caught Caeron's thought forms treading the same path as mine. As we looked at one another conspiratorially, he shrugged. I lifted my eyebrows and wiped the hair back from my forehead, and we both smiled. We walked in beside one another, each happy in the other's presence and mutual understanding.

We spent the morning wandering around the gallery and listening as each artist presented his work. I believe that an artist is an artist, no matter what his medium, and I felt at home with these people and experienced a momentary longing for what I had left behind. For an instant, a sudden mad desire to express myself in my music overcame me, but I pushed it away for the time being. The music had been sadly neglected.

†

Greg had thought that Romando and Benedikt were, between them, one of a kind. He couldn't believe his eyes when they arrived with their friends. Without exception they were each so uniquely attractive that it took the breath away. Each of them so politely cultured that they seemed like something that had stemmed from an author's imagination.

But without a doubt, Ethan shone above the rest of them. The impact of his beauty felt like a blow to the gut. It was a beauty so shocking that it seemed vulgar. Greg had never wanted anyone, as he now wanted Ethan.

Greg maintained his distance from Romando and Benedikt's friends. He was afraid that his dilemma would present itself for ridicule as he battled to keep his confusion hidden. He couldn't begin to understand his feelings, but each of the brothers held a magnetism that drew him and held him like a metal chip. The harder he tried to pull away, the more the magnet pulled, the more repelled he felt by his feelings. The pull to Ethan was such that he had to exercise extreme control not to prostrate himself before his new god.

He found Ethan alone, examining one of his paintings. A thrill coursed through him at the admiration he could see reflected on Ethan's face, especially because it was Ethan's face.

The opportunity had presented itself for him to single Ethan out.

"Hi. Do you like it?" He waited with bated breath for the reply - which took its time in coming as Ethan examined the painting.

"Greg? Yes, it's great. I feel your passion here - this one in particular. Through this painting I feel like I should know you, but I don't, do I?"

"No of course not, but you're not far off the mark. I painted this one, if you can understand, from the heart."

Ethan squinted at the painting, "I know! I see it!" He turned back toward Greg. "I do that in some of my more private music. It's the soul's medium for expression. Few understand the agony and the torment - the writhing. But in that way you're not like me are you?"

"I don't think so. Mine is more like the pouring out of the wonder of things, y'know?"

"Yeah, I wish I'd felt that way when I was still

writing - music that is. I don't think I had much happiness, at that time, to pour out. It would be better now. In fact I think I could do it. Haven't worked with my music for some time - it seems to be a part of my life that I would prefer not to remember. The music and the melancholy went hand in hand, sort of observers then players to my agony."

Ethan found himself voicing thoughts long forgotten and never before verbalised to a fellow human ... fellow human?

"Greg, you're different" he said softly. "You care don't you?"

"I hope so," Greg grinned. "Yes," the grin faded, "I do care. If you need to speak; if you need to work, then come to my studio and let's work together sometime. Often it's good to work with someone, even if the expression is dissimilar, with the same dedication. You have it - I can see that - the dedication."

Ethan replied, "Maybe. Haven't tried for a while. Greg, I'm happy now and don't think it's time for me to start working yet, really not the time, do you see what I mean?"

"Yes of course, in which case, come around anyway. I'd like to capture that past agony and your present happiness in one frame. It can be done, and you've got it there for me to do."

Greg invited, and Ethan, given his new nature, found it difficult to turn down an invitation, even if it didn't lead to capture. He voiced his thoughts, with a twist, for Greg's ear. "So what you're saying is that you'd like to capture me in paint, and leave me without the choice of capturing you?"

"Well, if you put it that way, yes. Bluntly, I'd like to paint you."

"Greg, look at your paintings, the genre is totally unlike me. It just wouldn't be you, you know, your type of thing, would it?"

"No, it's not my genre but I feel it's becoming my compulsion. I really want to do this. You've got a story to tell, I can see that, in fact I can feel it. That's what painting is all about, seeing and feeling. Inspiration is a funny thing, I'm sure you must know. It comes when you least expect it and sometimes leaves when you most need it."

"I wouldn't want to be the cause of disappointing inspiration - so okay, why not!" Ethan said playfully.

Greg was so pleased that he could barely keep the excitement from his voice. "So you'll do it?"

Ethan could see the enthusiasm in Greg's emanations. He had nothing better to do anyway and he liked Greg. "When do we start?"

Greg stuttered, "Why not tomorrow, how are you placed for Mondays?"

"Like I said, got nothing better to do."

"What do you mean, 'like you said'? You didn't say that; or wasn't I listening properly?"

"Sorry, I thought it." Ethan was accustomed to the brothers communicating with thought. "Forget I said it. It would be my pleasure. Does that sound better?" And added with a playful lift of the eyebrows, "This better be good."

"I believe I can do it." Greg fumbled in his pocket for a business card. "This is the gallery's address, but the telephone number at the bottom is mine. Ring me tomorrow morning and I'll give you directions."

Ethan took the card and turned to look for the others. Without further thought, he wiped the hair from his forehead and headed towards them. They were discussing a darkly oppressive painting on the far wall.

Amused, Benedikt turned to Ethan. "I see you've taken an interest in our friend's painting. If you want it, I hope you'll make an offer before I do. We would like to keep our little butterfly over there happy. Do you want to beat me to the offer, Ethan?"

"I hadn't thought about it really, but okay,

what are you offering?"

"Let us see what they ask. Romando, what do you think?" Each twin always included the other.

"I think Ethan wants that painting, brother. Leave it to him and let us discuss this one. It is more like us. Look hard Ethan, and feel it!"

Romando gestured to the shocking painting of a dark Lucifer gathering to himself golden cherubim, his crook a green snake with a red eye.

He stared piercingly at Ethan, a smile on his full red lips. Ethan shuddered as he looked at the painting, as he began to feel it, as he felt both Benedikt and Romando invade. His pupils began to narrow to slits as his killing-lust started to rise like bile in his throat. He turned his head away from the evil painting that brought forth self-recognition.

"What have I become?" he screamed silently to himself.

Kalin grabbed Ethan by the arm and led him away. "Keep your face down my beautiful one, come away from here. Romando and Benedikt are playing a game with you. As yet, you are not keen enough to recognise their wit for what it is. What is a light game for them is too much for you to absorb in your youth. Please recognise that they have planted those thought forms in your mind. Cast them away and let us make a bid for that painting of light that you like so much.

"Come my lamb, I feel your soul's shudder. You are not that evil caricature. Take my hand."

Ethan grasped Kalin's hand tightly and sought to draw the comfort that suddenly he felt he needed. He almost felt himself slipping into the quagmire of the confusion of the old Ethan.

The needle was piercing his skin, and he waited ...

Kalin shook Ethan and placed a finger on his forehead. "Ethan, snap out of it. Ethan!"

Ethan felt himself struggle to surface, and as his head broke water he saw Kalin's face. Happiness flooded his being, and he wondered what had happened.

"Kalin? Kalin, don't leave me." He gripped Kalin's arm.

"Come my lamb, I'm not going anywhere without you. We are all one forever, rest assured."

Kalin led the shaking Ethan back to the painting. Greg had moved away to the next one and was discussing it with potential buyers.

"You like this painting, Ethan?" Kalin said it

more as a statement than a question.

"I like its passion. Yes, I like it very much. But I also like the artist." He found he wasn't embarrassed to share this.

"Then it is yours. I will buy it for you as a celebration gift. A celebration for what we all shared of you this last evening. You have done well. The painting becomes you, and you should have it."

Kalin looked around for Guido, who was hovering here and there amongst the patrons like a little honey bird. He waved Guido over.

Guido gushed all over them. "Hello, hello! My name is Guido. Ah, I see you're interested in one of Gregory's paintings. Greg is a fine young artist. So ardent, darlings, that it makes me literally swoon."

Kalin answered him stonily, "Do I make the offer to you or to the artist? I see there are no prices on the pieces."

"Darling, why so sombre. Why, it's up to you of course. I have an arrangement with the artist and, either way, I will be happy for him if the picture is sold, especially to such a fine pair of gentlemen as you."

"It is Ethan who buys." Kalin turned to Ethan.

Guido felt himself squirm under Ethan's gaze. He thought to himself that it wouldn't take much to fall in love with someone this lovely, but at the same time he could see that Ethan was not his type. "My dear, this is the first time that Greg has exhibited with us, and I might say hopefully not the last, so this fine piece of work is selling at a good price. I am sure Greg would be happy with, say, two thousand Pounds. It's really quite a steal. What do you say? Do we have a deal?"

Kalin looked at Ethan, who nodded. They passed a thought between them. Kalin answered, "I will give you the two thousand Pounds, but as a gift to the artist, a further five hundred which goes only to him, compliments of my friend here."

Kalin could see that Guido was more than pleased with the offer and knew that Ethan was similarly so in favour of Greg.

"Well, Mister ...?" Guido gushed.

"My name is James Kalin."

"Mister Kalin. It was good to do business with you." He extended his hand to shake. After shaking Kalin's hand he turned, and to Ethan's surprise, placed a quick kiss on his cheek.

"Just had to do that, darling. My apologies. No, I'm not sorry." And then to Kalin, he whispered conspiratorially, "What a gorgeous boy. Where did you find him?"

Ethan turned away in disgust.

David came sauntering over, looking at each painting only briefly. He wasn't really interested in art, and Kalin knew this.

"David, brother. Go with Ethan to the car, I will follow. Benedikt and Romando have been playing their usual games, but their victim this time was not prepared. They're best played with Hadrian and Caeron who understand them better."

David laughed out loud. He knew their mind games as he had been caught up in them often enough. They were interesting. "This isn't my scene anyway. Whaddya say, Ethan? Let's go and grab a cup of coffee whilst these maniacs do their buying. Pig's teeth, this is boring!"

"Go, Ethan. I will arrange payment and delivery of your painting," said Kalin in dismissal.

Ethan lifted his eyebrows in agreement and left with David.

†

It had started raining outside. Ethan and David ran over to the double-parked limousine across the road. The coffee could wait.

"Ethan. I'm glad of this opportunity to be alone with you, brother. I have something I need to discuss, that I want to keep between us for now."

Ethan pushed the hair back from his forehead and looked into David's eyes. David was the brother that he knew the least - he was seldom around. He had the lightest eyes of all, pale green and lashed with black. His hair was a light golden brown and cut short unlike the rest of the brothers who wore their hair longer. Ethan felt the most uncomfortable with David as he represented all the things that he had been afraid of in his past life. "Well then, Dave. Let's get out of this rain, and then we can discuss whatever it is you think is so urgent."

The limousine door opened as they neared and, once inside, David pressed the button to isolate them from the driver. Rain drummed on the roof of the car.

"Alone with a cop," Ethan thought, and he half expected an interrogation.

"Ethan. You've learnt, in your short span of years, to be afraid of the wrong things. I am one with you, as are all the brothers. I have my purpose too, as do the others. The information I relay or fail to relay, one way or another, helps us to maintain our lifestyle. Understand this, and you will see that it is the sacrifice I have had to make on behalf of the brotherhood - and on your behalf - against the human race. I am the only one who feels so little for those weak mortals. Enough! Let me get to the point. Are you okay?"

"Yeah, fine. It's okay, David, I feel your kindred spirit. Go ahead, what's wrong? Or should I say, what's urgent? Have I fucked up? I usually do in some way or another?"

"For Chrissakes, Ethan, stop. It's not you; it's circumstances. It's Megan, your girlfriend!"

Ethan received his second shock of the day. The shocks were coming one after the other, to bombard an ego he was just beginning to discover and cultivate.

"Megan?" he whispered the question, almost as if he was afraid of being discovered. "What about her?" His heart thudded painfully against his ribs, and he felt his legs weaken. He hadn't thought he could ever react this way to the mention of her name. After all, hadn't he forgotten her?

Then he realised what had caused this insanity. David's emanations had gone as black as his eyebrows and, without saying, David had become a threat to Megan's existence. "David, please, not Megan. I thought it a rule not to touch friends."

David whistled a soundless tune under his breath as he scrutinised the rain pouring down outside, dripping and running like liquid diamonds against the window. He turned back to Ethan. "Ethan, besides the fact that rules are made to be broken, you are over-reacting.

"I wish Megan no harm, personally, but as a brother I look to our protection. In a way, I'm the protector. She is causing trouble with what she thinks is your disappearance. The police are ready to put out a missing person report on you. How would it go down with your face plastered all over every second bus stop? 'Have you seen this man ... Missing since ... Contact ...' and so on. So I say it only once, my friend. Sort it out before I bring her to the attention of the brothers. I assure you there will be no clemency, especially from Hadrian. He values his immortality and his skin, as do we all."

"David, if I'm causing trouble for the brothers, then perhaps I should go – leave, and return to my old life. You could explain to Kalin."

"There is no question about you going, and you know it," answered David emphatically. "There isn't even the faintest thought about it, my friend. You're part of us. We will never let you go. We love and covet you, Ethan, more than you could know."

David reached out and touched Ethan on the forehead, then shifted his hand to Ethan's neck and pulled him closer. He kissed him softly in the neck, and then pushed him away violently.

"Chrissakes, I'm going into attack mode! Blood is running. I'm sorry, forgive me."

"It's cool, Dave. I understand. I'll sort the Megan thing out. Give me until the end of this week." Ethan took David's hand in his and squeezed. "It's okay, I understand. You're right, of course. She can't be permitted to cause trouble. I am yours."

"Well, so be it. I leave it up to you." Ethan's answer seemed to satisfy David. "I'm sure you can placate her with no harm caused. I really don't want to see you unhappy. It is a state foreign to us Ethan, but such a state can become catching. Let it go. It's in the past, my friend."

Caeron tapped on the window, and the driver hastily opened for the dripping five.

CHAPTER 13

Snapped string

Down at the police station. Mick Courtley's landline rang. "Courtley!" he barked into the phone, as was his way.

"Mick, hey, it's Megan! How are things going? Well, first of all, how are you?" A pause, "You busy?"

"Oh hello, Meg. Yes, as usual I am bogged down up to the armpits in this cesspool of bleeding paperwork and hoodlums. You're calling, I presume, to find out about that boyfriend of yours?"

"Well, yes. I hadn't heard from you, and wondered if you'd found out anything yet?"

"Listen, my love, I handed it over to the brilliant David. He's been off for a few days digging around. I'm expecting him in later today, and then I'll have some more info for you. Believe me, Dave's good at what he does. I trust him. If there's anything to find out, Dave is the one to do it. Now patience is a virtue they say, so go and do something to spoil yourself and I'll call you later when I have more info."

†

Megan wandered around the flat, touching here and there. The guitar case lay where Ethan had last put it. She sat cross-legged on the floor and ran her fingers over it, flipped the catches and lifted the lid. This was Ethan's territory, and she hadn't opened it before.

If he was still alive - and she was sure he was - surely he would have come for his guitar? They had been inseparable! She lifted it out of the case, and almost dropped it as a string snapped; snapped like her nerves had been threatening to do these past months.

The rest of the strings lay taut across the neck of the guitar. She strummed her fingers over them gently, imagining Ethan's long fingers playing and teasing them back into life. But they remained tuneless and dead, like brittle bones of the past.

Her hand strummed harder and harder in panic, until she could feel the bite of the strings as they struggled against the life with which she was attempting to infuse them. Carefully, she laid the instrument back into its coffin and stuck her stinging fingers into her mouth.

For a moment she thought it was Ethan she could see nestled inside the case, inside this fluff lined box.

†

David breezed into the office. Everyone smiled a greeting at their favourite cop. "Hello, everyone. Your favourite person is here. Down, fans, down," he joked.

"Haven't seen you for a couple of days, Dave. What you been up to?" asked one from a littered desk.

"Ah, a little of this and a little of that. Where's the boss?"

"Where do you expect - in his office, of course, wrestling with the telephone and his computer."

David looked around for a willing face and, when he found one, put on his well-practised puppy dog expression. "Cath! How-about a cup of coff? I'm dying!" He grabbed at his throat, and with bulging eyes staggered across to where she sat.

"Okay, Romeo. One cup coming up. And this is the last until you make me one. I don't think you've ever made me one, y'no."

"Oh, fair Juliet! How can ye say such things? Sit! It will be I who will make thee a cup of coffee." He pushed her back into her swivel chair and spun her around. Everyone in the office chortled, glad he was back.

The 'self-server' belched its tepid water into the paper cups. He twisted the coffee server dial and a wallop of coffee plunked itself into the cup. "God darn machine gets cheekier every day. It should be called Hoocher. I dub thee Hoocher from this day forth." He carried the cup over to Cathy's desk, slopped it down and swaggered off to find Mick.

Mick glanced up from his computer screen to a gun-shaped hand pointing at his face.

"Gotcha, Boss."

"Bang yourself, David. I'm too tired to die now. Please sit." He continued scrolling through the files. "This bleeding case has got me baffled. The man has an airtight alibi, but two witnesses confirm seeing him at the scene. Ah, shit!"

He also had a paper file on his desk. He slammed it shut in frustration. "Where's my coffee?"

David yelled out the door, "Cath, the boss wants your coffee. Sorry." He turned back to Mick.

"Car's parked outside as proud as bloody hell. Had her cleaned this morning, and she's been preening all the way over. Spick and span." He handed the keys across.

"Thanks, bud. Glad you enjoyed her. How'd she go? Purred like a cat, I'm sure."

"Sure did Boss, just like you said. I think I charmed Sally just right."

"Well, what's news on Ethan Westwood? Found out anything?"

"Did a bit of snooping around. Nothing much really. I visited his mother. Sexy lady. She hasn't seen him. Popped into a few of the places he used to hang out and one fellow says that he saw him a couple of weeks ago, passing in the street. Seemed like an honest enough chap. All in all, Boss-man, I think he's chosen to just drop out of sight for a while - or maybe he's had enough of the girlfriend. Maybe he's on a bender and wants to hide out. No one else has reported him missing, have they?"

"Only Megan. If you could see her, Dave, you'd realise that she's not the type of woman someone has to run away from. Well, I certainly wouldn't. True, it seems he had been acting a bit strange, but then junkie types are wrong in the head anyway. What do I tell her?"

"I dunno Boss. Tell her to hold on for a couple of weeks, that we're still looking into it. In fact, give me her mobile number. I'll call, and maybe pop around to see her. Keep her satisfied that the police care."

"David, David. Why do you really want to visit her? I know that to you this is a Mickey Mouse case. Why the sudden interest?"

"Nah, just want to see this pretty lady you're so concerned about. Besides, I still have the rest of the day free, okay!"

"Okay. Just apologise on my behalf for not calling personally and that, seeing as you're the man with the info, you're the best one to talk to."

"Don't you worry. I'll handle it. You know me Boss, charmer with the ladies!"

Mick sent her contact card from his phone to David's. After a quick glance, Dave slipped his phone into his jacket pocket and breezed out of the station as effortlessly as he had breezed in.

†

It was a splendid day, with a cool zephyr weaving its way around and about the buildings. It teased here and lifted a skirt there, re-arranged the trees' hairdos and affectionately ruffled the heads of the lunch-timers, grabbing at their lunch papers and then letting go again in sympathy.

David decided to walk. He whistled tunelessly under his breath as he trudged up the street. He winked at the attractive women that passed and caught himself enjoying the way they clutched at their wind-caught skirts or hair. Yes, David enjoyed life all in all. Life was good, and today he felt that he was the master of destiny.

†

The building where Megan lived sported a small well-tended garden of creeping rose and a lush green lawn. David whistled his appreciation at the late nineteenth century design that had been renovated to the latest luxuries. He pressed the buzzer marked with Megan's name and waited; squinting up the side of the building to the flat that he imagined might be hers. He buzzed again and waited.

"Probably not here," he thought, and then she answered in a sweet-soft voice.

"Hello. Megan Sands. Can I help you?"

"Hi. Miss Sands?" He felt ridiculous bending over to speak into a box on the wall. "My name's Officer David Jacobs. Detective Inspector Mick Courtley sent me over. Police. May I come in?"

His heart skipped a beat as he waited for the invitation. Invitations of entry were always exciting as they hinted of pleasures still to be discovered.

"Yes, I've seen you before at the police station. Okay, push when you hear the buzzer and come up to the second floor - number 201, fern at the door."

The intercom died with a static snap, and David opened at the buzz.

She was standing in the passage waiting for him. Yes, he had seen her at the station with Mick, just the other day, an earthy and tempting girl.

With a slight tremble to her lips, she smiled her welcome. Dark circles under her eyes marred the honey complexion. "Mr Jacobs? David? Please come in. Mick has spoken of you, and I feel I already know you."

He returned her smile and stepped into the flat. "You've got yourself one helluva flat here. Great," he said, looking around in curiosity.

"Thanks. Come on through. I really hadn't expected anyone to come around this afternoon, so the place is in a bit of a mess. Mick said he'd phone, but I must say this is better. Over here - please take a seat. Can I get you something to drink? Tea, perhaps?"

The entire 'mess', as Megan had called it, was

a glass on the table and two open but empty compact disc cases.

"Yeah, a drink would be great – I walked over. Tall order, but do you have any tomato juice?"

Megan's eyes widened. "Oh, excuse me, Mr Jacobs. You caught me by surprise. Few people drink tomato juice, but Ethan, my boyfriend, always did. It's just really strange for you to ask. Yes, I do have. You wouldn't have thought, would you?"

"Truthfully? No! Hope it's warm, I don't like it cold."

"They're always warm, Ethan prefers them that way. Same as his wine. I think this must be a good omen."

She disappeared into the kitchen, and David looked around. There wasn't too much here that could be linked to Ethan. The compact disc player and its piled-up discs, the guitar in the corner, a poster of an obscure metal band - all still in their places where they had been left.

Megan came back with the juice and handed it to him. She smelt lovely, and he felt the beginnings of lust throb in his temples. He chided himself and concentrated on keeping his eyes normal.

"Thank you, Ma'am," he said, louder than he

had intended to. "As the boss has probably told you, I'm the investigating officer on this case - your missing friend, Ethan Westwood."

"Uh huh! Well?" She had taken a seat opposite and was leaning forward in anticipation of his answer.

"Well, we don't think he has in fact gone missing. I've had positive identification from an acquaintance of his that he has seen him recently, and no one else has reported him missing."

She fidgeted as he spoke, and then voiced her concern, "But his things are all still here? Surely he wouldn't leave without taking anything except a few clothes. His sound system, his guitar - these were things that were important to him. All he really has that is worth mentioning. I know most of Ethan's friends and have spoken to every one of them. No one has seen or heard from him." Her lip trembled, and she lifted her hand to cover it.

David's voice reflected his rising irritation. "Was there a quarrel, perhaps - between the two of you?"

She was on the defensive, as her emotions were playing havoc with her control. "Why, what makes you think that?" she snapped. "Or is this the usual police-type interrogation where the innocents are seen as the guilty? Just what Ethan has always said about you people."

David's eyes started slitting in anger. He didn't have the patience to sit here and pretend. "Do me a favour, Ms Sands, leave this alone. Your boyfriend is not missing, he's not murdered, and he's probably a lot happier wherever he went." He knew he'd said the wrong thing, so covered it up with: "Face it, he's a junkie and you can't trust any of them."

Megan was shocked by his response. "I can't believe this. How could Mick have spoken so highly of you? How can you speak to me like this? I think, David, that you should leave. I'd rather speak to Mick." She was confused and hurt.

David brought his temper under control, a worried frown now creasing his brow. He just didn't know how to throw her off without harming her. He didn't want to see Ethan hurt. "If you'll let me explain ..."

"Explain what?" she interrupted. "Just how busy you are, or how insignificant Ethan is in the whole scheme of things? To me he's the most important thing on Earth." A small sob escaped from behind her hand.

Her loyalty surprised him and, funny enough, warmed him a bit towards her. He gave her the most charming grin he was capable of and made a point of emanating his innocence. He spoke boyishly, as if he had been reprimanded. "Well, I'm really sorry if I've come across all wrong, Megan, truly. Obviously, I'm more accustomed to dealing with the baddies." He averted his eyes guiltily until she answered.

Megan blushed at the thought that she may have lost her cool for nothing. It was a build-up of all the worry over the past couple of months, and the disappointment that he had nothing positive to tell her.

"No. I'm terribly sorry. It's me that should be apologising, David, really. I think I'm losing it. I've just been so worried. I think I'm falling to pieces, to be honest."

"Megan let's look at this objectively: so far, so good. He's been seen fit and healthy, and at least he's not dead or arrested, or anything like that. That's good news, isn't it? Give it a couple of weeks, and in the meantime we'll keep an eye out. Okay?"

"Okay." she nodded. "You're right of course – no need to panic, huh? Thanks anyway." She stood up. "Let me see you out."

She ushered him to the door, barely able to contain the flood of tears that threatened to explode from her eyes.

His tomato juice was still untouched.

CHAPTER 14

Venus' Morning Star

Ethan

I am tired, really tired. For the first time in months I'm really worried. This is probably an accumulation of everything that has happened, and of course the strange situation I find myself in. I lie down on my bed, eyes heavy, and pull the covers over my head.

†

... I stand in the ever-stretching line of humanity - leading, I think; must be, I'm sure - to the Pearly Gates. As there is no such thing as time in this place, I cannot say how long I've stood here, but I can tell you that the queue is long, slow, and suffering.

We shuffle forward, foot by agonising foot, my fellow destiners and I. It could have been a few minutes, or perhaps it's been a couple of years that we have shuffled and scratched, waited, and watched, searching the illusionary horizon.

We watch the birth and death of stars, suns setting, moons waxing and then waning, the wailing of the unseen, the sun burning, the clouds cumulating and steaming away again. And we wait patiently, with not a word said. Each of us is alone with our thoughts, and distrustful of one another.

Again I shuffle forward, watching my shoes and measuring the distance to the shoes just ahead of me. They look pretty old and worn, and I imagine that their soles have neared their end. I try to catch a glimpse of their underside as they move forward again. But they scrape flat-footed, and my endeavours are thwarted.

I follow the leg up to the thin waist; search the withered hands that hang at the sides, up the emaciated arm to the bony shoulder, to the thin neck with a frizz of greying hair that covers it. This is all I see, the necks of my companions, with their sloppy skins, old and well-weathered.

I look back down at my shoes, and quickly slip my leg out sideways, then glance up clandestinely from under my bent brow to see if anybody noticed. They just shuffle forever forward, so I lose interest in my creativity and shuffle and wait, and shuffle and wait, and push the hair back from my forehead, as is my habit.

I sing endless songs in my head. Everything I've ever heard, everything I've ever written and everything I am still going to write. In snitches and snatches, they play themselves over and over until I feel they're taking possession of me. Taking from me the ability to think my own thoughts, or if I so choose, not to think at all. They allow me no respite with their endless words, their ongoing melodies, their poetry, and obscenities. I try to scratch them from my brain, both hands rummaging in my hair. They laugh and chant louder, whilst the new ones whisper their endless bizarre ideas.

When will this queue come to an end?

Then I see a brilliant light metamorphosing up ahead. It radiates a welcome, and those of us who have realised it, step a little quicker. We stretch out our arms to grasp its welcome with begging hands. The wearer of shoes, just ahead of me, disappears into the godly light. I wait my turn, scrabbling with my frantic paws at its door, just in case it doesn't open for me as well.

Finally my turn comes, and the door slides open on its obviously well-oiled hinges. I am engulfed in a writhing golden mist. But nevertheless I walk bravely forward with ever-extended arms, clasping, feeling, and just now and then, touching an illusive ghost of an imagination. I think that maybe this is it, eternity; promised immortality; and so I smile and try to make the best of it by swinging my arms and striding purposefully forward.

Suddenly I see Him sitting before and above me, resplendent on His throne of nebulous matter. The green nebula revolves slowly around him, and it seems that the throne is an illusion created for my benefit. I realise this. He leans forward, elbows on knees, and examines me keenly.

"Step closer, there's a good fellow," He says.

I step a little closer; He really isn't what I expected.

"So you're the clown I've been expecting!" He says down His nose at me.

I am surprised He recognises me for what I am. But then again why shouldn't He; He is 'He' after all, isn't He?

He snaps his fingers, and a winged angel appears at His side. I know this to be the Archangel because he carries with him a large leather-bound book that he hands to Him. He flips through it and seems to come to a page that satisfies Him.

"Let us see, um, what have we here?" His large-knuckled finger runs down the page. "Ethan Westwood!" He enquires, looking up from under his white bushy brows.

"That's me!" I reply.

"I know it's you. Haven't I just said it?"

I gulp and try to stop the silly giggle that threatens to explode from my throat.

He reaches up to adjust the white crown on his head. I notice that it's made of paper - possibly a Christmas hat, I muse to myself.

The angel reaches into the pocket of his white robe and withdraws a small penny whistle. He starts to play a song I once wrote. I am suitably impressed, just as he intends me to be. He smiles a cherubic smile."

I immediately know him for who he is: Venus' Morning Star.

He raises the lunate staff He holds it in his hand and conducts along with the rhythm of Pan's whistle. I wonder if I should sing along.

Abruptly he stops his playing. Again the angel reaches into his robe. This time his hand holds a bright orange pen that I think is rather out of place, given the situation. He hands the pen to Him. Whilst He thinks, He bites the end of the pen, snapping off pieces of the orange plastic. Venus' Morning Star reaches out to brush the odd orange bits from His robe. He scribbles something in the big black book and looks up at me. I give Him my most charming smile and raise my eyebrows. Again He scribbles.

"Are you dead?" He asks me seriously.

"Don't you know?" I ask Him back in the same tone.

He looks at the Archangel and complains, "Cheeky bugger, isn't he?"

The Archangel shrugs his shoulders, and in a display of nonchalance, glances away at nothing in particular.

I start feeling that I really don't want to be here. This isn't the place I want to be.

"Are you dead?" He asks again loudly, startling me from my thoughts.

"I might be dead. I really don't know." I answer. "I don't want to be dead, but don't know if I have a choice. I didn't think I could die, as dying is not in my nature" I add quickly.

"This is what I thought. I don't think you belong here. Where do you think you belong?"

I'm not sure what He means but get the hint when He steps down from the nebula on which He is standing. He takes my hand in his, and passes me over to the Archangel, who begins to lead me away. I notice that the Archangel has the word 'Lucifer' printed on his robe. Hadn't I recognised Him all along? Of course I had.

He says in his most perfect voice: "Come with me, Brother. Let us go back home where we belong. I have just recently fallen anyway, so your company is welcome!"

We walk back the way I had come, to my great relief.

†

I wake up with a jerk, remembering the weird dream. I look at my watch. Bejeezus, it's late, but I still feel exhausted. The dream has completely drained me. I drag myself onto an elbow and can feel the strain in the tightness of my face. Irritably, I shove the hair back from my face. The dream has left me confused and angry, and thoughts prior to the dream leave me puzzled over what is real what is actually a dream - are they separate or one? It feels like I exist in a plenitude of parallel worlds, and I am not sure which one I belong to anymore. I'm really fucked up, that's all there is to it. Nothing is going to change that!

I look up at the wall where Greg's painting now hangs. Kalin put it up soon after our return from the gallery. The writhing mass of colour explodes in my eyes and compounds my headache; a headache that I hadn't expected, given the circumstances of my new life. I have to look away.

My body feels in desperate need of something - a need not felt for quite a while now, and one

I thought well buried. A need that I thought had been replaced by bloodlust. Huh, the old need for a fix, one I had believed forever gone. Ah, well … seems that's the other me, huh? I'm kidding myself; this is emotional, not physical!

So what about the promises? Nothing has really changed. I'm just trying to be someone I'm not. Oh, the power of the mind! And they use it to brain wash me, to toe the line. Mind you, I've chosen where I am. All I'm doing is trading one queue for another, which is as disastrous in its reality as the first was. What kind of a fucking trade-off is that?

What is it they want of me? What is it that life wants of me, and why should I be the giver? Fuck that! I thought I was attaining my Nirvana, but instead I'm probably furthering my damnation. To eternally damn myself for what I do now, or be damned for what I did then - which one to choose? Or perhaps to be damned for that which I have not yet done. Hmm. I wonder if I still have a choice. Kalin says that there is always choice, and then David said I don't really have a choice, so do I have it or not? Is there even such a thing as choice?

†

The wagon wheels of Ethan's confusion reel about him, bouncing and bumping against his head, wreaking havoc on the fragile track that ego was attempting to birth, an ego that had to find escape, an expression within its own chaos. Multiple dimensions.

As Ethan sat, head in hands on the edge of the bed, Kalin brooded in his chamber and perceived the thoughts being emitted by his prodigy. Extremely concerned at the mutiny that pervaded the ethers, confused as to how this had come to be, he stretched out feelers of thought and crept into the recesses of Ethan's psyche, remaining disguised and well hidden in the maze of confusion.

Ethan threw aside the covers that had wrapped about his legs. Instinctively, he reached for the packet of cigarettes that usually lay next to the bed. His whereabouts were brought into sharp focus as his hand grabbed at the disappointing nothingness. Sucking in the clean air, but finding no release for his demanding need, he looked about in temporary madness, head snaking from side to side, eyes slitted in anger and discord.

As Ethan's thoughts beat out in howls of raging pain, he became aware of the interloper in his mind. He felt Kalin's presence as it prowled in disguise through his thoughts.

Ethan resented the intrusion and, in a

fit of aggression and revolt, immediately counteracted with a wall of pitch, allowing it to stickily ooze and engulf the intruder. The invasion halted as suddenly as it had begun, in defeat for the perpetrator - much to Kalin's surprise and annoyance.

Ethan had learnt too fast and was gaining power that he was far from ready to harness. Kalin shuddered in trepidation and cowered in his chamber as the image crushed his head between its fingers, unmercifully, then left him trembling anxiously.

Ethan jumped from the bed, taloned fingers tearing and raking at his head, pulling out chunks of hair, leaving raw scratches across his forehead and down his cheeks. Loose skin flaked like dried mud at the edges of the oozing scratches.

He sat on his haunches, staring up - snaking head, eyes fixed to his own hypnotic hallucinations. Slitted pupils focused on the agony of being. Ethan howled his misery of discovery to the ageless and unconcerned universe.

The forgotten son sat in the corner, no beam to penetrate his futile fate, the sun still shone like his gallant mourner, when the new moon rose it was too late.

There was no place for Kalin. There was no welcome for Kalin, and there was no need for him at this time.

Ethan was crystallising; metamorphosing like the gate in his dream - awakening to the horror of what he was; the pleasure of what he was. Spreading his wings of power, and encompassing the morass of his immortality. Venus' Morning Star led the way gleefully, enticing, innocently expecting.

†

Slowly, the early morning shadows caressed Ethan's kneeling form, trailing their fingers inch by inch over his body - then they were gone! The sun shone weakly through the window and past the blind, its awakening invitation warming Ethan's ice-cold limbs and frozen visage. The iced mask gradually melted, and Ethan fully awoke to the beautiful day with a wonderful mood upon him.

He was still leaning in the corner of the room, searching upwards, hands stretched out sideways on corded arms. Already the scratches on his face were healing, and at the very edges the skin had completely grown over in pink webs. The pupils of the eyes had turned from black to light brown and now formed droplet shapes in the eyes. His staggering beauty was now unmatched.

†

Ethan

I was kneeling, immersed in the kaleidoscope of colour and form that displayed itself before me. Thirstily, I drank in the wonder, but with the wonder came an aggression not previously felt, and an all-consuming itching deep down inside that demanded attention.

I wiped the hair back off my forehead and went in search of Kalin. The change in my body from the day before was quite remarkable, even to me. I knew that I walked more silently than I had ever done before, padding without sound down the passage towards Kalin's chamber. My hearing had increased at least threefold, and I could hear the breathing of all the living creatures that resided in the house. What the fuck? I could hear the insects in the wooden panelling, the birds nesting in the eaves and each brother as he breathed his way through his dreams. All were still asleep except for Kalin. I reached his room and could hear the heavy breathing of panic. I rapped on the door in newfound confidence and pushed it open before he could answer.

He sat in the corner of his chamber, staring in awe and something akin to fright. It was something I had never seen before, and don't expect to ever see again, from Kalin.

"Yes, I see it is true. My mind was not leaving me!" his voice quivered. Then he continued, "You have become much more than we expected or desired, Ethan.

"You have surpassed us, and in time will usurp each of us. It seems that you have attained a blend of what we are, what we were, what we will become, and most fearfully, all those same things that envelop the human animal. You are all of us *and* human. I don't know how this happened."

It seemed he recognised elements in me that I had not, as yet, had time to absorb. I felt the strength in my body begging for release. Without hesitation I knelt down beside him, took his arm in my hands and bit into his vein, sucking greedily at the blood as it pumped over my lips.

I chanced to look into his eyes and saw that the fright had gone and was replaced with pride. Pride in his prodigy, in the child of his creation; pride in his efforts at having produced much more than had been expected. Yes, it shone out of Kalin's eyes as he gave his blood. This was the day that I raped his soul!

I spun on my haunches to face the door.

The breathing patterns outside the room had changed. Someone was awake and moving soundlessly down the passage, blocking all thoughts to others. The vibration in the air rippled with his passage, and a faint aural glow began to reflect off the walls.

I knew this to be Hadrian. Kalin frowned as he waited, knowing as well of the presence, but not the identity. I looked back at him and said, "Hadrian comes."

"You have seen through his veil. I am surprised and pleased. I am the only one that can see through the veil once it has been enacted. Hadrian feels a danger he cannot explain and has 'veiled over'. If it is Hadrian, as you say - as yet I am not sure.

The words were barely out of Kalin's mouth when the emanations unveiled to reveal the owner: Hadrian.

"You were right, of course" stated Kalin. "Ah, Hadrian! Come and meet our metamorphosee."

Hadrian stepped into the room, the surprise on his face obvious. "Ethan. I nearly tremble to see you. If it were in my nature to be jealous, that would have to be the only way to explain how I feel right now. What say you, Kalin?"

"I find it difficult to say right now, as Ethan has

just planted his seed in me. This is new to me. A different Ethan?"

I could see the surprise on Hadrian's face. "I most certainly feel the energies at play here but will wait and see. I invite you Ethan, in your power and wonder, to take from me too. Take my soul, brother, and I will be yours without hesitation." As Hadrian said this, his face flushed with high colour, and he extended his arm in offering.

I acknowledged the passage of energy and took his arm, biting eagerly and deeply. After I had drunk his blood as well, I offered my neck to Kalin. He bit, and both in turn held me about the neck with a lacerated arm. Our blood flowed together, and our ties were renewed. There were still four to go. Another day; another time.

I had come to the realisation that I could be anything I wanted to be. I was a creature not governed by any law, not that of humankind nor that of the brothers. I could be as moral or immoral as I chose. Life was kneeling at my feet and begging to be taken. And I took as it came, took of its profferings - giving very little more than my soul as the trade.

†

CHAPTER 15

Charcoal sketch

Greg

The morning following the exhibition found me very excited at the thought of the new work I was about to undertake. I wondered if I was a capable enough artist to capture the wreathing soul of the tormented creature I had met. I call him a creature because of the feral qualities portrayed in those eyes. Ethan was so compelling that my hands shook as I anticipated re-creating him in oils. He truly thrilled me.

I started fixing myself some breakfast while I waited for my mobile phone to ring. Finished my eggs and bacon and waited; and waited. The phone remained silent, mocking me by its very presence.

I wasted some time by unwrapping a new canvas and placing it on my easel. I selected the tubes of oils that I would be using. Selected brushes and fanned them with my fingers. Twiddled those same fingers. Scratched my frayed chair. Got up and stared out the window. I watched the blank canvas, planning how I would start. I sat watching it and waiting. As I watched, the morning became afternoon, and the afternoon became early evening. The phone remained silent.

By that time the vendors in the street below my studio had started closing their stalls.

My disappointment was so keen that I anyway took hold of a charcoal pencil and despondently started sketching on the canvas. A face began to emerge; motivated by the very ethers of Ethan that had attached themselves to me. His eyes stared out at me from the white canvas; I their captive. I caught myself crying as I sketched, taken up by the astounding creature that developed before me; and of course because I was so disappointed that he hadn't called.

Well, it didn't look like he was going to call, so instead of dinner I opened a bottle of whisky to drown my disappointment. I sat in the old red chair, picking at the frayed edges with charcoal-smudged hands.

Finally the phone did ring and, even though I had been waiting so patiently for it, I felt nervous pinpricks run into my arms and legs. I knew it would be Ethan; I had just a little confidence in the way we felt about each other.

"Hey!" I croaked, dry mouthed.

"Greg. Hi. Ethan here." Silky smooth voice.

"Hey, Ethan." I didn't want him to know how I'd waited for his call, or how miserable he'd made me. "Is it to be an evening work?" I asked, as if everything was just peachy.

"Hell no Greg. There's a time for everything. For me, today wasn't the time to work."

My heart sank. Then he continued, "Give me your address, and I'll be there in about thirty minutes. Let's go for a drink or something. We can catch up on the painting tomorrow. Is that okay? You free, or up to it?"

"Gotcha! I'll be ready." I answered, no thought of admonition, and gave him the address.

The line went dead, and I threw the dregs of the remaining whisky down my dry throat. The beginnings of the portrait stared at me with blood-curdling awareness. I turned it around to face the back of the easel. Tomorrow we would come to grips, that portrait and me.

†

Ethan knocked. I hadn't expected him to. I

waited a few seconds and then opened the door. He stood straight and staring, amused, waiting for me to invite him in? His mask was gone, and he portrayed himself, for my benefit and in his friendship, as exactly the 'creature' I had expected he was.

His feral eyes gleamed a demonic iciness, and blood caked the corners of his mouth. He wiped his thick lustrous hair back from his forehead with slender hands. The remains of a cheek wound lay healing on his face; a wound that hadn't been there the day before.

"Er, come in," I invited.

He moved in fluidly and surveyed the room. I noticed the black bruises on his neck and arms. I couldn't help wondering what the hell he'd been up to that day, or if it would be rude to ask. I wondered how our friendship was going to develop, although I knew it would. I could 'so' feel Ethan. Wow, my senses reeled!

"Shall we go?" he asked after his scrutiny of my flat.

I walked to the kitchenette counter and retrieved my phone and wallet. "Let's do it then," I grinned.

We walked wordlessly down the road, each comforted by the presence of the other; he by what I presume to be my ordinariness and me by his extraordinariness. I couldn't help wondering what I had done in this life, or the previous one if there is such a thing, to justify the gift of his friendship. I knew, without question, that I had been granted his friendship.

He broke the silence with an unexpected question. "Are you a man that can be trusted?"

"Need you ask?" Even I could hear the truth in my voice. I felt like a Boy Scout. Even so, it was an odd question.

"Trust, Gregory, is rare," he said solemnly.

"I know," I nodded. "But yeah of course, Ethan, you can trust me. I need your trust too if we're to work together."

"You'll be working," he stated, "I'll be sitting staring at you."

I blushed, thinking of him staring at me for hours on end. "It will be difficult, but you can make it easier."

"How?"

"By not hiding the layers of you that I need to capture in paint," I explained.

"Do you know what you want to capture?" he asked.

"Yeah, I think so. I can see it in my mind, but I'm not sure how it will develop. I think it'll happen on its own, you see."

"You're perceptive Greg, and I wonder just how much you perceive without knowing it," he half asked, and half speculated.

I changed the subject somewhat. "I have the feeling that you could read my thoughts if you wanted to." This was part question, and part statement. I wasn't expecting an answer.

"True," Ethan agreed, "But that would be an invasion of your privacy and our friendship, so I refrain." He smiled mischievously.

"Thank you. I appreciate it. Yeah, I think I know you could if it's what you wanted. But why, Ethan? What makes you different?" I chanced the question.

He didn't mind. "I think you may know, Greg, but in any case if you're as good an artist as I think you are, or as good as that picture that now hangs on my wall says you are, you'll soon know. I won't be able to pull the veil on you, even though you're so, um, human."

"And you aren't?" I quipped.

"That's the funny thing, Greg. That's exactly what *we* are!" He grinned happily, and I wondered what the 'we' meant.

I laughed out loud. "Well, I'm glad of that."

And he laughed with me, a genuine warm laugh, which animated the previously dead eyes. Eyes that now sparkled with amusement and kinship. For just that moment he reminded me of a young boy – someone else entirely.

†

That night, we gloried in our newfound friendship, all strangeness gone. Any inkling that Ethan was not as entirely normal as anyone else was forgotten. In fact, he seemed to me more normal that anyone I had ever met. I questioned if just maybe he was the only normal one.

He was charming and fun, had a good sense of humour and was kind in friendship. A friend for sure, as we drank the night away and weaved our way home singing old songs that commemorated every forgotten dead star: Nat King Cole, Frank Sinatra, Louis Armstrong, and BB King - all found their melodies being made a mess of by our drunken voices.

We saw the morning in, sitting as inebriated as two tramps with a bottle between us, on a bus stop bench, singing at the top of our voices, *House of the Rising Sun*.

We slept the early part of the morning away,

each in his own dreams - me in my bed, and Ethan spread out on the carpet at the foot of the easel. He chose the floor instead of the red couch that belonged to the chair, black hair fanned out over his outstretched arm, matching the charcoal pencil that lay next to him. I awoke to find him in exactly the same position, eyes wide open and staring at me.

"G'd morning" I said with a thick tongue and furry mouth. Have you been awake for long?" I sat up groggily, grabbing for my head. "Ah shit, this is going to be a rough day."

He looked as fresh as if he'd had a full night's sleep with no alcohol to fuzz the senses, and answered, "Hang on there. I'll make you some coffee, or is there something else you'd prefer?" He sprang up easily.

"Coffee would be great. And Ethan, thanks. How come you're not suffering?"

"You wouldn't ask, if you knew how many hangovers I've suffered," he answered. "Most have been much worse than yours. Just say that I'm well practised at hiding them. I'll tell you about it one day, maybe."

I said no more and groaned into my cupped hands.

Ethan sang a raunchy blues number to

himself as he banged cups in my small kitchen. I had forgotten that this was his profession: music. It sounded good even though my head pounded. He came back with two steaming cups, put them down on the floor and reached out to touch my forehead.

"Hold on a sec. Here's something unpractised but should work." He closed his eyes in concentration, laying his warm palm on my forehead. I could feel the nausea rise from the pit of my gut, almost as if he was pulling it out by a thread through my head. The pain that throbbed behind my eyeballs soon followed, and I opened my eyes in surprise. "Shit, Ethan! How'd you do that? It's almost all gone."

"Dunno actually, Greg. Just something Kalin and the others seem to do often enough. Just picking up their habits, I guess." He reached for his coffee and took a sip.

"That's something I'd like to know a bit more about," I ventured. "I mean, Romando and Benedikt, Kalin and the other chaps that were with you at the gallery on Sunday. I can't quite piece it together."

I thought he might go cold on me, but he raised his eyebrows in humour and said, "Gregory, it's a long story that I might tell you one day, but for now leave well alone and let's get busy or else your painting will never get done. I'd like to be able to say that I've been painted by a famous artist."

"Hardly famous! Well anyway, I would like to know some time," I persisted. "And what about your music?"

"I think it's making a comeback," he answered. "I've started feeling it again. Playing with tunes. Yes, it's still there. Maybe soon."

With that, we began an easy and productive day. Ethan proved himself to be a patient and more than interesting model. The sketch that I had started the previous night seemed to grow of its own accord and we delighted over the replication of the many-faceted man within the painting.

CHAPTER 16

Breakfast special

It was a couple of days later that Megan decided to call Andrea to convince her to take the day off. She tapped in the number whilst sipping her coffee, half asleep and bleary-eyed. She hoped to catch Andrea before she left for work.

Andrea answered on the third ring. "Good morning, Megs. What's up?"

"Hi, Ands!"

"Megan, my goodness! Talk about the early bird catching the worm. Is everything okay?"

"Fine, everything's fine. Got a proposition for you, though. How about taking the day off?"

"I dunno, Megs. Why? I'm not sure my boss will be that impressed. We're hellish busy right now."

Megan persuaded, "How many days have you

had off this year? None, I bet! Come on then, give it a shot. Call him. One day won't hurt. For a friend? I really don't feel like today; just feeling so depressed. Let's just go out somewhere and have some fun. C'mon, pleeeez ...."

Andrea thought for a while. "Okay, let me phone you back in a couple of minutes. I'll just call through to the office to see if I can get a day off; without lying or playing sick. Speak to you in a couple of minutes then, okay?"

"Okay, but don't fade on me hey, I'm waiting and expecting a yes! Good luck!"

†

Andrea arrived at Megan's flat, and they left together, jabbering about nothing in particular and deciding what they were going to do with the day.

The streets outside were just clearing of the morning rush, and they both felt guilty, but at the same time elated by the freedom the day offered.

Birds fought over scraps of food on the pavement, pulling and chirruping through their squabbles. Mothers with prams peered into shop windows as they fantasised a better life. Drivers swore at one another for the same parking. Little children yelled in their play at the park.

It was a day that gave forth homely and everyday feelings. The smell of blossoms filled the air, intermingled with enticing breakfast smells that emanated from the local street cafés.

Andrea lifted her head, and sniffed the air, "This is wonderful! We should do it more often. Let's splurge with a big breakfast. Doesn't that just smell divine?" She spoke of the breakfast smells from the café they were passing.

"Fantastic!" Megan agreed. "Makes my mouth water." She peeped through the window, hand shading her eyes. "There are a couple of tables free. Let's go grab one."

They entered the small coffee shop and sat down at a corner table. Each picked up a menu to see what they'd have.

"Let's have *The Breakfast*," Andrea suggested. "Look it says here, 'two eggs, bacon, mushrooms, fried tomato, toast and tea or coffee' on breakfast special today! Ooh, that's making me hungry. That's what I'm gonna have; and you?"

"Sounds good," Megan agreed, "Okay, me too. What the hell." She was feeling much better already.

They ordered, and while they waited Andrea asked, "Okay, so what's up? Why're you so depressed? No, let me hazard a guess … Ethan!

That's it, isn't it? Always Ethan!"

"Okay, yes, I'm sorry! I suppose I do sound a bit like a stuck record most of the time" Megan agreed.

Andrea looked at her friend intently. "I don't mean it to sound that way, Meg, but honestly the guy's done a duck. He doesn't give a damn, either. I'm sorry, but that's the way I see it. Oh, and the 'stuck record' thing, that's a bit ancient," she chuckled.

"Ands, you know how I feel about him. I can't help being miserable. Sorry. Oh my gosh, I'm so pathetic!"

"Here we go again. I know how you feel. But for God's sake, Megs, as wonderful as you think he is, he's a bastard. You're a lovely person, so why waste your time and energies on him. Not to mention all the waterworks you've had to expend over him. Plenty more where he came from, you know."

"Ands, I can't just snap my fingers and the feelings all go away," Megan protested.

"Okay, you love him, I accept that. So then tell me what's happening, and I promise to keep an open mind. What have you found out? You went to Mick, didn't you?"

"I'll get to that in a minute, but for me, please

don't judge Ethan without knowing him," Megan appealed to her. "He's had a really rough time over the past few years, and I think he's done well for himself under the circumstances."

"Oh, alright," Andrea sighed, exasperatedly, "I stand scolded. You're right: I don't really know him. I've judged him by everything you've told me, and very little of it has been good. Convince me then."

"Andrea, I know that I've been quite negative about him when I speak to you, but that's only because you've been my sounding board. He's a great person once you get to know him properly - complex, but nice really, and is always judged negatively because he looks like an angel and is expected to act like one. He's human, Andrea. Just an ordinary mixed-up person who everyone seems to think will do just fine by himself; and he doesn't, does he? Am I making sense?"

"Yes! The little boy syndrome", Andrea answered, a little sarcastically. "So, back to what's happened. Have you heard anything at all from him or from Mick?"

"No, not a word from Ethan. Mick is still looking into it, half-heartedly I think. Strange, isn't it? Honestly, just when I thought that perhaps we were sorting things out, he does his disappearing act. Do you think it could be the dope, or just me? You know, he just doesn't want to be with me anymore and doesn't know how to tell me? Maybe I nag too much? I'm just not sure if I should be worrying about him, or just be giving up and letting go. The more I think about it, the more miserable I feel. Shit!"

Andrea reached out across the table for Megan's hand. "Just a thought: remember you told me he suffered a sort of memory lapse when you went out to the farm? Well, maybe he never got his memory back and just forgot where he lives, forgot he knew you, or something like that." She was being slightly condescending, but all the same was genuinely concerned about her friend.

Their breakfast arrived, and it looked just like the picture on the *Special Today* menu.

"Oh wow, this looks good." Andrea sniffed appreciatively. "Let's eat and talk later." She picked up her fork and stabbed at one of the eggs on her plate.

Megan perked up and tucked in too. She was grateful for Andrea's company, and generally pleased with their decision to enjoy the day, albeit marred by Megan's problems with Ethan. Then she glanced over at the table two away from theirs and noticed a man sitting alone, eating what looked like the same special. "Don't look now, but isn't that guy cute," she whispered conspiratorially to Andrea.

"Where?" whispered Andrea as she tried to follow Megan's gaze. She screwed her neck sideways to see.

"Just there, to the side of you, on the left." Megan indicated by raising her brows and indicating with her eyes. "But don't look like you're looking," she giggled behind her hand. "Pretend you're getting something out of your bag or something. Yeeks, he's cute."

Instead Andrea blatantly turned her head and looked in the direction Megan had indicated.

She grinned as she turned back to Megan. "More my type than yours, Megs."

"Who says?"

"I do. You were just saying how in love with Ethan you are."

"I'm just looking."

They giggled together as they cast furtive glances in the direction of the man at the table.

†

Greg started feeling uneasy as he caught the glances of the two women. They were both attractive, and that made him feel more embarrassed. Instinctively, he knew that he was the current focus of their attention as he ate his *Breakfast Special*. He lifted a forkful of mushrooms to his mouth, but at the same time kept his eyes glued to the fork. The fork bumped clumsily against his mouth and the mushrooms fell. He blushed. Intent on enjoying his breakfast, he decided that he'd not allow this harassment. He laid his knife and fork down on his plate and stood up.

Megan gasped when she saw him get up and look in their direction. "Oh my God, I think I've done it. Looks like he's coming over here! Save me, Ands!"

Now both of them were giggling nervously - Andrea because she had a foolish sense of humour anyway, and Megan in a release of tension.

He wiped his mouth with a serviette and sauntered over. "Morning ladies! I see you're enjoying your breakfast." He gave them a friendly smile and continued, "I'd like to enjoy mine too. I can either take my plate and go and sit somewhere where I won't be the focus of your amusement, or I can join you and then we can laugh together." He thought that sounded quite smooth and complimented himself. He bowed at them mockingly whilst waving his serviette in a royal circle.

Andrea smiled an apology and pursed her lips in the way people had told her was cute. "Sorry, really I am. You're not really the joke; we're the joke. We're just out having some fun. Sort of took a break from life today. Yes, please - why don't you come over and join us? We wouldn't want to be the cause of your having to find a lonely corner elsewhere."

Greg grinned, "Okay, forgiven. Make some room, I'll fetch my plate."

The two girls sheepishly shuffled and shifted their plates to make room for him.

Unceremoniously, Greg laid his plate, with balanced cutlery, on the table. He scraped up a chair for himself from the next table, sat down, grinned, gave a small wave with his fork, and immediately started shovelling the rest of his breakfast into his mouth. He was aware all the time of the two pairs of eyes focused on his every mouthful. After a couple of forkfuls he finished and looked up, tomato sauce smeared on one corner of his mouth. "That was great. You ladies finished?" He wiped at the tomato sauce with a grubby finger and popped it into his mouth. "Oh, by the way, I'm Greg. And you?" He looked from one to the other.

Both Megan and Andrea felt a bit foolish at being the cause of his inconvenience, the rest of their food forgotten.

"Hi there Greg, belatedly." Megan smiled. "Again, sorry about that, we're not usually so childish, are we Andrea?" Megan extended her hand. "Shake and make up? I'm Megan, and this is Andrea."

"Don't worry, it's okay. I was feeling lonely anyway." He picked up a crumb with his fingertip and ate it.

"You're not from around here, Greg?" noted Andrea. "It's the accent."

"Well I haven't been here for very long, but long enough to have settled in. From 'Down Under'. Fancied a change! You two ladies not working? Housewives?" he enquired.

Megan laughed, "No, not at all, just taking the day off. You know playing truant. And you?"

Andrea eyed the two of them. My, my, they were very focused on one another.

"Well, you could say that I work from home," Greg explained, "so as my hours are my own, they can be any time that I choose."

"Sounds good," said Megan. And then asked, "What kind of work do you do?" Her smile still creased her face.

"I apprehend old ladies in supermarkets and offer to carry their shopping home for them. Good tippers, old ladies."

"Oh, you're not serious, are you? Honestly, what do you do?" chortled Megan.

"I paint."

Andrea piped in, "What do you mean: houses, cars, fences or pictures?"

"Pictures, if you'd like to call them that," Greg explained.

"And you still manage to afford the *Breakfast Special*?" quipped Andrea.

"Just!" He laughed.

Greg noticed Andrea looking at the oil paint on his hands. He blushed. "It's a bitch to get off, and the turpentine eats hands if you're using it every day. They're quite clean really."

Megan asked "So, Greg. What do you paint? I mean, what are your themes? Do you have a particular theme, if you call it that?"

He turned to her. "It's called a 'genre'. But anyway, I'm really into the English landscapes and flowers at the moment, and one of the last two paintings that I've recently completed is along that line. The other is more of a London city scene – the market just down the road, in fact. But I sort of brighten them up a bit – don't go for the usual muted colours. I go bold and over-colour and add a bit of an impressionistic touch.

"I've just started a new one, which steps away a bit, but I s'pose that's what it's all about. Out of character for me. You know, creating what you're feeling at the time. In fact I'm busy with two just now."

He wondered if he was boring them, but they both seemed to be nodding for him to continue. "Also," he continued, satisfied that they wanted to hear, "I've just started sketching one, this morning in fact, of an old man that sits in Green Park grounds every day. He's really an impressive subject. The other is a portrait of a friend – a very personal thing, you understand - perhaps a bit off-beat." Was this too much information, he wondered. He stopped speaking and cleared his throat. He felt like a bore.

"Could we see?" Andrea ventured, already having forgotten what he was busy with, but hoping he would want to get to know her better.

"Well, there are two completed works in a gallery. Perhaps those would be the better ones to see," he offered. "The other two are in their infancy, really; and besides, the one is rather personal, as I said."

He reached into his pocket and took out a bundle of grubby paint-smeared business cards. He pulled one out of its elastic band bonds and handed it to Andrea. "This is the gallery's address. Go along sometime and tell Guido you're a friend of mine. He'll love it. Guido part owns the gallery with his partner, Simon."

He turned to look at Megan, "Both of you, of course."

Greg reached out for a serviette and wiped his mouth. "Where's that coffee?" he asked, looking around for the waitress. There was an awkward silence as they waited.

Greg impatiently spooned around in the sugar bowl. "Well, the breakfast was good, but I think our waitress has forgotten us. I live just over the road. How would you like to come up for a cuppa?" He looked at both of them in turn. "But if you do, I must apologise in advance – half studio, half living area. Not the neatest place on Earth, but the coffee is good I'm told." He grinned and added, "Or the tea, if you prefer."

Andrea audibly sighed her satisfaction. Megan kicked her under the table to convey her reluctance to accept the invitation. Andrea pulled her leg away and made a point of ignoring her.

"That would be wonderful, Greg," gushed

Andrea. "We've got the whole day to kill, haven't we, Megan?"

Megan moaned to herself but got up to leave with them. They paid and walked out of the café like old friends.

†

Greg's flat was unusual, even for an artist. Although neat, he had paraphernalia of oddments scattered about. Paper maché figures marched from the walls against a backdrop of artistic works that seemed to have been painted to enhance any ugly feature. Windowsills played stage to small sculptures, and mismatched furniture displayed bright colours. A tattered red chair and couch, oblivious of their condition, stood proudly side-by-side. Two neon green milking stools served as side tables, and in the centre of the room - if one could call it the centre - lay a sawn tree trunk slab with fairy carvings adorning the sides.

A large orange cat lay in a pot plant at the balcony door. It beamed its approval as Greg walked in. Greg turned and swept an arm around, indicating the innards of his flat. "Welcome to my humble abode" he announced.

"And this here is Marmaduke, my comrade in arms. Recently rescued from the drains and bins, where he got fat on rats it seems." He walked over to the cat and stroked its head. It started purring before he'd even touched it. Marmaduke stood up and stretched by arching his back, then ambled heavy-footed over to Megan with a meowed greeting.

"See, he likes you," said Greg, as he looked Megan up and down appreciatively. He thought he probably felt the same way as the cat did. Greg was in awe of the picture she made.

Megan bent over to stroke the cat. "Hullo, Marmaduke. What's up? Goodness you are chubby, aren't you?" she scolded kindly as she stroked his back. He purred louder than ever, pleased that he had so impressed her.

The sun poured through the balcony door in a beam that ended on Megan's head. Her golden-brown hair was reflected in wisps in her honey eyes; her lips flushed a coral pink. It was then that Greg lost his heart to the elf queen displayed in the sunny spotlight.

Andrea wandered around the flat, exclaiming her delight at almost everything she saw and touched.

Although shorter than Megan, she exuded a sexiness that was lacking in her friend's lanky figure. She hopped in and out of relationships, ending each one in a flourish of tears that were forgotten in a week when she started a new one.

Her hair was short and stylish, showing off small well-shaped ears that were usually adorned with outlandishly large earrings.

Andrea browsed, peeping in here and there, lifting lids, looking under and behind things, and generally being nosy. Greg really didn't mind. This type of woman fascinated him by her very femaleness. She reminded him of a little inquisitive mouse.

And though Andrea fascinated him, Megan had him enthralled in her mystery. She was the one who the 'good guy' married, and never regretted doing so as she amazed him year after year - as he unfolded time and again another layer of her petals, never to reach the core, but forever trying, and always surprised. He saw her through the eyes of an artist.

Andrea hissed excitedly, "Hey, Megs. Come here, quick. I want you to see something." She had lifted a sheet thrown over an easel-mounted canvas in the corner of the room. "You're not going to believe this."

She was peering, head sideways, under the sheet. She turned her head from side to side as she examined the sketch.

Megan walked over and bent to peep under the sheet as well, unprepared for what waited beneath its bland exterior. She found herself looking directly into Ethan's eyes.

It was unexpected, and such a shock. With shaking hands and a startled expression, she dropped the sheet, momentarily stunned. She turned slowly, afraid her legs might buckle, her panic-filled gaze locked on Greg's face. Her mouth twitched in an uncontrollable display of emotion.

Andrea hadn't expected quite such a dramatic reaction. She reached out for Megan, concern etched on her face. "Megs, you all right? Greg quick - get her a glass of sugar water."

Greg hurried to do her bidding, totally in the dark as to what was going on and somehow feeling that whatever it was, it was likely his fault and that to his mind sugar water was daft.

Andrea led Megan to the red couch and eased her down, where she stared ahead and said nothing. Her thoughts battled to put into order what she had seen. Tears formed in her eyes, and unabated they flowed in one unbroken stream, trickling into the corners of her mouth and out, down to the edge of her chin where they hesitated, then dropped onto Greg's wooden floor.

Clumsily, Greg rushed back with the glass of sugared water and knelt down in front of her. He took her cold hand in his and wrapped her fingers around the glass. "Hey, you okay? What's wrong? I'm sorry, have I done something? Here drink this, maybe you'll feel a bit better."

She whispered two words as she looked him in the eyes, "That picture!"

"The picture? You mean the sketch did this to you?"

She nodded her head up and down and sipped the water. Greg looked at Andrea in puzzlement.

"It's Ethan, isn't it?" Andrea asked Greg in a hushed tone.

"Yes, it is Ethan. Do you know him?" He was surprised and confused.

"He's Megan's boyfriend!" sighed Andrea.

"Her what?" Greg was astonished.

"I said, he's Megan's boyfriend. He's been missing for some time now, and she's been beside herself with worry. You can imagine her shock to find him here." She glanced back to Megan, who was now following the conversation with little nods.

Megan whispered, "When did you do it, Greg? When did you last see him?"

"About two days ago. Tuesday. We did this on Tuesday." He was starting to feel quite shocked himself.

"You did this on Tuesday?" she repeated, shaking her head, not understanding. "You said '*We did this on Tuesday*' - does that mean he was *here*?"

"Yes, he's agreed to pose for the portrait."

"Pose for the portrait ...." She again aped his words quietly but didn't intend it as a question.

"Yes. Are you saying he's your boyfriend? Ethan's your boyfriend?"

"Yes. Well, I don't know any more," she whispered, and took a sip of the sugared water, hands still trembling.

"You don't know? Why? What's happened? What's up?"

They spoke in a jumble of words as each attempted to grasp a situation they hadn't expected.

She spoke softly, "I don't know if he's still my boyfriend. He's been missing now for a couple of months. Just disappeared ..." Her voice trailed off as a new wash of tears splashed from her eyes.

"But he hasn't disappeared. He was just here," said Greg, clearly puzzled. "It's okay," he said, and leaned forward, feeling very uncomfortable about the situation. He put a hand on her shoulder. "It's okay. He's okay. He's not missing!"

"And that's just as hard for me, Greg," she sobbed. "Why?"

As Greg began to assimilate the pieces, he felt a well of pity build up inside him. Emotional by nature, his own tears pricked the corners of his eyes. He leaned closer and wrapped his arms around her. In a release of grief, she buried her head in his neck and sobbed. He patted her back, wondering what had happened between his friend Ethan and this lovely girl in his arms.

Greg couldn't believe that he held Ethan's girl in his arms, or that Ethan even had a girl. It just hadn't occurred to him. Just seemed odd, and he wasn't even sure why he thought that. Besides, he supposed that it was pretty obvious that he would have, but this particular girl? The girl he had decided he wanted more than he had ever wanted anything in his entire life. His girl!

Greg felt the beginnings of resentment flow through him - resentment of Ethan, the Ethan that she loved, and he worshipped.

"You love him so much?" Greg asked; his disappointment evident only to himself.

"I love him more than 'so much'," sobbed Megan. She moved out of his embrace and wiped her face with the back of her hand. Then in a complete turnaround, excitement lit her face. "Greg. When will you be seeing him again?"

"Tomorrow, actually," he replied.

"What time?" She could barely mask her eagerness, and sudden plan.

"He's coming for a sitting sometime in the morning, I think," said Greg. "Don't know exactly when." And he repeated dazedly, "Should be in the morning…"

"I'll be here early. I must see him," Megan quickly added.

Greg felt uneasy. This was stalking if he wasn't mistaken. "I don't know, Megan. I don't know what to say. I don't want to get involved in something that's got nothing to do with me. Please understand, I value his friendship and don't want to do anything to jeopardize it." Indecision played about his now rapidly blinking eyes.

Andrea had been a silent observer as she looked from one to the other of them and could barely conceal her anger and jealousy. *What the fuck?* She thought. *Everybody wants someone who doesn't want them.* And then she exploded.

"Well damn it, Greg. He doesn't know you know her. Throw them together, and let's see what happens. If he's your friend, then he's your friend. You won't lose his friendship, for goodness sakes, just because you know his girlfriend.

"Let's get real, they have unfinished business to sort out here. It's about time Ethan grew up and handled his responsibilities! It's about time Megan pulled herself together and faced reality, for fucking crying out loud! Why does everyone always step so carefully around Ethan, is he a God or something? Bloody hell!"

On that note she stormed to the door, wrenched it open and marched out, slamming it shut behind her and leaving Greg and Megan staring at one another in surprise.

Megan was clearly embarrassed. "Oh, Greg, I'm so sorry," she apologised, "I've been so wrapped up in my own problems just lately that I've really been neglecting my friends. Andrea isn't usually like that. She's always there for me, and I've probably come to expect it and take her for granted. Jeez, I'm pathetic. It seems I'm not very good at this human relationship thing. I should probably go after her. If you don't mind I'll pop in tomorrow morning, if I find the courage and don't change my mind. Andrea is right. Ethan needs to man up and let me know what's happening so I can put this whole thing to rest."

Greg felt he had no option but to agree. "Okay then, maybe you should. If you're determined to come over, please try to get here early before Ethan arrives - if he arrives. I won't be able to face him you know, if I have to wait for you. Thing is he'll know something is different, and that scares me."

"Why, Greg, Ethan's the last person you need to be afraid of! Or what do you mean?"

He shrugged, "I don't really know. I haven't known Ethan all that long. You probably know him a whole lot better than I do, but there's something about him. Don't get me wrong, I have the greatest respect for the man, and find him fascinating to say the least; I just don't want to get on the wrong side of him. Also, Megan, right now he's the best friend I have. I don't want to see him hurt either or lose his friendship. I just don't want to be involved. Sorry."

"So the Ethan bug has bitten you too, Greg! Don't worry, I'll take the blame if it's handed out. I just need to see him so badly. I need to know that he's okay. I need to find out exactly what's happening, and then go on from there, one way or another. This is just such a perfect opportunity to do that – corner him," she sniggered. "Briefly, I think it's one of two things: either he has high-tailed it away from me, you know, because he really doesn't want to see me anymore and didn't have the courage to say so, or he's in some sort of trouble. I have a sick feeling it's been me all along. Maybe I've been making a fool of myself thinking he could love me like I love him."

Greg didn't know how to answer, and stumbled on his words, "Look, I'm sorry, Megan. If it's like that, I'm sorry if he left you. I can't imagine it is like that though, and that Ethan wouldn't know what he had, when he had it. I just feel so terrible about this. What more can I say!"

"It's okay," she consoled, "I know it's got nothing to do with you and that it's not your fault – it's just the way things are." And with that, she rose to leave Greg to his thoughts. Greg noticed that she looked a lot happier than she had a few moments before. She left without a backward glance at him.

"Hope can be a sorry beast, and love an even sorrier one," he said out loud to himself.

CHAPTER 17

The strange ones

The previous Saturday ...

Ashley Constance did not know that the special day she planned to lose her virginity would also be the day she would lose her life.

That sunny Saturday morning, she washed her long brown hair, painted her toe nails, and creamed her body with her new sweet pea fragrance cream. Her face glowed, and her darkened lashes complimented her almond shaped eyes. She picked up her handbag, slung it over her shoulder and, with a bounce in her step, said her final goodbye.

"Bye, Mum. See you later," she chimed, as she walked towards the front door. Her hand rested on the door handle while she waited to hear if Mum had heard her above the drone of the vacuum cleaner. The mirror above the hall mantle caught her image perfectly – poised, pretty, excited. The salmon and cream roses in the vase on the shelf were the same colour as her lipstick and pale complexion. It was picture perfect. She admiringly blew herself a kiss.

"Don't be too late, luv. Remember that Da's knocking off early, and would like us all here for tea tonight," her mother called down the stairway. She was preparing for the overseas guests that would be arriving mid-morning.

Ashley was going into town. The man she was meeting had said he'd be there by ten and that he'd be looking out for her, but to keep it their secret. They were to meet outside the old bookshop. The door clicked closed behind her and, without a backward glance at the house where she was raised, she made her way up the road to town.

†

It was Saturday-morning-busy. Ashley checked her watch and quickened her step. She didn't want to be late. This was, from what she understood, their first real date. She felt like she'd known him forever, even though in fact she'd only spoken to him twice. She had memorised every line of his face, those green eyes, the soft drawling voice, the pale long-fingered hands with groomed nails and his breath-taking beauty. She'd never been so smitten with anyone before and was more than ready to give herself to him, body and soul.

She stopped outside the shop, adjusted her skirt, patted her hair, and then with a hand shading her face from the glare of the glass, peered through the window. He wasn't inside. But true to his word, she saw him walking down the pavement towards her. As he got nearer their eyes met, and she felt her legs weaken and a hot tingling flush creep up from her neck. She hardly knew him but did know that she loved him so much she could feel it as a pain across her chest. Smiling broadly, she raised her hand and gave a small wave, then gave a last look through the shop window and espied a book on the counter. It had a black cover, with gold lettering and a cross on the spine. She could see that much from where she stood. The elderly bookshop man stared back out at her. She turned away towards the approaching David. She would find herself holding on to the image of that Bible during the last few moments of her life.

†

When the old man behind the counter saw *the strange one* approach her, he called out a warning, but his words were lost in the noise of the traffic and the groan of the door closing behind a new customer.

†

David walked up to her, his mouth fluttering into a smile of pleasure. "I'm so glad you came," he said. He pulled her into his arms. She could feel his heart pounding wildly in his chest, and the tremor of his arms around her. He bent his head down and softly kissed her forehead. With eyes closed, she savoured his sweet smell and the feel of his lips against her skin; felt herself slip into his world and be engulfed by him. "Ashley. My God!" he gasped.

Holding her close with his arm about her shoulder, and hers about his waist, he led her up the road. Already she could feel the wetness of her body as it prepared for what she intended to give him.

†

They found her body four days later in an old barge on the river. A tramp discovered her, led there by his skinny dog. She had died in the throes of lovemaking, with a surprised look on her face. Bloated flies sucked on the crusted virgin blood on her legs, and on the deep bite marks where one of her nipples had been.

†

Present day

Old man Jason sat in the musty bookshop

that had been his father's, and before that had belonged to his grandfather. Pages of the past lay interleaved upon the floor to ceiling bookshelves. Here, some of them had resided for decades, awaiting their rightful owner. All well chronicled in Old Man Jason's brain.

He sat as he had sat the day before and the day before that, the week before and the week before that, the month before and the month before that, the year before and the year before that. He sat watching.

He knew all the people that frequented, or had frequented, this busy street. He had made up his own names for them, because it was seldom that they came in. But he did have his regulars, who had been coming year after year. He knew them by their names. There were *the lonely ones,* and then there were *the learney ones*, then there were *the loony ones*, and of course *the lazy ones*, *the lucky ones*, and so on and so forth. They were well-sorted on the shelves of his brain. But the ones he watched for most carefully, were *the strange ones*. He had known years before that they were different because theirs was the only name that did not begin with the letter *L*.

It cannot be said that Old Man Jason was so idiotic that he only knew they were strange because he categorised them thus; it was also what he saw over the years. He noticed them, yes he did. He saw their comings and goings, yes siree, he certainly did.

As he had done many times before, and as had his father and his grandfather, he walked slowly down the aisles of the shop each day, searching for any of his books that might be in the wrong place. He knew their places as well as he knew which braces he would clip to his baggy trousers each morning.

All *the ones* kept coming and moving the books a couple of inches perhaps, but sometimes more than a foot away from where they rightly belonged. He watched them doing it and said nothing, his resentment never showing. As soon as they left, he would laboriously remove himself from his stool behind the counter, and once again traverse the aisles muttering under his breath, to replace the books where they belonged. Some of them had lived in one particular place since his grandfather's days. Yes, they each had their place.

There was, of course, a shelf for the new books - *the modern ones* that slouched into his shop in their shoddy soft covers. These books had lost all pretence of nobility. No more gold etched hard spines, no more meticulous language. Ah, these books, the traitors that peered out from their bright covers, enticing readers with their decadence. They sat upon their shelves leering and encouraging their uncomprehending victims.

Old Man Jason could keep them under control. Never once was he seduced by their provocative bodies. He understood them and had reserved a special place for them where they could be watched. He didn't care much how they ranked themselves; he didn't care for their disarray. Fate had decreed that they should never feel the security of having a right place on the shelf.

And as he kept an eye on the rebel books, so he watched out of his dirty window each day. At times he would walk up close to the window, remove his scented handkerchief from his pocket, spit on it, and polish a new peephole in the dust. Through this peephole he would sometimes stare for a full two hours, until such time as his bandy legs would become so painful that he would return to his place behind the counter, on his stool.

He would use that same handkerchief that had a 'J' embroidered in one corner, to clean the dust off his spectacles. The place got dustier by the year.

It wasn't every day that he saw *the strange ones*. No, indeed not. But he saw them - he most certainly did, as he had for the past forty years. There had been seven of them, the same ones year after year - and then there had only been six. One had never come back.

He quickly did a re-shuffle of his thoughts. Yes, he remembered now, there had been a time when they had all disappeared for close on fifteen years. He had thought they had gone for good and was somehow pleased. But as surely as God made little apples, they returned - but only six of them.

Now, just recently and of a sudden, there were seven again. That was their number now.

The new *strange one* was the most beautiful he had yet seen. He reminded Old Man Jason of those decadent books that he had to keep check on. So it became obvious to him that he would also have to keep check on number seven in particular. This was his mission, he was sure. Though it had been his mission all these years to keep check on all *the strange ones*, he knew that his purpose had now been magnified.

As he had grown older over the years, *the strange ones* had never changed. They had thought that by disappearing for those fifteen years, his vigil would have been forgotten. No siree, definitely not, he had known them even after fifteen years. They had tried to pull the old wool over his eyes, that was for sure.

Old Man Jason knew, as sure as God had made

little apples that they would come for him one day. That was their purpose. They already knew he was there. He was sure they wanted *the old ones* - the special books that resided on his very back shelf. They were crafty, the demonic seven, as they waited patiently over the years for him to weaken.

He had seen the murders that they had committed. No one else knew. They were Satan's own children, those seven, living right here, blatantly defying the whole order of things, going their bloody way, and still having the audacity to act like aristocracy itself.

Yes, that pretty young girl who had looked through the window at him had gone off with the one who pretended to be a policeman. He knew he'd never see her again.

Old Man Jason had bought himself a 1911 .45 pistol on the black market. He kept it under the counter, well-oiled and polished, with seven cartridges laying in wait in the gun's magazine. The bullets were silver. It must have been an omen, because when he bought the gun it held exactly seven cartridges – and at the time there had been seven *strange ones*. Yes siree. One of his oldest friends on the farthest shelf had warned of their coming and had suggested the silver bullets. He considered himself well prepared.

Once, just about five months ago, one of *the strange ones* had come right here into his store and stared at him as if the time had come, and then gone to look through *the old ones*, right at the very back of the shop. He had selected one, as if he cared, and placed it on the counter.

Old Man Jason had seen those hands. Not a blemish, not a wrinkle, nary an age spot to tell of *the strange one's* age. Old Man Jason knew him to be older than he himself was, older by many years, he was sure. Ah yes, he had stood there, that *strange one*, with a challenging sneer, just waiting for Old Man Jason to comment.

The strange one had paid for the book and had left the shop rudely, without speaking a word and without looking back. The old man was livid that after all these years, these years of watching and waiting, that *the strange one* had hardly acknowledged his existence. When he thought about it later, he realised that it was all part of their plot.

As he grunted in thought, the large wolfhound, lying at his feet on his hessian sacks, wagged his powerful tail.

"We are waiting for the right time, aren't we Peego?" He laboriously leant over to pat Peego's large diamond-shaped head. The yellow eyes stared up at him and, as if to answer, powerful jaws parted to seemingly pant out his agreement. A long pink tongue dangled from between the ferocious canine teeth, dripping saliva onto the dusty floor.

Peego, the large hound, was a fairly new addition to the musty book shop. In fact, he was more than a little out of place, but gratefully accepted his new home and the man who gave him pork sausages to eat on some nights.

Now and again, the man would take him for a walk along the pavement, in amongst the busy people with shopping bags. He would endeavour to pee up against every pole he saw, nearly dragging Old Man Jason from his feet in his haste to reach the next pole, and if luck was in, a tree.

The local animal shelter had despaired of finding a home for Peego. It had seemed to be a year for puppies and their cuteness. Peego had peered out eagerly from his cage, growling his pleasure as the children came past. But his growls were misinterpreted, and without fail the human pups went screeching off to their parents. Peego remained, and his name had been penned to the bottom of the 'death-row' list.

But it was at about this time that Old Man Jason had decided that he needed a good strong watchdog: one that would sense the coming of *the strange ones*; a dog that would equal them in strength and cunning. He had nearly taken the white bulldog, but Peego had growled out a welcome and Old Man Jason knew he had his dog.

Never had Old Man Jason walked home so fast, as Peego dragged him along in his new-found freedom.

It was on one such day, when Old Man Jason was being pulled hectically along the pavement, that Peego first espied his Master. The Master was walking on the opposite side of the busy road, intent on wherever it was he was going.

At first Peego wasn't sure, as he vainly tried to get a better glimpse between the cars that zoomed to and fro. The scent was strong, though, and so familiar. Now you see him, now you don't; then he's one place and, when you manage to look again, another. The traffic cleared fleetingly, and the large dog was able to better see the familiar and still beautiful face.

He lifted his muzzle into the air wolf-like and sniffed. Yes, the scent was very familiar, the little of it that wasn't disguised by the strange fumes coughed out by the cars. He pricked up his ears as far as they would go and listened, but all he could hear was the cacophony of sounds emitted by humans clustered together in one place, as they did here.

And then he received a thought form that only the Master could emit. He wagged his tail furiously to himself and felt himself go silly with joy.

The large wolf-dog shivered in anticipation, stretched his neck up, and without losing sight of the evasive Master, howled out a greeting; howled out his need.

Old Man Jason was feeling decidedly irritable as he careened down the road after the powerful dog. His skin itched from the final and unexpected August heatwave and sweat ran from his brow and ringed his hat. He thought that things really couldn't get much worse, as sure as God had made little apples. But they did.

Firstly, he happened to glance to the other side of the busy road - had felt impelled to glance to the other side of the road. There, walking in all his conceited glory was the new *strange one*. Oh, he loved himself, he did, strutting like that down the road pretending not to see Old Man Jason. But Old Man Jason could see him squinting sideways, see him plotting, but as ever pretending not to notice.

And then to compound the situation, the dog had stopped in the middle of the pavement, heedless as dogs are to the tugs of the chain, and howled at the passers-by. He tugged on the choke chain, but the dog would not budge. He pulled until the dog's howl became a gurgle, and still he would not move.

Then Old Man Jason lost his temper and kicked the dog in the ribs as hard as he could. He dragged the dog back into the shop. Into the safety of the musty book shop they scuffled, and then Old Man Jason shortened Peego's chain and tied him to the back of the counter, muttering all the time about the coming demise of *the strange ones*.

†

Ethan was on his way to Greg for a sitting. He had decided to walk to release some of the pent-up energy that threatened to erupt, and which he had not as yet learnt to properly control. His mind was busy translating what his newly honed senses perceived. The sharpness of his vision enthralled him, as did the heretofore unheard sounds.

As people passed, he could hear the distinctive beat of their hearts and the rushing of the air in their lungs. He could hear the trees creak within their trunks and became aware of the myriad of creatures that inhabited this busy place. His eyes caught the scuttle of a rat a block away; the feelers of a cockroach as it inspected the terrain outside its rubbish pile; the eye and the beat of the wings of a bird that flew overhead. The world was truly a wonderful place and, without a doubt, a gift to be appreciated at all times.

Ethan watched the people rushing about, faces uncomprehending of the wonder of creation about them. Most of them stared at the ground as they walked, intent on not meeting the eyes of their fellows; brushing past and bumping, apologising "Sorry," and the other "No, not at all, I'm sorry," not looking up, and then purposefully walking a straight line on the pavement that they thought their personal possession. Irate drivers honked horns, muttered oaths, and gesticulated at the inhabitants of the car up ahead. They were really quite a sorry bunch but amusing in their humanness.

As Ethan mused to himself, a smile on his lips, he understood what Kalin had said. Yes, out of the chaos of creation had come order which, if one looked around, was really the order of chaos. The simple yet also complex lives of the brothers were definitely a drop of order within this chaos. But his thoughts did not dwell on anything in particular, as he was in a light-hearted mood, and happy.

Then he heard the cry, faint at first but rising in crescendo as it sought and found his thought pattern. Ethan looked around in surprise. He recognised the voice, even though it spoke in an archaic language of grunts, howls, and groans. He understood what it said even in its frenzy to reach him, but he could not find the owner.

In wonder, Ethan searched the faces that passed him by, but the wonder changed to disappointment as the cries grew softer and soon disappeared. Ethan walked back the way he had come, now desperate - searching and listening, emitting wave upon wave of thought form, directed to his target, to his friend.

"Master!" it had called. He understood without knowing how he understood. "I have found you, but am forsaken in discovery," it howled. "Find me, and let us run together again," it growled. "It is I, Thalem. It is I, Thalem ..."

Ethan forgot about his appointment with Greg as he searched the streets the rest of the day, not stopping once to rest or take nourishment. He found himself possessed by the pathetic cry and a need to find and nurture. He sought Thalem, not knowing how Thalem looked. Finally, completely despondent, and as the sun was saying its final farewell, Ethan made his way home with a questioning soul.

†

The house was cloaked in dark, and no glimmer of light issued from the windows. Ethan was disappointed, as he had intended speaking to Caeron about his new discovery; or lack of discovery, it seemed.

He entered and walked through to the study. The door was open, but he could feel no aural emanations. On this night, there was no welcome to be found here. He walked over to the bar and poured himself a whisky from the crystal decanter, took the glass over to the fireplace and placed it on the mantelpiece. The embers were still glowing but wouldn't last for much longer. He added a few pinecones from the bucket on the side of the fireplace. Flames licked up immediately and caressed the pinecones. The fire spat back to life with orange flames, casting welcome warmth upon Ethan's face. He extended his hands to the warmth.

The whisky was good. Kalin bought only the best. He sat sipping, watching the flames, and soaking in the restful ambience of the room. He felt a hunger come upon him, which could not be sated by the food in the house.

The fire was rapidly digesting the cones, and he placed two pine logs above them. This would last a while. He settled comfortably into the armchair and sipped. His attention was so focused on the fireplace that he did not notice Caeron, veiled over, at the door.

Caeron had been standing framed in the

doorway for about ten minutes. He had veiled so as not to disturb the picture Ethan made as he sat absorbed by the fire.

Caeron examined his profile. It appeared to be in flame as the ruby shadows played about Ethan's face and hair. A pinkish hue reflected and combined with the aural glow, the emanations themselves playing shadow-world in pulsing patterns with the furthest corners of the room.

Caeron was overcome with what he saw before him. He had not been witness to the metamorphoses as had Kalin and Hadrian, so he stood at a loss for words, but started to remove his veil. He felt like he was spying on Ethan.

He had barely begun to unveil when Ethan felt his presence and, as he did so, a humming filled the air. In a movement as quick as a flash of light, Ethan leaped to his feet and spun around to face the intruder.

Caeron smiled and stepped into the room.

"Caeron, it's you! You caught me unaware. I was so deep in thought."

"I intended catching you that way. I thought, much earlier on, that I detected a thought form from you. There was confusion, and I knew you sought me. However, I arrive here and find you bathed in a light of contentment."

"Well you're not wrong, Caeron. I came home specifically to talk to you. The strangest thing happened today. I'm not sure what it means, or if it has anything to do with my situation here, but thought that perhaps you may have some answers for me."

"And what is it of which you would desire knowledge?"

"Today, as I walked the street, a voice beckoned for me in a language I didn't understand. The voice knew me well and called me 'Master'. The strange thing is that I also recognised the voice and understood the language, even though I know that I haven't heard either before. Does this make sense to you?

Ethan continued before Caeron could answer. "I searched for the owner of the voice and found nothing. I searched the faces and re-walked the route that I had taken, but again came up with nothing. The voice communicated telepathically, of course, as we do. Can anyone else communicate with us like this, and why would it call me 'Master'?"

Caeron sat down by the fire, staring in as had Ethan, as he listened. He turned in concern, and said, "The truth is Ethan, I don't know. I don't remember something like this happening to one of us before.

"What do you drink there my lad?"

"Whisky, not Tullamore Dew. Can I get you one?" Already, Ethan had approached the drinks cabinet and was pouring for Caeron.

"Yes, I would like that, thank you. Tell me Ethan, did this silent communicator of yours leave a mental calling card with his name?" Ethan could sense that Caeron was interested.

"Well yes, he said, 'it is I, Thalem', if I interpreted the name correctly. As I said, the language isn't one with which I feel familiar."

Caeron hesitated, and in a pleasantly surprised voice whispered the name to himself, "Thalem. It can't be, not after all these years. Ethan, here is a story to tell, indeed, if you would like to hear it?"

"But of course, Caeron, I have felt bothered by the calling, and have a feeling that it might become an obsession to find the caller."

And so they sat, without a doubt the two of the brothers who were the most alike and the least alike - alike in their equal beauty, but unalike in their self-expression. Until the small hours of the morning, they sat, whilst Caeron related the tale as he could remember it, in shared memories. Memories that he awakened in Ethan - that had been there all along, part of the kindred spirit, waiting like the fire in the hearth for re-kindling.

And to share these memories they had to share their blood and revelled in so doing.

CHAPTER 18

Disappointment

Megan arrived early, as Greg had requested. She knocked, hoping that Ethan would not be there yet. Greg opened immediately, and a similar concern was etched on his face. "Oh, Megan, thank heavens. Come in. Ethan isn't here yet."

"Hey, Greg. Oh good. If you haven't noticed, I'm as nervous as hell."

He kissed her on the cheek, then stuttered, "I don't know why, but I am too. Hope I'm not doing the wrong thing. Ethan trusts me and in a way I feel I'm betraying his trust, if you can see what I mean."

"No Greg, I don't think so. I really don't think you're betraying him. Aren't we friends too?" It was more of a statement than a question. She took off her jacket and stood holding it.

He didn't notice the jacket. "Yes, of course,

Megan, but our friendship is newer than the one I have with Ethan. My friendship with Ethan is reaching the point where we're beginning to feel comfortable with one another. Ethan is opening up to me. I wouldn't want to hurt him."

"Then, Greg, you're one of the few people who feels the same way I do. I love Ethan, and he's the last person I would want to see hurt. But I really need this confrontation. I can't begin to tell you how worried I've been over the past few months. Please understand, I need to satisfy myself that he's okay. One way or another, I have to finalise our relationship, even if it means that I get hurt - which is really what I'm expecting. I need closure, Greg." She was still standing in the doorway holding her jacket.

But deep in the recessed parts of him that nurtured guilt, Greg wept to himself. He somehow knew that he was the Judas. This particular deed in itself was unimportant, it was what he knew - without knowing - would follow.

With his misgivings well concealed, Greg ushered her in and took her coat. He flung it over the armchair where Marmaduke was lying, licking his paws. Marmaduke scuttled off in a large puffy ball of orange annoyance. They then made small talk whilst they waited for Ethan to arrive. But, as Greg was becoming accustomed to - and as he perceived it might be a habit of Ethan's - Ethan never came. They waited the whole morning, both of them nursing their fears and doubts, but keenly aware of each other listening for his step in the hallway, the knock, his face framed in the door. It never came.

Megan became more and more fidgety as time wore on. "Greg, are you sure Ethan said he was coming today, because it really doesn't look like it?"

"He definitely said today. I wonder what could have happened."

"You don't really believe that something has happened, do you?"

"No."

"Neither do I."

"So what do you think?"

"The truth is, Greg, I don't think Ethan cares one way or another. I don't think he truly cares about anything."

"I think you're wrong, Megan," answered Greg. "He does care, but in a different way to us. Come over here and look at this sketch. Tell me what you see. Or are you still upset about it?"

"No, it was just a shock. Ethan's eyes were the last thing I expected to see peering out from under your sheet. Okay, let's look."

Greg walked over to the easel and lifted the sheet.

Megan's eyes widened. "It's quite astonishing really, y'know, Greg. The likeness is unreal. So far you've managed to capture something I couldn't quite put into words. What does Ethan think of it?"

"He praises me for being a good artist, and for creating the likeness. He knows himself, so doesn't see the apparent truth that we're experiencing. You see, he had it in him all along, so it's nothing new to him."

She stared at the sketch silently whilst Greg examined her in appreciation. She broke the silence. "He really isn't like us is he?"

"No, I don't think so."

"Greg, you know him now. How is he? I mean, what kind of person is he? You know he was changing rapidly - it was so apparent. I just couldn't handle the change, didn't understand it. Was he just growing up, y'know, maturing?"

"Well, Megan, I didn't know him at the same time that you did, so can't imagine him any different. I tell you this, though: Ethan is something not quite of this world. Every time I think I've pinpointed it; it slips away again before

I can grasp it. It's so illusive, this thing that Ethan is, but at the same time compelling. He draws me, on a personal level, like no one has done before."

"He has always drawn me, Greg. He used to be different, though. Now, I don't like admitting, but there is something to be afraid of. I also can't put my finger on it. It's almost like he's gone out of his mind, or his personality is splitting. Enough said. It's really difficult putting my feelings into words. I just can't explain it."

Greg was also afraid of displaying to her the deep emotion he felt for Ethan - the holiness that, for him, permeated Ethan. He also couldn't say that Ethan had, in his way, become his Owner, Destiner, and Angel. Guiltily he looked up at Megan, afraid she might read his feelings on his face.

"Look, he's not coming. It's already midday. How about I take you for lunch if you don't have plans? We can take a drive to the coast and sit on the beach with a bottle of wine. What do you think of that?"

"I think that would be wonderful. We deserve it, don't we?"

"Of course we do!" He took her hand and lifted her from where she had sunk down on the floor.

†

Megan and Greg drove a way up the coast, with neither admitting to the other their disappointment, but both knowing how the other felt. They shared their common self-doubt and mutual love for Ethan. Each of them drew comfort from the other and, by sharing their mutual rejection, their relationship grew.

By sunset, they were laughing, and Ethan was being mentioned less. But they went their separate ways that evening, each to their own thoughts and home, and each to the ever-lurking shadow of Ethan.

†

Greg

It was to be five days before I heard from Ethan again. As he had never given me a contact number, I hadn't been able to call him for an explanation.

I had gone down to the gallery that afternoon to collect the cheque that Guido owed me from the sale of two paintings, the one being from Kalin for Ethan. Guido was excited about the public interest in the paintings and nagged for more. He could obviously see the Pound signs in the air. And there I found my friend, and Ethan's companion, Benedikt. He was still negotiating the price of the "devil itself" painting that hung on the wall, opposite to where mine had been displayed.

I walked over to greet him, feeling slightly apprehensive and not knowing why. It seemed that I was getting a lot of these feelings just lately and it wasn't like me. I usually take things as they come.

"Did you ever go home Benedikt?" I asked as I approached.

As he turned, I shuddered at the maleficent look on his face, retained from his intense perusal of the painting. But I had hardly acknowledged it before his visage had changed to one of open friendliness.

"Well, if it isn't our old friend Gregory. Hello, Gregory. Good to see you, bambino. We almost thought we'd lost you, heart, and soul, to Ethan our beautiful companion."

"I have seen a bit of Ethan. He's agreed to sit for a portrait."

"He surprises me, then. Such a quiet one, and shy too. I never expected. Nevertheless, I trust the portrait will be as good as you have proved you can do. Look here, Greg. What do you think of this - we have bought it. Romando and I are quite taken with it. Do you perhaps know the artist? I mean, do you know him personally?" Benedikt had turned to continue his examination of the painting, his face an expressionless mask.

"I've seen her around and have said a couple of words to her, but don't know her. It's quite a painting but a little too merciless to appeal to me."

"A woman painted this?" Benedikt asked in surprise.

"Yes, and you wouldn't say, looking at her, that she would paint like this. She's a small little thing."

"I would like to meet with her." He licked his lips as he said this.

I noticed that as his interest in the artist had piqued, he no longer looked me in the eyes but kept his head averted. I had seen similar behaviour in Ethan and wondered at it.

I thought I'd ask about Ethan. "Ethan was supposed to come around a couple of days ago for a sitting. I waited, but he never arrived. Is everything okay? Have you seen him? I've been a bit worried."

"Of course I've seen him, Gregory. Don't worry yourself about nothing, Ethan is quite capable of looking after himself, trust me."

"When did you see him, Benedikt?"

"I see him every day, bambino. We live together."

"I don't understand. What do you mean, you live together?"

"We all live together – share an abode if you like. Don't misunderstand, Gregory - we're family."

Megan had said nothing about Ethan having any other family besides his mother, and the brother who was overseas. I didn't understand but thought better of questioning any further.

"Well then, Benedikt, could you please ask him to give me a call? I've waited for five days for him without word. Perhaps he's annoyed about something or has chosen not to continue with the portrait. I did give him my mobile number, but here it is again." I handed him a gallery business card with my number at the back. Ethan hadn't given me his number, so I didn't know if he had a mobile.

"Ah, Gregory. I sense here some petulance. Ethan has been extremely tied up with some personal business. It's not like him to forget a friend. I'll speak to him for you this afternoon."

"Perhaps I could call around to see him?" I asked, expecting him to agree and give me the address. But Benedikt turned from me in dismissal and walked over to where Guido sat babbling away - with waving hands - to Simon. I wondered if Benedikt was jealous of my friendship with Ethan. I found them a strange, but magnetic, group of people.

†

True to his word, Benedikt had obviously asked Ethan to call me. No more than two hours from the time that I had asked him to. And as I had arrived home with the packet of extra oils and brushes that I needed, my mobile rang in my pocket. I dumped everything on the floor to dig for it, expectantly.

"Greg speaking!" I gasped breathlessly.

"Hi!" he said, and waited. I recognised his voice of course.

"Hey, Ethan. I waited for you. Did you forget?"

"I'm sorry, Greg. Something important came up. You know, family matters that needed sorting out. Can we make it for tomorrow - if you don't already have something planned, of course?"

"Yes, that's fine, providing you don't let me down. Remember, this is my living."

"Sure, I understand. But remember, Greg, it was you that wanted to paint me, not me who wanted to be painted."

I was momentarily shocked at the truth of his statement. There was no anger in his voice, he was merely pointing out a fact that I, in my emotional state, had overlooked. He was right of course, it was he who was doing me the favour, and I who was becoming possessive.

"Crikey, you're right Ethan. It's me that should be apologising."

"That's cool. Absolutely no need. We're friends, and I give you my guarantee that I'll be there tomorrow. Greg, I have to go now as I have some pressing business to attend to that hopefully will be complete before tomorrow. I'll see you at about eight. Hope you'll have some breakfast ready?"

"That's early for me, but okay the deal's on. Cheers!"

I contemplated whether or not I should tell Megan. He was coming early and would find it strange to find her there at that time. But the rising Judas in me insisted, and I called her. After a time, she answered, her voice vague and sleepy.

"Hello. Megan Sands."

"Megan. Hi. Greg here! Were you sleeping?"

"No, Greg. Just got home, in fact. It's been a

helluva busy day. You know, I haven't worked for a few days now, and needed to do a lot of catching up. I had clients bitching down my neck the whole day: 'Where's this, what's that, and blah blah blah.' And you?"

"Ethan called." The phone went too quiet. "Megan, are you there?"

"Yes."

"I said Ethan called."

"Yes, I heard. You know every time I think I'm learning to cope with this whole darned thing, I surprise myself." She gave a nervous giggle.

"Is he still going to sit for the portrait?"

"Yeah, he's coming tomorrow morning - for breakfast."

"That's early. I have a client to see. Can you try to keep him there until late afternoon?"

"I'll try, but I doubt he'll stay that long. Something curious that Benedikt said today...."

"Who's Benedikt?"

"Oh, yes. I haven't mentioned him, have I? He's actually the chap who sort of introduced me to Ethan. Hasn't Ethan ever mentioned him?"

"No."

"Well, he said today that he and Ethan are family, and that they stay together. I'm surprised you don't know him."

"I've never heard of him. Sounds a bit odd. Did he say anything else?"

"No. Megan, I know Benedikt, and his brother Romando. They're definitely brothers - and if I think about it, there is something about them that Ethan also has. You know, their ways and expressions, if you can see what I mean."

"I still think there's something strange here, Greg. Ethan has never mentioned anyone except his mother, and his brother Andrew who is overseas. His father has been dead for a few years now. He never had any family whatsoever visiting, or interested in him, before this 'Benedikt' person."

"Look, I don't know. Anyway maybe you can ask him if you see him tomorrow."

†

And so I spent another night alone, longing for no company except for Ethan's - or maybe Megan's. I looked forward to the following day, and the time I would be spending with him.

CHAPTER 19

Caeron's tale

Caeron

On the night that I found Ethan sitting in the library, engrossed by the fire, I had felt the wonder of him and recognised the metamorphoses that I had not yet personally had experience of. I had communicated with both Kalin and Hadrian earlier in the day, all three of us together, and so had foreknowledge of what to expect.

As I stood absorbing his very being from the doorway, I understood their awe and knew that I too would give myself to him willingly. Because Kalin had always been our unacknowledged leader due to his age and wisdom, never before had any one of us seen any other as leader. Both Kalin and Hadrian had recognised it and expected that I would too. We were not sure of David, Benedikt, or Romando, and felt it too soon to communicate our thoughts.

When Ethan had mentioned Thalem's name, I had immediately communicated my thoughts to both Kalin and Hadrian. Yes, it was true; the coming of Thalem had made it evident. We had waited hundreds of years for the sign that we kept sacred in our memories - the memory that Ethan, in his youth and innocence, had not yet acknowledged. It had obviously fallen to me to assist in reawakening it for him. He had sought me out, and I was humbled by his need.

As is our way, we exchanged blood, and in our symbiosis I permitted his seeding. Whilst we ambled in and out of euphoria, the memory of Thalem took strength, and soon we were enveloped by the remembrance as once again we ran with Thalem.

†

In an early epoch, when the ages were still dark...

The C'raether, Kalin, had remained still while his pursuers with their horses and hounds stamped around his spring-fed sink hole. Here, he had submerged and started the meditation whilst he waited for them to pass on.

After a while, all became still as Kalin's pursuers left. But so he remained in rest, his lips turning blue not only from the cold, but from the lack of oxygen. All that moved were the masked eyes that fluttered weakly in the dark murk.

The wolf watched from cover of the reed bed. He saw the humans, many with wolf-skins about them that stank of cadaverous decay. Upon their tamed beasts and calling to their hounds, they went about their business of hunting the C'raether. He watched with his diamond-shaped head and yellow eyes; his scent masked by the plains mud in which he had rolled. His fur, now drying, stood out from his body in caked spikes, lending to him an unreal quality. And unreal he was, this mythological beast, for he was Thalem, the messenger. His calling had come from Cernunnos, the God of Beasts.

Thalem waited patiently until the air was clean of the perverseness of those that had passed. He gave a final sniff and padded to the edge of the sink hole where the C'raether had entered. His sharp eyes searched for the place where the submersion had taken place.

Stepping into the water, he swam strongly to where the man of his calling lay immersed. As he reached the place, he became aware that the faint thought patterns of his new Master were getting weaker. In haste, he dove like an otter, his eyes immediately falling on the still C'raether.

Thalem was large and strong. He took into his mouth the arm of the brother, gently so as not to harm, but firmly enough not to lose his hold. With strong strokes of his hind legs, he pushed against the muddy silt of the sink hole and started dragging the man to shallower waters. The C'raether's arm lifted and encircled the wolf's neck as he placed both his trust and life into the jaws of his saviour.

The wolf found some purchase for his limbs and managed to drag his burden from the arms of death. The C'raether gulped cold air into his imploring lungs, after vomiting out the water that he had knowingly drunk to help stop their aching.

Slowly, warmth crept back into his cold nimbus of being, and the failing heart began a slow weak tapping in his chest. Thalem's rough but welcome tongue licked continuously at his body bringing the cold blue flesh back to life.

All the while, the C'raether's hand continued to clutch at the spiky fur in fear that he would find it but a dying dream.

As night came, and with it winds to chill the marrow, Thalem lent to the brother his warmth, and kept constant vigil. At times he would lift his muzzle to the moon to howl out his purpose.

As the moon faded to welcome the sun now casting its rays above the horizon, Thalem scanned the face of the C'raether to establish whether he would awaken. The eyes were fluttering, and the man was whispering in his sleep. There would be time before he awoke. Thalem lifted his stiff body from its place next to his new Master, stretched, yawned, and padded off into the trees to hunt. He knew his Master's need would be for human blood, but this was not the prey he was accustomed to hunting.

†

The forest was a bunched knot of closely growing oak and beech trees, so ancient that they alone, like the brothers, could tell of the passing of the aeons. It lay nestled in a small valley at the foot of the hills and provided the first cover at the edge of the plains. It was into these trees that Thalem loped in search of prey.

It was the first morning of the seventh day of the seventh month of the seventh year - a day of religious awe and celebration for the human inhabitants of this small forest that lay at the foothills of the Risjnak mountains. They awoke early to begin their preparation for the sacrifice and feast that would ensue this day. In their secularity, they spoke little as each pondered, in awe, their God and his seven cherubim that roamed freely and took from their kind without malice or greed.

Theirs was a simple life that revolved around

the seasons and the beasts that inhabited the forest with them. Their God was the one of beasts, Cernunnos. They were pleased with their God because things had gone much better for them since his choosing.

As was their way, they proceeded in a long pious line to the collection of stones that lay in the very heart of the forest. Stones that had stood in their vigilant ring for longer than any could remember. None knew how they had got there. In the midst of the stones lay the most hallowed one. It formed an altar worthy of praise, in its richness of colour and smoothness to touch. It was to this stone that they made their way, in a chanting snake-line through the forest.

Thalem's consternation grew as he searched for a suitable one to take. None wandered alone in the forest, as they kept to their tight queue. He sat watching them as they shuffled past, crooning together in unison. Soon the last one passed Thalem's secret place, and he followed with hope in his brave heart.

They arrived at their holy place, where all gathered together within the circle of stones. Thalem sat in the shadows at the periphery of the circle of worshippers, searching intently. Being the beast he was, he understood nothing of the proceedings, but his growing concern for the Master who lay waiting for him increased. He sat with bunched haunches, and in frustration he kneaded the ground with his front paws.

By this time, the sun had risen to its zenith. Still the worshippers chanted and flayed themselves.

†

The C'raether woke and looked about. He was weakening fast in his need for succour. The wolf creature had left - he did not know when. His heart was growing weaker, and his blood flow barely reached his numbed limbs. Even though the sun was well risen and was warming the day, he grew colder. Weakly, he rose to an elbow.

He knew that soon his time would come, and he did not know how this could be happening to one of his kind. He thought of the other six brothers who must be searching for him. Using the last vestiges of energy he possessed, he closed his eyes and concentrated on the ethers about him, projecting both his thought forms and aural pattern for any near that would understand.

†

Thalem pricked his ears as he responded to his Master's mind-search. Without a backward glance, he left the humans to their strange ministrations and ran back through the forest to the call. He arrived at the place where he had left the Master, his tail tucked between his quarters in guilt for not having procured the sustenance the Master needed.

The C'raether lay in the coldness and loneliness of death's stare. The wolf crawled the last couple of feet towards him, whining all the while as he pulled himself slowly forward with his front paws, ears now lying flat on his head in misery.

Thalem understood death's call. He stretched his neck forward to the C'raether. The C'raether lifted his head as the wolf leant forward to lick his forehead and, with a weak arm, pulled the wolf in closer.

"I am weakening, and need your invitation, Thalem. Is this what is meant to be? I know not, in my delirium. We have never taken from your kind before."

"Master. I have tried to procure a kill for you but think that Cernunnos meant otherwise. His calling was for me to be here for you, as he predestined your need."

The C'raether responded, "My human body can no longer harbour this soul. Will you share, and perhaps there will still be respite?"

Thalem responded with a howl of welcome,

all thought form vanishing for the moment.

"I thank you, Thalem," whispered the C'raether, as he took the wolf about the neck. He bit through the thick coat, and the wolf shuddered in ecstasy. The C'raether's bite was weak, and he took time to gnaw through the beast's thick pelt. The blood spurted from the severed artery in the wolf's neck. The C'raether died as he took his last gulp.

The wolf lay still, waiting, blood still seeping from his neck. He was unsure for what he waited, and was confused that, with his offering, the Master had died anyway. Instinctively, and with an agonised whine of comprehension and lost time, he turned his head to the still warm body. With lips lifted from his teeth, he bit into the exposed abdomen, and took the spirit of the C'raether into himself.

The C'raether and beast had now shared each other's blood, and destiny was being fulfilled. Thalem's body stiffened as the wandering soul of the C'raether returned and entered. The wolf began to wag his tail wildly in understanding and glee. And so they were the two of them, co-inhabitants of Thalem's strong body. The severed artery healed almost immediately.

†

By the time they again reached the stones in

the centre of the forest, the youth had climbed upon the central stone. He stood naked, chest marked with a cross of red, screaming out his need to be taken. Those about him lay prostrate on the floor, awaiting the acceptance from the gods of their sacrifice. The youth was now an elated being, enthralled by his personal offering, afraid that it would not be accepted. It would be a disgrace to his clan.

They watched from the cover of the last standing stone, both together as one, Thalem and the C'raether. The golden body of the youth beckoned, and their blood lust became so intense that they could not withstand its need. Without fear or misgiving, they walked forward between the prostrators. Untouched, they reached the altar.

The worshippers gasped in pleasure as the wolf jumped upon the altar. The golden youth fell to his knees and thanked the gods for their mercy as the two ripped his throat open and together drank his blood and ate his flesh. He died in a state of complete happiness and fulfilment.

The fusion was now complete as, together and as one, they fed.

Strength flowed, and they were ready for the journey that would return them to the brothers, where they could receive help to retrieve the body that still lay by the waters. A journey that must be made immediately, before the body began its putrefaction.

Thalem and the C'raether returned to the body to pay their farewell, and to drag it into an icy pool to retard the decay. They placed about it a veil of protection and went on their way.

†

The body of the wolf provided the C'raether with a powerful and fit medium for the return. By nightfall of the next day they had almost reached the abode of the brothers. The C'raether had all returned safely and knew that the seventh was on his way to re-join them. Already, the thought forms had grown strong as they communicated over the distance. At the same time they perceived the primitive thought patterns of the beast that ran with him. Not knowing what to expect, they waited.

Thalem trotted into their camp, and they jumped up in surprise at the form in which their brother had returned. They were ready to accompany him.

†

For the rest of the next day and that night, they ran without stopping. They found the body where it had been hidden in the glacial pool. They were surprised to find that there had been no decay whatsoever. Never had they experienced death of one of their own kind and had expected the decay that they usually found in the cadavers belonging to their fellow creatures. But theirs was an immortal nature, and the body had remained in a suspended state, awaiting the return of the soul and for the combined healing power of the seven.

Together they formed a circle about the head of the body. Each reached forward and placed a finger, and the wolf a paw, upon the cold lifeless forehead. Soon the ethers about them hummed, and the life spirit flowed back into the body down the limb and through the paw of Thalem, the wolf. The C'raether who had co-inhabited with the wolf returned to his now warm body and awakened to life as it was before. This was Kalin.

In appreciation, the C'raether hunted for Thalem and brought before him a kill of the most succulent kind. Their gift accepted; the wolf ate in friendship.

Thalem was pleased with the awakening and re-seeding of the brother. His task complete, he bid them a thought form farewell, which they interpreted as: "Goodbye, C'raether. It has been my pleasure to have run with you. I go now, but in my going, know that we will meet again. Our meeting will be in dire circumstances and will hearken the recognition of He who will be acknowledged - the one that will be the strength of all, and he who will take upon himself, in suffering, the misdemeanours of your kind. Until then, I leave you with love in my heart."

He left them as the wolf he was, never to remember that he had once been Thalem. They never saw him again, but it was told between them, and in the lore of their kind that they carried in their minds, that he would come again as he had promised. It was told that when he came, it would be in obeisance to the Master that they would then have among them. They were to prepare and remain strong for his coming."

†

Here, Caeron had ended the memory tale, which he had shared with Ethan. Together, they acknowledged the return of Thalem, and the portent it carried. Caeron fell to his knees before Ethan in recognition.

CHAPTER 20

Desertion

Anne Westwood sat at the desk that had been her late husband's. She tapped her pen as she read through the report. Although she had kept the business together over the past years since Dirk's death, her heart wasn't in it.

Fortunately, the senior management of the company were good people who had been with the firm since Dirk's days. All she really had to do was confirm the decisions they made. She completed reading the last page of the report, flicked back to the first and signed her name across the bottom of the covering letter.

She spun her chair around to get a better view from the window. Swallows swooped past the two-storey building. How she longed for their freedom. It was a huge responsibility keeping the business going. She'd been so lonely since Dirk had passed, and of course since the boys had left home.

Still she had not heard from Ethan, and after the visit from the police a few weeks back she'd found herself worrying more about him than she usually would.

Anne couldn't understand why Ethan had betrayed her so. She had given him everything and more - what else could he want? He had talent, good looks, was intelligent, and had the love and wealth of his family. She wondered what it would take to make him happy. Perhaps if Andrew came home? Ethan hadn't been happy since Andrew left. They'd been so close. Andrew was the only person Ethan had ever allowed into his own personal space.

She tapped a button on the telephone that would connect her to her secretary. "June, could you get Andrew on the line for me please, even if you must call him out of class. It's important."

"Yes, of course, Anne. Is anything wrong? You haven't been sounding like yourself lately?"

"Just a bit worried about Ethan. Otherwise, everything's fine. Get Andrew on the line if you can, sweetie. He may be tied up, so you could leave an urgent message."

Anne disconnected, and June immediately began scrolling through the contacts on her computer. Anne had been preoccupied lately, June thought, and she was worried about her.

June had started with the company about five years ago, and in that time had met Ethan only once. She'd met Andrew when he had come home on vacation a couple of years ago.

She wondered at Anne's loneliness but said nothing. It appeared to her that Anne's family had abandoned her in her time of need. With a shrug of the shoulders, she picked up the telephone and dialled the number of the university in Paris. As usual, she was informed that Andrew wasn't available. She left a message. She dialled through to Anne. "Anne. He's not available now, but they'll get him to return your call soon. Sorry. Is this okay?"

She could hear Anne sigh on the other side of the phone. "I s'pose it'll have to be okay. Please could you get me a cup of tea – strong with extra sugar? Bring yourself a cup too, June, if you don't mind. I need someone to talk to until he phones."

"Okay, will do" said June.

"Oh, June? Before you get the tea, could you get David Jacobs on the line? He's one of the officers at the police station."

June had the number and dialled.

"Police station" an irritable voice answered.

"Hello. I'm looking for David Jacobs; he's a policeman at your station."

"Hold on!" the unfriendly voice said, then after a while came back on the line. "He's not here right now. I'll put you through to Detective Inspector Courtley."

The connection was made after a few seconds.

"Mick Courtley!" Mick barked into the telephone.

"Oh, hello Detective Courtley. One moment please. I'm connecting you to Anne Westwood." June transferred the call through to Anne and told her it was Detective Inspector Mick Courtley not David Jacobs.

"Detective Inspector Courtley. Good day to you. Anne Westwood here. I recently had a visit from one of your young policemen, David Jacobs. It's about Ethan Westwood, my son."

"Ah, yes. How do you do, Mrs Westwood? Of course I know who you are," Mick said in a congenial tone.

Anne continued. "Officer Jacobs said that Ethan's girlfriend, Megan, has lodged a missing person report on Ethan. I haven't heard from the police again and have been wondering if you've come up with anything. I've neither seen nor heard from Ethan. Quite frankly, since being contacted by Officer Jacobs, I've started to worry."

Mick answered, "I must be honest, Mrs Westwood, I haven't spoken to Dave for a few days, but he did say that someone had confirmed seeing your son. So we're not sure that he is missing at all. Maybe he's just keeping a low profile."

"I really don't think that's good enough, Detective Courtley." She was irritated as she was accustomed to getting results.

"Well Ma'am, it would be taken a lot more seriously if you would lodge a missing person report yourself, you know - you being family, and all. Besides, I think I should talk to Megan again. Maybe she's heard from him, although I doubt it. I'm sure I would have heard from her if she had."

Anne's voice softened. "Detective Courtley, I have never met Ethan's girlfriend. I wonder if you would be so kind as to ask her to telephone me. Maybe we have something in common after all."

"Believe me, Mrs Westwood, she's a girl in a million. Ethan couldn't have chosen better."

"It seems that he's deserted her as well, Detective. He seems to make a habit of deserting the people he loves."

Mick could hear the bitterness in her clipped tone and couldn't help feeling sorry for her. "I'm sure there's more to it than meets the eye Mrs Westwood. I'll speak to David, the officer who is looking into this for me; and Megan Sands. If I have anything further of value I'll call you back. We have your number on file."

"Thanks. I appreciate it. Oh, one more thing, Detective, when David and I spoke, I gave him Ethan's bank account number. You know, he receives a trust from his late father, and gets some money from the company. I took it upon myself to do some checking up, and the bank confirms that he hasn't drawn any money for a while. This concerns me."

"That's strange, Mrs Westwood. Dave didn't mention anything about the bank account, and it's not in the file. In any event, I suppose that's both good and bad news."

"And why is that?"

"Because as you know, Mrs Westwood, your son is a reformed drug addict. If he were drawing money, it would mean that he might have gone back on the dope. He would need the money, don't you agree? On the other hand, it concerns me that he hasn't drawn any money, as he still needs to live. It appears he hasn't got a job."

"Yes, I suppose you're right." Her voice dwindled away, and he could hear her sigh. "But it could also mean that he hasn't been able to draw the money, and that something has indeed happened to him."

"Anyway, Mrs Westwood, before you go getting yourself all worried about nothing, let me speak to Megan and David, and get you an update on the situation. I'll need you to come down to the Station to fill in some forms to officially give us the go-ahead to look for him - nothing too complex, a mere formality. That is, if he's not around."

"Thank you. Oh, and Detective, our family is one of long standing. I would appreciate it if you could keep this discreet and, of course, ensure that Ethan isn't hounded. You know what I mean. He had a drug problem, and we're aware of that. He doesn't need harassment if drugs have become his problem again - he'll need help. Our family has long supported, from a money viewpoint, the local community. We have connections."

"I understand, Mrs Westwood. Believe me, regardless, I will do everything I can to help. You see, Mrs Westwood, Megan Sands and I go back a long way, and that's why I've taken a personal interest in this case."

"You've made your point," she responded. "Thank you, anyway. Let me know if there's any trace of him. Please!" With tears of frustration,

Anne put the telephone down. She had tried to ignore Ethan's drug problem. Personally, she thought that this was what the whole damn thing was about. He was probably on a binge, and too embarrassed for anyone to discover his lapse. She wished Andrew would telephone, as she needed to share her problems and worries with someone equally concerned.

June gave a light tap on the door and entered with the two cups of tea.

"You okay, Anne? Anything I can do?"

"Oh, June!" Anne couldn't control the tears and scratched in her desk drawer for a tissue. "I just don't know. I don't know if I'm overreacting. I'm having terrible guilt feelings, as if I'm the cause of all this. You know Ethan is supposedly missing, don't you?"

"I gathered as much. You're not to blame, Anne, Ethan is a grown man now, and has a mind of his own. I'm sure he's just fine, you'll see."

"Thanks, but I've just got this strange feeling that things are going to get worse - that things can still go terribly wrong. I'm his mother. I know there's something funny going on. Oh, my God." She wiped her eyes with the crumpled tissue as she battled to compose herself.

They both jumped as the telephone rang.

Anne grabbed for it.

"Hello, Mum. What's up?" It was Andrew.

"Andrew! Thank heavens you've called back. It's Ethan!"

"What?" Andrew asked in panic. "What's happened to Ethan?"

"Hold on, Andy. Nothing has happened to him - that we know of. He's just missing, and I'm worried."

"But Mum - he hasn't bothered with us for a few years now. You know that."

"Andrew, this is different. The police have been to see me. It seems that his girlfriend has reported him missing. He isn't drawing the trust money any longer, either."

"Do you think it's 'The Horse', Mum?"

"The what, Andrew?"

"Sorry. Slang. Do you think it's the drugs?"

"I don't know. I have this terrible feeling, Andy, and I'd like you to come home. I think Ethan needs you. In fact we probably both need you."

"Of course I'll be there for you. When?"

"I'll book you on a flight for next week. Is that

too soon?" she asked.

"I'll manage. Will have to sort out a few things, cancel some lectures and make replacement lecturer arrangements first. You've really got me worried too, Mum."

"Believe me, son, I am worried. Anyway, maybe I'll have some further news for you later in the week when I call you with the flight times. I'll arrange for the ticket to be at the airport. And Ands ..."

"Yes?"

"Thanks, love. This means more to me than you can imagine."

"I know, Mum. Love you. Bye."

†

Anne left the office earlier than usual that evening. She arrived home to an empty house. This was once a home that had been filled with the voices of her family. Ethan's never-ending curses as he attempted to play something new on the guitar or the piano; Andrew, who would inevitably be sitting in front of the television with a sketch pencil and paper talking to himself; and Dirk who would be calling for coffee from the study - the coffee that always preceded the heavy drinking.

She switched on the television for company and made her way up the staircase to her bedroom. It was still the same bedroom she had shared with Dirk when he was alive.

Anne peered into the bathroom mirror as she creamed her face. She looked closer at the telltale wrinkles about her eyes. They weren't too bad. She wiped the cream off. With a couple of swipes of her brush through her thick hair, and a kick that sent her shoes flying through the bathroom door and across the bedroom, she meandered back down the staircase to the kitchen.

As usual, the maid had prepared a solitary meal for her earlier and had put it in the warming drawer. She felt sick at the thought of eating it, and instead poured herself a straight gin. Sipping her drink, she wandered back through to the lounge. The television blared its usual rubbish, and she switched it off.

Squatting down beside the cabinet that housed the hi-fi, she selected an old favourite: Nat King Cole. She slipped the compact disc in. He crooned, "Ramblin' Rose, Ramblin' Rose, how I ramble ...." She felt herself relax, and lay back on the floor, one arm over her eyes. She attempted to recall the memories of Dirk. This was his kind of music, old fashioned just like he was. She preferred something more modern, like U2. Instead, another face filled her mind's eye. A smile creased her weary face. And so she fell asleep, to waken in the small hours of the morning, cold and stiff. The sad memories of the previous day were put aside as she looked forward to Andrew coming home the following week.

That morning, as she crept alone into her bed, and fell asleep with that same smile on her face - the beloved face was still etched on her mind, as it had been over the past years; the same enticing memory of his warm and inviting body next to hers. Kalin.

CHAPTER 21

The white mare

Although the thing Ethan wanted to do most was continue his search for Thalem, he had promised Greg that he would go for a sitting. He was sorry now, but he liked Greg and respected his feelings. He had already let him down twice before.

Before leaving the house, he found David in the kitchen eating a bowl of cereal.

"David. Hiya. I see you're ready to take humanity by storm." He smiled and pulled up a chair, sitting facing the rear of the chair with his arms resting on the back.

"Hey, Ethan." David scooped the last of the cereal into his mouth. "Just grabbing a bite," he chortled impishly, "Before going off to work. Real busy day ahead."

"So, what're you doing this evening, then?" asked Ethan.

"On duty. Why?"

"Thought we'd spend the evening together, but if you're on duty …" His voice tapered away.

"You got anything special planned?" David noticed something different in Ethan, and found himself more humbled than usual, so he added, "I s'pose, if you really need it to be me, then I can arrange something."

"It is you who I need, David. We need time together." Ethan walked up to David and touched a finger to his forehead.

David felt a thrill course from the area of the touch to his solar plexus. His loins contracted in arousal. "Me?" he asked feverishly.

"Yup you, brother of mine." A humorous twitch played at the corner of Ethan's mouth. He wiped his hair off his forehead.

"Okay, then, I'll give you a buzz later today - see what I can arrange. What have you got planned today?"

"Promised Greg I'd go over for a sitting."

"Oh yes, he's doing that painting of you. How's it coming along?"

"I've only been once. Still just a sketch, but he's good. It does look a bit like me."

"Shit man, I wouldn't mind getting my teeth into him."

"Rules, Dave! He's my friend" chided Ethan.

"I know, just a joke. Must go now, or I'll be late. Enjoy *him*," a huge grin, "I mean *it*."

Ethan wanted David - he had not yet become his. He needed him to further the plan that destiny had mapped out for them all. With slitted pupils, he cast his yellow gaze at the retreating form and swallowed the saliva that poured into his mouth.

David turned briefly, as he felt the intensity of Ethan's eyes burn into his back. "Giving me the evil eye, my brother? Or is it the lustful eye? Until later then," he said over his shoulder in pleasure. He shook his head to clear his thoughts and made for the exit.

Ethan laughed out loud, and called after the retreating form, "Sorry, Dave. Didn't mean to startle you. You know we have some unfinished business here, don't you?"

Dave whispered to himself, "Yes, I know," and then, whistling a little tune of joy under his breath, slammed the kitchen door shut and made his way to the garage.

It was now that David began to come to the awareness of Ethan. He thought that the change in Ethan was remarkable. He had been ordered, and would definitely not be working tonight. He reversed the police car out of the garage, his stomach knotting as it screamed in anticipation. "Pig's teeth!" he said out loud and, with a joyful grin, went tyre-screeching down the road.

Ethan remained in the kitchen for a while, concentrating on controlling the blood that threatened to burst from his temples. Adrenaline coursed through his body and left his heart racing and hands shaking. As his eyes returned to a semblance of normality and his heartbeat slowed to its usual rhythm, he popped open a can of tomato juice and poured the liquid down his still convulsing throat. Not as good as blood, but it would suffice.

†

Greg was busy frying eggs when Ethan walked in. He heard the door shut and called, "Hey, Ethan. It is you, isn't it?" His focus was on the egg he was flipping.

"Why? Were you expecting someone else?" Ethan called back.

"Nope. Eggs are nearly done - bacon and toast are ready. We've got a meal here fit for a king." He flipped the egg that remained in the pan.

"Hmmm, smells good." Ethan complimented.

"Oh by the way, Greg, forgot to tell you I don't eat bacon. Okay with you?"

"All the more for me. Got some fresh orange juice in the fridge - help yourself."

Ethan poured the orange juice into a glass and watched as Greg, face flushed, clumsily went about the business of clearing up the kitchen. Paint was still smeared up one arm. He didn't look like he belonged here, and Ethan couldn't help comparing him with the picture he had of Megan doing the same thing just a few months back. She had looked as if she fitted in a kitchen - it was a female thing somehow, or was that chauvinistic? He felt himself longing for a brief glimpse of her and shook his head to clear the thoughts.

Ethan hadn't eaten much since he'd moved in with the brothers. He hadn't needed to and seemed to survive extremely well without it. It was almost as if he were drawing the food he needed from the air around him. Every time he breathed in, he could feel life's bounty filling his guts. After a few forkfuls he started pushing his plate away.

"Not good?" Greg asked disappointed.

"No, just not much of an eater Greg, sorry." He could sense Greg's disappointment and forced himself to pull the plate back and take another forkful.

"You don't have to eat it, you know," said Greg.

"I know that. It's really good though, Greg." He grinned and added, "I'm trying, so stop worrying about it."

They looked at one another across the small table. Both stopped eating as they sensed their parts in the play. Greg broke the short silence. "You know, you make me feel strange at times."

"I know." Ethan sensed that Greg was hiding something but wasn't quite sure what it was. He refrained from entering Greg's mind, leaving him to reveal it in his own time.

Greg forced down the last of his meal, as his hunger had also left him. He couldn't explain the trickle of fear and awe that pervaded his being and put it down to the guilt of knowing that Megan would be coming later. He wondered how he could keep Ethan busy that long. He felt his stomach flip over as he thought about her arriving. Christ!

"Hope you've got nothing planned. Must put in a full day's work, and it'll probably go into the evening," said Greg hopefully.

"Nope. Nothing planned until much later this evening."

"What's on this evening?"

"Nothing that needs discussing. Personal business" Ethan cut off Greg's line of questioning.

"Oh, okay - sorry." He shrugged, pretending nonchalance but emitted hurt.

"Greg, it's okay man, just something I don't want to discuss. You okay?"

"Of course, but how did you know how I really felt?"

"Friends always know, don't they, Gregory?"

"Well, then thank you for your friendship, I suppose."

They smiled at one another and began the day on a note of shared friendship - and soon to be betrayed trust.

†

As the day wore on, and the painting received the beginnings of the oils that would immortalise it, Greg's trepidation grew. He wondered what time Megan would come. Ethan sensed his uneasiness, wondering what was bothering him. Knowing that, if he wanted to, he could enter and find out, but looking forward to the revelation that Greg was keeping hidden.

Nevertheless, the worry did not seem to affect the progress of the painting, as it slowly went through the same metamorphosis that Ethan had. Greg didn't understand how he was doing it, but saw. Ethan knew. Knew the story it would tell as it grew over the days it would take to complete. He understood the plane it had now uncovered, and would understand each plane as it unveiled itself.

The footsteps in the hall, and the knock that followed, came much earlier than Greg had expected. In panic he dropped the brush he was holding, and looked first at the door, and then back at Ethan. Ethan could see by Greg's face and aural emanations that the time of revelation had come. Still he did not enter his thoughts but waited patiently to see what could be upsetting Greg to such a degree. He also felt faintly familiar emanations coming from the area of the door.

In truth, Greg felt like taking a flying leap out of the window into the late afternoon drizzle. He did not want to be here any longer - did not want to see his two friends face each other. He just did not want to, at all.

"Want me to get the door for you, Greg?" Ethan asked calmly.

"No. No, it's okay," he stuttered, "I'll get it." He gulped and felt a bead of sweat drop from under his armpit.

"Okay, then, you get it. Go on then - whoever is there is waiting." Ethan still played the game, knowing full well that something was about to happen. He wondered what Greg was up to.

The visitor knocked again.

Greg walked over to the door and opened it. Megan looked lovely; she had excelled herself for the occasion.

"Oh, hi! Come on in." Greg spoke loudly, with pretended surprise. "I wasn't expecting you. How nice."

"Hey, Greg. Just thought I'd pop in to see how you are." Megan hoped they wouldn't notice that her legs were shaking uncontrollably. She followed Greg into the studio.

Although Ethan was expecting something out of the ordinary, he hadn't expected Megan. For just a moment his heart stopped, whilst he collected himself.

"Ethan, let me introduce you. This is Megan, a friend of mine," babbled Greg.

Megan stood still, staring at Ethan. She lifted her hand feebly in greeting.

"Why introduce me, Greg. You know I

know her." Ethan's voice dripped the venom of betrayal. Why hadn't Greg told him? The betrayal wasn't that they knew each other, wasn't that he didn't want her here - the betrayal was that Greg had abused the trust he had placed in him and used it as a weapon of deceit. He endeavoured to maintain control. "Hello, Megan." he greeted. "You look good."

Ethan did not hold this event against her. They had never traded the trust of friendship, as had he and Greg. He could read the love she transmitted and was suddenly overcome with emotion. In his previous state he couldn't have done this, but in his changed state of awareness he was surprised at her intensity.

"Fuck, I never realised Megs!" he gasped.

"Ethan?" was all she said as she stepped hesitantly towards him.

He reached out, grabbed her hand, and pulled her forward into his arms. They hugged warmly. As he stood stroking the back of her head, her face pressed wetly against his shoulder, his feelings became much like those when he was about to kill. Excitement!

†

Ethan

She filled my senses. Her smell; the beat of

her heart and gush of her blood; her hair; and those deep honey eyes! I had to control the urge to take her then and kill her, or make love to her perhaps? The excitement of the kill was all I really knew or understood now, so the lust was confused with the kill - to take her blood, or to eat of her flesh to sustain mine; or to make love to her body to satisfy mine.

For a time, in my musings, I forgot about Greg. He said nothing, and I imagine he stood there looking at us, at a loss for words. By the time I released her from my embrace and looked his way, I could see the admiration he held for her in his eyes. Even though the love was fresh and innocent, it was there all the same.

I also saw that, for that instant, there was no jealousy. He loved me too, but in a different way. I say this because I abused the friendship and briefly entered his thoughts. Yes, he revelled in me, as I expected. A pity!

His betrayal lay over me, and I harnessed my thoughts of revenge and took a deep breath. I had to take control and, in doing this, I had to push Megan away. I had to escape them both as I felt the other Ethan slip in.

Eyes averted from their gaze, I walked to the bathroom. There I stood for a long while, concentrating on taming the feral eyes that I could see peering out at me from the mirror - wondering what the fuck I had become.

I sat down on the toilet seat and cried. This was the first time I had really cried for years, and I couldn't stop the fucking tears. I'm talking 'sobbing' - not just the leaking of tears. I wondered how those evil eyes could still emit tears, and that they were still crystal clear. I had expected tears of blood - the blood that I had so heedlessly taken over these past months. I was the very old me talking to myself again. Welcome back!

The jacket I was wearing was the same one that I had grabbed the day I had left Megan's flat, and I was sure that I would find, in the inner pocket, the thing I had dreamt about all along. I scratched to the depths - felt, yes it was there, my friend, my pony. Where it had waited and tempted, faithfully.

I recognised the clown in me, the impostor!

Why had I been given the gifts that I now possessed? Why, of a sudden did they all hold me in awe? This is not what I'd wanted; this is what I'd had my whole life – awe! Yes, I finally acknowledged my destructive beauty.

I hated it - the cause of my need for self-destruction, as well as the loneliness. And now those men, the brothers, doing the same fucking thing, putting me somewhere I really didn't belong. I thought I belonged, but I don't. I am not part of them - they have become part of me.

It is now me, placing my seed as usual, in their feeble old brains. How could they have allowed it? How could Kalin have permitted my seeding when it isn't what I'd wanted - deep down inside? And Megan, out there with Greg - was she the one who truly loved me? I didn't know. After all, I was the impostor that my mother created - my nefarious mother, creeping into my bedroom at night in an attempt at seduction; perhaps the reason for my battle to retain my purity of body.

Where was Andrew, my real brother? He loved me for what I was, and not for what I could offer. Oh, where was Andrew, my brother?

As the tears rolled down my cheeks, and the snot oozed from my nose, I slipped the belt from around my waist, looped it around my upper arm and clipped it into the used hole, far down on the belt.

I emptied the inner pocket of its contents, pushed aside the cigarettes, and poured the contents from the small bag I found there into the spoon. A couple of water drops trickled from the tap. My flame licked the bottom of the spoon until the contents sizzled. Part of the contents spilt, falling in a droplet on my shoe. Carefully I drew up my heaven into its cylinder of agony.

I sat down on the closed toilet seat, holding that syringe in my shaking hand, and hating myself the more for it. Just hating myself. Hating this old Ethan. The vein pulsed and beckoned. I lifted the syringe to the light, tapped, and pushed the plunger. A couple of drops oozed from its tip.

With a final moan, I eased the needle into the vein, and plunged back into my old nightmare - the nightmare that I understood; an escape from the hellish nightmare of life as it was, and the horrendous nightmare of life as it had now become - a nightmare of my own making.

†

And there she was waiting for me, my fine mare. Pawing the ground in her haste for me to climb, once again, upon her back! A wind came from nowhere and blew her silky mane upon my face. Taking a handful of it in my shaking hands, I whispered, "Here I am, girl - back again. Let's go!" And with that, she reared, and we were off, once again, the two of us alone in our world of rushing air and mutually beating hearts - my true friend, my beautiful white horse.

I quickly dismounted and gathered myself when - from far away on the other side of our dream - I heard the knock on the bathroom door. Feebly, I fumbled for my gear that lay on the floor about where I had sunk, stuffed it back into the inside pocket, and pulled myself up on the basin.

The eyes that looked at me now, in the mirror above the basin, were tamed. No more oblique yellow pupil. I was grateful for the small mercies life had to offer and splashed cool water over my face.

I noticed how grey the once white towel was; noticed the texture of the towel. I wiped the towel over my face, appreciating the roughness of it, pushed my hair back, lit a cigarette and dreamed my way out of the bathroom, taking with me the horse, controlled by the reins in my hand.

†

They didn't notice that I led the horse out with me. They also didn't notice that this was a different Ethan. As you may have realised by now, there are a few of those Ethans.

There they sat, the two of them, equal looks of concern on their faces. Waiting to see what it was that Ethan was all about. What I was all about. Their looking, prying eyes. Always. Why?

"What?" I said, looking from one to the other.

"You were gone for a while. Everything okay?" Greg asked.

"Yeah, sure, why shouldn't it be?" I retorted, somehow remembering God and how he'd interrogated me once.

I was battling to control my thoughts but noticed in my battle that the horse was pawing the ground to get going again. Though, considering the time we'd had apart, not half as much as I would have expected. My new nature was a controlling and cleansing one, but it was not in full control now - I was.

I floated over to the settee where Megan sat, and dutifully sank down beside her. She sat rigid, hands clasped between her legs and eyes darting from Greg, to me, and back to Greg again. He was my betrayer; she was my destroyer. I had to take control again, and let Ethan, the brother, back in.

I had seen this look on the victim's face when we killed: the 'what the fuck?' look. The horse nudged the back of my neck, seeking attention. Why had I let this happen again? I could feel my hair stand on end as she persisted. Goose bumps broke out on my arms. Without being too obvious, I glanced down at the already healing puncture mark on my arm. Megan followed my gaze. I looked her in the face as I rolled down my sleeve.

"What?" I asked again, in an edgy voice. Words were becoming a bit easier, but at the same time it was becoming difficult to concentrate on the people here with the animal in me demanding attention. I felt my legs begin to shake, so I rested my elbows on them. Riding does this to me. My uncontrollable eyes narrowed in consternation. My C'raether eyes were surfacing, so I hid my face in my hands, elbows still on shaking knees.

I thought I felt the horse nuzzle my neck again, but realised it was Megan's hand as it slowly traced patterns on the exposed part of my neck. Looking up at Greg, I feebly mind-voiced the word "Traitor". He read the thoughts without realising what they were, probably thinking they were his own perceptions, but anyway clearly startled at the accusation.

Even in my confused state of mind, I could still play the mind games so recently learnt from Romando and Benedikt. So, revelling in my returning power, jumbled as it was at this time but also seeing no limits as the horse was revealing, I continued, cold-hearted to the friendship he had to offer.

"Fucking coward!" I mind-hissed.

He started fiddling with the broken material of his chair.

I continued, knowing myself for what I was becoming again. Going with Satan's flow.

"You are treading where angels fear to tread, my foolish and traitorous friend. Do you not know me for the beast I am?" I was no more the clown, I chortled to myself - never to be again. Now I was the beast!

Megan still stroked. I turned my head towards her, careless of masking my eyes for what they had become. She gasped. Smiling, I took her hand in mine and raised it to my lips, keeping an eye fixed on Greg's face. I turned her hand, palm up, and began kissing it, permitting the thick spittle that invaded my mouth to leave traces of slime. I could see my tongue as the snail creeping about her paw.

Greg's eyes barely masked their horror. My sweet Satan, I was enjoying this - the exhilarating pleasure of allowing the evil to run rampant. Not caring to hide what I had become, nor what I had always been. Trying so hard all those years to mask what they had all made of me - The Beast, the beautiful beast. Not beauty and the beast - the beauteous Beast himself. I let out a howl of pleasure.

No sooner had they mind-shrieked their dismay to one another did my pony demand my attention. I forgot about them for a while and became Ethan again. I slid from the place where I had been sitting on the sofa onto the floor. I clasped my arms about my legs and began rocking, backwards and forwards, on my horse. We seemed to stay in one place, my horse and me. She scolded me with her sensitive lips, telling me that I was a 'bad boy' for leaving her. Simultaneously Venus' Morning Star entered the picture, his usual seraphic smile upon his face.

"Come, Ethan. Let us away for a while. Here is a lesson well learnt."

I asked silently, "From whom do you come?"

"Do you not know? You have had the pleasure of his company."

"Oh, from him?"

"Yes."

"I thought he didn't care."

"You thought wrong. Also, I am not the star you think I am!"

"Oh, yes! Then who the fucking hell are you?"

"I am your guardian angel. Don't you think you need one?"

"I know I need one but thought myself forsaken."

"Of course not. You are not forsaken. Why would you think that?"

I was slipping in and out of my different

personas. "I am evil. I am the beast. I have drunk the blood and eaten the flesh of the people you would protect. Where were you then?"

"I was there, but you kept bad company. Their will is strong. You have not yet killed, Ethan. Do not be misled. You have only partaken of their victims. You, you have not yet killed!"

"Eating the flesh, drinking the blood, and desiring the kill is evil unto itself. The thought, surely, is the deed?"

"Not quite. There is still salvation for you. Are you going to take salvation by the hand and atone for your indiscretions, or are you going to take Thalem upon yourself?"

"Thalem? what has he to do with this?"

"He was sent by the one who is making you that which you are not sure you want to be - the one who has put the reins back in your hands. Is this what you want?"

"This is the wrong time to ask me. The horse and I are one right now. She is me, my mare, and I am her. We are one."

"You enjoy oneness, don't you?"

"It is all I have."

"Boing! Wrong."

"Is this a quiz show?"

"It's anything you want it to be."

"Anything?"

"Well yes, there is always 'choice'."

"I have heard that before. Kalin. I think I need Kalin. I am confused."

To my way of thinking this conversation with that part of me had to come to an end. I veiled so that the guardian couldn't enter my thoughts. No time had passed, it seemed. Both Megan and Greg still sat staring at me, petrified as stone. Thalem's ringed circle of stones - Kalin's stones. I needed Kalin to heal me and make me whole again. This was my choice; there was no going back.

"Stop! Talk. Return," I pleaded. "I'm so very sorry," I implored. "I didn't want this. It's something I have no control over. I'm so sorry!"

The spittle crept in oily traces down the side of the painting, from the grinning mouth.

"Shuddup!" I yelled at the painting, pointing as if he was the cause of all this. "Fuck off, you creep!" And then back to them. "I'm sorry, really I am."

†

Greg

Yes, I was shocked. Ethan had always appeared so controlled to me, someone to look up to. Actually, this is what I had been doing; worshipping the ground he walked on.

But here was an unexpected revelation. I couldn't believe the reaction, and I felt more the Judas than ever. At the same time, I was mortally scared. I couldn't recognise certain elements in Ethan's behaviour. It seems that the entire change had come about whilst he had been in the bathroom. It was almost as if he was slipping in and out of himself.

He was sitting still now, the ranting and raving toned down to sobs in his hands. Megan had woken from her apoplectic state, and sat down beside him, also crying. I could see just how much she loved him. Fuck, but they had a chaotic relationship I couldn't understand! I was sure she wasn't aware of what I could see clearly. She was stroking his arm all the time, and saying, "Ethan, Ethan. I'm sorry." He would then sob out "No, I'm sorry." They would then repeat their sorriness to one another. I was merely the astonished outsider.

I got up and went through to the bathroom to see what could have happened there. They didn't notice my departure, so taken up were they in their own individual obsessions. There was nothing untoward in the bathroom and everything looked untouched, as I had left it. I couldn't understand, walked out, and went to the kitchen. Maybe a glass of sherry each would ease whatever it was that was tense. I poured a good measure of the sherry into three mismatched glasses and walked back through to the lounge.

I suppose it was a stupid gesture, but I tried anyway, at loss what to do. "Here, let's drink and try to sort this all out. I must say that I don't know what the hell's going on here." I sat down on the floor as well, cross-legged and facing them, and placed the glasses between us.

Ethan seemed to have calmed down, and now had a dreamy look. The face that had scared me earlier on now seemed angelic and fragile. His head, which was resting on Megan's shoulder, slowly slipped down to rest in her lap. He seemed to fall into a sleep of sorts.

She looked up at me. "You see, Greg? This is what Ethan's all about. It's difficult to understand."

"I can't believe it," I replied, not really knowing what else to say. "Briefly I was scared of him, really scared. Christ, I just don't get him."

"I feel like that too sometimes, but it never

lasts. He does no harm."

"But why is he like this, Megan. Has he always been like this?"

"No, not really. There are times when he goes off into a world of his own, but for a few weeks before he disappeared things were becoming stranger than usual. I didn't know him anymore. Today isn't any worse than a couple of other times that he's 'gone off'."

She lifted Ethan's arm and pushed up the sleeve. No new puncture wounds, only old scars. Wordlessly she looked back up at me with relief in her tear-filled eyes, then continued stroking his face.

"He's an addict," she said. "I think this is the whole problem. He started up again just before he left. Dunno, really."

My heart gave a sick lurch. I couldn't believe this. "Those are old marks, Megan." I wasn't a complete ignoramus.

"He could be spiking anywhere on his body, Greg. He's been through rehab. I met him when he was in hospital recovering from an overdose."

"Well then that explains it, I suppose, but does it make his behaviour forgivable?"

Ethan groaned my name, "Greg?"

"Yes mate, what can I do for you?" I asked, relieved to hear him speak.

He spoke softly through swollen lips, "Greg. Will you get hold of Kalin for me? Things going wrong. He must fetch me. Will you do that for me, Greg? You must get Kalin or Caeron." He fell asleep again.

"Who are Kalin and Caeron?" asked Megan, confused.

"They're two of the guys he's living with."

"Probably the one's feeding him the dope."

"No, I don't think so, Megan. You'd have to meet them to understand that they're not like that."

"But you didn't think Ethan was like that."

"I suppose that's true. But believe me, you would have to meet them. You'll see."

"I'm feeling a bit hurt, Greg. Well a 'bit' is an understatement, I suppose. Why has Ethan asked for this person, or people?"

"Maybe Kalin has been helping him to get through this, or something. I don't know. Again, you would have to meet Kalin to understand just how compelling he is."

"Well then, let's call him, and I can see

for myself. Maybe I can talk to him and start understanding what the hell's going on here."

"Megan, I don't know where they live. I don't even have their phone number. I think they're family of Ethan's, so perhaps you could get the number from Ethan's mother?"

"In the meantime, Greg, maybe he should come home with me. I'm worried. Ethan said some strange things. Really strange!"

"I think it's my fault, Megan. He trusted me, you know. Seems this entire thing has just freaked him out."

"Greg don't start believing that you're to blame. Where it concerns Ethan, everyone believes it's their fault. I always think the same thing. I realise now that Ethan needs help. It's not our fault; it goes deeper than that. He needs professional help, Greg; help we cannot possibly give him."

It seemed that Ethan wasn't as out of it as we thought and had been following our conversation. He slowly sat up, and Megan's hand fell from his shoulder.

"It's neither of your faults," he said, looking from Megan to me, and having become completely rational again. "Greg, I was going to speak to you but now I can't. I know you for what you are. I don't think you chose to play the part that has been written for you, so I suppose I'll have to forgive you."

Well, I didn't know what part I was supposed to be playing - but, anyhow ...

Ethan continued, now speaking to Megan, "Megan, I've hurt you without knowing how much you cared. I apologise. It has never been your fault. I am 'the fault", as you said."

Megan begged, "What's been going on, Ethe?"

"There's nothing to tell, Megs. Nothing at all."

He seemed to know what we both thought but didn't enlighten us. I could hear by his tone that he was again becoming confused.

He turned to me. "Greg, please get Kalin to come for me before I lose my grip here."

"Ethan, I don't know where to find Kalin. You've never given me the telephone number."

"Oh! Ooh, yeah," he said, again confused. He didn't offer the telephone number but got groggily to his feet. "Come, Megan. Please take me home."

"Home? Where's home, Ethan?"

"Home, you know. Our place."

"I thought you didn't live there anymore, Ethe?"

"Could we go anyway? I'm not feeling right. Greg, Kalin knows where Megan lives. If you can find Romando or Benedikt, they'll contact him. Tell them where I am. Please."

I asked, "And, Ethan, do they know about the dope?"

"Yes they do - of course, they know everything. We have no secrets. We're brothers in all."

"Well, I don't know about that, but yes, I'll go down to their shop and ask them to get hold of Kalin for you. And Ethan ..."

"Yeah?"

"I know how you feel about me now. I don't understand it all, but I'm sorry. Megan, if you need me again, I'll be here. Look after yourself. Remember, I care."

She smiled and, putting her arm about Ethan's waist, half walked with him, and half supported him out of the flat. It would be quite a while before I saw Ethan again.

And, from being a happy person before I met them, I felt the weight of depression and loneliness as they left. Like them, I felt on the verge of tears - tears of frustration and confusion. I drank the rest of the sherry.

CHAPTER 22

Bloody landscape

Ethan

Maybe it was better that I had gone home with Megan that day. At least it put a halt to her constant harassing of the police. And I supposed that it would put a stop to their search for me, and of course would soothe David's concern.

The day that I permitted the old Ethan back, rode the horse and went home with Megan, was the day that I had felt it appropriate to seed David. Of course he waited and I never went home, which explains me perfectly. I just keep on letting people down. Oh, well …

It was only the following day that Greg was able to get a message to Romando and Benedikt, and so it was the evening of the following day that Kalin came to fetch me. By that time I could have got back on my own but, the truth be told, I was enjoying myself far too much.

I had finally relaxed and allowed my nature to take control of my longings.

So before I tell you about Kalin, let me tell you about the evening of the day that I went home with Megan. And also, let me tell you that I have, for the first time in my life, learnt what it is to love a woman.

My return to ride the horse was part of my growing process. I think I had to release the barriers of the past, and the only way to do that was to embrace it. The funny thing is that the horse had been so much a part of what had gone wrong in my previous life, that it was the thing that needed reckoning with the most, and that had the most likely influence. You know, they say that once a junkie, always a junkie. It's the same as alcohol or cigarettes, once these substances become part of your life, they inevitably remain part of it, even if it's only the constant vigil one must keep over one's own actions. So anyhow, I had to put that Ethan on the back burner.

Now that I think back, I am sure Kalin had been aware - all the time, as he knew my thoughts - that I would inevitably slip into that other person, and spike again. With the growing power that I was experiencing, I began thinking of myself as being able to cope with any situation - or should I say, being able to control any situation. I suppose I had to prove myself wrong.

Any creature has its limitations, and I had a couple of these creatures to deal with.

I had to decide between living a full and wholesome life with what I had or degenerating back to riding and again become the obsessive and complexed person that I had been. Enough said.

†

Megan drove me back to the flat in her Mini. I barely fitted into the passenger seat, not because I have extra-long legs but because the car was so small. Also, the passenger seat had jammed and was immovable. So I sat all the way back to the flat with legs jarring uncomfortably against the dashboard. This was reality.

I watched her as she drove, glasses perched at the tip of her nose, head held high as she squinted at the road. Her fingers clutched the steering wheel so hard that her knuckles showed white. I could see she was stressed and had to admit to myself that I had been a bastard.

She drove, muttering to herself about the manners of other drivers, grating her gears and generally driving atrociously. She was nervous about me being there, I could tell. I was nervous too - not sure just how much I could tell her, or how much I was permitted to tell her. Also, I wasn't sure of my intentions, but thought that I would probably surprise both of us. And so we arrived at 'the flat'. Sounds like something out of a movie, doesn't it?

We hadn't said much during the drive, but now Megan decided that a long speech was necessary. I watched her delightful mouth.

"Nothing much has changed, you'll see. Your things are still exactly where you left them. I knew you'd come home. Did I tell you; I snapped a string on your guitar? Well, I didn't snap it, it sort of snapped itself. It just 'twanged' when I opened the lid of the case. I was checking if it was okay."

She continued in a voice that sounded, perhaps, as if she was close to tears. "You know, I went to the police. Was so worried that something might have happened to you. Would still like to know what's been going on.

"Isn't it strange that Andrea and I should meet Greg, and that he should know you? That painting is something, isn't it?" And so on and so on.

I wasn't really listening, just watching her intensely; the drug in my system keeping me mellower than I knew I would be if it wasn't there. Even my eyes had returned to normal.

As I mentioned earlier, given the beastly thing

that I had become, I healed quickly. I wondered just how far this healing process would go. It was certainly giving the horse a bit of its own medicine, kick for kick, neutralising the effects and sharpening my brain again.

By the time we arrived, I was sufficiently compos mentis to wrap my arm about her waist, swing her up into my arms, and carry her over the threshold. Rather gallant, I thought at the time. Well, she seemed to like it.

We ambled to the bedroom, hugging each other as if it was our last moment. We sat on the edge of the bed, and this time I made sure that I kissed her gently. She responded with equal gentleness, and her lips moved sensuously against mine. I felt the pupils of my eyes begin to tighten in their orbs, starting the transformation to which I was becoming accustomed.

As you have probably realised by now, I find difficulty discerning between bloodlust and sexual lust. They almost seem like one to me. But it came, the lust, out of all proportion. I must admit that it did occur to me to kill her, but that would have been digging my own grave, so to speak. So instead, I permitted nature to take its course, and soon we were undressed and lying together under the bedclothes.

"Ethan, I'm so glad you're here," she whispered

into my ear.

"I am too. You know, of course, that I've never done this before - made love to a woman."

"Don't talk rubbish." She was grinning against my cheek at my supposed joke. "You don't have to hide anything you've done in the past. I don't care how many women you've had, as long as you're mine now."

She ran her hand up my leg. Oh the pleasure! I carried on anyway, perhaps to prolong the time before we would finally consummate our relationship.

"But I'm serious, Megan. Honestly. I'm even a little afraid that I might do this all wrong. You know there's so much that I have done that, probably, most people haven't. But this - this I haven't done." I traced the curve of her breast with my hand, softly at first.

"I don't believe you. Serious?" She spoke deep into my ear as she nibbled.

"Dead serious. Have I ever tried with you?"

"You did, just that once."

"I had ample opportunity, didn't I?"

"Yes, you did. I suppose it's obvious how much I've always wanted you."

"I knew. I'm sorry that the only time I responded I ended up hurting you. Fucking up, as usual."

"Shh, that's over now. We can take it from here."

"Megan, I've wanted you more than I've ever wanted a woman before." We were both breathing hard.

"Then why?" she gasped, as my caresses became rougher.

"At first, I suppose, it was a battle with my own confused ideas of morality. I've just had this thing in my mind that has always forbidden it. A sort of pre-conditioning that I can't explain. I have also been afraid that allowing myself to become close to anyone - and how much closer could one get? - that I'd be opening myself up to be hurt. I don't have any close relationships, Megan. I feel more comfortable without them. I've always desired them, though - wished for them, fantasised about them, but never been able to reach out and have them. They've proved so illusive, especially as I never trust. Maybe it's because I know how untrustworthy I am, that I expect other people to be the same. The truth is, I don't know. I've just been so afraid." I think I used up all the breath I had left.

"And now, are you going to be able to go

through with this, or leave me dangling again?"

"Nothing could stop me now. I'm veritably wallowing in lust and love."

I made love to her. It was wonderful, and totally carnal. That is what I enjoyed most, the carnality.

Afterwards, the sexual arousal brought forth in me an intense hungering for what I had become accustomed to - the sweet ambrosial blood and flesh of the kill. The feeling was almost the same as desiring a cigarette or dessert after a meal to round it off. It needed rounding off. Instead, I reached for the cigarettes that were again becoming part of my life. Oh wait - they were part of my old life. Damn it!

†

After I had gone through the change, that night in my chamber, I had also come to the realisation that there was nothing to stop me doing anything I wanted to. Only myself. As far as I was concerned, I had taken unto myself the epitome of evil. I really didn't believe I could do anything worse than what I had already done.

But this said, I suppose I could still be saved, as the voices had said. I might have assisted and tempted and enticed the victims of our desires, but I had not killed. Eaten and enjoyed, yes I had, in blissful appreciation.

They say that if the thought has been formulated, the deed might as well have been done. So this is how I looked at it. In thought, I had killed, and joyfully so.

Of course, I intended to go right ahead and permit the beast in me to run rampant. You remember that earlier on I admitted to being the Beast? No more the clown. I felt better about relinquishing my clown outfit, as it was no longer comfortable. The beast outfit imposed no restrictions, and isn't that the absolute state of nature?

You might also be wondering how it is that I have become 'chattier'. Before, I was still suffering from my disillusions. But now, with all the discoveries that are making me more a man - or should I say, more the Beast - I don't feel quite so inhibited.

Since then, I have also made love. Remember, I hadn't done this before, and felt less for it. Now, I feel more. I am beginning to feel fulfilled, as I fight nothing. I can even mount up and ride with very little repercussion to myself, as an individual. All I need is to make the switch to that Ethan. I can make love to a woman, without repercussion. I can kill without repercussion. I can even smoke my cigarettes and then leave them for a week, without repercussion. I can love a man and share his soul, without repercussion.

Hell, I could be any fucking thing I wanted to be. I can say any fucking thing I want to. After all, I am without morality, especially now. I can be all those Ethans put together. So I snigger to myself in satisfaction.

For once, I allow my thoughts and desires to run amok. I imagine killing Megan but think that her discovery is not worth risking. I even imagine the pleasure it would give me to take Kalin's soul upon myself, but then wonder if he has a soul of his own - or if I have one? Has Venus' Morning Star taken them unto himself? I am sure this is just what he has done. Really, when all is said and done, he is obviously the 'brother supreme': the star that is. So that makes us eight, doesn't it? With pleasure, I say I am glad of it. He is part of me, after all.

I seem to be getting a bit carried away here. Let us go back a bit to our lovemaking. Gentle? No! It is not within me to be gentle anymore. I ravished her physically and raped her mentally. In her love, she invited with abandon and ignorance of what I was - which makes me feel all the better.

You know this beauty thing of mine? Well, you haven't seen me. I am just as beautiful as they say, and I've always hated myself for it.

You might ask "Why?" The answer is because it's like wearing a perpetual mask. The mask that hides the multiple 'people' within. Judged by that mask, and loved for that mask - can you see what I'm saying? And deep down inside you're just a little lonely person. No, I'm not feeling sorry for myself.

I used to. Today I have stopped it.

Megan loves me for what I am. She said it. She proved it as she looked into my immoral, obscene face. She saw, and I allowed it. She knew I took her without compassion, again tasted the blood in her mouth, but she never voiced displeasure. Her arms tightened about me, and she whispered in a bloody gurgle, right into my ear, "Ethan, my demon incarnate. I love you."

Can you believe it? I think she does love me, and now I can truly love myself. If I can be anything with her and still be acceptable, even loved - blessed Satan, 'loved!' - then fuck me! I can be anything within myself, and still love.

Our lovemaking took almost the entire night, and I found myself insatiable. I awoke the following morning to find that we were still wrapped in one another's entwined limbs. Her head was resting on my chest, and her face was turned up to mine. The bruised lips added to her loveliness.

I bent my head down and, even though she still slept, kissed her full on the lips, forcing her mouth open. Her arms tightened about me, and she whimpered her pleasure. We repeated the events of the night before, much quicker this time and certainly with more urgency. I found her to be as demanding as I.

†

It was later that I remembered David. In my gratification, I had completely forgotten about him.

"Megs, I have to make a call. A friend of mine was expecting me last night." I disengaged myself from her legs.

"A girl friend?" she asked, her voice still husky with just a little edge of worry.

I laughed. "No. You don't have to worry about that. Never has been, and never will be." I said this in all sincerity.

"That makes me happy. Go, then - go and phone your friend. Who is he, Ethan?" She had turned onto her stomach next to me, tracing the line of my lips with a finger.

"One of the guys I live with. David."

"We must speak about this when you're through calling him. I'll make some tea in the meantime."

She rose naked from the bed, and without any shame walked through to the kitchen. She did not have a perfect body, but to me it was the best I had yet seen. Pulling my eyes away, I grabbed for my clothes and searched the pockets for my mobile to call David. He wouldn't be at home, so I Googled the police station's number. I couldn't get through.

"Megan!" I called through to her. "Do you have a number for the West End Central police station? One that gets you straight through to them. I'm battling. Perhaps you have one of those emergency numbers or something? Didn't you once tell me you have a mate who works there?"

"What do you want the police station's number for?" she called back.

"My friend works there. He's a police officer."

"What did you say your friend's name is?"

"David."

"I know him, Ethan. The number is jotted down on the front of my contacts book on the bedside table. In purple pencil. I usually get through on that number."

†

Megan

I stood in the kitchen making the tea and purring with satisfaction. What more could I want out of life if I had Ethan. Of course, I had realised by then that Ethan was different from anyone else. I think I even acknowledged that he wasn't quite human - well you know what I mean, human like everyone else. I had seen it in his eyes, but I wasn't scared. I loved him no less.

His lovemaking had made up in passion for what it lacked in sensitivity. By now, acceptance of his behaviour had become part of my life. Rather this than nothing.

The kettle steamed and hummed in tune to my happiness - which was suddenly shattered as a thought formulated itself. He had said 'David'. David was the cop who Mick had sent around; the one who was investigating the case. I could feel my heart doing queer flutterings in my chest.

David had never admitted knowing Ethan; so why had he been investigating Ethan's disappearance if he'd known where he was all along. Why the farce? What the hell? I thought it best not to mention this to Ethan, but I would call Mick later to see what was going on. Were they, Mick, and David, having me for the fool? Ethan had said that David was one of the guys he lived with.

Then I relaxed, chatting to myself. *God, I'm such a fool! There are probably a hundred Davids that work at that police station. After all, it's a common name.* With that I felt much better and carried the tea through to the bedroom.

Ethan had grown colder now that he had had enough of me. Or that's how it felt. He still cared, I knew that, but was just withdrawing again. I was used to it. Even though I had wanted him to tell me what was happening, I didn't expect it when he suddenly broke his silent stare out the window.

"Megan, there are things you should know about me. I think it would be only fair, given the new nature of our relationship. I might be untrustworthy, but generally I try to be truthful. The truth is I don't know where to start and wonder if you'll understand. I'm also afraid that if you knew more about me - that would be it! Perhaps you wouldn't want to know me anymore, and suddenly that means more to me than you can imagine. Because I am becoming familiar now with what I am, it's easier for me to accept it for what it is. But I don't think you could accept it."

"Why don't you try me, Ethan? There's a lot I know that you don't even realise I know. Have I ever turned my back on you? And we've been through it all! What makes you think that I would now?"

"You see, Megs; it's a whole perception thing. What I perceive to be acceptable might be totally objectionable to you."

"Again, try me!"

"You want it bluntly?"

"Start off by giving it to me bluntly. You can always sugar coat it afterwards."

"You sure you want this? Sure you'll still be there for me?"

"Absolutely sure. I love you."

"Do you know what love is?"

"I think more than you do."

"You're probably right. I've only discovered love recently."

"You mean …?"

"Kalin. The rest of my friends. Caeron. You!"

"I'd like to meet them, if they're so worthy of your newly discovered love."

"I'd like you to meet them. They're more than I could ever put into words."

"So special?"

"More."

"Are they part of it?"

"Very much so. They are it."

"Then what is it? Who are they?"

"I think, perhaps, it would make more sense if you were to meet Kalin first. Maybe he can explain better than I can."

"Ethan, you're hedging again. Just tell me."

He shook a cigarette out of the packet, lit it and squinted at me through the rising smoke. He'd found a whole packet of cigarettes he'd left behind. He took his time, and like old, tried to blow a smoke ring through a smoke ring. He was thinking how to do this, I could see that. He broke the silence. "Megan. There is a way I can tell you so that you'll understand and experience. I have the ability to enter your mind, to plant a mental seed. Do you love me enough to permit me?"

"Well, I have been to a hypnotist before, and it was a complete failure. Seems I can't be hypnotised," she said. "But yes. I'll say it again. I love you! I'm happy to go along with it. What does it mean?"

As Ethan spoke, I realised that his diction was changing, becoming almost - for lack of a better word - 'archaic'. "It means that I am not what I appear to be. There are layers of me if that makes sense. Megan, I am also not wholly human. I have abilities not yet discovered by others. They are there to be discovered, it's just too early. But wait, I'm confusing you. Let me enter your mind, and you can share with me the things I am trying to tell you."

"Ethan, I am trying very hard to accept what you're saying. I'm trying to keep an open mind. So okay, I'll play along for now. The questions can wait. How will you do it? Can I really trust you?"

"Trust me? Well, that's your choice. The only promise I can make is that 'we' won't hurt you."

"Do you mean physically or mentally?" She wondered about the 'we'.

Ethan answered. "Physically. Only you can control your own mental hurt - that's beyond my power or control."

"How does it work?"

"Very simple, really. Come here!"

He opened his arms, and I walked into them with trust. His hug was warm and kind, even though his face had become a mask of concentration. He laid his forehead against mine, eyes never wavering as they stared, until the vertigo had me in its thrall. Never before had I felt such power in any person, or such awe springing from within myself. I wondered how he could possibly love someone as simple and ordinary as me. And then his mind started its bombardment.

I felt like I was spinning through the mists of make-believe, as the phantoms of his psyche revealed themselves in all their horror. I thought I might go mad as I read the stories they had to tell. They also made it known that this was but the beginning of his connection with hell. I wondered what it would do to my soul, should I allow these thoughts to ingrain themselves within my mind.

Through the bloody landscape of his madness, I followed, shrieking as each new horror unfolded itself before me.

Here I stop, as to relate what one sees in another's mind is to go mad oneself. I witnessed for the first time and probably the last, pure unadulterated layers of hysteria. The very discord disclaimed by the powers of good, but innocent in the very ignorance of its own character.

I also met the other parts of him that made up the seven. They were all one, just as he had said. Now I could understand the message, barely scraping the surface, attempting its revelation through the canvas of Greg's painting.

I screamed and pushed Ethan away from me. He blinked in surprise. He had been right, of course; he was accustomed to what horrified me. Never could two minds be so dissimilar in their make-up.

"For Christ's sake, Ethan. Get away from me!" I screamed, backing frantically away from him. "Get out of here! Oh, Jesus help me, help me," I sobbed, not heeding the hurt that Ethan took no pains to hide.

He turned without a word and left the flat.

He left me with the horror and the malice; he left me with the decay that pervaded his being. I could not erase the pictures from my mind. The blood: the murder and the evil companions he kept. Mostly, he left me with a fear so intense that I could not move from where I stood.

†

Ethan

I walked slowly down the stairs, noticing their cracks and blemishes and the small dust particles that had settled in the corners; the tufts of the sum total of life; wisps of nothing, waiting in corners to be swept away, or perhaps, never noticed or ever having the pleasure of the motion of being swept away. I really couldn't feel anything at that point in time.

Of course, Kalin was waiting in the limousine, parked just outside. I should have known he would be there. He certainly was the predator. Well, here came the prey, down the dusty stairs, devoid of emotion. It was Kalin who had planted the visions in my mind - those that had horrified that woman up there. So what! I am saying that to apportion blame is pointless, because ultimately all blame is mutual. Really, it's as it should be. When all is said and done, does anything really matter?

I climbed in beside him but had no desire to meet his gaze. I veiled my mind and, as the car pulled away from the curb, looked out at humanity as it teemed about its usual business.

The day had passed quickly, and it was already dusk. The green and red traffic lights on each corner flashed their commands at the obeyers. I suddenly felt so very sorry for Mother Earth as she perched in the heavens like a ripe fruit, teeming with the rubbish of her creation. These very traffic lights pricked into her bountiful flesh like toothpicks, and perched above the toothpicks, the green and red onions.

So really, this teeming mass of humanity was being 'godded' by a bunch of toothpicks headed by onions. Strange to think of it this way, isn't it? As one onion made way for another, so the disciples stopped, and went, and stopped and went - quite pointless, really. All in their usual little queues, following blindly, one behind the other.

The spitefulness of it all as, just now and then, they jump their place, and break their necks to get before the other. These things really make an impression on me because they're so pointless. Here they have this wonderful and powerful universe about them, ready to be gloried in, and they plod along their self-created lanes of habit.

I looked at Kalin.

"It is best this way," he said sadly.

"Best for who, Kalin?"

"Us. We."

"And me?"

"You are us; don't you see? We are you."

"We are not individual?"

"No, of course not."

"Yeah, I see. You're saying that we're just like those fools out there. All part of one foolishness."

"If you'd like to put it that way - but at least we're aware of our foolishness, and secure in it."

"That would depend on whether security is the desire."

"Ethan, my lamb. What is your desire when you have been given everything?"

"Everything? Everything I've never wanted."

"Then, to rephrase: what is it that you want?"

"I want the freedom to be whatever I choose to be."

"But being as you are, you have that choice, surely."

"You have just taken it away from me again."

"To use your words to Megan, it's a matter of perception."

"So, Kalin, you were with us?"

"We are always together. At any time you could be with us too."

"Surely an invasion of privacy?"

"What does it matter?"

"You're right, of course. What the fuck does it matter? Nothing really matters, does it?"

"No, not really. That is why we have the ritual to life that we have. To make things matter."

"And, to what end?" Ethan snapped back.

"Ethan, when I can answer that I will be the perfect being."

"So you're admitting that you're not the perfect being?"

"Of course. I've never claimed to be."

"Then what right do you have to meddle like a god? Surely gods are perfect beings."

"I think that it's the very imperfections in gods that make them approachable. The Christian God forsook his son. I will not make that mistake."

"Am I your son?"

"It is because of me that you will survive to become what destiny has planned."

"But Kalin, you cannot know what destiny has planned for any of us."

"It's in the memories, Ethan. After you ran with Thalem in Caeron's thoughts, you must have realised that there are greater things for you than that woman."

"She is great in her simplicity and love."

"What love, Ethan, my lamb? Did she not say that she would love you for better or for worse?

Where is that love now? The chaos of our minds drove her away. How loving is this? A true lover would have rejected the opportunity of the weakness perceived."

"Not the chaos of our minds, Kalin. It was the chaos of your mind."

"Our mind."

"Whatever."

"I am still here, am I not?"

"Still here after my indiscretions, I suppose."

"Yes."

"Maybe I don't want you here."

"Oh yes, you do, because what would you be without me?"

I turned again to look out of the window at the streetlights. The futility of everything was blatant.

CHAPTER 23

Checkmate

Caeron moved his queen decisively, then took a sip of his coffee. The waitress hovered nearby with a refill jug.

"Check." he said quietly, and then looked up at Hadrian.

"What the ...? I didn't see that." Hadrian's cheeks were flushed, and he continuously licked his lips. "Caeron, you always do this to me. I'll get out of this, don't you worry."

"Hadrian, you've got no chance and might as well give up. We've been playing this game for two days now, with you running around the board. I'm tired of it. Come, admit defeat. Tomorrow we can start another."

"But I'm far from finished."

"You're just bluffing. You have two more moves to make and you'll be checkmated. Save yourself the humiliation."

"What is that? I never feel it. Humiliation!" Hadrian puffed.

"I know." Caeron shook his head in mock wisdom. "Anyway, let's pack it in. I'm hungry. If you really are adamant about finishing this, let's do it tomorrow, okay?"

"Sure, if that's what you want. I'm hungry too. Didn't David say he was meeting us here?"

"He was going to, but he's working tonight. Was supposed to work last night but spent the whole night waiting for Ethan - who never came. Did you not receive his thoughts? He was disappointed."

"I was doing my own thing last night; wasn't really tuned in. I can understand, though, why he waited. After all, we've had our turn, I suppose. Truly Caeron, what do you think?"

"About what?"

"Now who's playing a game? You know what I mean."

"Hadrian, look again at the memories. It is what is destined. Thalem is among us once again, there is no doubt about that. I am sure Ethan will find him. Ethan's part in our little passion play is undoubted. We must let things take their course. Wait and see what happens."

"Caeron, I was the first after Kalin to be seeded by Ethan. I took his seed gladly, but I can tell you now, he will sow a seed of discontent among us and there will be trouble. I know this."

"I don't doubt your foresight, Hadrian, but as I said before, we will just have to wait for the karma to manifest itself in its own time and way. I am prepared to wait, and that is all you can do. You love Ethan as much as we do, don't you?"

Caeron needn't have asked. He had heard the change in the timbre of Hadrian's voice when he had spoken about Ethan and had seen the excited projection of aural emanations at the mention of Ethan's name. Yes, he loved Ethan as much as they all did.

"True, I love him, but that hasn't stopped me from feeling uneasy about something."

"I feel it too. Let's forget it for now - you were just saying that you were also hungry. It is my turn to hunt tomorrow. Should we make it tonight, or wait? There is more pleasure in waiting, don't you think?"

"No, I don't enjoy waiting. For me there is more pleasure in killing. All the same, if you would like to wait until tomorrow, then I must abide by your wish. After all, my time isn't yet for two weeks. Can I accompany you tomorrow?"

"Why Hadrian, need you ask? By so saying I had offered, hadn't I?"

"I knew, of course. I was just being polite."

"The truth is, Hadrian, I need some exciting companionship, and I enjoy hunting with you when in such a mood."

"And Caeron, what mood is that?"

"A mood that only you would understand." He looked into Hadrian's eyes and touched his finger to Hadrian's forehead. Hadrian responded immediately by grabbing his hand and pulling it towards his mouth. He kissed each finger in turn and, like the other, didn't take his eyes from Caeron's face. They locked gazes and thoughts in mutual appreciation and camaraderie.

The spell was broken when the waitress, wide-eyed, approached closer with her jug of coffee. She thought that they were as gay as they came, fawning all over one another like that. Staring into each other's eyes every so often. They had been coming here for two weeks now, to play their chess games. It always ended in the same way, with the two of them mooning over one another. Inevitably, they would leave holding hands and smiling happily.

She couldn't help thinking it a waste. They

were really two amazingly handsome men. There were two others that had joined them six evenings ago, whom she would never have thought were two separate individuals, but merely a trick of the eye, as they were so alike.

The twins were also good looking, but in a much darker way than the two sitting here now. They had come in laughing and joking, flushed with happiness. She was sure that it was a bloodstain that was smeared down the lapel of the one's jacket. She had peeked at them from under her frizz of black hair, just to see what the others would say about the blood. Well, it must have been all right, because no one else seemed to notice.

All four had then taken hands as they chatted. Their chatting was strange, and she couldn't understand it. Often, one would answer a question as though another had asked it. But questions hadn't been asked. It was almost as if they could read one another's thoughts. She chided herself for allowing her imagination to run riot. Anyway, they had left soon afterwards. A large black limousine had picked them up. With a chauffeur, mind you. *The life of the rich and famous!* she had sighed, as she wiped down the table where they had sat, those six evenings back.

And, just as she thought back, the present

surprised her as the devils themselves entered the coffee bar. Romando and Benedikt pushed the door open, and walked in. A cold breeze followed them. Autumn was on its way, and the coffee bar offered a retreat from the growing evening chill. They wound their way through the groups of people huddled together over their steaming cups, seeming to search for their friends.

But it was a show. Matty had noticed that they always sat at the same table, the one in the corner where the lighting was particularly flattering. They didn't need lighting to show off their astoundingly handsome faces anyway. She moved away and pretended to be doing something or other behind her counter but watched them all the while.

As before, they were warmly welcomed, and took their seats next to one another as usual. The twins were dressed more formally than the other two, Hadrian and Caeron.

The door swung open again. Matty's attention was diverted from the four at the table as two more men came in, searching the crowd as newcomers always did. She had thought that there couldn't be a better-looking group on the face of this Earth than those four at the corner table, and so was surprised by the new arrivals. She felt her insides contract in delight as she examined the two newcomers. *Well, I'll be! The bloody angel of all*, she whispered to herself.

Ethan and Kalin joined the table of four. Romando moved his chair closer to Benedikt to make more space.

The pleasure on Benedikt's face was obvious as he greeted the newcomers. "Brothers Kalin and Ethan! To what do we owe this pleasure? The two of you have been keeping very much to yourselves these past couple of weeks. Well, the pleasure is certainly ours."

Benedikt grabbed Kalin's hand and pulled him closer, a mischievous gleam to his eye. "So you have managed to bring Mohammed to the mountain - or, should I say, the mountain to Mohammed?"

Kalin grinned, and patted Benedikt affectionately on the shoulder. He looked affectionately at each of them. "Hello all. We felt for you and found you here. New place?" He asked Caeron.

"New to you, Kalin, but not so new to us. This is the place where I am vanquishing Hadrian on the chequered board" said Caeron and cast an equally mischievous look at Hadrian.

"Not so," Hadrian quipped, with a feigned look of imagined victory. "I remain unbeaten as yet.

Caeron most certainly had the upper hand, but there was still life in my two pawns, knight, and rook - bravely defending their king and master, I might add."

Kalin chuckled. "Hadrian, is that all you have left? And Caeron, what part of the army remains for the black side?"

"The black side still has its queen, a pawn, and the evil bishop in defence of their king. But a fiery queen for sure, rampaging in a black mood over her lands. Taking here and knocking down there. A frightful woman."

They all guffawed. Both Caeron and Hadrian were terrible chess players, far too impatient and impulsive, even though their moves were just as brilliant at times. Kalin still remained undefeated at chess within the brotherhood as, with the patience of a saint, he painstakingly planned each move strategically. Needless to say, their private rules forbade the reading of minds whilst they played.

And when the brothers hunted, it was like the playing of their chess games: Kalin with patience and perfection, Hadrian cruelly and on impulse, and Caeron playfully and with abandon.

Ethan smiled as they flung friendly insults at one another.

"So, Ethan, bambino, beautiful but woebegone," said Romando, "what sad tale do you have for us tonight? Although, I see there a glimmer of a smile. To tell the truth, brother, I never expected it after what happened today." He played with Ethan's hair as he spoke to him.

"So you were also there, Romando? Funny, but at the time I could have sworn that I was alone. Now I realise why she reacted like she did."

"We were all there." Romando chuckled. "We joined with you too late to experience the lovemaking. More's the pity.

"Our dear friend Gregory called at the shop. Such a sad countenance did your little betrayer bear upon his humble face. In any event, he spilled the beans, brother." He turned to Benedikt, "Benedikt, you tell him."

On cue, and as if he had predicted the request, Benedikt continued, "Of course, we hastened to lock thoughts with you. Ah, Ethan, if only you knew how long it has been since Romando and me have had a woman. I'm sure you did us all proud."

Hadrian keenly joined in the conversation. "I have had a woman recently."

Kalin grinned in his usual benevolent way. He enjoyed it when they joked and played with one another. There had been too much tension and serious debate just lately. He also joined in. "So tell us, Hadrian, when was this? We were not party to it. Don't you think that's rather selfish of you? Were you well veiled, or was she an imaginary woman?"

"Kalin, it was at the time when you were so taken up with the seeding of Ethan. Everyone was so busy concentrating on his conversion that, just for a few hours, I took my pleasures of a woman before I killed her."

Ethan laughed out loud. All heads in the coffee bar turned in pleasure at his laugh. He wiped the hair back from his forehead. "You killed her, Hadrian," he questioned mischievously, "after making love to her?"

"Why not?" Exclaimed Hadrian. "It's not like I connected with her emotionally. Ethan, there is a distinction."

"Well, I wouldn't know," Ethan countered. "It seems the endeavours of the brothers succeeded in keeping me a virgin for close on twenty-seven years. I didn't know what I was missing, it seems. But all the same, Hadrian, I can't believe you killed her. Did you eat her flesh as well?"

"You know me, I never take much of the flesh anyway. I only took some of her blood, you know, just a taste."

A further roar of approval from the five brothers seated about Hadrian.

Caeron looked comically aghast. "Are you sure, Hadrian - just her blood?"

"Cernunnos strike me down dead right now if I lie," proclaimed Hadrian ceremoniously, and crossed himself.

Kalin no longer found the situation funny. He did not want them to think that relationships and murder were the same thing. Love was hallowed and should be treated that way.

"Hadrian, I'm sorry I have to say it, but you were wrong. Never mix business with pleasure my brother. If you love, then you love. When you kill it's an entirely different matter. Don't mix the two."

Ethan added. "But Kalin, I must admit that if I had felt any less for Megan, I would have killed her. Even knowing her as I do, the thought did pass through my mind, that the lovemaking would have been made all the better with the letting of her blood. I had to restrain myself from doing it. Really what stopped me is that I knew that if I did it, there would be no more Megan for me to enjoy. A selfish sentiment, I know.

"I actually think I felt love for her. Well, I think I do love her. Not of course like the intense love

I feel here between us - this is far more special. I can't explain; it's just different. What say you, Kalin?"

"Believe me, Ethan, we have all had women, but we were all virgins up until after the seeding. It is our way. But it is shallow, this woman thing. It cannot be compared with what we have here." He searched each of their faces. Each nodded his agreement and looked at Ethan.

†

Ethan

At this point in the conversation, I thought it appropriate to veil my thoughts. I had become a master at doing this and could veil some and reveal others. I knew that only Kalin could do this as I had stolen the recipe from his mind when I had seeded him. I also knew that he hadn't realised that I could do it too. So they read what I wanted them to.

What I wasn't revealing is that I was deeply hurt and troubled by what had happened, and that I loved Megan almost as much as I loved them. Even though I would never give them up for her, I loved her with a tenderness that only our lovemaking could have encouraged. I could have a physical closeness with her that was similar to the mental closeness I had with the brothers. It was different, though. Sometimes one needs that physical melding.

I suppose I contradict myself. Could anything be better than the sharing of blood as we did? No, in retrospect, they were right. All the same, it was still there, this longing for Megan; this longing to undo the harm that had been done; this very private yearning to go back in time before Kalin had seeded me - to start again, with her. But have I ever been happy with what I've had? This thought cheered me up somewhat, and I re-joined the conversation.

"Never mind," I said, "I am glad you were all with me at the end. I wish you could have been with me at the beginning as well. It was great. She was great."

They all sighed and, as one, looked about the room at the women that were seated about them. Lust shone from their eyes.

I continued, "And it is true what Kalin says, though, nothing can be as great as the love we have here between us. Regrets I have. I am sure you have all had them."

I touched my forehead and projected my intense feelings of love to them. Their faces softened as they looked at me with renewed respect and longing. Such sheep!

Romando and Benedikt squeezed each other's

hands as both recognised their new master. This was He. The power of my thoughts had them enthralled. I knew it, but as yet did not know what to do with it.

Hadrian voiced what we had all been thinking, "This calls for a celebration. What say you all? Let us hunt together, all of us, tonight."

"Well said, Hadrian. It would be wonderful," hissed Romando.

"Brothers," I said, "There are seven of us, not just the six sitting here. We will wait for David. He will be here soon - I can feel his emanations."

Surprised, they acknowledged what I had said. David's emanations were there amongst us. He was on his way. I had felt them before they did.

No more than twenty minutes passed before David entered. By this time it was already 10pm and the coffee bar was on the verge of closing its doors.

With a happy smile, David joined us. I moved aside for him and sent him a silent apology for the previous evening. He accepted it graciously and touched my forehead as he pulled up a chair beside me.

Within moments we had let him know, silently as we do, of all that had been discussed that evening. Even the most trivial details were not kept from him. Unanimously, we agreed that tonight would be the hunt.

The waitress called Matty approached our table. "Gentlemen. The manager has asked me to tell you that we are going to close now." She battled to keep from looking at me.

I stretched out my hand and held her by the arm, squeezing in a personal manner whilst examining her deep brown eyes. The way the lid puffed slightly at the crease, and the short stubby lashes blinking thickly and often. The generous mouth and extremely white teeth; the rise and fall of her large breasts as she breathed her excitement; and the small chubby fingers that clutched at a tray. "What tender prey?" I mind-voiced to the others. I could feel their excitement growing out of all proportion. It would be she.

"Matty, is it?"

"Yes," she blushed. "How did you know?"

"Well, I just couldn't imagine a name that would suit you better - suit your sensitive and passionate nature. But, secondly, and honestly, I heard someone call you by name just a bit earlier on."

She blushed again as she wondered at my interest in her.

"Matty," I spoke in a voice that had become

uncontrollably harsh in its lust and excitement. "Come with us, my pretty girl. Let us show you the beauty of life. Just for a short time, and you will understand how plain life has been without us."

She looked like a mouse, seeing the trap perhaps, but wanting the cheese so badly that her greed bested her. "But I don't know you. Where are you going? Why must I come with you?"

She didn't know that she already spoke with the death rattle. We could hear Death Himself, banging away in our heads. Like an orchestra he pounded his drums, rattled his calabash, and clashed his cymbals. I wondered that she couldn't hear the sounds of Him, the feel of Him. I wondered how it was that she couldn't hear the blood rushing madly through our hearts in excitement.

She looked like she was on the verge of dropping everything and running away.

"Matty," I spoke softly, "come here, my darling." I pulled her onto my lap and slowly, with a gentleness I didn't feel, stroked her upper arm; brushed my fingers very lightly over her extended nipples; leant my face in towards her, and sensuously nibbled at her neck.

"Matty, look at me," I commanded. I took my

hand and turned her head in such a manner that she was looking directly into my eyes. "What do you see here?"

She just stared. I could hear the hysterical pounding of her heart near my chest. So could the others.

Caeron rose from where he sat. He came to kneel beside us, running his hand up her leg - reaching under her skirt. She opened her legs as if to welcome us.

We were so taken with our game that we did not notice the manager as he approached. He spoke without fear - he could do this I suppose, as I had never seen such a big giant of a man before - a hairy man. A true gorilla, if you know the type.

"Stop that," he growled loudly at us. "Matty, get back there at once. These fellows here are up to no good."

She scrambled from my lap and trotted back to the counter, visibly shaken. Her lips were quivering. She was ready to burst into tears.

"Now get out, you evil sons of bitches. I don't want to see any of you here again," the manager spluttered. "Get out!"

He slapped our bill on the table and stormed off. We could hear him ranting and raving under his breath. He was telling Matty off as if the entire thing had been her fault.

Death shrugged His shoulders, for now, and stopped his orchestral crescendo. Until later then!

†

Giggling madly, we left. We were mostly so old but could be so childish. At least I had an excuse - I was only 27. Matty had been lucky that night. We went in search of less protected prey. Her time would come. This was our time, and we were not going to give it up for her.

We prowled in our pack, as of old. On this night we killed with malice, uncaring of the pleas of our prey, just like it had been at the beginning. His time came swiftly. With a soft gurgle, his lungs gave up their last moisture from between the crushed ribs. We lapped greedily at the pink froth, and then tore from the abdomen. After the feast, we lifted our heads to the moon, and as one howled our ecstasy.

Faintly, within the din of our mutual enjoyment, I could hear Thalem's call. He called and called, and I knew that too much time had been wasted. I would continue my search for him as soon as the sun rose the next day.

That night we all arrived home, shared our blood, and in perfect harmony curled up together on the floor. All seven of us slept together that night, fully clothed and warmed by the fire that smouldered its companionship.

†

It was in the early hours of the morning that I took David to me and seeded him. It was what he had been waiting for so patiently. What better time. I cannot now say whether the physical thing of making love to Megan could ever have been as exotic, or as rapturous, as the seeding of the brothers. David seeded especially well, and now our blood ran together as it had never done before.

Tomorrow, Thalem must be sought.

CHAPTER 24

Seeking Thalem

The weather had turned colder. Old Man Jason now wrapped up warmly each morning before venturing out.

Peego was also wrapped up warmly; Old Man Jason made sure of that. Jason had a tweed jacket of an indistinguishable brown colour with slight red flecks here and there. He had managed to find a material almost identical, and he'd had a doggy-coat made for Peego. Peego didn't like it much. Not to hurt Old Man Jason's feelings, though, he would wag his tail eagerly as he was tucked into his coat at the beginning of each day.

They would share a breakfast of sausages, eggs, and toast, normally from the pan in which it was fried. Peego would get one half to eat as he stood on his back legs against the table, while Old Man Jason forked other half into his mouth as quickly as Peego gulped. The rule was that the one who finished first could start on the other's meal. Then they would wash down their greasy breakfast with a strong cup of percolated coffee for the old man, and a bowl of milk for Peego.

The day was spent in much the same way as any other. As they arrived at the shop, Peego peed against the pole just outside the door. Old Man Jason cleared his phlegmy chest and spat a projectile of goo into the gutter.

Then, whilst he fiddled with his bulky bunch of keys (why he needed so many only the good Lord knew, and he certainly wasn't telling), Peego would wait patiently. Old Man Jason had made it a habit to try each key even though he knew which one would fit. There were about twenty keys on his large brass keyring. It was always the last one that would finally slip into the hole to open the door. In they would go.

Peego would be tied behind the counter to lie for a good part of the day on his now acrid sacks. Old Man Jason would immediately patrol the aisles to see if anything untoward had happened during the night. He would inspect each row minutely, just to make sure. This whole process would take him a good part of an hour. Then, with a self-satisfied grunt, he would pump his paraffin stove to make his morning cuppa - not, of course, until after all rows had been paraded, no siree.

Old Man Jason sat on his stool behind the counter, sipping away at his cracked and stained mug. He could feel that the day of reckoning was drawing closer, as sure as God made little apples. He leant over to pat Peego's head, and simultaneously peeked under the counter. Yes, it was still there: the gun, still waiting. He put his mug down on the dusty counter and reached for the weapon. Checking inside, he saw that the bullets were still there. He was faintly surprised that he had a gun with bullets. "So very lethal, yessirree. Ain't that so, Peego?" he asked of the mute dog.

Peego had the whole day, each day, to ponder and dream. And dream he did. Old Man Jason would watch him as he dreamt. Always, his paws would work in fits and starts. Yessirree, he was a busy dog in those dreams. Old Man Jason thought that he was probably dreaming about the day that they would vanquish their foes, *the strange ones*. He would have been surprised at what Peego really dreamt.

Peego dreamt of a large valley in another land. He dreamt of the river that ran through it. He dreamt of the still pool where the C'raether had sunk in disguise. He dreamt of the rescue.

Now and then, a booming voice would call in a beastly fashion. At these times, Peego would whimper in his sleep, an odd smile of fear playing about the large canines. These were the times when Cernunnos appeared to him.

He could never see the God's face, but the body was frightening enough. He would cringe and scrape the floor, in his dream, at Cernunnos' feet. Normally it would be at this time that his bladder would relax in terror, and he would pee on his sacks. This is why they were smelling so.

Then there were times when he dreamt of running with the pack. Through the dense forest they would lope, smoothly and soundlessly, all creatures hiding from their passage. Their nostrils would be flared to catch the scent of their prey. As they ran together, their eyes weaved the same eerie pattern in the pitch dark - searching, alert for every tell-tale movement.

Mists swirled about them until only their heads could be seen, seemingly floating between the ancient groves, bodiless and haunting. Yellow eyes gleaming, pink tongues lolling, and silently panting.

At these thoughts, Peego would growl under his breath in his sleep, eyelids flickering. It would inevitably end with one of them catching the scent of a deer, or maybe something smaller.

Ever sensitive to the others, each would flow with the next, as if they were all part of the same creature. At these moments, their thoughts would plan in unison, until such time as they would part into two snake-like columns, each forking, one to the right of the victim and one to the left. The lead animals in the separate columns would re-join just past the victim, to close the noose. Now there was no hope. The prey was surrounded, and death to the victim was inevitable.

But these were the early days when he was just more than a pup. These were the good times, before the two-legged hunters came to the forest and began their ruthless hunt for wolf pelts: the dark days when neither the wolves nor the C'raether were safe. What a trophy it was for these hunters to take home to their dens the pelt of a wolf, or a beautiful, staked head of a C'raether.

In the early days, the C'raether roamed freely in the forest as fellow predators to the wolves. There was no competition as their prey differed. There were times that they would even run together, the C'raether and the wolves. There were times that the wolves crept up, one by one, to share the fires of the men that weren't men, so similar in their nature were these creatures.

However, communication was difficult, except for the aged few who had mastered the art. So, soon the two species would once again drift apart, each to go their separate way and to hunt in the fashion that most pleased them.

But Peego's thoughts did not encompass the complexities of what had been. He knew only that his real name was Thalem, and that he had always been The Messenger. He was the communicator in the world of beasts. He had become the mediator as he grew older. The gift of silent thought form was his to command.

He had managed to assuage, on several occasions, the ruffled fur of a wolf who had misunderstood the intentions of a C'raether whom he had mistaken for a man. Of course, there were times when it was the quick temper of the C'raether that had to be soothed when the wolves, unintentionally, of course, would drive away a victim that the C'raether had been painstakingly tracking.

Thalem woke with a whimper. He looked up from where he lay. Yes, there sat the old mad man. He liked the man's sausages, but there was very little else he liked about him. His smell was one of decay; that the large dog found extremely unpleasant. In truth, he had an instinctual feeling that he was living with the enemy.

Thalem knew he was here for some reason beyond his canine comprehension. He would bide his time until the Master came for him, and come he would, of this he was sure. Thalem's thoughts had travelled well and made their impression. The Master was already seeking and being the Master, would find.

He fell asleep again to the chatter of Old Man Jason's small radio.

The announcer on the radio read the news in his usual monotonous voice. Old Man Jason was not interested in the news in general. He waited to hear news of *the strange ones*. It never came. Well, they were never mentioned by name, but he knew that these evil perpetrators in his neighbourhood committed the countless murders that the announcer spoke of. Even in distant cities, where there were so many murders. He was certain it was also them. And he was probably right.

The day passed with few customers. Every so often, Old Man Jason would shuffle over to his dirty window, take the handkerchief from his pocket, spit on it, and wipe clean his peep hole to the street. He would bend slightly to get a better view and spend the next thirty minutes or so scrutinising the passers-by. Ever expecting a glimpse of *the strange ones*, whom he had now renamed *the evil ones*.

He was sure that they were playing a game with him, yesiree, these spawn of hell. He knew they lurked in this very street, ever watchful of his shop, and of him and his brave hound Peego. They were as cunning as they were evil. Yes, he could play their spiteful game. He would stop peeking through his hole for the next few hours and they would soon become concerned with his absence.

He chuckled to himself as he made his way to the back of the shop to greet his old friends.

Thalem also knew that the time was coming closer when he would be reunited with the Master. Under what circumstances, he did not know - that was for the Master and their shared god to decide. He hoped it would be soon. The hunt beckoned, and he was becoming uneasier by the day. Exhausted as he was from the endless dreaming, he once again made the supreme effort to call the Master, telling him in no uncertain terms that he was growing agitated with the delay, conveying his loneliness and need.

The day drew to a close, and the streetlights awoke with the night-time prowlers.

Old Man Jason inspected his rows of books one more time before locking his old till and untying Peego. He carefully folded the crumpled handkerchief and placed it neatly into his pocket. "Peego, my boy, time to go home. I think tonight we'll have sausages. What do you think of that?

Yesiree, sausages it will be." He chuckled to himself and snapped his braces in defiance to any argument that might present itself from the dog.

They left the shop, locked the door after trying countless keys, peed up against the pole and spat into the gutter. With all their ministrations complete, the two careened off down the pavement in their usual fashion, with the large dog pulling and sniffing and the old man barely keeping his hold on the lead.

And so it was that Ethan began his search in earnest the next day: the search for Thalem.

†

Ethan

The following morning, I eased myself from the tangle of arms and legs. The fire had died, and the morning was cold. Everyone still slept soundly, sated from the feast of the night before, and warmed by their mutual blood.

I ran myself a steaming bath and, after soaking away the gore that smeared my body and hair, invaded Hadrian's cupboard for clean clothes. Most of mine were still at Megan's flat, along with just about everything else I possessed. These were things that still needed collecting.

It was a chill, fresh morning; unusually cloudless. Already, I could hear the incessant hum of the traffic as the morning birthed.

My senses were particularly honed on this Saturday, probably given the glory of the previous night's kill and the sharing of our mutual blood, and of the spirit of the victim. It was with a feeling of satisfaction and confidence that I made my way to the garage that housed the limo, confident that I would find Thalem and pleased with myself for what I was. The feeling of well-being pervaded me as I soaked in the smells and sounds of this wonderful day.

The garage was set some way from the house, and above it lived Joseph, the chauffeur. I don't think I had ever spoken more than a couple of words to him and hadn't noticed that anyone else had either. I'd never wondered or thought about him before but did so now as I heard the strumming that came from the garage.

I pushed open the side door and was immediately assailed by the smells of the garage. Oil, petrol, grease, and the unmistakable soapy smell of the black man who sat in the corner, still strumming.

Joseph was old, his peppercorn hair well-salted with grey. I was surprised to see that today he wore crisp blue jeans and a red chequered shirt. It was a change from the usual immaculate navy suit and cap. His face was lined, and these lines were now broken by a huge white smile as he saw me enter.

"G'd morning, Joseph." I said. He stopped playing the guitar.

"Good morning Mastah Ethan. Will you be needing to go somewhere today?"

I could see that he hadn't expected a call, and I hoped that he had nothing planned. "You're looking casual today, my man."

"Mastah Kalin said that yous wouldn't be needing me today. Just used to getting up early and checking on my lady here. Thought I'd give her a little song this morning."

"It sounded good, Joseph. Mind if I have a look at your guitar? I play as well."

He was pleased, and gladly handed over the aged instrument. I sat on the edge of the workbench, and ran my fingers over the strings. They were well tuned - he obviously knew his music. The licks came easily, given the neglect of my music over the past months.

"Well, Mastah Ethan, you s'prise me. Your fingers, they are working like lightning. You play a long time?"

"Yeah, most of my life." I handed the guitar back to him. "Come on, Joseph. You know your guitar better than I do. Play for me. Please."

With a broad smile, he took back the guitar. "This here is an old blues number you might know." He started singing in a raspy voice ... *"I went down to the St James Infirmary; I saw my baby there; She was laid out on a cold white table ..."*

I knew it and joined in at this point. We both sang ... *"So cold, so white so fair; Let her go, let her go, God bless her ..."* Both of us laughed in enjoyment as we continued with the song.

"Eh, you know it? Then you are a music-maker."

"Yeah, of course I know it." We grinned our delight to one another.

The music was still in me, and I realised how sorely it had been missed. Today, I would fetch my guitar from Megan and start working again. The time was right, and life seemed so bountiful.

"Joseph, I need to do a couple of things today that would be made a lot easier if you could drive me. Or perhaps, if you're busy, I could catch the bus?"

"Eh, no, Sir. I will take you. An old man like me has nothing better to do with his time. What is it you want to do? Where will you be wanting to go?"

"Firstly, I want to go to the bank. Then I want to drive around and look for my dog. He's been missing for some time, and I'm hoping I might catch a glimpse of him somewhere. I know the general area where he went missing," I lied. "You game to do some dog spotting?"

"That sounds like easy work, Mastah. I really like dogs," he grinned.

"Perhaps we could drive by some of the local parks. Dogs like these places, don't they? People who have stolen dogs will surely go to these places?"

"I'm sure you're right!" Joseph answered. "If you'd like to play this here instrument of mine for a while, I'll go to the kitchen and fix us a lunch to take along."

I was amused by his eagerness. He obviously enjoyed company. "Yeah, you do that Joseph. That'd be great. And Joseph ..."

"Yes, Mastah?"

"Please just call me Ethan ... and Joseph, thanks. I know this is your day off."

"Ethan ..." he tested the name. "It's a good name." He went to prepare our 'picnic lunch'.

I felt like a small boy again in the anticipation of a picnic with Joseph in the park, and I couldn't wipe the happy grin from my face as I ran through 'St. James Infirmary Blues' once again.

Joseph soon returned, and we climbed into the limo. The electric doors of the garage slid up effortlessly, and we purred out.

In friendly silence, we drove the streets in the area where I had last sensed Thalem. The car interfered with the thought forms that I might receive from him, and so there was only silence. We drove anyway, with both Joseph and I peering out of the window in our search for the elusive canine.

The fact of the matter was that I didn't even know if Thalem had come in canine form, so I didn't really know what I was looking for. I presumed canine and assumed that he would look very much like I had seen him in Caeron's dreamscape.

After unsuccessfully combing the area, I asked Joseph to detour to the bank where I had previously drawn the trust money. The account balance had escalated considerably, and I withdrew a substantial amount of money and stuffed it into my back pocket. This money would go to Kalin. It was only in the last couple of days that I had thought about giving him some money for my keep.

The past months had been so new and exciting that money hadn't crossed my mind. Most of the brothers worked, if not to bring in money, then to keep themselves amused it seemed. Romando and Benedikt had their shoe shop; Kalin was an interpreter and translator; David was in the police; and who knows what Caeron did. Hadrian had a small workshop in the house, where he did carpentry. It was mainly restorative work where he resurrected old furniture, that was then sold.

I asked Joseph to return to the area where I had sensed Thalem, thinking that perhaps it was still too early because as hard as I concentrated, I could feel little of his presence. He wasn't calling now.

The day was young, and it would be better to return later. I gave Joseph directions to Megan's flat, as I thought it a good opportunity to collect my guitar and amp, along with a few other things I needed. Joseph sang to himself as we drove and I soon joined him, singing some of the old blues numbers that we both knew, and even Eric Clapton and Cream's "Sunshine of your Love". We enjoyed that, and while Joseph imitated the guitar with a "dah, dah, da, da …" I played drums on the dashboard. I hadn't had so much fun in ages.

Megan wasn't there, but I still had a key to the flat. I let myself in and, without permitting myself memories, gathered some clothes that still hung in the same place in the cupboard, a few personal memorabilia that I had carried from place to place, and of course my guitar. I found myself feeling heart sore.

I wondered what had happened to my amplifier, as it wasn't there, but then remembered that it had last been used when I had played on that fateful evening with The Sock. I would have to go to Exodus tonight - hopefully the band would still be playing there, and I could collect it.

Joseph helped me to disconnect my old hi-fi, and we loaded it as well. I hoped Megan wouldn't mind. Perhaps I could buy her another one, but this one had been painstakingly put together and I wasn't going to leave it behind. The three hundred odd compact discs were lovingly packed into a box that I found in the kitchen, and we were on our way.

There is nothing much more to tell of that day except that we finally settled for lunch in one of the parks that I had decided needed searching. Joseph and I sprawled out on the grass in the sun, popped a beer each and ate some of the food he had brought along. It seemed like a feast, and I ate more than at any other time since I had joined the brothers.

The human in me was having a field day, and it was almost as if I was the same person I had been years ago. The years when Andrew and I had sat in our tree house, whispering of ghosts, and eating the biscuits that we had raided from the pantry for our midnight feast.

"You're thin, Ethan, so I'm glad to see yous eating like this. You'll put on some weight."

"I'll never put on weight, Joseph. It doesn't matter how much I eat; I've always been on the thin side."

"Eh, you young people, always on the move like that. Coming home so late every night. How can yous expect to get fat?"

"But I don't want to get fat, Joseph. Don't you like me like this?"

"Eh, Ethan. You have the pretty face, but a body like a scarecrow." He passed me another sandwich.

"Really, Joseph, I've had enough. It was great. You eat it."

He stuffed the sandwich into his mouth and took another gulp of his beer. "So, Mastah Ethan: tell me, where is your family? I have only ever seen yous alone. All of you people there in the house are always alone, keeping to yourselves like that. I've never even seen a friend. And look at yous, such a friendly and pleasant boy. Eh, I don't understand. And where are your girlfriends? I have never seen one lady friend at the house."

I didn't mind his questioning. It was innocent. "Joseph, relationships and me don't work out. That's why I was collecting my things from that flat. I was sharing it with a woman, Megan. Basically she's given me the boot. It was pretty much finalised yesterday. So you see I did have a girlfriend."

"But how can you have a girlfriend if you're always with the other Mastahs? This poor girlfriend never saw you. What can you expect, that she wait for you forever? I can see why that poor girl kicked you out. Eh!"

"Nah, it wasn't like that at all, Joe. She just finally knew me for what I was and didn't like what she saw. It's like that, you know. Once you let people know who you are, they go running scared. Once they know they have your love, it's not good enough."

"Eh, but I can tell that yous a special boy, Ethan. They will still love you when they know yous."

"Joe, if only you knew me, you'd change your

mind quick enough."

"But Ethan, I's never wrong about people. Yous a good boy deep down inside. Mischievous maybe, but with a good heart."

"What makes you say that Joe?"

"Ethan. I's an old man, and I've seen a lot of life. Some people, they're bad; and some people, they are good. And it's always the same. I can spot them - see them a-coming. I know them. I's knows the good ones, and I'm never wrong. The bad ones have a certain curtain of badness that they wear. You know what I's saying …?

"You mean an aura. I can see auras, Joe - yours is a good one."

"I believe you, Ethan, that yous can see these aura things. My old grandmother said that children that are born with a caul can see these things. You must be one of them."

"Well, I don't know about that, Joe. This aura thing is quite new, though. I haven't always seen them. But tell me about yourself. You always seem to be there when we call for you. Don't you have a family or anything?"

"No one. The car, she is my family - her and the guitar."

"You must have had family once, Joe?"

"I once had a wife, many years ago when I was still in Africa. She was a beautiful Zulu girl who died when she was still a young woman. The lungs." He paused here with misty eyes, obviously reminiscing.

"There were no children. I was hard on that woman. Came home late at night, full of beer. Never telling her how wonderful or needed she was. Never noticing how hard she worked to make our poor house a home. Never noticing how special that woman was until she was gone. Then it was too late. It is always like that, Ethan, we only realise how special they are when they're no longer there. And this lady of yours?"

"Ah, Joseph, it's such a long story. Very much like yours, I suppose, except it's not she that is dead. It is me."

"Eh, I don't believe it. You have much life left in yous, Ethan. Yous a strong young man. Even if you're too thin, I's sure that your woman still likes yous. I can see the hurt on your face. You still love this woman?"

I suddenly felt the tremendous sorrow that I had chosen to keep hidden from myself and had to look away from Joe as the tears gathered. The park misted, and I furiously blinked.

"Yeah, I love her. I think I've lost her, though. Left it too long, Joe. I've allowed myself to become too evil, and she knows it."

"Eh! Now, Ethan, you're talking bad things. How can you say that you're evil? There's not an evil bone in your body. I'd know if there were. You're just a young man, and young men do things that they later regret. They're experimenting with life, that's all. If your woman loves yous, she will think on it and still love you even if you've been naughty."

"You think so, Joseph? I dunno so much. There's naughty, and there's pure unadulterated evil. I'm afraid to say that I'm the latter."

"Eh, I don't believe it."

"What if I told you I was a murderer?"

Joseph moistened his lips with his tongue and gazed off into the distance. Then he started talking in a voice fraught with emotion. "I remember once when I was a young man like you. We'd been drinking heavily that night, Alpheus and I. We fighting mad that night, with the beer. I can never remember exactly what happened, but a fight broke out. We were at a shebeen. We were all arguing about something.

"Alpheus was a mad one when he'd been drinking. He broke a bottle and stabbed the other man right in his face. And mad I was as well, although I can't remember why. When that man went, down I kicked him; kicked him so hard until he begged for mercy. But I carried on kicking, and so did Alpheus. We kicked until he stopped begging for mercy; until he was still. *Dead!*

"And then we ran home, and nobody ever asked if it was us that'd killed him. That night, everybody told the police that they didn't know who had killed him, but that he'd surely deserved it. I can't remember why he deserved it, because I think I blanked him from my mind from that day. Can't even remember how he looked; but I killed him!

"To this day, I'm sorry for doing that thing to him. Think now that I didn't have no right to take his life away from him, even if it was miserable.

"Ethan. I've killed a man, and you're the first person I's ever told. Only old Alpheus and I know about this. Alpheus is dead now hisself. He's left me alone with the guilt of that man. Now you see I was an evil man myself. Killed that man.

"Ethan, you can't ever say one man is more bad than another. Kill is kill, no matter why you did it or no matter whether that person deserved it or not. So you say you killed a man? Tell old Joe here about it, boy. I have done it too!"

"Joe, I haven't personally killed, but have

partaken in the urging of it - thrilled to it. Not once, Joe; many times." Suddenly I felt extreme remorse. I felt sick.

"I don't know what you're telling me, young Ethan, but know this thing: men get excited when they see other men doing bad things. They egg them on and shout them along. It's like a bull fight. Bad thing, that. I's know of the bad things at the house, Ethan.

"You're still a good boy, and rightly I think you should go back to your girlfriend. Make her see she still loves you. Go back to her before those people make you bad. They're already bad, and you'll go bad if you stay there. I know what goes on there. I've seen the blood for many years. It's like a lion has been and gone some mornings.

"I's been taking blood money from them for a long time - was a young man when I started taking it. I needed it - I was a political refugee in those days. I've grown older, and they've stayed the same. I think they're devils: 'tokoloshi', as we say. But me too, I'm a devil for taking their money for so long. I's a bad man who belongs with those men who're yours friends.

"But you, you're still good. Go away, I warn you, before you're also a bad man who never grows old."

I sat shocked as he said these things and

wondered if Kalin had any idea of how much Joe knew. However, Kalin must have chosen Joe knowing how much, or how little, he could be trusted. Kalin wouldn't have erred. I personally believed that he was beyond mistakes.

I wondered why Joe was telling me these things and said as much to him.

"Joe, maybe you're wrong about what you perceive here. All the same, if it is as you say, why are you telling me? Aren't you afraid for your own life? Should I mention to the others what you're telling me here? Aren't you afraid of me? I am a killer like they are! They have made me like themselves. I am as bloodthirsty and malicious as they are.

"Unlike you, I feel very little guilt for the people we have murdered. So, why are you telling me this?"

Joseph nodded his head as Ethan spoke, and then responded, "Maybe I's taking a chance, Ethan. You still have true youth, not stolen youth. I don't want to see your innocence stolen. This is what those peoples are going to do, and yous won't see it, so in love you are with them. Let me warn you, young Mastah Ethan - don't trade your lovely soul for nothing. It is nothing that they live for!"

Well, he was making me think. I silently

packed together the few things we had with us.

"Let's leave it at that, Joe, and say no more. We have some more driving to do before it gets dark. I think we're more likely to find my dog now, because it is later in the day, and he is more likely to be out and about."

"And what about this dog, Ethan? Where does this dog fit into all this?"

"Just a dog, Joseph. Nothing more, and nothing less; just a dog."

"And you love this dog too?"

"Reckon so, Joe. More like I feel responsible for him."

We left the park, still friendly with each other, but much warier - me with him, and he most certainly with me. He looked as if he expected me to launch at his throat. I saw him glancing sideways at me, while driving, and I started to smile. "Really, Joe. What do you think me? I've made myself sound far worse than I really am. We're okay. Hey, maybe you're going to kick me to death when we get home, huh?" I chortled, trying to salvage our relationship. He gave it some thought and was soon also giggling.

"You know, Ethan, for one moment there yous had me believing all that wild rubbish you were talking."

"Joe, it's been a great day, and you've given me a lot to think about. I mean, about Megan. Maybe I'll go back and try. Maybe I won't leave it until it's too late, like it was for your wife and yourself. What was her name, Joe?"

"She had a simple name from the bible, Ethan. It was Mary."

I thought to myself, "My God! Mary and Joseph. How appropriate."

Well, we were obviously not going to find Thalem on this day, as all thought form projections from him were still. I hoped he was still okay, and that nothing had happened to him. I knew though, without a doubt, that we would find one another.

When we arrived home, Joseph again cautioned me regarding my relationship with the brothers. I promised to think on it, and to report back to him at another time.

†

Everyone was out except for Kalin, who sat alone in the study busy with some papers. I couldn't help feeling a sudden rush of renewed fondness for him. He had obviously bathed, as I had done earlier, and all traces of the slaughter of the night before were gone. His hair gleamed in the low light. and when he looked up his eyes seemed greener than usual. He pursed his mouth, and then gave me a welcoming smile.

"Why, Ethan. Hello. You have been out with Joseph." He stated, without a question.

"Yeah, looking for Thalem. What you doing there?"

"A translation. When the time is right, you will find Thalem. Personally, I think you're wasting your time going out looking. He will come to you, one way or another. And Joseph?"

"Friendly old man. You know, Kalin, before today I didn't know his name. There he was all along, and I didn't even acknowledge his existence."

I walked closer and sat on the floor, cross-legged, at Kalin's knees. He reached out and rested his hand on my head.

"Yes, he is a pleasant old man, but he rambles. It might be better if you don't listen to some of his apparently well-intentioned advice. He knows nothing of us or of our beliefs. He has seen a lot over the years, of that I am aware. You are still young. Don't be misled by how he perceives things. I talk of things he would never understand but you have experienced. We are one. Remember!"

"Kalin, believe me, I would choose nothing

else. I admit he gave me some food for thought. But here I am, back and wondering how I could ever have doubted. My love for you is as strong now, if not stronger, than it has ever been. Kalin, I love you."

"And I love you too, more than you could know. We have spent little time together lately. Come closer."

I rose on my knees and reached for him.

CHAPTER 25

Cradle Blues

Ethan

Later that night, I persuaded Joseph to drive me to Exodus. He waited outside – I said I was going to run in to see if The Sock were still playing. I was greeted at the door as if I'd never been away.

"Hey, Ethan! How're you doing? Haven't seen you for a while mate," Creep greeted me enthusiastically. He was the bouncer at Exodus; had been there for as long as I could remember. The name came from something to do with him being found creepy by the younger girls. He was a little aged, skinny but still ripped, with thin long black-to-greying hair. He usually wore cutaway shirts whatever the weather, had a large gold hoop in one ear, and had the meanest tattoos I'd ever seen. His arms and upper body were covered with tats. He'd organised the wolf I had on my arm. I can truly say mine is also one of the finest tattoos around.

"Hey, Creep. Yeah, it's been a few months. And you, how're you doing?" He grabbed my hand and shook it vigorously, then pulled me close and slapped me on the back. Huh, never knew he liked me that much!

"Well, I'm still here, aren't I? Go in, my man. It's on the house. Good to see you." He stepped back and looked over my shoulder at the person behind me. Then, as I walked through the door, he turned and added under his breath, "If you're buying, the man is here."

I hesitated and turned back to him. "Doubt that I will tonight, Creep. The Sock still playing?"

"Yeah, sure thing. You should hear their new stuff. Good music! Of course, we miss you though."

Now that I knew they were still playing, I turned to walk back to the limo to let Joseph know that things were cool.

Creep called after me. "Hey, Ethan. Not going in?"

"Coming right back. Just organising a lift for later," I replied.

"Still haven't got your own wheels?" he asked my back.

"Never needed them," I called back over my shoulder.

I walked over to the car, and the electric passenger window slid down. I bent to speak to Joseph, "It's okay, Joe. They're still here. Come back for me at about two. I'll have to chat a bit before I take the amp. You know, get friendly, buy a couple of drinks, socialise. That okay with you?"

"Sure thing, Mastah Ethan. I's thinks I'll park just up the road and get mahself a drink or two at the pub. That okay with you?" he said with a smile, copying my question.

"Sure thing, Joe," I copied, "You do that. See you later then!"

I gave the roof of the car a couple of slaps in farewell, and turned to go back in. He pulled away with a wave, his polished white grin still apparent on his face. I shook my head in affection.

Creep let me in, and I walked down the passage to the main room of the club. The music came pounding up the walkway, reverberating against the ghoulishly painted walls and into my newly sensitive ear drums. I caught myself wanting to hold my ears like a kid, to block out the din. Hear no evil! After a few glasses of wine, I'd be okay. The smells of the past assailed me, stronger than I had ever noticed them before. Weed, alcohol, perfume, damp, and bodies. It was sickening, and I had to control an urge to run back out into the fresh night air.

A girl wove drunkenly towards me. "Well, if it isn't the great Ethan hisshelf," she slurred. Haven't seen you in a while, gorgeous. What you been doing with yourself?" She came up close to peer up into my face, a little too close for my liking, a drink in one hand and a cigarette in the other, bloodshot eyes, spiky hair, and a sour breath.

"Been busy." I was abrupt and hoped she would go.

"Been too busy to come over and say hi to me. Hope you're going to give us a song later. Will you do that, 'speshially for me?" She stroked my neck with a long fingernail. I could've vomited.

"Yeah sure, maybe." I gagged. "Sorry, what's your name again?"

"Oh my gaash, he doesn't even remember my name" she announced to no one over her shoulder. "It'th Roxy, remember? Little Roxy. We got sick together wunsh, outside in the alley. You wrote a song that I know is about me. Remember now?"

Talk about sick - she sickened me. Besides, I

couldn't remember ever having been sick in the alley with her, and none of my songs were about her. But I suppose if she said so it must be true, the alley thing. There was a lot I couldn't clearly recall, of the times when I had spent most of my evenings drunk or doped to the eyeballs.

I brushed her away with my hand to get past. "Good seeing you again, Roxy. Till later …"

With a pout on her face, she swooned off in the other direction. Soon she was gushing over someone else who stood alone at the edge of the dance floor, spilling drink down his shirt, and trying to brush it off with a be-cigaretted and ringed hand. So it wasn't that I was the flavour of the day after all.

The lights pulsed about me like heartbeats. From what I could see, most of the faces that I saw briefly displayed in the strobe were new, with only the odd person here and there greeting me disinterestedly. So much for being noticed!

I pushed my way through the throng to the bar and raised my hand for attention. With a nod of his head, the barman acknowledged that he had seen, and continued serving at the other end. I leant against the wooden bar top and turned to look at the band, wiped the hair back from my forehead, and reached into my pocket for my cigarettes. Hang on - which Ethan is it now? Oh this one! Tapped one out, and lit it, causing an angry face next to me. Fuck you!

The band's music sounded good but had become a lot heavier since I'd played with them those months back. Yeah, they were better, far better than they had been then. I found myself enjoying what they put together.

The barman finally approached with lifted eyebrows and a dish cloth over one shoulder. I ordered a bottle of red wine and a tomato juice. My drinks and wine glass came and, after downing the tomato juice, I poured a glass of wine and sipped while I gazed out over the crowd. This was my haunt.

Soon the band begged forgiveness of their audience to take a break. They made their way over to the bar, and immediately saw me.

"Well, look here! It's the man himself," exclaimed Bryan. He pulled me closer and gave me a man hug and pat on the back.

I grinned. "Bryan. Good to see you. Music sounds great - you've got it together well, man."

"More's the pity you're not with us," he grinned. He reached back to pull someone forward.

"Meet Chris. He's the mean guitarist that you heard playing earlier. Chris, this is Ethan. He played with us for a while, just before you joined. But I'm sure you know who Ethan is?"

Bryan asked me, "How many times was it, Ethan, that you played with us? Only once, maybe twice, if I remember correctly?"

"Gig-wise only once. Then I let you down. Sorry about that Bryan." Though we had only played together for such a short time as The Sock, I had known Bryan, as a friend and fellow musician, for a few years. He was one of the best and so easy to love.

"I just didn't make the cut, Chris." I added, "These chaps were just too good for me. Oh, and pleased to meet you!" I extended my hand to shake. "Was listening - I like what you're doing."

"Hiya," answered Chris self-consciously. I've been to one of your gigs, when you were playing with Obliviously Mad. Great stuff." I could hear he was a Scot like Bryan.

"Yeah, that was a long time ago, in my 'obliviously mad' youth." I grimaced and took another sip of my wine. Over the top of the glass, I could see Blue weaving his way towards us. Yeah, you got it, 'The' Blue.

He was clearly surprised to see me. "Holy crap, Ethan. Last time I saw you, I left you for dead. Sorry about that man, just kinda freaked, ya know?" He put his arm around my neck and squeezed affectionately.

"It's cool, Blue. As you can see I'm here, alive, and well," I said in my iciest voice.

"So, what you been up to?" Blue asked. "Must say, you look a lot better than the last time, man." He plastered a concerned look on his face.

"Nothing really." I brushed him off. "Where's Dill?" I asked to change the subject. I felt like saying much more but it just wasn't worth it. After all, it had been my choice. He didn't force me to take the shot that nearly killed me.

Chris answered. "Chatting up someone over there," he pointed vaguely, "who's been admiring him for a while. Cute girl. Wouldn't mind getting to know her myself."

Bryan called to the barman, "Hey Mac, a round here for all." The barman nodded in a non-committal way and started pouring drinks for us. He remembered my drinks preference and gave me another tomato juice - the wine bottle was still mostly full.

Bryan continued. "So, Ethan my man, with the all-time lovely Megan, I see."

I was puzzled. "No, actually I'm not with her. Why do you say that?"

"Well, she's here," he said, nodding over the crowd to the dance floor. "Could see her from the stage. When I saw you here, I assumed you were together. You're not?"

I couldn't help showing my dismay. "Bryan, Megan and I are just not so cool together right now. It's a long story!"

Chris looked uneasy and I wondered what he was thinking. "Time's up, chaps," he said, "Gotta get back. You going to come and do a number after this break, Ethan?" He placed his glass down on the counter, wiped his mouth with his sleeve and started making his way back to the stage, looking back expectantly for me to follow. "Come on, Ethan," he beckoned, "The kids here would love it if you did a couple of songs for them. We'll do two of yours - oldies. Okay?"

Chris was trying, and I appreciated it. He was a good man. Sincere. "Yeah, okay. Why not!"

"Cool," he said, and turned to search over the crowd for Dill.

I walked with them to the stage, memories crashing in around me, good and bad. The good overrode the bad, and I jumped onto the stage with pleasure, now looking forward to doing a couple of my old favourite tunes. Blue handed me the semi-acoustic and I quickly tuned to drop D.

"I've dropped to D," I said to them. "Cradle Blues first, followed by Massacre Molly. Can you still do them? We covered both in practice sessions. Chris, you okay with this?"

He nodded and gave me the thumbs up. He had been following me in my previous band and seemed to know the songs.

They nodded. I tested the microphone. "One two, one two ..." and began Cradle Blues, a number that started soft and built to a passionate plea. It always got the crowd going and had a beat that could be danced to, in parts - okay they could stand parts of it out and just appreciate ... me?

As is my way, I sang close to the microphone in a slow, smooth voice, building up to the climax of the song to end in a guttural agonised scream, straight from hell. I was fortunate to have the range. I think I enjoyed it more than the audience, and wished I could get rid of the guitar and give the song what it needed - action! Good to be doing this again: letting off steam. Just after the climax, the song again slowed down and Dill did some wonderful drumming to change the tempo to what it needed. His timing was perfect. It's such a good feeling when a drummer has such rhythm.

As I again started, the slow deep drone that

the song required, I glanced around looking for Megan. The crowd was enjoying it, and I thought how easy it would be to get back into this.

I found her. She was dancing in a slow hypnotic way to the song. It was a song she knew well, and she was doing with her body exactly what I had longed to do with mine - give the music life. I found myself singing to her, matching the movements of her body, singing to the swaying hair and to those sensual limbs. She was doing it for me, and I was doing it for her. She was giving life to the words and the slow, sweet rhythm that accompanied them. Without anyone being aware of it, we were making musical and passionate love - her down there with the throng about her, and me up above for all to see. There were only the two of us, consumed.

I ended the song with the crescendo it deserved, screaming into the microphone in primeval release. She stopped, and looked up at me, straight into my eyes - and then with a sad smile she turned and stumbled the other way. It was as if she was giving me a final farewell, and what a farewell it had been! A total mind-fuck!

My instincts told me to jump from the stage and follow her - crush her in my arms, kiss her like our lives depended on it. But, I had promised another song, and already the band was beginning the primitive strains of 'Massacre Molly': the weirdest and to me, most perfect song I had ever written. We were doing my song; how could I leave?

Megan must have heard the song; it was her favourite. I saw her turn and weave her way back through the crowd to the dance floor. She couldn't resist it. It almost seemed that I had written the song, all that time ago, especially for this night. For her! Ah hell, destiny does some strange things.

†

A woman stood at the foot of the stage - watching, not moving, and not blinking an eye. She was dressed entirely in black and had shoulder length black hair. Even her eyes were black and lined with the same lack of colour. The look she was giving me was colourless.

She turned her eyes to look from me, to Megan, and back again. Purposefully, she walked onto the dance floor to stand opposite Megan, and to add her rhythmic message to the one Megan was transmitting. With snaking limbs, she imitated Megan's movements.

The song was taking forever to reach completion and I had no heart for it any longer, just fear for Megan. If ever I had thought I was evil, then I'd met my match down there - that woman. It seemed this devil's spawn had stepped straight from the decaying doors of hell. My fear increased as I watched her covet Megan. Fierce cramps of concern gripped my stomach.

The band had come to expect the unexpected from me. I threw the microphone down and leapt from the stage, bashing my way through the crowd towards Megan to save her from the woman in black. Was I truly going mad?

But there was no need for concern after all. The dark lady turned away and continued her dance with someone else. Was this an excuse to wrap my arms around Megan? She fell into my embrace, clutching at me to keep her balance. Another mind-fuck moment.

Megan doesn't do drugs; thanks be to whomever I now belong. No, she was drunk, and had reached the point of consumption when one is suddenly overcome by the drunkenness. No greeting, only clutching. I held her tighter, and the band struck up a number especially for us, a slow one.

I glanced up at the woman in black. She was still there, intent on her snaking weave. Her face turned puppet-like and dead, to stare in our direction. Suddenly her visage changed, and she became Venus' Morning Star. Was she just another me?

She mind-voiced across the crowd, "So, it took *me* to bring you to her. You coward! I don't think you could have done it yourself. Always been a bit of a yellow-belly, haven't you? Cluck, cluck cluck cluck ..."

"And who are you to know, you piece of chicken shit?" I mind-voiced back, lips tightly closed and eyes glaring hate.

"Me? *Me?* How dare you ask? I know you better than most, my insolent friend. Was it not I who led you from the doors of despair? Was it not I who spoke to you when you rode your horse? Is it not always I who is always there, to guide your ways ...?"

"I've never seen you before tonight," I replied, but I knew.

"Ah, but of course you have. It is I."

It was then that I stopped playing the game and acknowledged him for what he was. Of course, he was Venus' Morning Star. Why had I always thought he was male when, truly, he could be female. He could be anything, as could I, as we were one. Tonight he had been the shadow of Megan.

"I see your thoughts, Ethan; black Ethan. You are right, of course ..."

What was I right about? I was seldom right

about anything. With that, she disappeared. I don't know where - he or she just disappeared, along with the face that had once again become male; away with the black clothes. Even the barren aural remnants of him disappeared, and soon I began to wonder if he had been there at all. But of course he must have been - he was my guardian and shadow. Our shadow now, it seemed. I had a sneaking suspicion that they were all 'me'.

†

"Megan. You all right?"

"Uhuh"

"You don't sound all right." We swayed together as one.

"Ethan, I feel sick. I need you. I love you. Hold me!" I was holding her - up. "Don't ever leave me again," she said in a rush, as if to hesitate would be to forget that she wanted me to stay. Why would this fantastic woman want me anyway?

I said, confused, "But didn't you leave me?" Where the hell had he gone? Why couldn't I remember what he'd said? I was back-tracking again. *"Present, Ethan; present,"* I scolded myself.

I whispered against her hair, "I never wanted to leave you. I love you. I want to look after you. I promised, remember? You promised."

"Ethan, I love you. I'm sorry I ran. I don't care. I'll be with you forever ..." She lurched, and nearly fell. "Ethan?"

"Yes? Shh. My God, I love you." I held her tighter. My body was responding to her.

"You said, 'My God'. Is He your God?" she whispered against my chest.

"How much does that matter to you?" I asked.

"Right now, the way I feel, nothing matters except you. I think I've had too much to drink." She swayed against me.

"And nothing matters except you, too. Come, let's go. Come home with me."

"Ours or yours?" She giggled as she ran her hands provocatively across my backside; pressed my hips against her.

"Anywhere you like." I answered huskily.

"Yours. It's about time, Ethe."

I swallowed. "And you think you'll be okay with that? Okay with me? You won't freak out on me again? Remember who you're speaking to, my love. It's your choice." I ran my fingers gently up her arm.

"I don't care. The devil can have my soul as well. As long as we're together; forever."

"Forever? I think the drink speaks here!"

"Forever. For sure, drink or no drink. The alcohol is merely the means of acceptance. You better take me now, before the booze wears off." She giggled drunkenly and pulled me closer than I thought I could get.

We left together. Joseph was waiting patiently outside in the limo. We fell in, laughing.

"Joseph," I introduced her, "meet Megan. This is the lady I was telling you about earlier today. The one who I'll never leave again!" I turned to Megan and explained, "It's Joseph here that we have to thank." Then back to Joseph, "I wonder if it is not you who is my guardian angel."

He grinned his pleasure as he shut the door behind us. What a confusing aural glow emanated from him. No time to wonder, as the connecting panel slid up and he left us in privacy.

Megan was unused to such opulence. "Ethe! Ooh, now I can see why you went away. You left me for all this luxury," she said playfully, before pulling my head down to be kissed.

I mumbled against her lips, "All the luxury on earth wouldn't make me leave you." Then I kissed her gently, and with more love than I had ever done before. She wrapped her arms around my neck.

This time, there was no 'killing lust', I am surprised to admit. Only carnal lust, and love. Right now, we were just a man and a woman in love.

Forget the brothers, forget the power, forget the immortality, forget the pain, forget the suffering, forget the dope, forget the mother, forget the Gods, forget Thalem, and forget Joseph's confusing aural emanation.

Remember, just us - two creatures made for one another, at this moment, both bodily and mentally. Why had I never seen this before? But let's face it, lust speaks in loud words.

I wondered how, or if, my blood brothers would accept this. I realised I didn't care, and kissed her mouth, her neck, her ears, then slipped the shirt from her shoulder and kissed the swell of her breast. I could have kissed her all night.

†

I slipped her into my chamber, sure that the others would feel her vibe. There was no dissension in the air, and I wondered at it. Concentrating, I veiled, and attempted to veil on her behalf, hoping it would work but not knowing if it was in my power.

We made love that night, and it was beautiful.

I cannot explain the tenderness that I felt for her, nor the need to protect. Tomorrow, I would face the music, as I had broken one of the cardinal rules: to never bring someone back to the house.

CHAPTER 26

Wood scrapings

Megan woke the following morning with the after-effects of the night before pounding thunderously in her head. Waves of nausea brought on a need to rush to the bathroom. Where was the bathroom? Ethan still slept but woke enough to put out a hand to pull her back as she got out of his bed.

The house was silent, except for two voices coming softly from somewhere in the distance. She shook Ethan gently. "Ethan. Ethan, wake up for a sec."

He opened his eyes, and the previously passive face became suddenly animated. "Oh shit. Megan. Shit!" He sat up, irritably wiped the hair from his forehead.

She looked at him questioningly. "What's wrong? It's because I'm here, isn't it?"

"Yeah, I shouldn't have brought you back

here."

"But why, Ethe? What have you got to hide?"

"Nothing. Just need to get you out of here before they find out - before they come. I must have relaxed the veil when I fell asleep."

"Find out what? What's wrong with me being here? What veil? What're you on about? Besides, I need the bathroom, and I don't know where it is."

"Forget it! Throw on your clothes, and let's get out of here. I'll grab you a cab. Have you got your mobile phone with you? I'll phone so that a taxi will be waiting." There was an unexplained urgency in his voice.

"Ethan, what's wrong?" His urgency was catching, and her voice became a little frantic. "What's up? Are you ashamed of me, or are you having a scene with one of these guys that live here?"

Sighing in exasperation, he softened his tone, feeling crap for her. "No, definitely not ashamed of you, crazy woman. You're beautiful, Megs, and I love you." He rubbed a finger tenderly across her cheek.

He reached out for her, trying desperately to get his thoughts into order - trying to recapture the wonderful evening they had just had together. Trying. The quickening of his heartbeat; the spittle in his mouth! "One quick kiss," he whispered against her cheek. He felt a slip taking place. Which Ethan would come out now? He felt the rise of panic.

She placed her hand in the warmth of the nape of his neck, and gently massaged with her fingers while they kissed.

Ethan pulled away. "Oh, fuck it! Fuck them! Let me just pull on some trousers, and I'll go with you to the bathroom. Then I'll get you a glass of orange juice; or would you like some tomato juice?"

"Still the tomato juice?" she smiled. So unsure of herself.

"Yeah." He zipped up his trousers irritably and stood up.

†

The bathroom seemed to be further from his bedroom than he could remember. Senses alerted, he led her by the hand down the passage, him in front, her behind. He just wasn't sure what the others might do; wasn't sure what he would do with the black lust that was coming upon him.

They were all killers, and he had brought tender prey right here amongst them. It was almost like lowering an unsuspecting mouse into a snake tank, and he knew it was irresponsible to have brought her. He knew this to be the biggest mistake he had ever made. Beads of sweat glistened on his lip.

David had warned him. Hadrian was ruthless. There was no telling what Romando or Benedikt might do; they had very little compassion. Kalin was unpredictable, but wise enough to weigh up the situation; and Caeron, Ethan knew, wouldn't harm Megan if she were with him. Under normal circumstances, they would all be well controlled, but this was their domain, so to speak. Their lair. His lair!

Ethan could feel the pull as his pupils drew tight together to form the oblique he was always trying to hide. This always preceded expected violence, or the kill. With face averted from Megan, he pushed her into the bathroom, closely following before closing the door and locking it.

"You're acting a bit paranoid, aren't you?" Megan asked. She reached up and turned his face towards her, gasping in confusion at what she saw. "My God, Ethan! Have you seen your eyes?"

Roughly, he pushed her hand away and muttered "I'm sorry. I couldn't stop it."

"Couldn't stop it? Is this something you have control over? What's going on?" she whispered urgently.

"Sometimes I can control it." He was battling to keep his mind on their conversation. "It's difficult to explain, Megan. As I told you before, I'm different now - from other people. You've either got to accept me for what I am or get going very quickly." His voice was becoming thick with the spit that was rushing into his mouth. "When I get like this, I become unpredictable." It was a half-hearted attempt to warn her.

He could feel the blood rushing madly through his veins; could hear both the crazy beat of his adrenalized heart and the slower beat of hers. There was something in the air that was catching, and he was becoming infected. A surge of energy and primeval desire coursed through his body, and his hands shook in anticipation of a kill.

Ethan's thoughts ran wildly. *They know. They sense the prey and have become excited. They're invading my psyche. Will I be able to protect her, or will I become so involved that she won't be safe? Sweet Satan! What have I allowed myself to become? I beseech you, not this time!* "Megan, I want you to do something for me," he said anxiously.

"What Ethan? For God's sake, what is it?" Bile was rising into her throat as she felt an inexplicable urgency, and a terror. His obvious unease was infectious.

He spoke slowly to keep the words lucid. "Go back to my bedroom; close the door, and lock yourself in. Now!" He could feel he was losing it.

She spoke in a desperate whisper, searching his coldly animated face. "Ethan, you're scaring me. Why?"

"Time's running out," he responded hoarsely. "They're awakening and know you're here. I don't know what they'll do, or what I'll do. Their mania is compelling and infectious. We're not entirely human, Megan." His voice was changing to a coarser, thicker diction. He looked up at the ceiling as if to beseech an unseen observer. *I'm too young for this part I must play; haven't learnt to control it, and them, yet.* His fists clenched and unclenched - flexing, testing.

"Come." He took her by the hand, dragged her up the passage and pushed her roughly into his bedroom. Viciously, he called out behind her. "Lock that door like I told you to. Don't hesitate! Now!"

"But, Ethan, I ..."

"Just shuddup, and lock it," he hissed, as he consciously stopped himself from pulling her back towards him.

The door shut, and he heard the key grate in the lock.

†

Ethan

I turned in time to see Hadrian stalking silently up the passage, followed closely by Kalin. All humanity had disappeared from both of their faces and, for the first time since I had met them, I saw them for what they really were - and I was horrified, and ecstatic. I was such an animal too.

I battled for control, but felt the weak human in me relenting, permitting the beast to open itself up to welcome them. They padded soundlessly towards me with changed faces and bared teeth. Their slitted eyes conveyed their excitement - the same excitement I could feel enthralling me.

The air was filled with the static of their combined power - our combined power. It portrayed itself in an aural emanation of a magnitude that I had never seen before, but nevertheless relished. Mine was reaching out to welcome and join theirs - the undulation was rebounding along the rays of mine and entering at my fingertips. A beam penetrated my solar plexus and began its possession. I could feel my lips pull back in a shared snarl as we became one. I could feel them all, and at the same time lost that part of me that was the Ethan who was in love with Megan.

Benedikt, David, and Romando had materialised as if the air itself had birthed them. We were all together and revelling once more in our shared ecstasy and the promised delight of the kill.

I turned to bash at the door. They joined me, and in turn we scraped at the door with our bared fingernails. A pile of wood shavings was already gathering at our feet as we scraped away.

†

On the other side of the door, Megan stood petrified as she listened to the scraping and the combined hoarse panting of the pack. Try as she might, she couldn't fathom what was going on out there on the other side.

They didn't speak; Ethan didn't plead her case. She didn't know if he was even there. Her mouth twitched in terror, and she felt a trickle of urine run down the inside of her legs. A slow crooning of horror and helplessness escaped from her lips.

It seemed to her that she watched the scene of her own tragedy impassively, as if from a distance. This could not be happening, not to her. What were these people? What was Ethan? But surely she had known. She had said to him the night before that nothing mattered, as long as she could have him. Without knowing, she had invited.

†

Ethan

As the wood of the door wore away, we became more excited. All rationale had left me, and I joined in with glee and anticipation. So excited were we by this time that we turned to one another to snarl and snap our delight. This was the kill, in every sense of the word.

It was usually too easy as we ensnared our prey with pretty and seductive words: it was too controlled. This was primitive and brought forth in us the very nature to which we were made.

We were predators supreme. And me ... well, I'm sorry to say that I was encouraging our actions.

We could hear the frenzied heartbeats and breathing from the other side of the door; smell the fear, as it permeated the air about us. It did nothing to allay our anticipation, and by this time we were climbing all over one another to get at that door. It couldn't withstand our onslaught for much longer.

A small hole appeared in the wood and, whimpering, we tore at it with hands that were now stained with their own blood. I reached in and felt for the key and turned it. The door swung open.

We stood still, all seven of us, as still as any predator stands just before it launches into its final spring. The victim edged back slowly with heavy limbs that seemed to be made of the very wood we had just destroyed. She could barely sustain an upright stance as she slithered and slid backward.

In unison, we shared bloodlust - communicating telepathically, planning - and licked our lips as the drool issued from the corners of our mouths. Romando and Benedikt were the first to move. One crept to the left and one to the right, followed closely by Kalin and Caeron. David, Hadrian, and I were left as the middle thrust.

We edged forward, not taking our eyes from the prey for one second. It became obvious to me when David and Hadrian dropped, just behind me that this was to be my kill - they had acknowledged it. My excitement grew out of all bounds and my groin tightened painfully in absolute lust. MINE!

Slowly, and with control, I stepped forward, holding her eyes all the while - hypnotising. She stepped back once more and fell to the ground.

One moment I had been crouched before her, and the next I was upon her, straining to get at her throat. The others had closed in about us.

She offered only a little resistance and kept saying something incomprehensible to me at that time: "Oh, Ethan, no! Oh, Ethan no, not you! Ooh, Ethan." And blah blah blah, the same chatter of fright; eyes liquid pools like those of a doe. A mist passed over those eyes as she comprehended her coming demise.

Her entreaties became a chant, a chant that encouraged me to end it. I grasped her arms by the wrists and fell upon her throat. The chant became a gurgle as my teeth closed on her windpipe. Her eyes soon clouded over completely, and her limbs twitched in a final death throe. A gurgle: then a stream of blood ran from her nose. We were then able to gorge on the sweet warmth of the body.

As the satiation coursed through me, so did the sudden remorse of the deed. I lifted my head and howled my grief. My eyes relaxed their obliqueness to allow a flood of tears that ran unchecked down my cheeks; onto the bloodied hands that I now clutched to my face, and down over my fingers: torrents of grief; effluent of decay. One Ethan and left and another had returned.

In those moments, I knew myself to be without forgiveness. Nowhere was Venus' Morning Star to offer me solace. Kalin only looked on with a satisfied smile. The desecrated body lay before us, spread in the gore and blood that surrounded it – lay crucified on the floor of my bedroom.

†

I knew then that my life would never be the same again.

Ethan's tale continues in Book Two, Blood Brothers, Resurrection.

Printed in Great Britain
by Amazon